喚醒你的英文語感！

Get a Feel for English !

喚醒你的英文語感！

Get a Feel for English !

閱讀高點

旋元佑 高點建國
閱讀・寫作名師

英文閱讀通

IELTS ● TOEFL ● TOEIC ● GRE ● GMAT

作者序

　　學英文，尤其是在非英語的環境學英文，需要大量的閱讀。要想眞正學好英文，一定要有大量的閱讀來支撐。通過閱讀，可以熟習單字、文法、句型、文章結構，並且爲最終的挑戰──寫作──打下紮實的基礎。這本《閱讀高點：旋元佑英文閱讀通》，在學習英文過程中可以扮演閱讀材料的角色。書中收錄的文章分屬各種不同的領域，讀者一定可以找到有興趣的文章來看。

　　另外，坊間各大英文考試幾乎都有考到閱讀測驗，本書採用閱讀測驗加上題解的方式編排，就是爲了輔助考生累積閱讀測驗的答題經驗與技巧，在考試時能夠最有效地把握時間、選出正確答案。一般中高級以上程度的英文考試，測驗型態都受到托福考試的影響，閱讀測驗也不例外。不過，托福 iBT 的閱讀測驗，其中有一些最新型態的考題設計比較特殊，不易模仿。坊間諸如研究所、後醫、公職、英檢等等考試的英文閱讀測驗則還是停留在一些比較傳統的題型上。這種趨勢短時間內不容易有變化，本書設計的閱讀測驗題型採用的主要就是坊間各大考試容易碰到的典型題型，例如問主題、細節、推論等等。詳細的題型分類與答題策略，請參看下文「方法論」。

　　英文考試，尤其是如果有考作文，對一般平均程度的考生而言會構成相當的時間壓力。要化解時間壓力，閱讀測驗是個關鍵。平時多做廣讀，考前大量做閱讀測驗，可以提升閱讀速度、磨練答題技巧，在考場上就可以從容不迫地作答，並且留下充分的時間來寫作文。這本《閱讀高點：旋元佑英文閱讀通》，就是提供給讀者作爲閱讀訓練的材料以及練習閱讀測驗的工具，具有廣讀與準備考試的雙重功能。

　　本書的方法論整理出閱讀測驗最常看到的 11 種題型，包括各種主流題型的特色以及答題策略，並且分別舉例說明。請讀者先看完方法論之後再開始練習做題目。後面的閱讀測驗分爲 10 章，每章有 6 篇閱讀測驗，文章內容廣泛涵蓋各種領域。每篇所附的題目有 5 到 12 題，分成 11 種題型。在每一篇閱讀測驗之後皆附有中文翻譯與題解，請讀者在挑戰閱讀測驗後自行參看題解。做練習時最好給自己設定時間限制以模擬考場實況並且提升閱讀速度。

旋元佑

文章主題分類概覽

章別	文章	主題分類	章別	文章	主題分類
第1章	1	自然科普（動物學）	第6章	1	人文歷史
	2	自然科普（自然生態）		2	自然科普（地球科學）
	3	自然科普（地球科學）		3	社會科學
	4	文學藝術		4	自然科普（生物學）
	5	自然科普（應用科學）		5	自然科普（自然生態）
	6	人文歷史		6	社會科學
第2章	1	人文歷史	第7章	1	文學藝術
	2	自然科普（應用科學）		2	藝術／人文歷史
	3	社會科學		3	社會科學
	4	社會科學		4	文學藝術
	5	自然科普（地球科學）		5	自然科普（應用科學）
	6	社會科學		6	人文歷史
第3章	1	人文歷史	第8章	1	人文歷史
	2	人文歷史		2	自然科普（生物學）
	3	自然科普（動物學）		3	社會科學
	4	文學藝術		4	自然科普（地球科學）
	5	社會科學		5	社會科學
	6	社會科學		6	社會科學
第4章	1	社會科學	第9章	1	社會科學
	2	社會科學		2	自然科普（生物學）
	3	自然科普（應用科學）		3	人文歷史
	4	人文歷史		4	自然科普（應用科學）
	5	人文歷史		5	人文歷史
	6	自然科普（醫學）		6	自然科普（自然生態）
第5章	1	自然科普（動物學）	第10章	1	社會科學
	2	自然科普（地球科學）		2	人文歷史
	3	人文歷史		3	自然科普（地球科學）
	4	自然科普（應用科學）		4	社會科學
	5	自然科普（應用科學）		5	文學藝術
	6	自然科普（生物學）		6	人文歷史

CONTENTS 目錄

閱讀測驗篇

方法論

本書設計的閱讀測驗題型，涵蓋坊間英文考試閱讀測驗的主流題型，
每種題型有其特色以及相應的解題策略，分別說明如下。

1 主題型

問主題的題型，一般是作如下的包裝：

- **What is the main idea of the passage?**
- **What is the passage mainly about?**
- **What is the author's purpose in writing this passage?**
- **Which of the following would be the most appropriate title for the passage?**

主題型題目的答題關鍵在於找出主題句，包括全文主題句與段落主題
句。答題策略是先略過這種題型不做，把其他題目都做完之後，對整個文
章已經有初步的了解，再看一下全文主題句與段落主題句，比對一下哪一
個答案最能夠涵蓋全文主題，就是最好的答案。例如下面是把一篇文章各
段開頭的句子摘錄出來：

第 1 段：

Researchers surveyed more than 2,000 physicians in various specialties regarding their beliefs about unnecessary medical care. On average, the doctors believed that some 20% of all medical care was unnecessary.
研究人員調查 2,000 多位各種專長的醫生，問他們對於「多餘醫療」的看法。平均起
來，這些醫生認為所有的醫療當中大約 20% 是沒有必要的。

第 2 段：

Nearly 85 percent said the reason for overtreatment was fear of malpractice suits.
將近 85% 的醫生表示，過度治療的原因是醫生怕惹上業務過失訴訟。

第 3 段：

Almost 60 percent of doctors said patients demand unnecessary treatment.
將近 60% 的醫生說，病人要求過多的治療。

第 4 段：

More than 70 percent of doctors conceded that physicians are more likely to perform unnecessary procedures when they profit from them.
超過 70% 的醫生承認，如果有錢賺，醫生比較容易做沒有必要的治療。

　　完整的文章中，第 1 段開頭有可能是開場白，像前面「研究人員調查 2,000 多位各種專長的醫生，問他們對於多餘醫療的看法」這句就是開場白。接下來是全文主題句：「平均起來，這些醫生認為所有的醫療當中大約 20% 是沒有必要的」。由此看來，這是一篇關於調查研究結果的報導，研究的主題是醫生對「多餘醫療」的看法。接下來從第 2 段起進入文章的發展部分，各段第 1 句就是段落主題句，分別報導研究中醫生對「多餘醫療」提供的 3 項理由：怕吃上業務過失官司、因為病人要求、因為要賺錢。

　　如果考出這麼個題目：

What is the main idea of the passage?

答案可能會是：

Research finds much medical care unnecessary
（研究發現許多醫療並無必要）

　　這是個好答案，因為涵蓋性剛剛好：可以包覆整個主題，但範圍又不會太大。反之，下面這個答案就不好：

Doctors give unnecessary medication for profit
（醫生過度醫療為了謀利）

這個答案不好是因為它只能涵蓋第 4 段的主題 (請參閱段落主題句)，範圍太小。另外這個答案也不好：

The current status of medical care
(醫療照護的現況)

它不好的原因在於範圍太大，超過原文真正主題的範圍。

 **2** 細節型

問細節的題型，可能作如下的包裝：

* **According to the passage …**
* **According to the author …**
* **According to the second paragraph …**
* **The passage states …**
* **The author mentions …**
* **The third paragraph says …**

這是直接問原文有說到的某項細節，答案限於原文裡面找得到的資料。這種題型最常見的出題手法是用同義表達 (paraphrasing) 來增加答題的困難度。所謂同義表達，就是意思相同，但是措詞不一樣的表達方式，例如單字換成同義字、句型構造改變、主動被動互換之類，都可以製造出同義表達。

這種題型的答題策略首先要按照所問的細節找出相應的本文句子。通常不會太難找，因為大部分的題目排列順序會和原文中出現的順序相同，而且題目經常會標明出在原文的第幾段。找到細節所在的句子之後，判斷一下當中哪個部分是要找的答案，然後比對答案選項、找出同義表達就是正確答案。例如文章中如果有下面這個句子：

In the dry season, hunter-gathers dig for roots and tubers and eat lots of meat, because it is easier to hunt for animals on a parched landscape.

在乾季，狩獵採集者挖根莖並且吃很多肉，因為在乾燥的地形上比較容易獵捕動物。

如果考出這麼一個問題：

According to the passage, why do hunter-gatherers consume a large quantity of meat in the dry season?

（根據本文，狩獵採集者在乾季為何要攝取大量的肉類？）

有經驗的考生可以從句首 according to the passage 字樣看出這是問細節的題型，答案要找同義表達。首先，問題本身就已經開始運用同義表達：題目的 consume 是原文中 eat 的同義字、題目的 a large quantity of 是原文中 lots of 的同義詞。經過同義表達的比對，可以判斷這題的答案應該是原文這個部分：

because it is easier to hunt for animals on a parched landscape

（因為在乾燥的地形上要獵捕動物比較容易）

但是，正確答案往往還要經過同義表達的偽裝。這題的正確答案很可能是這樣的包裝：

because game has more difficulty escaping hunters in a dry terrain

（因為獵物在乾燥地形想要逃脫獵人比較困難）

仔細比對會發現：答案中的 dry 是原文 parched 的同義字，答案中的 terrain 是原文中 landscape 的同義字，而答案中 game has more difficulty escaping hunters 就是原文 it is easier to hunt for animals 的同義表達。

問細節的題型，只接受同義表達作為正確答案，也就是原文中必須有直接提到這項細節，偽裝答案的手法頂多只能換換同義字、改變一下句型，

但原文裡不能沒有。答題步驟是先從問題的同義表達找出原文的相關細節，再從原文細節的同義表達找出正確答案。

如果考出來的東西原文並沒有明確講到，只是暗示、或者要經過推論方能得知，那就不是問細節的題型，而是下一種題型：推論型。

3 推論型

這種題型經常作如下的包裝：

- **It can be inferred from the passage that …**
- **It is implied in the second paragraph that …**
- **Which of the following can be inferred from the passage?**
- **The author suggests that …**

它和細節型的問題不同，差別在於：細節型的問題所問的內容必須是原文中有直接提到的事情，頂多只能做同義表達的偽裝，不能用暗示的。如果問的是原文沒有直接提到的事情，要靠推論才能推出來，就屬於推論型的問題。這裡所謂的推論只是簡單的文意推論，不涉及真正的理則學或複雜的邏輯推論。例如：

Plastic bags have been found in the guts of dead sea turtles, which mistake them for jellyfish.
在死海龜腹中找到塑膠袋。海龜誤以為那是水母。

根據這句話可以設計一個推論型的問題如下：

Which of the following can be inferred about sea turtles and jellyfish?
（關於海龜與水母，可以推論出什麼？）

一個合理的答案是：

Sea turtles like to eat jellyfish.
（海龜喜歡吃水母。）

原文並沒有明說海龜愛吃水母，只說海龜把塑膠袋吃下去的原因是誤以為那是水母，這就暗示牠會吃水母。

推論型的題目和細節型的題目類似，差別在於細節型的題目原文中可以找到同義表達，推論型的題目則只能找到根據，要經過推論才能得出答案。再看一個例子：

Researchers found that people with greater exposure to stress over their lifetimes had worse mental and physical health. But they also discovered that if people were highly forgiving of both themselves and others, that characteristic alone virtually eliminated the connection between stress and mental illness.
研究人員發現：一生當中接觸壓力較多的人，心理與生理健康會比較差。但他們也發現：如果對自己、對別人都比較寬容，光是這一項特質幾乎就可以完全消除掉壓力與精神疾病之間的關聯性。

根據上文，有一道推論題型如下：

What does the passage imply about a person who has to deal with heavy stress on a long-term basis and is determined to seek revenge for every small wrong?
（本文暗示一個長期面對重大壓力而且睚眥必報的人可能會怎樣？）

合理的答案如下：

The person is at a higher-than-usual risk of developing mental illness.
（此人發生精神疾病的風險高於一般。）

原文只說「寬容的人會怎樣」，但是據此可以推出「不寬容的人會相反」，這就是推論。

 4 消去法的細節型或推論型

細節題型與推論題型有一種變相的考法，包裝如下：

* **According to the passage, all of the following are true EXCEPT …**
* **According to the author, which of the following is NOT an accurate statement?**

* **All of the following can be inferred from the passage EXCEPT …**
* **Which of the following is NOT implied by the author?**

如果題目中有全部大寫的 EXCEPT 或者 NOT 字樣，就是採用消去法的變化題型。答法大致與前述細節型與推論型相同，以細節型為例，如果問的是：

According to the author, which of the following is NOT true?

從 according to the author 可以看出這是問細節的題型，但是 NOT 一字表示這是要採用消去法的變化形。答法是：如果是 4 選 1 的選擇，要在選項中找出 3 個同義表達（就是 true 的部分）消去，剩下 1 個找不到同義表達的才是答案。如果是這樣的問法：

Which of the following CANNOT be inferred from the passage?

從 infer 一字可以看出這是推論題型，但 CANNOT 表示這是採消去法的變化形，要找出根據、刪去 3 項可以推出的結果，剩下的就是答案。

採取消去法的變化形，不論是細節型還是推論型的題目，出題根據比較常見的是限於一段以內的範圍，所以並不會太難找答案。但是因為要找出 3 個正確答案消去，確實會多花一點時間。當然，如果能夠看出某個答案和原文牴觸、明顯是錯的，就可以直接選出、省下作答時間。

5 單字型

　　這種題型通常作如下的包裝：

- **The word X in the second paragraph can best be replaced by which of the following?**
- **The phrase Y in the third paragraph is closest in meaning to …**

　　這是在閱讀測驗當中考單字或片語，通常會告訴考生這個單字或片語出自哪一段，而且往往所考的單字或片語會加上特別標示如註明行數、加上黑體字或底線等等，所以不必花時間就能很快找到。一般說來，這種題型就和純考單字的考題情況差不多，關鍵還是在於考生是否認識考的單字與答案選項中的單字。但是有時候上下文會扮演關鍵的角色。例如，一個很簡單的字可能有多種解釋，在單字型的題目考出來，主要是在測驗考生會不會從上下文來判斷它是其中哪一種解釋。例如：

The theory is **apparently** sound, until closer examination.
這個理論乍看之下是紮實的，但禁不起仔細檢驗。

　　設計一題單字型考題如下：

The word "apparently" is closest in meaning to which of the following?

考的單字 apparently 本身很簡單，但它有肯定（很明顯就是）與否定（乍看之下似乎是）這兩種解釋。答案選項中如果有 evidently，意思是「明顯是，看得出來是」，屬於肯定語氣；另一個選項 seemingly 意思是「表面上是，乍看之下似乎」，屬於否定語氣。如果光看 apparently 這個字，無法判斷該選哪一個，但是從下文「但禁不起仔細檢驗」可以看出應該採用否定的語氣，所以比較好的答案是 seemingly。再看一個例子：

How can we tell if people are happy or **despondent**? Well, the expression on someone's face will show you whether he or she is glad or sad.
如何能夠判斷別人是高興還是悲傷？其實臉上的表情就可以顯現此人是快樂還是傷心。

設計一道單字題型如下：

The word "despondent" can best be replaced with which of the following?

這題考的單字 despondent 比較難，可能許多考生會不認識，出題的人也知道這點。但是仍然要考是因為這是閱讀測驗裡的單字題型，考生只要有好的閱讀能力，就可以看出原來那兩個句子中，前面的 happy or despondent 是和後面的 glad or sad 對照的。其中 happy 就是 glad，那麼 despondent 當然就是 sad 的意思。因此，考生儘管不認識 despondent，答案仍然不難選出來（就是 sad）。

以上這 5 種題型是坊間各大英文考試閱讀測驗中的主流題型，佔絕大多數的題目。接下來還有幾種出現頻率稍低一些的題型。

 **6 指射型**

這種題型經常作如下的包裝：

- Which of the following does the word X refer to?
- The expression Y refers to which of the following?

考出來的有可能是個代名詞（包括關係代名詞）、要找先行詞，也有可能是同一個東西的另一個名稱。這種題目通常要從上文（較少數情況是從下文）去找指射的對象，看哪一個代入比較合理。例如：

If men remarried, their heart risk did not go up, while for women who remarried, their chances of having a heart attack remained slightly higher, at 35%, than **those** of divorced women.
男人如果再婚，心臟病的風險並不會升高。再婚的女人得心臟病的風險仍比離婚婦女稍高，在 35%。

設計一道指射型題目如下：

What does the word "those" in the paragraph refer to?

指射型題目的答法是要找上下文。原文是比較句法，這種句法要求比較的雙方平行對稱。前面比的是得心臟病的風險 (chances)，後面和它相比的 those 也應該是風險，所以指射的對象就是 chances。再看一個例子：

Darwin's theory of evolution implies that monkeys are descended from a common ancestor with humans. Many find it hard to accept that **these caricatures of humanity** are indeed our cousins.
達爾文的進化論暗示猴子的祖先和人類相同。許多人很難接受這些扭曲人類的拙劣模仿確實是我們的表親。

設計一道指射題型如下：

Which of the following does the expression "these caricatures of humanity" refer to?

指射題型要從上文去找對象。指示限定詞 these 表示這個名詞片語指的是上文出現過的東西。再從意思判斷，these caricatures of humanity 只能是 moneys 才合理（而且也符合 these 是複數的要求）。

7 修辭目的型

這種題型常見的包裝如下：

- **What is the author's purpose in stating/saying/mentioning …?**
- **The author mentions X in the third paragraph in order to do which of the following?**

作者在發展主題時，可能會提出數據、舉例說明、引用實驗、引述權威等等。如果題目問到作者提出某個部分的 purpose 或 in order to 是什麼，問的其實是這個部分的修辭目的，答題策略是要從直接上文去找答案。這種題型通常也會標示出在文章中的位置，所以不必花太多時間去找。若直接上文找不到合理的答案，就要看一下該段的段落主題句，因為段落中所有的細節歸根究柢都是為了發展段落主題句。例如：

Good questions that break the ice require more thought and more than a simple one-word answer. If you ask questions that need more details to answer, the conversation will go on longer. For example, if you are at **a summer pool party**, don't ask people if they like summer. Instead, ask them what they like or dislike about summer. So, instead of getting a one-word answer, you might have the chance to share in a memory.

打破尷尬的好問題需要讓對方動點腦筋、而且不能只用一個字回答。如果問的問題需要比較多的細節來回答，對話就可以進行得久一點。例如，如果你參加夏日泳池派對，不要問別人喜不喜歡夏天。應該問他們喜歡或不喜歡夏天的哪一方面。那麼，對方不是用一個字就能回答，你也就有機會分享對方的一段回憶。

設計一道修辭目的題型如下：

What is the author's purpose in mentioning "a summer pool party"?

這種題目要從上文找答案。句首的 for example 是很明顯的線索：這是一個例子，目的應該是舉例說明上文。直接上文與再上一句的段落主題句是在教讀者如何在社交場合中打破尷尬、該用怎樣的問題和別人搭訕。所以下面會是個好答案：

To illustrate what good ice-breaking questions are like.
（舉例說明好的打破尷尬問題是什麼樣子。）

8 組織結構型

這種題型典型的包裝如下：

● **What would a paragraph preceding this passage be about?**
● **What would the author most likely discuss in a paragraph following this passage?**

基本上問：上一段或下一段可能是談什麼？這問的是組織結構。答題策略是要先找出全文主題（若有主題型的問題，先做出該題的答案，再用答案來判斷組織結構型的問題）。不論是上一段還是下一段，談的主題應該還是與原文同一個大主題，不能改變。其次就是上下文要能夠銜接。若問的是上一段講什麼，正確答案要能夠銜接本文的開頭。若問的是下一段，則要能夠銜接結尾最後一句。例如，下面是把一篇文章的全文主題句與段落主題句摘錄出來，最後一段並且附上結尾句：

第 1 段：

A new study reports that working out during a language class amplifies people's ability to memorize, retain and understand new vocabulary.

一項新的研究報導：上語言課同時運動，對記憶、保留與理解新字彙有幫助。

第 2 段：

In recent years, a wealth of studies in both animals and people have shown that we learn differently if we also exercise.

近年來，有許多對動物與人類進行的研究都顯示，如果一邊運動的話，學習效果大不相同。

第 3 段：

Many scientists suspect that exercise alters the biology of the brain in ways that make it more malleable and receptive to new information. ... However, further research is needed before we can capitalize on the correlation between exercise and language acquisition.

許多科學家猜測：運動會改變大腦的生理，使它更有彈性、更能接受新資訊。……然而還需要進一步研究，才能真正利用運動與語言學習之間的連帶關係。

設計一道組織結構的題型如下：

What would a paragraph following this passage most probably deal with?

組織結構的題型要先整理出全文主題。第 1 段全文主題句點出「運動有助於語言學習」這個主題，第 2、3 段引用科學家的研究來發展這個主題，所以下一段應該還是屬於同一個主題，並且要能夠銜接結尾句。一個好的答案是：

The kind of research that may help language learners benefit

from exercise.
（這種能夠幫助語言學習者從運動中獲利的研究是什麼。）

這個答案可以繼續發展「運動與語言學習」這個大主題，並且能夠銜接結尾句「需要進一步研究，才能真正利用運動與語言學習之間的連帶關係」，所以是好答案。

9 安插句子型

這種題型最常見的包裝是：

- **In which position would the following sentence best fit in paragraph 5?**

然後會有一個通常用黑體字標出的完整句子要被安插。同時在指定段落中會事先留下四個位置，如 W, X, Y, Z，問考生這個黑體字的句子要安插在何處比較合適。

這種題型也是修辭題型，與組織結構有關。答題策略在於觀察插入句的句首與句尾。最常見的一種答題根據是：插入句句首與上文有重複、句尾與下文有重複，或至少有關係，可以銜接得上。

例如下面這道題目：

In which position would the following sentence best fit in the paragraph?
"Fitness is measured by an organism's ability to survive and reproduce."
（適應能力是用生物生存與繁殖的能力來衡量。）

下面這個段落中有個 X 位置，我們來看一下這個插入句為什麼應該放在這個位置。

The central concept of natural selection is the evolutionary fitness of an organism. _X_ However, fitness is not the same as the total number of offspring.

（天擇的主要觀念就是生物進化的適應能力。 X 不過，適應能力和生出後代的總數不一樣。）

插入句放入之後，成為這麼一段文字：

The central concept of natural selection is the evolutionary fitness of an organism. <u>Fitness is measured by an organism's ability to survive and reproduce.</u> However, fitness is not the same as the total number of offspring.

天擇的主要觀念就是生物進化的適應能力。適應能力是用生物生存與繁殖的能力來衡量。不過，適應能力和生出後代的總數不一樣。

由此可以看出，上文提出適應能力這個觀念，可以銜接插入句句首的「適應能力」。下文說到「生出後代的總數」，可以銜接插入句句尾的「生物生存與繁殖的能力」，所以插入句卡在中間剛剛好。

 **10 語氣態度型**

這種題型常見的包裝如下：

* Which of the passage best describes the author's tone in the passage?
* The author's attitude toward X can best be described as ...

問作者的語氣與態度，要看文章的用字與措詞，基本上可以分成「肯定、中立、否定」三大類，常見的答案有：

- 肯定

  enthusiastic, admiring, warmly approving

- 中立

  objective, noncommittal, disinterested, unbiased, neutral

- 否定

  skeptical, critical, condemning, hostile

　　從用字中判斷出作者是肯定、中立、還是否定的態度，問題就容易回答了。例如：

EPA Administrator Scott Pruitt's expanding ethical cloud is one reason he should not be the nation's top environmental officer. The other is that he seems determined to ruin the environment. Two major EPA announcements last week illustrate his pattern of siding with industry over experts.
環保局長史考特·普魯特涉及的道德問題，疑雲越滾越大，這是他不應擔任全國最高環境首長的一個原因。另一個原因是他似乎決心要毀掉環境。上週環保局做出兩項重大宣告，可以說明他那套不理睬專家、與工業同一陣線的模式。

　　設計一道問態度的題型：

Which of the following best describes the author's attitude toward Scott Pruitt?

　　這種題型要判斷是肯定、中立還是否定。原文首先指出此人涉及道德問題因而不適任。然後說他要毀掉環境、與工業同一陣線，這都是嚴重的指控，反映出來的是極為否定的態度，所以一個好的答案是：

Condemning「譴責的」

再看一個例子：

America hasn't always, or even usually, been governed by the best and the brightest; over the years, presidents have employed plenty of knaves and fools. But I don't think we've ever seen anything like the collection of petty grifters and miscreants surrounding Donald Trump. Price, Pruitt, Zinke, Carson and now Ronny Jackson: At this point, our default assumption should be that there's something seriously wrong with anyone this president wants on his team.

美國並非一直是，甚至並非經常是由頂尖的人才在治理。多年來，當總統的人聘用過的惡棍與蠢材多得是。但我不認為我們曾經見識過像 Donald Trump 身邊這麼一批小騙子與無賴。Price, Pruitt, Zinke, Carson，現在則是 Ronny Jackson。到了這會兒，我們預設的認知應該是：這位總統想要拉到他的團隊中的人肯定都有嚴重的問題。

設計一道語氣型的問題：

Which of the following best describes the author's tone in the passage?

語氣，主要從用字措詞透露出來。本文的用字包括惡棍、蠢材、騙子、無賴等等，對美國川普總統的團隊是極為負面的態度，語氣也是高度負面。所以一個好的答案會是：

Sarcastic「挖苦的，譏嘲的」

 **11** 句子改寫型

這種題型常作如下的包裝：

• **Which of the sentences below best expresses the essential information in the boldfaced sentence in paragraph 1?**

然後在相應段落中有一整個句子作黑體呈現。這種題型可以視爲「同義表達句」的選擇。正確選項要包含原句主要的內容，可以忽略細節，但不能缺少重要內容，也不能出現和原句有衝突的內容。答題策略就是摘出原句的重點，然後尋找同義表達。例如考的是這一句：

As long as maple syrup does not have an off-flavor, is of a uniform color, and is free from turbidity and sediment, it can be labelled as one of the A grades.

（只要楓糖漿沒有怪味道、顏色一致、不混濁也沒有沉澱，就可以標示爲 A 級。）

改寫句子的答案可能是這樣的：

A-grade maple syrup must meet criteria of flavor, color, and purity.

（A 級楓糖漿必須符合味道、顏色與純度的標準。）

改寫句子的正確答案通常會比原句短，因爲不重要的細節可以略去，但不能少掉任何一個重點，如此才是正確的同義表達。

第 1 章

Not all birds fly the same way. The least **sophisticated** form of flight is gliding. The pterosaur, primitive forerunner of all flying creatures today, probably flew like a hang glider, launching itself from a cliff or the top of a tree and gliding along for short distances. Some modern birds, notably pelicans, often glide while migrating **in formation**, to save energy until the loss in altitude forces them to flap their wings for a climb.

Most birds can be likened to airplanes with flapping wings. Their densely feathered arms and hands perform the dual function of airplane wings and propellers. Like **a swimmer** using the butterfly stroke, the bird uses semi-circular, flapping motions in its arms and hands to drive itself forward while maintaining altitude.

Larger birds usually flap their wings more slowly than smaller ones do. As a result, when an especially large bird like a swan wants to take off, it needs a long runway like a lake surface to build up speed. That is why swans swimming freely in small ponds in the zoo do not fly away: the runway is not long enough for **these jumbo 747s**.

The humming bird, the smallest bird in the world, is not so much an airplane as it is a helicopter. Its wings move in two complete circles instead of the half circles used in typical flapping action. Therefore, it can lift perpendicularly off the ground, hover in mid-air, or even fly backwards by tilting its "propeller blades."

The champion flier, however, is the eagle, which flies like a hot balloon. On sunny days, there are rising columns of hot air surrounded by upward spirals of air currents. Riding these currents on extended wings, the eagle soars in expanding circles without flapping. Even the swift swoop for prey is nothing but an effortless albeit guided free-fall. All the energy, meanwhile, is saved for the arduous task of carrying off the prey, which may be up to half the eagle's own weight.

✏ Exercise

① Which of the following titles best summarizes the passage as a whole?
   (A) Varieties of Bird Flight
   (B) The Champion Flier among Birds
   (C) Evolution of Flight in Birds
   (D) Birds and Aircraft

② The word "sophisticated" in the first paragraph is closest in meaning to
   (A) philosophical
   (B) artistic
   (C) investigated
   (D) complicated

③ The phrase "in formation" in the first paragraph can best be replaced by
   (A) in certain seasons of the year
   (B) with particular information
   (C) in allotted positions in a group
   (D) in the process of taking shape

④ According to the passage, when would migrating pelicans have to flap their wings?
   (A) When they encounter rising columns of hot air
   (B) When the runway is too short for take-off
   (C) When they are doing the mating dance
   (D) When they are gliding too close to the ground

⑤ In the second paragraph, the author mentions "a swimmer" in order to
   (A) indicate that some birds also swim
   (B) describe how flapping flight is done
   (C) illustrate how birds swoop down at the sight of prey
   (D) suggest that birds are just like butterflies

⑥ The author suggests that swans in the zoo do not escape because
  (A) they are kept in cages
  (B) there are airports nearby
  (C) the ponds there are too small
  (D) there is a steady food supply there

⑦ "These jumbo 747s" in the third paragraph refers to
  (A) huge airplanes
  (B) great lakes
  (C) swans
  (D) pelicans

⑧ Which of the following does the author compare to helicopters?
  (A) eagles
  (B) hummingbirds
  (C) pelicans
  (D) pterosaurs

⑨ According to the passage, the hummingbird can do all of the following EXCEPT
  (A) take off without a runway
  (B) fly backwards
  (C) suspend itself in the air
  (D) ride rising columns of hot air

⑩ Which of the following is probably most tiring to an eagle?
  (A) bringing its victim off the ground
  (B) flying backwards
  (C) climbing currents of air around hot columns
  (D) swooping down at its prey

題解

文章翻譯

　　鳥類飛行方式不盡相同。最簡單的飛行是滑翔。始祖鳥是今日所有飛行生物的原始祖先，飛起來可能像具滑翔翼，從懸崖上或樹梢起飛、作短距離滑翔。有些現代鳥類，尤其是鵜鶘，在遷移時編隊飛行經常會滑翔以節省精力，直到高度降低太多，不得不鼓翅爬升。

　　大部分鳥類都像飛機，但翅膀會拍動。密生羽毛的臂膀和手兼具機翼與螺旋槳的功能。像游蝶式的選手一樣，鳥用臂膀與手的半圓形拍動來推進，同時維持高度。

　　大型鳥類鼓翅的動作通常比小型鳥慢。因此，特別大的鳥像天鵝之類想要起飛時，需要像湖面那樣的長跑道來加速。所以，動物園的小池塘中自由游動的天鵝不會飛走，就是因為跑道太短，不夠這些巨無霸 747 起飛。

　　蜂鳥是世界最小的鳥類，與其說牠像飛機，不如說是像直升機。牠的翅膀不像一般鼓翅飛行那樣作半圓形運動，而是畫出兩個完整的圓圈。所以牠可以從地面垂直起飛、懸浮在半空、甚至後退，只要傾斜一下「螺旋槳葉」就行。

　　不過，飛行冠軍還是老鷹，牠的飛行方式像熱氣球。晴朗的日子，上升的熱空氣柱周圍有盤旋而上的渦狀氣流。老鷹張開雙翼乘著氣流繞著圈子上升、越繞越大，完全不用鼓翅。就連急撲而下獵食的動作也只不過是毫不費力卻有導向的自由落體運動。同時，牠所有的精力都節省下來準備進行一件吃力的工作：把獵物帶走，獵物有可能達到牠自己體重的一半。

練習題翻譯與詳解

① 下列哪個標題是全文最佳的摘要？

　　(A) 鳥類飛行的種類　　　　　　　(B) 鳥類飛行冠軍

　　(C) 鳥類飛行的進化　　　　　　　(D) 鳥與飛機

【答案】**A**

【解析】這是問主題的題型，要找全文主題句與段落主題句。第一句「鳥類飛行方式不盡相同」是全文主題句，而後面各段的第一句（段落主題句）則分別發展幾種不同的鳥類飛行，故選 (A)。

② 第一段中的 sophisticated 一字意思最接近

　　(A) 哲學的　　　　　　　　　　　(B) 藝術的

　　(C) 被調查的　　　　　　　　　　(D) 複雜的

【答案】**D**

【解析】sophisticated 的意思是「複雜的、世故的、先進的」（字根 soph=wise）。

③ 第一段的片語 in formation 可以換成

    (A) 在某些季節   (B) 有特殊情報

    (C) 在團體中指定的位置   (D) 在成形的過程中

【答案】**C**

【解析】片語 in formation 的意思是「編成隊形」。

④ 根據本文，鵜鶘什麼時候必須鼓翅？

    (A) 碰到上升熱空氣柱時   (B) 跑道太短無法起飛時

    (C) 進行求偶舞蹈時   (D) 滑翔太接近地面時

【答案】**D**

【解析】這是問細節的題型，要找同義表達。第一段最後一句說「直到高度降低太多，不得不鼓翅爬升」，選項 (D) gliding too close to the ground 與原文的 the loss in altitude 是同義表達。

⑤ 第二段中作者提到 a swimmer 的目的是

    (A) 表示有些鳥類也會游泳   (B) 描寫鼓翅飛行的作法

    (C) 說明鳥類看到獵物時如何俯衝   (D) 暗示鳥類和蝴蝶完全一樣

【答案】**B**

【解析】這是修辭目的的題型，要找出上下文與段落的主題句。第二段的段落主題句講到鼓翅 (flapping wings)，下文說「鳥用臂膀與手的半圓形拍動 (flapping motions) 來推進」，說的也是鼓翅，故選 (B)。

⑥ 作者暗示，動物園裡的天鵝不會逃走是因為

    (A) 關在籠子裡   (B) 附近有機場

    (C) 池塘太小   (D) 有食物供應

【答案】**C**

【解析】這是推論的題型，要找「根據」。第三段說「動物園的小池塘中自由游動的天鵝不會飛走，就是因為跑道太短，不夠這些巨無霸 747 起飛」，這是把池塘比喻為跑道、天鵝比喻為飛機，因此是暗示「池塘太小」。

⑦ 第三段中 These jumbo 747s 指的是

    (A) 大型飛機   (B) 大湖泊

    (C) 天鵝   (D) 鵜鶘

【答案】C

【解析】這是指射的題型,要看上下文。解說參看上題。

⑧ 作者將下列何者比喻為直升機?

(A) 老鷹　　　　　　　　　　　(B) 蜂鳥

(C) 鵜鶘　　　　　　　　　　　(D) 始祖鳥

【答案】B

【解析】這是問細節的題型,要找同義表達。根據第四段開頭「蜂鳥是世界最小的鳥類,與其說牠像飛機,不如說是像直升機」,故選 (B)。

⑨ 根據本文,下列的事蜂鳥都能做,除了

(A) 不需要跑道,直接起飛　　　(B) 後退飛行

(C) 懸浮在空中　　　　　　　　(D) 騎乘上升的熱空氣柱

【答案】D

【解析】這是問細節、用消去法的題型,要刪除三個同義表達。選項 (A) (B) (C) 在第四段都可找到同義表達,只有選項 (D) 是原文用於描述老鷹的文字被張冠李戴拿來描述蜂鳥,不是同義表達,選選 (D)。

⑩ 下列何者可能是令老鷹最疲倦的事?

(A) 帶著獵物離地　　　　　　　(B) 後退飛

(C) 繞著熱空氣柱爬升　　　　　(D) 俯衝抓獵物

【答案】A

【解析】這是問細節的題型,要找同義表達。最後一句說「牠所有的精力都節省下來準備進行一件吃力的工作:把獵物帶走」,其中 arduous 是 tiring 的同義字,carrying off the prey 是 bringing its victim off the ground 的同義表達,故選 (A)。

Reading 2

Acid rain is precipitation containing sulfuric acid or nitric acid. Whether acid rain induces baldness is debatable, and so far it has not done any damage to crop cultivation. However, it has killed off aquatic life in some lakes, caused whole forests to shed leaves and die, and accelerated erosion of buildings, monuments and outdoor sculptures.

Acidity in rain is a result of chemical pollution of the air. The burning of fossil fuels produces sulfur dioxide and nitrogen monoxide, which are released into the atmosphere from automobile exhaust pipes and factory smokestacks. These chemicals are wafted high up where they dissolve in tiny water droplets, turning into sulfuric acid and nitric acid. When such droplets come down to earth, they become acid rain.

Apparently, cleaner air should reduce the amount of acid rain. The passage of the Clean Air Act in the U. S. in 1970 seemed the answer to the problem of acidity in rain. By now, nearly half a century later, artificial emissions of sulfur dioxide into the atmosphere has been cut by over 90%, thanks to rigorous industrial standards. Yet, to the **dismay** of environmentalists, acidity in rain remains high. How is it that cleaner air does not make cleaner rain?

Paradoxically, the reason acidity in rain does not go down is that we have made the air too "clean." Complying with the Clean Air Act requirements, factories set up scrubbers in their smokestacks to sift pollutants out. An **unforeseen** consequence is that the alkaline materials that can help neutralize acidity in water droplets are removed alongside the pollutants. In addition, land surface in industrial nations is increasingly turned into buildings, paved with asphalt, or planted over. **This** has greatly reduced the amount of alkaline dust that used to be blown to high altitudes. With the sources of alkaline materials cut down, acidity in rain fails to be neutralized.

✎ Exercise

① What does this passage mainly discuss?

(A) Environmental damage caused by various forms of pollution

(B) Air pollution, its causes, and measures to prevent it

(C) The serious damage of acid rain on lakes in the U. S.

(D) Acid rain, its causes, effects, and attempted solutions

② Which of the following can be found in acid rain?

(A) sulfur dioxide

(B) nitrogen monoxide

(C) sulfuric acid

(D) alkaline nitrogen

③ Which of the following is LEAST affected by acid rain?

(A) natural forests

(B) lakes

(C) outdoor sculptures

(D) agricultural crops

④ According to the passage, which of the following is emitted from automobiles and factories into the atmosphere?

(A) nitrogen monoxide

(B) acid rain

(C) sulfuric acid

(D) water droplets

⑤ It can be inferred that the passage was written in

(A) the 1970s

(B) around 1985

(C) around 1995

(D) the 2010s

⑥ The word "dismay" in the third paragraph can best be replaced by
   (A) joy
   (B) disappointment
   (C) amazement
   (D) indignation

⑦ The word "unforeseen" in the fourth paragraph most nearly means
   (A) unexpected
   (B) unfortunate
   (C) unusual
   (D) invisible

⑧ Why has the Clean Air Act failed to cut down acid rain?
   (A) Factories did not follow its requirements but kept on polluting the air
   (B) The Act did not require that land surface be paved with asphalt
   (C) Climatic patterns did not change after passage of the Act
   (D) Alkaline substances were reduced along with acid-forming substances

⑨ The word "This" in the fourth paragraph refers to
   (A) the planting of vegetation
   (B) the paving of asphalt
   (C) the change in land surface
   (D) the construction of buildings

題解

【文章翻譯】

　　酸雨是含有硫酸或硝酸的降雨。酸雨是否會引起禿頭，尚無定論。截至目前為止酸雨也沒有對農作物的栽培造成傷害。但是酸雨在一些湖泊中造成水中生物死亡、整座森林落葉枯死，並且加快建築物、紀念碑和戶外雕塑的侵蝕。

　　雨的酸性來自於空氣受到化學污染。燃燒化石燃料會產生二氧化硫與一氧化氮，這些化合物從車輛排氣管與工廠煙囪排放到大氣中。飄到高處後溶解在小水珠裡面，就變成硫酸與硝酸。當這些小水珠降到地面就是酸雨。

　　空氣若乾淨，看來應該可以減少酸雨量。美國在 1970 年通過空氣清潔法案，似乎正可以解決酸雨問題。過了將近半個世紀，如今二氧化硫人為排放進入大氣層的量已經減少 90% 以上，因為工業標準很嚴格。但是，令環保人士相當失望的是：雨水的酸度仍然很高。為什麼空氣乾淨了雨水卻還不乾淨？

　　原因很矛盾：雨水酸度居高不下，是因為空氣太「乾淨」了。工廠遵照空氣清潔法規定，在煙囪裡裝了過濾器，把污染物篩檢出來。這造成一項始料未及的後果：可以中和小水珠酸度的鹼性物質也和污染物一同排除了。此外，工業國家的地面快速蓋上建築物、鋪上柏油路、或者種上植物。這造成鹼性灰塵量大減，從前灰塵會吹到高空。因為鹼性物質來源減少了，雨水的酸度無法中和。

【練習題翻譯與詳解】

① 本文主要討論的是什麼？
　　(A) 各種污染造成的環境破壞
　　(B) 空氣污染的原因，以及預防措施
　　(C) 酸雨對美國湖泊造成的嚴重破壞
　　(D) 酸雨的成因、影響、以及嘗試的解決辦法

【答案】**D**
【解析】這是問主題的題型，要找全文主題句與段落主題句。全文第一句「酸雨是含有硫酸或硝酸的降雨」是酸雨的定義，後面各段第一句（段落主題句）的內容則分別是「酸雨的成因與解決辦法」，故選 (D)。

② 酸雨含有下列何者？
　　(A) 二氧化硫　　　　　　　(B) 一氧化氮
　　(C) 硫酸　　　　　　　　　(D) 鹼性氮

【答案】**C**
【解析】這是問細節的題型，要找同義表達。根據第一段開頭「酸雨是含有硫酸 (sulfuric acid) 或硝酸的降雨」，故選 (C)。

③ 下列何者最不受酸雨影響？

    (A) 天然林   (B) 湖泊

    (C) 戶外雕塑   (D) 農作物

【答案】**D**

【解析】這是問細節的題型，要找同義表達。第一段提到「截至目前為止酸雨也沒有對農作物的栽培造成傷害」，其中 acid rain has not done any damage to 是 is not affected by acid rain 的同義表達，crop cultivation 是 agricultural crops 的同義表達，故選 (D)。

④ 根據本文，下列何者從車輛與工廠排放到大氣中？

    (A) 一氧化氮   (B) 酸雨

    (C) 硫酸   (D) 小水珠

【答案】**A**

【解析】這是問細節的題型，要找同義表達。根據第二段「燃燒化石燃料會產生二氧化硫與一氧化氮 (nitrogen monoxide)，這些化合物從車輛排氣管與工廠煙囪排放到大氣中」，故選 (A)。

⑤ 可以推論這篇文章寫在

    (A) 1970 年代   (B) 1985 前後

    (C) 1995 前後   (D) 2010 年代

【答案】**D**

【解析】這是推論題，要找根據。第三段說「美國在 1970 年通過空氣清潔法案，似乎正可以解決酸雨問題。過了將近半個世紀，如今……」，可以推論本文寫作年代是 1970 加上 40 幾年，也就是 2010 年代。

⑥ 第三段中的 dismay 一字可以換成

    (A) 喜悅   (B) 失望

    (C) 驚訝   (D) 憤怒

【答案】**B**

【解析】這是單字題，dismay 的意思是「失望，沮喪」。

⑦ 第四段中的 unforeseen 一字意思最接近

    (A) 未料到   (B) 不幸

    (C) 不尋常   (D) 隱形

【答案】**A**

【解析】這是單字題。unforeseen 是 not before seen 組合的古英文複合字，意即「事先沒有看出來」。

⑧ 空氣清潔法為何沒有減少酸雨？

    (A) 工廠不遵守規定，持續污染空氣

    (B) 法案沒有規定土地要鋪上柏油

    (C) 氣候型態在法案通過後並未改變

    (D) 鹼性物質和致酸物質一同減少了

【答案】**D**

【解析】這是問細節的題型，要找同義表達。根據第四段，「可以中和小水珠酸度的鹼性物質也和污染物一同排除了」(the alkaline materials that can help neutralize acidity in water droplets are removed alongside the pollutants)，其中的 alkaline materials 是 alkaline substances 的同義表達，removed 是 reduced 的同義表達，pollutants 是 acid-forming substances 的同義表達，故選 (D)。

⑨ 第四段中的 This 指的是

    (A) 栽種植物   (B) 鋪設柏油

    (C) 地表改變   (D) 建造建築物

【答案】**C**

【解析】這是指射的題型，要找上下文。This 的直接上文是 In addition, land surface in industrial nations is increasingly turned into buildings, paved with asphalt, or planted over.，This 指的也就是這整個句子，最接近的同義表達就是 (C)。另外三個選項分別是該句中的三項細節，只有 (C) 能夠涵蓋整句。

The Magellan spacecraft sent back a treasure trove of information that unveiled the mysteries of Venus, our sister planet. Scientific knowledge aside, however, the historic Magellan mission itself is **a saga** full of its own surprises.

The Russians were the first to explore Venus. In 1962, at the peak of the Cold War years, they sent the first of more than 20 spacecraft to Venus. For their Venera 15 and 16 missions in 1983 they even invited American scientists to participate—the same scientists who were also on NASA's own Magellan project. These Russian projects and international joint-ventures undertaken in the Cold War years provided valuable data and experience for the Magellan project.

On the American side, NASA established its own Venus project—Magellan—in 1969. After nine years of preparation, NASA launched the Pioneer Venus Orbiter, **to scout the terrain** for Magellan. In the early Reagan years, after hundreds of scientists and engineers had spent millions of dollars of government money on the project, Magellan was in danger of being halted due to budget tightening. NASA, however, was determined to get Magellan launched.

Faced with shrunken funding, NASA officials looked through their **inventory** and found an antenna on a Voyager probe which they could use on Magellan. A computer was also dismantled from a Galileo craft and set up on Magellan. With other bits and ends secured similarly, Magellan was finally assembled and successfully launched on May 4, 1989.

✎ Exercise

① The best title for the passage would be
   (A) How NASA Helped Win the Cold War
   (B) The Magellan Mission
   (C) Supremacy in Outer Space
   (D) Russian exploration of Venus

② The phrase "a saga" in the first paragraph most nearly means
   (A) an age
   (B) a lecture
   (C) an epic
   (D) a mystery

③ According to the passage, the earliest space mission to explore Venus was a spacecraft launched in the
   (A) early 1960s
   (B) late 1960s
   (C) early 1980s
   (D) late 1980s

④ It can be inferred that international cooperation on exploration of Venus occurred in the year
   (A) 1962
   (B) 1969
   (C) 1978
   (D) 1983

⑤ According to the passage, which of the following was a NASA probe that was a forerunner of the Magellan spacecraft?
   (A) Venera 16
   (B) Galileo
   (C) Voyager
   (D) Pioneer Venus Orbiter

⑥ The phrase "to scout the terrain" in the third paragraph means most closely
(A) to look for the enemy
(B) to gather information
(C) to collect soil samples
(D) to get ahead of competitors

⑦ The passage mentions that the Magellan project was almost canceled at one time because of
(A) a serious accident at lift off
(B) the Cold War
(C) insufficient funding
(D) faulty parts

⑧ The word "inventory" in paragraph 4 can best be replaced by
(A) stock
(B) invention
(C) purse
(D) shopping list

⑨ All of the following are mentioned in the passage EXCEPT
(A) A computer on Magellan was taken from Galileo
(B) An antenna on Magellan was originally on a Voyager craft
(C) A spaceman on Magellan was a specialist from Russia
(D) Several parts used on Magellan were not new

題解

【文章翻譯】

　　麥哲倫太空船傳送回來一座資訊寶庫，揭開了我們姐妹行星金星的神祕面紗。撇開科學知識不談，歷史性的麥哲倫任務本身也是個充滿驚奇的傳奇故事。

　　最早探測金星的是俄國人。1962 年，正值冷戰時代的高峰，俄國人派出頭一艘太空船前往金星（後來總計有 20 幾艘）。1983 年俄國的 Venera 15 與 16 這兩次任務甚至邀請美國科學家參加——這批科學家正是美國航太總署本身的麥哲倫計畫的科學家。這幾次的俄國計畫與冷戰年代進行的一些跨國合作，為麥哲倫計畫提供了寶貴的資料與經驗。

　　美國方面，航太總署在 1969 年建立了自己的金星計畫，就是麥哲倫。經過 9 年的籌備，航太總署發射出先鋒號金星軌訊船，目的是為麥哲倫偵察地形。到了雷根政府初年，幾百名科學家與工程師已經花掉政府數百萬美元的經費，麥哲倫計畫卻面臨叫停的危機，因為預算緊縮。不過航太總署決心要發射麥哲倫。

　　面對資金縮水，航太總署官員在存貨中四下翻找，在旅行者太空船上找到一架天線可以用在麥哲倫上。又從一艘伽利略太空船上拆下一台電腦裝到麥哲倫上頭。另外還有一些零件也是這樣弄來的，麥哲倫終於組裝成功，在 1989 年 5 月 4 日成功發射。

【練習題翻譯與詳解】

① 本文之最佳標題是

　　(A) 航太總署如何協助打贏冷戰　　　　(B) 麥哲倫任務

　　(C) 外太空霸權　　　　　　　　　　　　(D) 俄羅斯的金星探測

【答案】**B**

【解析】這是問主題的題型，要找全文主題句與段落主題句。第一句（全文主題句）是「麥哲倫太空船傳送回來一座資訊寶庫，揭開了我們姐妹行星金星的神祕面紗」，後面的段落主題句分別說明俄國與美國兩方面的金星探測，仍以美國的麥哲倫計畫為主，故選 (B)。

② 第一段中的片語 a saga 意思最接近

　　(A) 一個時代　　　　　　　　　　　　(B) 一場演講

　　(C) 一部史詩　　　　　　　　　　　　(D) 一個謎

【答案】**C**

【解析】名詞 saga 源自北歐語，字根與 say 有關，原意是「故事」，暗示長篇、複雜的傳奇故事，最接近的同義字是 epic「史詩」。

③ 根據本文，最早探測金星的太空任務是在什麼年代發射的太空船？
(A) 1960 年代初
(B) 1960 年代末
(C) 1980 年代初
(D) 1980 年代末

【答案】A
【解析】這是問細節的題型，要找同義表達。根據第二段開頭「最早去探測金星的是俄國人。1962 年，正值冷戰時代的高峰，俄國人派出頭一艘太空船前往金星」，其中 1962 與 the early 1960s 是同義表達，故選 (A)。

④ 可以推論，國際合作探測金星發生在哪一年？
(A) 1962
(B) 1969
(C) 1978
(D) 1983

【答案】D
【解析】這是推論題，要找根據。第二段說到「1983 年俄國的 Venera 15 與 16 這兩次任務甚至邀請美國科學家參加」，這是最早的跨國合作。而且下一句的 international joint-ventures 是本題所問 international cooperation 的同義表達，故選 (D)。

⑤ 根據本文，下面哪一個是航太總署的太空船，成為麥哲倫太空船的前導？
(A) Venera 16
(B) Galileo
(C) Voyager
(D) Pioneer Venus Orbiter

【答案】D
【解析】這是問細節的題型，要找同義表達。根據第三段「航太總署發射出先鋒號金星軌道船 (Pioneer Venus Orbiter)，目的是為麥哲倫偵察地形」，可以看出 Pioneer Venus Orbiter 是麥哲倫號的先導，故選 (D)。

⑥ 第三段的片語 to scout the terrain 意思最接近
(A) 尋找敵人
(B) 收集情報
(C) 採集土壤標本
(D) 搶先在競爭者前面

【答案】B
【解析】這是單字題。to scout the terrain 字面上是「偵察地形」，引申為「了解情況」，最接近的是 to gather information「收集情報」。

⑦ 文章提到麥哲倫計畫一度幾乎被取消，因為
(A) 起飛時發生嚴重意外
(B) 冷戰
(C) 資金不足
(D) 零件瑕疵

【答案】C
【解析】這是問細節的題型，要找同義表達。根據第三段「麥哲倫計畫面臨叫停的危機，因為預算緊縮」(Magellan was in danger of being halted due to budget tightening)，其中 in danger of being halted 是 almost canceled 的同義表達，due to 是 because of 的同義表達，budget tightening 是 insufficient funding 的同義表達，故選 (C)。

⑧ 第四段中的 inventory 一字可以換成

    (A) 存貨   (B) 發明

    (C) 錢包   (D) 購物清單

【答案】A
【解析】這是單字題，要找同義字。inventory 是「存貨」，選項 (A) stock 可以解釋為「股票、存貨」，是最接近的同義字。

⑨ 以下各點原文中都有提到，除了

    (A) 麥哲倫上有台電腦是從伽利略號拿來的

    (B) 麥哲倫上有組天線原本用在旅行者號太空船上

    (C) 麥哲倫上有位太空人是俄羅斯來的專家

    (D) 麥哲倫上有幾樣零件不是新貨

【答案】C
【解析】這是採用消去法、問細節的題型，要刪去三項同義表達。(A)(B)(D) 選項在最後一段都可找到同義表達，只有選項 (C) 是無中生有，故為正解。

# Reading 4

From the 1970s to the mid-1980s, Brice Marden painted primarily in a **set** format which was also employed by many other abstract artists: blocks of color, one built upon another. The interest lies in the play of colors and proportions. During this period Marden worked with oil colors mixed with wax, a technique he learned from Jasper Johns, whose paintings he admired. The addition of wax gives his paintings a wonderful **luminescence**, as if a very dim light were diffused under the surface. The colors themselves are subtle and remind one of the sky, sea water, trees and old stones.

Around 1985, Marden's interest in Chinese calligraphy led him to experimenting with lines instead of blocks of color. He was especially fond of the poetry of the Zen Buddhist Han Shan, or literally, Cold Mountain. Marden reconciled calligraphic lines with the kind of webbing he found in Jackson Pollock's art, which was an important influence on Marden.

Marden first tried calligraphy painting with tender twigs and branches of the ailanthus, and then switched to long-handled brushes like those used in Chinese calligraphy. From 1988 to 1991 he painted six such works and called them the Cold Mountain Series. The coloration in this series is further **toned down**, mainly in the silver-gray of snowy mountains, although subtle variations of shade are visible from painting to painting.

In the Cold Mountain Series, Marden did not use wax in his oil paint, but scraped and sandpapered the canvas so that old lines are but shadows in the background; he then added new, crisscrossing lines on top of them. Interwoven with lines drawn with a slight change in hue, his lines on the canvas can evoke pictures of dense, snowy woods, with light coming from deep within, glowing through row after row of branches weighed down with snow.

✎ Exercise

① A paragraph preceding the passage would probably deal with
   (A) another of Brice Marden's master series, in the 1990s
   (B) Brice Marden's art before 1970
   (C) American realist painting
   (D) abstract artists other than Brice Marden

② The word "set" as used in the first paragraph is closest in meaning to
   (A) fixed
   (B) arranged
   (C) agreed-upon
   (D) custom-made

③ The author mentions that before 1985 Marden
   (A) primarily did watercolor painting
   (B) used the technique of scraping and sandpapering
   (C) imitated Chinese calligraphy in his art
   (D) painted in a way similar to that used by other artists

④ The word "luminescence" in the first paragraph is closest in meaning to
   (A) brightness
   (B) subtlety
   (C) shallowness
   (D) dimness

⑤ According to the author, which of the following prompted Marden to shift from blocks to lines as the main components in his paintings?
   (A) Pollock's webs
   (B) Zen Buddhism
   (C) Chinese calligraphy
   (D) ailanthus brushes

⑥ According to the passage, all of the following statements are true EXCEPT
(A) Marden liked Jasper Johns's art
(B) The color of the Cold Mountain Series is chiefly silver-gray
(C) Cold Mountain is the name of an actual mountain in China
(D) Marden liked to use subtle coloration in his paintings

⑦ According to the author, all of the following had an influence on Marden's art EXCEPT
(A) Jackson Pollock
(B) Jasper Johns
(C) Han Shan
(D) Christianity

⑧ How many paintings are there in the Cold Mountain Series?
(A) Five
(B) Six
(C) Seven
(D) Eight

⑨ The phrase "toned down" in the third paragraph most closely means
(A) subdued in brightness
(B) lowered in pitch
(C) directed downward
(D) increased in vividness

⑩ It can be inferred that Marden scraped and sandpapered the canvas primarily to
(A) get rid of excess wax
(B) correct errors
(C) imitate Jackson Pollock
(D) create depth in his paintings

⊡ 題解

【文章翻譯】

從 1970 年代到 1980 年代中葉，布萊斯‧馬登主要採用一種固定格式作畫，那也是許多別的抽象畫家愛用的格式：層層堆疊的色塊。趣味主要在於色彩與比例之間的變化。在此時期，馬登用的是油彩摻上蠟，這項技法是他學雅斯培‧強斯的，他很欣賞強斯的作品。因為摻了蠟，他的畫裡面有一種神奇的光澤，仿佛在表面下有很黯淡的光在漫射。色彩本身很含蓄，令人聯想到天空、海水、樹木與老岩石。

在 1985 年左右，馬登因為對中國書法有興趣，開始實驗線條畫、捨棄了色塊。他特別喜愛禪宗詩人寒山的詩，寒山字面上就是冷山。馬登調合了書法線條與他在傑克森‧波拉克作品裡面發現的網狀線，波拉克的作品對馬登影響很大。

馬登嘗試書法畫，最早用的是檉樹的嫩枝條，然後改採中國書法用的長桿毛筆。從 1988 到 1991 年他用這種手法畫了 6 張作品，稱之為寒山系列。該系列的配色被他進一步壓抑，主要呈現的是雪山的銀灰色，雖然不同畫作間可以看出細微的色調變化。

寒山系列中，馬登沒有在油彩中摻蠟，而是將畫布括擦、用砂紙打磨，老線條因此成為背景中的暗影而已。然後他在上面加了新的、交叉的線條。裡面穿插著色調稍有改變的線條，交織在一起，這些線條令人想起濃密森林覆雪的景色，光從林中深處傳來，穿過一排又一排被雪壓彎的樹枝透出微光。

【練習題翻譯與詳解】

① 本文前一段的主題可能是

(A) 布萊斯‧馬登另一個主要作品系列，作於 1990 年代

(B) 1970 年之前布萊斯‧馬登的藝術

(C) 美國寫實畫

(D) 布萊斯‧馬登之外的抽象畫家

【答案】 B

【解析】這是問組織結構的題型，要看各段的主題句。因為問的是上一段，所以第一段的主題句尤其重要，就是「從 1970 年代到 1980 年代中葉，布萊斯‧馬登主要採用一種固定格式作畫」。下一段主題句說到 1985 年馬登的畫，再下一段主題句說到 1988 年馬登的畫，可以看出這篇文章的組織結構採用的是「時間先後順序」，全文主題是「馬登的畫」。所以，若往前推，上一段應該是第一段的時代 (1970-1985) 之前馬登的畫，故選 (B)。

② 第一段中 set 一字的用法最接近

(A) 固定的   (B) 經過安排的

(C) 已經同意的   (D) 訂製的

【答案】 A

【解析】這是單字題，要找同義字。set 在此是過去分詞，意思是「固定不變的」，最接近的同義字是 fixed。

③ 作者提到，1985 年以前馬登

(A) 主要畫水彩畫

(B) 採用括擦與砂紙打磨的技法

(C) 模仿中國書法來作畫

(D) 畫法類似其他畫家的畫法

【答案】 D

【解析】這是問細節的題型，要找同義表達。第一段第一句提到「從 1970 年代到 1980 年代中葉，布萊斯‧馬登主要採用一種固定格式作畫，那也是許多別的抽象畫家愛用的格式」，其中 from the 1970s to the mid-1980s 就是 before 1985 的同義表達，而 painted primarily in a set format which was also employed by many other abstract artists 就是 painted in a way similar to that used by other artists 的同義表達，故選 (D)。

④ 第一段中的 luminescence 一字意思最接近

(A) 明亮

(B) 含蓄

(C) 淺薄

(D) 黯淡

【答案】 A

【解析】這是單字題。luminescence 的字根 lumin 是 light，單字的意思是「光亮」，最接近的同義字是 brightness。

⑤ 根據作者，下面哪項因素促使馬登離開色塊，轉而採用線條為他畫作中的主要成分？

(A) 波拉克之網

(B) 佛教禪宗

(C) 中國書法

(D) 檸樹毛筆

【答案】 C

【解析】這是問細節的題型，要找同義表達。根據第二段第一句話「在 1985 年左右，馬登因為對中國書法感興趣，開始實驗線條畫、捨棄了色塊」，其中 prompted Marden 就是 led him，而 experimenting with lines instead of blocks of color 就是 to shift from blocks to lines，故選 (C)。

⑥ 根據本文，下列每句都正確，除了

(A) 馬登喜歡雅斯培‧強斯的藝術

(B) 寒山系列的色調主要是銀灰色

(C) 寒山是中國一座真實山名

(D) 馬登作畫喜歡採用比較含蓄的色彩

【答案】**C**

【解析】這是採用消去法刪除三個同義表達的細節題型。其他選項都找得到同義表達，只有 (C) 與原文牴觸。第二段說到寒山是個佛教禪宗 (Zen Buddhist) 的人名，選項 (C) 卻說是山名，所以不是同義表達。

⑦ 根據作者，下列都對馬登的藝術產生過影響，除了

    (A) 傑克森·波拉克   (B) 雅斯培·強斯

    (C) 寒山   (D) 基督教

【答案】**D**

【解析】這也是要用消去法刪除三個同義表達的細節題型。其他選項都找得到同義表達，只有 Christianity 從頭到尾沒有提過，屬於無中生有，故選 (D)。

⑧ 寒山系列共有幾幅畫作？

    (A) 5   (B) 6

    (C) 7   (D) 8

【答案】**B**

【解析】這是問細節的題型。第三段說「從 1988 到 1991 年他用這種方法畫了 6 張作品，稱之為寒山系列」，所以答案為 (B)。

⑨ 第三段中的 toned down 這個片語意思最接近

    (A) 壓抑亮度   (B) 降低音調

    (C) 方向朝下   (D) 增加鮮明度

【答案】**A**

【解析】名詞 tone 可以是音調、也可以是色調。在此上下文 toned down 應該是壓抑色調，使其明度降低，所以最接近 subdued in brightness。

⑩ 可以推論，馬登括擦與砂紙打磨畫布主要是為了

    (A) 除去過多的蠟   (B) 訂正錯誤

    (C) 模仿傑克森·波拉克   (D) 創造作品的景深

【答案】**D**

【解析】這是推論題，答案會比較不明顯，要找根據。最後一段說馬登「將畫布括擦、用砂紙打磨，老線條因此成為背景中的暗影」。由此可推知，在這個背景上添加新線條，最後的效果是好像有光從森林深處傳出，成功在平面畫布上創造出景深，故選 (D)。

Medical and nutritional consensus holds that a diet with a high content of whole grains provides such important nutrients as fiber and antioxidants, which can help fight obesity, heart disease, diabetes and cancer. However, fewer than 10% of American adults eat three servings a day, as is recommended by the Department of Health and Human Services.

Not that the people distrust authorities or ignore their own health requirements. It is simply not that easy to find whole-grain foods that **live up to** their claim. Marketers are capitalizing on people's increasing health consciousness. Walk in any grocery store, and you'll find plenty of breads, cereals and crackers with "made with whole grains" printed on their boxes. Problem is, such products are not necessarily made with whole grains. How can they, you might ask, get away with such blatantly false claims? The reason is that there are few standards guiding whole-grain claims.

A grain kernel comprises three parts: the bran, the germ, and the core. The Food and Drug Administration (FDA) accepts as a whole-grain food any product that contains the three components in the same proportion found in the kernel. This means that a food made of finely ground grains, laced with sugar, containing all sorts of unhealthy ingredients, can still be labeled "made with whole grains" with impunity.

Exercise

① According to the passage, the U.S. government suggests that grownups should eat three servings per day of
(A) nutrients
(B) whole-grain foods
(C) fiber
(D) antioxidants

② The phrase "live up to" in the second paragraph is closest in meaning to which of the following?
(A) look up to
(B) surpass
(C) fulfill
(D) survive

③ What does the author suggest is the cause of the unreliability of supposedly whole-grain food products?
(A) Whole-grain foods cannot really prevent cancer.
(B) Many whole-grain foods are tough to digest.
(C) There are few foods labeled as whole-grain in grocery stores.
(D) There aren't clear guidelines over what can be labeled as whole-grain.

④ It can be inferred from the passage that the FDA would consider which of the following as a whole-grain food?
(A) A loaf of bread with an unusually large amount of fiber in it
(B) A box of crackers with "whole grains" printed on the back
(C) A box of cereal that contains the bran, the germ, and the core
(D) Finely ground flour with all the grain constituents in natural percentages

⑤ What does the author seem to feel about FDA oversight of whole-grain foods?
(A) It should be strengthened.
(B) It has been an effective safeguard against various diseases.
(C) It should no longer exist.
(D) It is unnecessarily detailed and intrusive.

🡒 題解

醫療界與營養界的共識主張：富含全穀類的飲食提供像纖維質與抗氧化劑之類的重要營養素，可以對抗肥胖症、心臟病、糖尿病與癌症。但是美國人每天遵照美國衛生及公共服務部建議、有吃到三份的人還不到 10%。

倒不是因為人民不信任權威、也不是忽視自己的健康需求。只是因為要找到名符其實的全穀食品不是那麼容易。行銷人員在利用人民日增的健康意識。隨便走進哪家雜貨店，就會看到許多麵包、穀片與餅乾，包裝盒上印有「全穀製造」字樣。問題是，這種產品不見得就是全穀製造。你可能要問：如此公然說謊，怎麼能夠過關呢？原因在於：哪種食物可以號稱全穀食品，這方面的指導標準很少。

一粒穀仁含有三種成分：麩皮、胚芽、胚乳。美國食品藥物管理局 (FDA) 接受認定全穀食品的標準是裡面這三種成分要和穀仁裡面的比例相同。這表示：用精研穀粉製造的食品，摻了糖、含有各式各樣不健康的成分，仍舊可以標示為「全穀製造」而不受罰。

練習題翻譯與詳解

① 根據本文，美國政府建議成年人每天應該吃三份

    (A) 營養素   (B) 全穀食品

    (C) 纖維   (D) 抗氧化劑

【答案】B

【解析】這是問細節的題型，要找同義表達。第一段說「富含全穀類的飲食……美國人每天遵照美國衛生及公共服務部建議、有吃到三份的人還不到 10%」，其中 a diet with a high content of whole grains 就是 whole-grain foods 的同義表達，故選 (B)。

② 第二段中的片語 live up to 意思最接近下列何者？

    (A) 尊敬   (B) 超越

    (C) 達成，實現   (D) 存活

【答案】C

【解析】這是單字題。片語 live up to 的意思是「達到，實現」，同義字是 fulfill。

③ 作者暗示，所謂全穀食物製品其實不可靠，原因在於什麼？

    (A) 全穀食品不能真正預防癌症

    (B) 許多全穀食品不易消化

    (C) 雜貨店裡標示為全穀的食品很少

    (D) 什麼食品可以標示為全穀，沒有明確的指導原則

【答案】**D**

【解析】這是推論題,要找根據。第二段說「問題是,這種產品不見得就是全穀製造……原因在於:哪種食物可以號稱全穀食品,這方面的指導標準很少」,可以看出原因在於缺乏明確的標準,故選 (D)。

④ 由本文可以推論,FDA 會認為下列哪一種是全穀食品?

   (A) 一條麵包含有特別高的纖維

   (B) 一盒餅乾背面印有「全穀」字樣

   (C) 一盒穀片裡面有麩皮、胚芽、胚乳

   (D) 精研麵粉裡面穀子所有的成分按照天然比例

【答案】**D**

【解析】這是推論題,要找「根據」。第三段說「FDA 接受認定全穀食品的條件是裡面這三種成分要和穀仁裡面的比例相同」。因此,若精研麵粉符合這個條件,FDA 就會認定為全穀食品。

⑤ 關於 FDA 對全穀食品的管理,作者似乎覺得怎樣?

   (A) 需要加強

   (B) 一直是對抗各種疾病的有效保護

   (C) 不應該繼續存在

   (D) 太過詳細、擾民

【答案】**A**

【解析】這是語氣態度題,要看用字來判斷肯定或否定。第二段說「哪種食物可以號稱全穀食品,這方面的指導標準很少」,已經暗示 FDA 管理不力。第三段說「用精研穀粉製造的食品,摻了糖、含有各式各樣不健康的成分,仍舊可以標示為全穀製造而不受罰」,更是直指 FDA 管理無效,故選 (A)。

The U.S. is a nation of immigrants. Some 19 million people arrived in the U.S. between 1890 and 1920. By the early 1920s, however, competition from unskilled foreign-born workers had forged an alliance between wage-conscious organized labor and those who called for restricted immigration on racial or religious grounds, such as the Ku Klux Klan and **the Immigration Restriction League**. The Johnson-Reed Immigration Act of 1924 permanently curtailed the influx of newcomers with quotas calculated on nation of origin. **The law reduced permissible immigration from outside the Western Hemisphere to 150,000 per year, with national quotas based upon three percent of each group's population in the U.S. according to 1920 census results.** This formula was designed to limit the flow of workers from Southern and Eastern Europe.

The Great Depression of the 1930s dramatically slowed immigration still further; many newcomers even returned home. The number of immigrants dropped about 90 percent over three years—from 242,000 in 1930 to 23,000 in 1933—and totaled only 528,000 for the entire decade, 1931 to 1940. Half a million people returned to Mexico; almost as many Europeans left the U.S. as arrived.

In 1930, President Herbert Hoover requested that American consuls abroad use administrative procedures to **curb** immigration to well below the level legally allowed. State Department officials, eager to protect the American economy and political system from foreign incursion, proceeded to reject vast numbers of applicants on the grounds that they were "likely to become a public charge." With public opinion opposed to immigration and President Franklin D. Roosevelt unwilling to take the political risks attendant upon making exceptions for persecuted European minorities, relatively few refugees found sanctuary in the U.S. from the Nazis after Adolf Hitler's ascent to power in 1933. During the period from 1932 to 1945, only 250,000 Jewish refugees were issued visas for the U.S., a **paltry** number, though still the largest of any Western nation.

Postwar refugee policy was also ungenerous. The Displaced Persons Acts of 1948 and 1950, for example, **admitted** only 405,000 Europeans out of an estimated five million left homeless by the war. In 1953 a Congress crusading against communism voted to admit another 205,000, many of them refugees from Eastern bloc nations. This paved the way for special legislation to admit Hungarians after the abortive uprising of 1956 and Cubans after Fidel Castro's revolution in 1959.

Throughout the postwar decade, the U.S. clung to nationality-based quotas, justifying the restrictions ideologically in the McCarran-Walter Act of 1952. Senator Patrick McCarran and his supporters argued that quota relaxation might **inundate** the U.S. with Marxist subversives from Eastern Europe. New, though tiny, quotas of Asians were permitted, usually totaling 100 or fewer per year. Special preference was given to those with "exceptional" skill or ability, such as scientists and engineers.

President John F. Kennedy, the grandson of Irish immigrants, proposed a major revision of immigration law in the early 1960s. In 1965, two years after his assassination, Congress abandoned national quotas. The Western Hemisphere was allotted 120,000 immigrants annually, though countries in North and South America were generally permitted to exceed the quot(A) The Eastern Hemisphere had a 170,000 quota, with no nation allowed to exceed 20,000 annually. Relatives of U.S. citizens received preference, as did immigrants with job skills in short supply in the U.S. In 1976, amendments to the 1965 Act redressed statutory inequities between the hemispheres by extending the preference system and the 20,000-per-country quota to all nations of the Western Hemisphere. In 1978 the hemispheric limits were replaced by a worldwide ceiling of 290,000, a limit reduced to 270,000 after passage of the Refugee Act of 1980.

__W__ Since the mid-1970s, the U.S. has experienced a fresh wave of immigration, with especially large numbers of arrivals from Asia and Latin Americ(A) __X__ As the U.S. disentangled itself from the Vietnam War, refugees fled the political and economic turmoil. __Y__ The Asian population of the U.S. increased 70 percent from 1980 to 1988. __Z__

During the late 1970s and throughout the 1980s, economic stagnation and political instability in Latin America **loosed** a flood of immigrants and refugees—legal and illegal—northward to the U.S. The great majority are Mexicans, with over 95,000 legal immigrants arriving in 1988.

Exercise

① The author mentions "the Immigration Restriction League" in paragraph 1 in order to
(A) provide a contrast to the Ku Klux Klan
(B) support the argument that the U.S. is a nation of immigrants
(C) cite a social force that was against immigration
(D) explain the origin of national quotas on immigration

② Which of the sentences below best expresses the essential information in the boldfaced sentence in paragraph 1?
The law reduced permissible immigration from outside the Western Hemisphere to 150,000 per year, with national quotas based upon three percent of each group's population in the U.S. according to 1920 census results.
(A) The law allowed only 150,000 immigrants a year from the Eastern Hemisphere.
(B) The law put a ceiling on immigration and set national quotas by a formula.
(C) The law used 1920 census results to reduce total immigrants to 150,000 per year.
(D) The law set national quotas to three percent of total annual immigration.

③ Which of the following can be inferred from paragraph 2 about Europeans during the Great Depression?
(A) The number of European immigrants was reduced to only 10% in three years.
(B) There were only about half a million European immigrants throughout the 1930s.
(C) Nearly half a million Europeans left the U.S.
(D) Slightly more Europeans immigrated to the U.S. than left the country.

④ The word "curb" in paragraph 3 is closest in meaning to
(A) raise   (B) limit
(C) stimulate   (D) bring

⑤ The word "paltry" in paragraph 3 is closest in meaning to
(A) substantial   (B) insignificant
(C) sickly   (D) surprising

⑥ The word "admitted" in paragraph 4 is closest in meaning to
(A) agreed   (B) recognized
(C) accepted   (D) confessed

⑦ According to paragraph 4, which of the following made it easier to pass laws to accept Hungarian and Cuban refugees in the 1950s?
(A) The lack of generosity in postwar refugee policy
(B) The large number of European war refugees that came to the U.S.
(C) The dislike Congress felt for communism
(D) The failure of Fidel Castro's revolution

⑧ The word "inundate" in paragraph 5 is closest in meaning to
(A) drown   (B) supply
(C) flood   (D) harm

⑨ According to paragraph 5, which of the following was never changed throughout the 10 years after World War II?
(A) Immigration quotas based on country of origin
(B) The voters' support for Senator Patrick McCarran
(C) The number of Asian immigrants in the U.S.
(D) The definition of "exceptional" skill or ability

⑩ According to paragraph 6, in which of the following years did the Eastern and Western Hemispheres begin to receive relatively equal treatment in terms of immigration to the U.S.?
(A) 1965   (B) 1976
(C) 1978   (D) 1980

⑪ In which position would the following sentence best fit in paragraph 7?
Vietnamese emigration, however, has been dwarfed by the numbers of arrivals from South Korea, China, the Philippines and India.
(A) Position W   (B) Position X
(C) Position Y   (D) Position Z

⑫ The word "loosed" in paragraph 8 is closest in meaning to
(A) lost   (B) unleashed
(C) created   (D) stopped

☐ 題解

文章翻譯

　　美國是移民國家。在 1890 到 1920 年間大約有 1 千 9 百萬人來到美國。然而到了 1920 年代初期，出生在外國、沒有技術的勞工帶來了競爭，造成兩股勢力結盟：一是很注意工資的勞工組織、一是基於種族或宗教立場呼籲限制移民者，例如三 K 黨與移民限制聯盟。1924 年的詹森李德移民法案設下配額，永久限制了移民的湧入，配額根據來源國計算。該法將來自西半球以外的移民准許人數降低到每年 15 萬，各國的配額計算基準是 1920 年人口普查中該國在美國人口總數的 3%。這套公式的設計就是為了限制從南歐與東歐來的工人潮。

　　1930 年代的經濟大蕭條更進一步、大幅度減緩了移民的腳步，許多新來的人甚至又回去了。三年間移民人口大跌約 90%（從 1930 年的 242,000 到 1933 年的 23,000），整個 30 年代 (1931-1940) 總共只有 528,000 人。有 50 萬人回去墨西哥，離開美國的歐洲人只比來到的人數稍低一點。

　　1930 年，胡佛總統要求駐國外的美國領事，利用行政程序遏止移民人數到遠低於法律准許的水平。國務院官員很想保護美國經濟與政治制度不受外國入侵，於是拒絕大批移民申請，理由是他們「可能成為政府的包袱」。因為民意反對移民，羅斯福總統又不願意冒政治風險（如果破例收留被迫害的歐洲少數民族就會帶來政治風險），所以 1933 年希特勒上台後，能夠在美國找到庇護、躲避納粹的難民不多。1932 到 1945 年間，只有 25 萬猶太難民取得美國簽證，少得可憐，雖然在西方國家之中仍是最多的。

　　戰後的難民政策同樣小氣。例如 1948 與 1950 年的難民法案，在因為戰爭無家可歸的 500 萬歐洲難民中只接受了 40 萬 5 千人。1953 年，國會正值反共熱潮，又投票接受了 20 萬 5 千人，其中許多人來自東歐集團國家。這為將來的特別立法鋪了路，在 1956 年的匈牙利流產抗暴、1959 年古巴卡斯楚革命之後接收了一些難民。

　　整個戰後的 10 年，美國緊抓國家配額不放，用 1952 年麥卡倫華特法案當作理念依據來合理化限制移民的措施。麥卡倫參議員與支持他的人主張，一旦放寬配額，美國將被東歐來的馬克思顛覆分子淹沒。亞洲國家也出現了新配額，雖然很少，通常一年在 100 人以下。擁有「特殊」技能者如科學家與工程師有最惠待遇。

　　甘迺迪總統是愛爾蘭移民之孫，在 1960 年代初期提議大幅修改移民法。1965 年，甘迺迪遇刺兩年後，國會取消了針對國家的配額。西半球每年允許 12 萬移民，但南北美洲國家往往可以超出配額。東半球的配額是 17 萬，但是單一國家不能超過一年 2 萬。美國公民親屬有最惠待遇，擁有美國短缺技能的移民亦然。1976 年，1965 法案獲得修訂，解決了東西半球之間法律規定不公平的問題，將特惠制度與國家上限 2 萬的配額擴大適用於西半球所有國家。1978 年，半球上限取消、換成全球上限 29 萬，後來通過 1980 年難民法之後降低為 27 萬。

　　W 自 1970 年代中葉以來，美國見識到新一波的移民，來自亞洲與拉丁美洲的特別多。X 隨著美國撤出越戰，難民也逃離政治與經濟混亂。Y 美國的亞裔人口從 1980 到 1988 增加了 70%。Z

在 1970 年代晚期以及整個 1980 年代，拉丁美洲經濟停滯、政治動亂，釋放出移民與難民的洪流（有合法也有非法）北上到美國。絕大多數是墨西哥人，1988 年合法的墨西哥移民就超過 9 萬 5 千人。

練習題翻譯與詳解

① 第一段中作者提到「移民限制聯盟」的目的是
　　(A) 為三 K 黨提供一個對比
　　(B) 支持「美國是移民國家」一說
　　(C) 舉出一股反移民的社會勢力
　　(D) 解釋移民的國家配額是怎麼來的

【答案】C
【解析】這是修辭目的的題型，要看上下文。第一段說到「兩股勢力結盟：一是很注意工資的勞工組織、一是基於種族或宗教立場呼籲限制移民者，例如三 K 黨與移民限制聯盟」，所以移民限制聯盟與三 K 黨同樣，都是「限制移民」的勢力，故選 (C)。

② 下列哪個句子最能夠表達第一段黑體字句子的主要內容？
「該法將來自西半球以外的移民准許人數降低到每年 15 萬，各國的配額計算基準是 1920 年人口普查中該國在美國人口總數的 3%。」
　　(A) 該法只准許東半球每年 15 萬移民。
　　(B) 該法設定移民上限、並且按照公式設定國家配額。
　　(C) 該法使用 1920 人口普查結果將移民總數降低到每年 15 萬人。
　　(D) 該法設定國家配額為年度移民總數的 3%。

【答案】B
【解析】這是句子改寫的題型，要找句中重點的同義表達。原句有兩個重點：一是西半球以外的移民上限、一是計算出國家配額，也就是選項 (B) 中的兩點。至於上限的數字以及公式的算法，那是不重要的細節，可以忽略。

③ 關於經濟大蕭條期間的歐洲人，從第二段可以推論出什麼？
　　(A) 3 年內歐洲移民人數減少到只剩 10%。
　　(B) 整個 1930 年代只有約 50 萬歐洲移民。
　　(C) 將近 50 萬歐洲人離開美國。
　　(D) 歐洲人移民到美國的人數比離開美國的稍多一點。

【答案】D
【解析】這是推論題，要找「根據」。第二段說「離開美國的歐洲人只比來到的人數稍低一點」，反過來說就是來到的人數比離開的稍多，故選 (D)。

④ 第三段中的 curb 一字意思最接近

(A) 提高

(B) 限制

(C) 刺激

(D) 帶來

【答案】**B**

【解析】這是單字題。curb 是指「阻撓，限制」，同義字是 limit。

⑤ 第三段中的 paltry 意思最接近

(A) 大量的

(B) 微小的，不重要的

(C) 不健康的

(D) 驚人的

【答案】**B**

【解析】這是單字題。paltry 是指「微小的，極少的」，同義字是 insignificant。

⑥ 第四段中的 admitted 一字意思最接近

(A) 同意

(B) 承認，辨認

(C) 接受

(D) 坦白，招供

【答案】**C**

【解析】這是單字題。admit（構造：to/send）可以解釋為「承認」，但是在此上下文應解釋為「接納」，同義字是 accept。

⑦ 根據第四段，下列哪項因素使得後來在 1950 年代較容易立法接受匈牙利與古巴難民？

(A) 戰後移民政策很小氣

(B) 來到美國的歐戰難民人數眾多

(C) 國會不喜歡共產主義

(D) 卡斯楚革命失敗

【答案】**C**

【解析】這是問細節的題型，要找同義表達。第四段說「國會正值反共熱潮，又投票接受了 20 萬 5 千人……這為將來的特別立法鋪了路，在 1956 年的匈牙利流產抗暴、1959 年古巴卡斯楚革命之後接收了一些難民」，其中 a Congress crusading against communism 就是 The dislike Congress felt for communism 的同義表達，故選 (C)。

⑧ 第五段中的 inundate 一字意思最接近

(A) 淹死

(B) 供應

(C) 淹沒

(D) 傷害

【答案】**C**

【解析】這是單字題。inundate（構造：in/wave/(v.)）字面上是指「淹沒」，與 flood 一樣都是用「淹水」來比喻「大量湧入」。

⑨ 根據第五段，二次大戰後的 10 年，下列哪一項一直沒有改變？

(A) 針對國家的移民配額

(B) 選民對麥卡蘭參議員的支持

(C) 美國的亞裔移民人數

(D)「特殊」技能的定義

【答案】**A**

【解析】這是問細節的題型，要找同義表達。第五段說「整個戰後的 10 年，美國緊抓國家配額不放」，其中 nationality-based quotas 就是 quotas based on country of origin 的同義表達，故選 (A)。

⑩ 根據第六段，在移民美國方面，東西半球在哪一年開始獲得相對平等的待遇？

(A) 1965　　　　　　　　　　　　(B) 1976

(C) 1978　　　　　　　　　　　　(D) 1980

【答案】**B**

【解析】這是問細節的題型，要找同義表達。第六段說「1976 年，1965 法案獲得修訂，解決了東西半球之間法律規定不公平的問題」，所以答案是 (B) 1976。

⑪ 下面這個句子最適合放在第七段什麼位置？

「但是越南移民相形之下在少數，大宗是從南韓、中國、菲律賓、印度來的。」

(A) W 位置　　　　　　　　　　　(B) X 位置

(C) Y 位置　　　　　　　　　　　(D) Z 位置

【答案】**C**

【解析】這是安插句子的題型，要看上下文。Y 位置上文說「隨著美國撤出越戰，難民也逃離政治與經濟混亂」，可以銜接要插入句句首的「但是越南難民……」。Y 位置下文說「美國的亞裔人口從 1980 到 1988 增加了 70%」，這可以銜接上插入句句尾的「大宗是從南韓、中國、菲律賓、印度來的」，故選 (C)，成為：「隨著美國撤出越戰，難民也逃離政治與經濟混亂。<u>但是越南移民相形之下在少數，大宗是從南韓、中國、菲律賓、印度來的</u>。美國的亞裔人口從 1980 到 1988 增加了 70%」。

⑫ 第八段中的 loosed 一字意思最接近

(A) 失去　　　　　　　　　　　　(B) 釋放出

(C) 創造出　　　　　　　　　　　(D) 停止

【答案】**B**

【解析】這是單字題。動詞 loose 字面上是「放鬆」之意，unleas 字面上是「解開」之意，同樣比喻「釋放出」。

NOTES

閱讀測驗篇

第 2 章

The American colonists at first had to pay various taxes to the British government. However, by 1770, the British Prime Minister Lord North had abolished most taxes on the colonists. Britain's King George III, nevertheless, insisted on **retaining** the tax on tea imported to the colonies. He saw this tax as symbolic of Britain's right to tax the colonies, and hence of British sovereignty in America. On the American side, however, public sentiment was: no taxation without **representation**. The colonists considered it highly unfair that they should be made to pay taxes to the British government while they had no right to send their representatives to Parliament. The 3-pence-a-pound tea tax itself, meanwhile, did not generate much revenue for the British treasury, nor did it cost much to the colonists. Over 90% of the tea entering the colonies was smuggled in and therefore tax-exempt.

Things **came to a head** in 1773, when Parliament gave the British East Indies Company a monopoly over the import of tea to the colonies. The American merchants were outraged by the special treatment and worried about additional monopolies to come. When ships carrying monopolized tea came into harbor, the colonists plotted their revenge. In Charleston the tea was locked into a warehouse. In Philadelphia and New York the tea ships were forced to turn back. In Boston, 50 citizens, disguised as Native Americans, boarded a tea ship at night and poured all 343 boxes of tea into the harbor. The "Native American" disguise was **half-hearted at best**; the Bostonians made an open challenge to British law and authority. This direct forerunner to the War of Independence came to be called the Boston Tea Party.

Exercise

① Which of the following would be the best title for the passage?
   (A) The American War of Independence
   (B) The Boston Tea Party
   (C) History of Colonial America
   (D) The Tea Monopoly of 1773

② The word "retaining" in the first paragraph is closest in meaning to
   (A) reducing
   (B) expanding
   (C) abolishing
   (D) continuing

③ The author mentions that George III considered which of the following as symbolic of British control of America?
   (A) the abolition of most taxes
   (B) the amount of tax money collected on tea
   (C) the right to collect the tea tax
   (D) Parliament's monopoly on tea export

④ The word "representation" in the first paragraph refers to which of the following?
   (A) Having one company represent others in importing tea
   (B) Receiving presents for having paid taxes on time
   (C) Sending members to the British Parliament
   (D) Presenting the colonists' case directly to King George III

⑤ It can be inferred from the passage that, until 1773, the British government did not collect much tax on tea because
   (A) tea was inexpensive in the colonies
   (B) tea parties were infrequent in America
   (C) Lord North had declared tea tax-exempt
   (D) a lot of tea was illegally shipped to America

⑥ The phrase "came to a head" in the second paragraph is closest in meaning to
(A) came to a standstill
(B) went ahead
(C) reached a crisis
(D) came to the notice of someone

⑦ The author mentions that the colonial merchants were worried in 1773 that
(A) more monopolies might be granted
(B) their smuggling could not continue
(C) the tea tax might be resumed
(D) a revolution looked inevitable

⑧ According to the passage, who actually poured tea into Boston Harbor?
(A) Native Americans
(B) Citizens of Boston
(C) British merchants
(D) Guests invited to the Tea Party

⑨ By saying that the "Native American" disguise was "half-hearted at best" in the second paragraph, the author implies that
(A) these Native Americans did a sloppy job while putting on disguise for war
(B) these people did not really expect to fool the British government as to who they really were
(C) these merchants lost heart when they saw Native Americans coming
(D) the rebels did not really have the heart to pour all that tea into the harbor

⑩ According to the passage, which of the following is a correct statement about the Boston Tea Party?
(A) It involved 50 Native Americans
(B) It occurred shortly before the Revolutionary War
(C) It forced some tea ships to turn back
(D) It locked 343 boxes of tea in a warehouse

↱ 題解

文章翻譯

　　美洲殖民地人民一開始得向英國政府繳納各種稅金。不過到了 1770 年，英國首相諾茲爵士已經廢除了對殖民地課徵的大部分稅捐。英王喬治三世卻堅持要保留殖民地進口茶葉的稅，他認為這象徵英國對殖民地課稅的權力、因而也象徵英國對美洲的主權。但是在美洲這邊，民意是：沒有代表權就不交稅。殖民地人民認為很不公平：他們得向英國政府納稅，卻無權派代表進國會。同時，每磅區區 3 便士的茶葉稅，本身產生不了多少稅收給英國國庫，殖民地人民也不感覺有負擔。超過 9 成的進口茶葉都是走私進來的、免稅。

　　到了 1773 年，情況爆發了。英國國會授予英國東印度公司專賣權，可以專營進口茶葉到美洲殖民地。美洲商人對此特權深感忿怒，並且擔心還會有新的專賣出現。船隻載著專賣茶葉進港時，殖民地人民正在策畫報復。在查爾斯頓市，茶葉被鎖進倉庫。在費城與紐約市，運茶船被迫折返。在波士頓，50 名市民偽裝為美洲原住民在半夜登上茶葉船，把 343 箱茶葉全部倒入港中。所謂「原住民」偽裝也不是很認真的：波士頓人等於是公開挑戰英國法律與英國權威。這是獨立戰爭的直接導火線，後人稱之為「波士頓茶葉事件」。

練習題翻譯與詳解

① 下列何者是本文最好的標題？

(A) 美國獨立戰爭　　　　　　　　(B) 波士頓茶葉事件

(C) 殖民地美洲史　　　　　　　　(D) 1773 年茶葉專賣案

【答案】**B**

【解析】這是問主題的題型，要看主題句。本篇按照時間順序敘述，全文主題句在最後一句的結論：「這是獨立戰爭的直接導火線，後人稱之為波士頓茶葉事件」。

② 第一段中的 retaining 一字意思最接近

(A) 減少　　　　　　　　　　　　(B) 擴大

(C) 廢除　　　　　　　　　　　　(D) 繼續

【答案】**D**

【解析】動詞 retain（構造：back/hold）的意思是「保留」，最接近的同義字是 continue。

③ 作者提到，喬治三世認為下列何者是英國統治美洲的象徵？

(A) 廢除大部分稅捐　　　　　　　(B) 茶葉抽到的稅金額度

(C) 抽取茶葉稅的權力　　　　　　(D) 國會出口茶葉的專賣權

【答案】**C**

【解析】這是問細節的題型，要找同義表達。根據第一段「英王喬治三世卻堅持要保留殖民地進口茶葉的稅，他認為這象徵英國對殖民地課稅的權力、因而也象徵英國對美洲的主權」，所以應選 (C)。

④ 第一段中 representation 一字指的是

(A) 由一家公司代表別家來進口茶葉

(B) 準時納稅可獲得禮物

(C) 派出代表進入英國國會

(D) 直接向英王喬治三世提出殖民地人民的訴願

【答案】**C**

【解析】這是指射題型，要看上下文。直接下文是「殖民地人民認為很不公平：他們得向英國政府納稅，卻無權派代表進國會 (they had no right to send their representatives to Parliament)」，其中 representatives 就是選項 (C) 中 members 的同義字，故選 (C)。

⑤ 由本文可以推論，直到 1773 年，英國政府都收不到很多茶葉稅，這是因為

(A) 茶葉在殖民地賣得不貴

(B) 茶宴在美洲不常舉辦

(C) 諾茲爵士已經宣告茶葉免稅

(D) 許多茶葉都是非法運到美洲

【答案】**D**

【解析】這是推論題，要找「根據」。原文有兩項線索，都在第一段。「每磅區區 3 便士的茶葉稅，本身產生不了多少稅收」，以及「超過 9 成的進口茶葉都是走私進來的、免稅」。由這兩項可以推知英國政府收不到多少茶葉稅，選項 (D) 是原因之一，故選 (D)。

⑥ 第二段中的片語 came to a head 意思最接近

(A) 完全停止   (B) 向前進

(C) 發生危機   (D) 引起某人注意

【答案】**C**

【解析】這是單字題。come to a head 是個片語，表示「爆發」。

⑦ 作者提到，1773 年殖民地商人擔心

(A) 政府可能會授予更多的專賣權   (B) 他們的走私無以為繼

(C) 茶葉稅可能恢復   (D) 革命看來在所難免

【答案】**A**

【解析】這是問細節的題型，要找同義表達。第二段說「美洲商人對此特權深感忿怒，並且擔心還會有新的專賣出現 (additional monopolies to come)」。其中 additional 是 more 的同義表達，to come 是 might be granted 的同義表達，故選 (A)。

⑧ 根據本文，是誰真正把茶葉倒入波士頓港？

    (A) 美洲原住民   (B) 波士頓士民

    (C) 英國商人   (D) 應邀參加茶宴的客人

【答案】**B**

【解析】這是問細節的題型，要找同義表達。第二段說「在波士頓，50 名市民偽裝為原住民在半夜登上茶葉船，把 343 箱茶葉全部倒入港中」，所以是波士頓市民做的。

⑨ 作者在第二段說 "Native American" 的偽裝是 "half-hearted at best"，這是在暗示

    (A) 這些原住民穿上偽裝要上戰場時很不用心

    (B) 這些人並不真正指望他們的真實身分能夠瞞過英國政府

    (C) 看到原住民一來，這些商人就害怕了

    (D) 這些叛徒並非有心想要把那麼多茶葉都倒進港中

【答案】**B**

【解析】這是單字題，考的是片語 half-hearted at best。首先，"Native American" 一詞在原文加上了雙引號，意思是「所謂的」，已經帶有反面的意思。其次，at best 是「充其量、最多」，然後 half-hearted 是「並非很認真」，整個的意思就是「並不指望能騙得了誰」。

⑩ 根據本文，下列哪一項是關於波士頓茶葉事件的正確陳述？

    (A) 它涉及 50 名原住民   (B) 它發生在獨立戰爭前夕

    (C) 它迫使一些運茶船返航   (D) 它鎖住 343 箱茶葉在一間倉庫

【答案】**B**

【解析】這是問細節的題型，要找同義表達。文中最後一句「這是獨立戰爭的直接導火線 (direct forerunner)，後人稱之為波士頓茶葉事件」，其中 direct forerunner 就是 occurred shortly before 的同義表達。

Engine noise in cars has been a headache to automobile designers. Drivers like smooth and quiet rides. The traditional way to reduce engine noise is through **sound insulation**. In other words, designers add enough material to the body of the car to cut off engine noise. However, if enough weight is added to the car to make it quiet, the car becomes so heavy that it is no longer fuel efficient.

There is a high-tech approach to this problem. Sound is produced through vibrations, or variations in air pressure. With the help of computers, engineers at the Lotus Group, a sports car manufacturer, have successfully produced anti-sound to **wipe out** irritating sound.

The Lotus engineers place an electronic sensor under the engine hood to monitor engine noise. Microphones in the interior of the car pick up the noise as it is heard by the driver or passenger, and transmit it to a computer, in which the noise wave-form is analyzed and identified. The computer then creates electronic signals for the production of anti-noise, which has wave-forms exactly the **reverse** of the noise. When the signals are played through the car's stereo system, the wave-forms of the anti-noise exactly cancel those of the engine noise. The result is a lack of variation in air pressure, and hence, complete silence.

✏ Exercise

① What does the passage mainly discuss?
   (A) A sports car manufacturer
   (B) The causes of engine noise
   (C) Quiet technology in cars
   (D) Automobile stereo systems

② The term "sound insulation" in the first paragraph is closest in meaning to
   (A) blocking of noise
   (B) healthy states of isolation
   (C) thorough investigation
   (D) stereo system installation

③ A drawback to the traditional way of reducing engine noise is that
   (A) it is too expensive to install the technology
   (B) it makes the car consume too much gasoline
   (C) it reduces smoothness of the ride
   (D) it replaces one kind of noise with another

④ According to the passage, what produces sound?
   (A) faulty engine design
   (B) weighty car bodies
   (C) changes in air pressure
   (D) electronic sensors

⑤ The phrase "wipe out" in the second paragraph is closest in meaning to
   (A) cancel
   (B) forget
   (C) pardon
   (D) purify

⑥ The author mentions that microphones are set up
(A) under the engine hood
(B) inside the computer
(C) in the automobile
(D) under the front passenger's seat

⑦ In the Lotus anti-noise system, a computer does all of the following EXCEPT
(A) analyze the noise wave-forms
(B) identify the noise wave-forms
(C) create signals for anti-sound
(D) play the anti-sound on its speakers

⑧ The word "reverse" in the third paragraph is closest in meaning to
(A) back
(B) copy
(C) opposite
(D) amplitude

⑨ It can be inferred that riding in a car equipped with the high-tech system described in the passage would be
(A) sporty
(B) fast
(C) quiet
(D) smooth

題解

文章翻譯

　　汽車引擎噪音一直是令汽車設計師頭疼的問題。駕駛人喜歡開起車來平穩無聲。降低引擎噪音的老辦法是靠隔音。換句話說，設計師添加足夠的材料到車身以隔絕引擎噪音。但是，如果車子加了很多重量來造成安靜的效果，那就太重而不再省油了。

　　要解決這個問題，有個高科技的辦法。聲音來自於振動，也就是空氣壓力的變化。借助電腦之力，跑車廠商蓮花集團的工程師成功製造出反聲音來抹去刺耳的聲音。

　　蓮花集團的工程師在引擎蓋底下放一個電子偵測器來監聽引擎噪音。車子裡面有麥克風可以接收駕駛或乘客聽到的噪音、並且輸入電腦，在電腦中分析並且辨認噪音的波型。然後電腦再製造出電子訊號以產生反噪音，它的波型和噪音波型正相反。訊號經過車子的音響系統播出，反噪音的波型剛好抵消引擎噪音的波型。結果是空氣壓力無變化，也就是完全安靜無聲。

練習題翻譯與詳解

① 本文主要談的是什麼？

　　(A) 一家跑車廠商　　　　　　　　(B) 引擎噪音的原因
　　(C) 汽車內部無聲科技　　　　　　(D) 汽車音響系統

【答案】**C**
【解析】這是問主題的題型，要看主題句。本文第一段是開場白，說明背景。全文主題句在第二段：「聲音來自於振動，也就是空氣壓力的變化。借助電腦之力，跑車廠商蓮花集團的工程師成功製造出反聲音來抹去刺耳的聲音」，所以選 (C)。第三段則是在發展細節。

② 第一段中的 sound insulation 意思最接近

　　(A) 封鎖聲音　　　　　　　　　　(B) 健康的孤立狀態
　　(C) 徹底的調查　　　　　　　　　(D) 音響系統裝設

【答案】**A**
【解析】這是單字題。insulation 字根與 island「島」相同，意思是「絕緣，隔絕」，所以接近 blocking「封鎖」。

③ 降低引擎噪音的傳統辦法有個缺點在於

　　(A) 裝設這項科技成本太高　　　　(B) 會令車輛耗油太凶
　　(C) 會減低行車的平穩度　　　　　(D) 會用一種噪音取代另一種

【答案】B

【解析】這是問細節的題型,要找同義表達。第一段說「如果車子加了很多重量來造成安靜的效果,那就太重而不再省油了」,其中 no longer fuel efficient 就是 consume too much gasoline 的同義表達,故選 (B)。

④ 根據本文,是什麼造成噪音的?

(A) 引擎設計不良

(B) 車體沉重

(C) 空氣壓力變化

(D) 電子偵測器

【答案】C

【解析】這是問細節的題型,要找同義表達。第二段說「聲音來自於振動,也就是空氣壓力的變化」,其中 variations 就是 changes 的同義表達,故選 (C)。

⑤ 第二段中的片語 wipe out 意思最接近

(A) 取消

(B) 忘記

(C) 原諒

(D) 淨化

【答案】A

【解析】這是單字題。wipe out 字面上是「抹去,擦掉」之意,也就是「消除」,最接近 cancel。

⑥ 作者提到,麥克風裝設在

(A) 引擎蓋下

(B) 電腦裡面

(C) 汽車內

(D) 前乘客座底下

【答案】C

【解析】這是問細節的題型,要找同義表達。第三段說「車子裡面 (in the interior of the car) 有麥克風可以接收駕駛或乘客聽到的噪音」,其中 in the interior of the car 就是 in the automobile 的同義表達,故選 (C)。

⑦ 在蓮花集團反噪音系統中,電腦做的事不包括

(A) 分析噪音波型

(B) 辨認噪音波型

(C) 製造訊號以產生反聲音

(D) 在電腦揚聲器播放反聲音

【答案】D

【解析】這是問細節、採用消去法的題型,要刪去三個同義表達。由第三段提到「訊號經過車子的音響系統播出」,可知選項 (D) 不是同義表達。

⑧ 第三段中的 reverse 一字意思最接近

    (A) 背部   (B) 拷貝

    (C) 相反   (D) 幅度

【答案】C

【解析】這是單字題。reverse（構造：back/turn）的意思是「相反」。

⑨ 可以推論，搭乘配有本文描述這套高科技系統的車輛會很

    (A) 輕快   (B) 快速

    (C) 安靜   (D) 平穩

【答案】C

【解析】這是推論題，要找「根據」。這套系統是無聲科技，所以效果應該是「安靜」。

2

As over-fishing became an increasingly serious problem in the 1980s, the National Marine Fisheries Service (NMFS) of the Unites States developed a plan to manage the seafood resources on all three coasts. This was known as individual **transferable** quotas, or ITQs. The NMFS had long been keeping records of the fishing history of any sizable fishing boat. It now decided to issue permits to boat owners allowing them to catch a certain amount of fish each year, the precise amount depending on the recorded amount caught by the boat the previous year. The ITQs could be leased or sold for profit, or passed on from father to son. It would appear that the ITQs were making fishing more like international trade, a business in which transferable quotas had been a set practice. According to Richard Schaefer, however, who was the NMFS conservation chief directly responsible for the ITQ system, the basic idea behind the ITQs was to encourage fishermen to act more like farmers. It was hoped that, with ITQs in hand, the fishermen would start looking on fish in the sea as farmers regarded their crops: with protective care in both cases. "Fishermen don't own a fish until it's on the deck," said Schaefer. "If they own it before it is caught, they will manage it rationally."

Most fishermen, however, did not react positively to the idea initially. They were in favor of suspending licensing operations indefinitely, to keep new boats from entering the already overcrowded waters. Besides, many were worried that the ITQ system would mean an end to their independence. Major fishing corporations, it was feared, would buy up ITQs and put fishermen out of jobs, just as Big Business had bought up farmland and evicted the farmers. In addition, American fishermen considered themselves true heirs to the cowboys of the Old West. Their hard job on the sea was rewarded as much by fun and adventure as by money. To **these cowboys**, the new system was degrading.

Exercise

① A paragraph preceding this passage would most probably deal with which of the following subjects?
(A) Cowboys of the Old West
(B) Problems caused by over-fishing
(C) The quota system in international trade
(D) Farmers on the West Coast

② According to the author, the amount of fish that a boat could catch under a permit was
(A) decided by the amount recorded for the boat the year before
(B) unlimited whatsoever, as long as the boat owner had an ITQ
(C) dependent on how well the boat owner did conservation
(D) determined by the tonnage of the boat

③ It can be inferred that the ITQs were called "transferable" because
(A) they were issued to every boat
(B) they could be freely bought or sold
(C) they were based on previous records
(D) they decided the legal amount of catch

④ The author implies that ITQs would appear to make fishing similar to international trade because in the latter
(A) ITQs were already used to export fish
(B) a lot of money could be made
(C) quotas could also be bought and sold
(D) the NMFS was also in control

⑤ Which of the following can be inferred to be true if one compares fishermen with farmers?
(A) Both conserved resources equally well
(B) Both neglected environmental issues
(C) Fishermen took better care of the sea
(D) Farmers took better care of their land

⑥ The author quotes Schaefer's words in the first paragraph in order to
(A) prove that fishermen are just like farmers
(B) describe the organization of the NMFS
(C) explain the goal of the NMFS in promoting the ITQs
(D) argue that fishermen should own their boats

⑦ Most fishermen supported suspending the giving out of licenses probably because
(A) they were ready to change jobs
(B) the NMFS had told them to do so
(C) they were as conservative as farmers
(D) there were too many fishing boats already

⑧ The fishermen were against the ITQ system for all of the following reasons EXCEPT
(A) Big Business would evict them from their homes
(B) It would spoil the fun and excitement of fishing
(C) They cherished their independence
(D) Big fishing companies would drive them out of jobs

⑨ "These cowboys" in the second paragraph refers to
(A) American fishermen
(B) farmers
(C) major fishing corporations
(D) cowboys of the Old West

題解

　　過度捕撈在 1980 年代成為越來越嚴重的問題，於是美國國家海洋漁業部研發出一套計畫來管理三條海岸線上的海產資源，這套計畫稱為「個人可轉換配額」(ITQ)。漁業部早就在持續記錄大型漁船的捕魚史，這時漁業部決定要核發許可證給船主，有證就可以每年捕撈定量的漁產，至於是怎樣的量，取決於這艘船前一年記錄捕獲的量。ITQ 可通過租售賺錢，也可以由父傳子。看起來，採用 ITQ 好像會讓捕魚變成比較接近國際貿易，國貿早就固定採用可轉換配額。不過，根據當時漁業部保育局長理查·薛佛的說法（就是他直接主管 ITQ 制），ITQ 背後的基本概念是要鼓勵漁民多多向農民看齊。主管機關的期望是：漁民有 ITQ 在手，會開始像農民看待農作物一樣，用同樣的眼光來看待漁產，也就是會同樣地保護、照顧。「漁民要把魚拉上船才算是自己的」，薛佛表示。「如果在抓到之前就已經是自己的，就會比較理性地管理漁產」。

　　但是大部分的漁民一開始對這種做法的反應並不是很肯定。他們支持的是無限期停止核發新執照，不要讓新船進入已經過度擁擠的水域。此外，許多漁民還擔心 ITQ 制會結束他們的獨立性。他們害怕大型漁業公司會收買 ITQ，漁民就得失業，正如大企業早已收買完農地、驅逐走農民。而且，美國漁民自認為是老西部牛仔的真正傳人。他們艱困的討海生活，報酬一半是金錢、一半是樂趣與冒險。對這些牛仔而言，新制會貶低他們的身價。

[練習題翻譯與詳解]

① 本文的前一段可能是處理下列哪一項主題？
　(A) 老西部的牛仔　　　　　　　　(B) 過度捕魚造成的問題
　(C) 國際貿易的配額制　　　　　　(D) 西海岸的農民

【答案】**B**
【解析】這是組織結構的問題。首先要看出本文的主題是什麼，前面一段應該屬於同樣的主題。其次要看開頭第一句，上一段要能銜接得上開頭。本文的主題從兩個段落主題句來看（兩段的第一句），談的都是漁業。然後，全文第一句是「過度捕撈在 1980 年代成為越來越嚴重的問題」，要能銜接上這句，又要和漁業有關，就只有 (B)。

② 根據作者，許可證准許漁船的捕魚量是
　(A) 由該船前一年記錄的漁獲量決定
　(B) 全無限制，只要該船擁有 ITQ
　(C) 取決於船東保育工作的成效
　(D) 由船隻的順數決定

【答案】A

【解析】這是問細節的題型，要找同義表達。根據第一段提到「有證就可以每年捕撈定量的漁產，至於是怎樣的量，取決於這艘船前一年記錄捕獲的量」，其中 depending on 是 decided by 的同義表達，the recorded amount 是 the amount recorded 的同義表達，the previous year 是 the year before 的同義表達，故選 (A)。

③ 可以推論，ITQ 稱為 transferable 是因為

    (A) 每艘船都發給　　　　　　　　　　(B) 可以自由買賣

    (C) 建立在以往的紀錄上　　　　　　　(D) 可決定合法的捕魚量

【答案】B

【解析】這是推論題，主要根據是 transferable 的字義「可轉讓」，但下文也有「ITQ 可通過租售賺錢 (could be leased or sold for profit)」，這是 could be freely bought or sold 的同義表達，故選 (B)。

④ 作者暗示，ITQ 好像會讓漁業變得像國際貿易，因為在後者

    (A) ITQ 已經用來出口漁產　　　　　　(B) 可以發大財

    (C) 配額也可以買賣　　　　　　　　　(D) 也是由漁業部主管

【答案】C

【解析】這是推論題，要找「根據」，第一段：「看起來，採用 ITQ 好像會讓捕魚變成比較接近國際貿易，國貿早就固定採用可轉換配額」。這裡雖沒有直接說到買賣，但前面有說 transferable 就是可以買賣，兩句放在一起就可推出 (C)。

⑤ 如果拿漁民和農民比較，下列何者可以推論為真？

    (A) 兩者同樣成功地保育資源　　　　　(B) 兩者同樣忽略環保議題

    (C) 漁民照顧大海比較成功　　　　　　(D) 農民照顧土地比較成功

【答案】D

【解析】這是推論題，原文沒有明說，要找「根據」。第一段說「主管機關的期望是：漁民有 ITQ 在手，會開始像農民看待農作物一樣，用同樣的眼光來看待漁產，也就是會同樣地保護、照顧」。主管機關顯然認為漁民應該向農民學習，所以是農民做得比較好。

⑥ 作者在第一段引述薛佛的話，目的是

    (A) 證明漁民就和農民一樣　　　　　　(B) 描述漁業部的組織

    (C) 解釋漁業部推動 ITQ 的目的　　　　(D) 主張漁民應該自有船隻

【答案】C

【解析】這是修辭目的的題型，要看上下文。引用句的直接上文說「ITQ 背後的基本概念是要鼓勵漁民多多向農民看齊。主管機關的期望是：漁民有 ITQ 在手，會開始像農民看待農作物一樣，用同樣的眼光來看待漁產，也就是會同樣地保護、照顧」。主要內容是敘述主管機關（漁業部）的目的，故選 (C)。

⑦ 漁民大都支持暫停發放新執照，可能是因為

    (A) 他們想改行　　　　　　　　　(B) 漁業部叫他們做的

    (C) 他們和農民同樣保守　　　　　(D) 漁船已經太多了

【答案】D

【解析】這是推論題型，要找「根據」。原文雖然沒有直接說明原因，但是第二段有這句「他們支持的是無限期停止發新執照，不要讓新船進入已經過度擁擠的水域」，其中 already overcrowded waters 就是 there were too many fishing boats already 的同義表達，故選 (D)。

⑧ 漁民反對 ITQ 制的原因不包括哪一項？

    (A) 大企業會趕他們離家　　　　　(B) 捕魚的樂趣和刺激會受到破壞

    (C) 他們珍惜自己的獨立性　　　　(D) 大漁業公司會逼他們失業

【答案】A

【解析】這是問細節、採用消去法的題型，要刪除三個同義表達。由第二段內容「大企業早已收買完農地、驅逐掉農民」可知，大企業驅趕的是農民、不是漁民，所以 (A) 不是同義表達。

⑨ 第二段中 these cowboys 指的是

    (A) 美國漁民　　　　　　　　　　(B) 農民

    (C) 大漁業公司　　　　　　　　　(D) 老西部的牛仔

【答案】A

【解析】這是指射題，要看上下文。直接上文說「美國漁民自認為是老西部牛仔的真正傳人」，所以指的是美國漁民。

U.S. agriculture went through a series of changes in the first half of the twentieth century that accentuated many of its problems. From "parity years" and the period surrounding World War I to the distressing 1920s, the tragic 1930s and the recovery with World War II, farmers plunged from the heights to the depths and then **cautiously** watched the recovery of the 1940s and rising production and rising costs of the 1950s. During this period scientific farming as taught in colleges of agriculture and practiced in the experimental stations had a profound effect everywhere, **not just on the larger or more progressive farms**. Improved farm machines, especially the combine harvester and thresher, and, more than anything else, the introduction of the rubber-tired tractor and the extension of electricity, led to a revolution in farming.

In the new west, twentieth-century homesteaders continued to press on, primarily into the semiarid lands around west Texas and the Oklahoma Panhandle. Wheat was their principal crop. Dry farming techniques were developed which enabled farmers to conserve the meager moisture in the soil; **the process of dust mulching** was developed and land was allowed to lie fallow in order to build up moisture for the following crop year.

In the older states of the northeast, farming continued to contract, at least as far as the number of farms and total acreage were concerned. Despite the strident cries of alarmists, this **contraction** was regarded as healthy by most agricultural economists. Poor unproductive land reverted to forest. Farmers prospered on the more productive land. The growing demand for dairy products and the extension of paved roads made possible the extension of urban milk sheds so that few farmers in the northeast were too distant to feel the pull of the city market.

In the south, produce from Florida was shipped north in refrigerated cars to the rapidly expanding urban markets. A complex transportation network developed to bring the great cities the seasonal produce raised in the warmer climates of the South. Specialty crops, including vegetables, fruits, and nuts became big business.

Exercise

① What can be inferred about the years 1900-1920?
   (A) They were good years for U.S. agriculture.
   (B) They were the bottom of the agricultural cycle.
   (C) The World War hurt the prices of farm produce.
   (D) U.S. agriculture was on par with European agriculture.

② In the first paragraph the word "cautiously" most nearly means
   (A) anxiously
   (B) carefully
   (C) scarcely
   (D) enthusiastically

③ What do the words "not just on the larger or more progressive farms" mean in the first paragraph?
   (A) Smaller farms led the way in productivity gains.
   (B) Some farms did not become progressive as anticipated.
   (C) Scientific farming techniques were widely applied.
   (D) Even small farms could afford the new machinery.

④ According to the passage, what was primarily responsible for the increased farm production of the 1950s?
   (A) The combined harvester and thresher
   (B) Newly improved farm machines
   (C) A revolution in some rural areas
   (D) Increased electrification of farm areas

⑤ Why does the author mention "the process of dust mulching" in the second paragraph?
   (A) To illustrate why farmers abandoned their land
   (B) To recommend a novel solution to a farm problem
   (C) To describe old arming practices in Oklahoma
   (D) To provide an example of a dry farming practice

⑥ The author implies which of the following about farming in the northeast?

(A) Some of the land was replanted with fruit trees

(B) The number of farms fell but productivity increased

(C) Fewer farms sold milk to the residents of the cities

(D) The agricultural economists were proven incorrect

⑦ In the third paragraph the word "contraction" is closest in meaning to

(A) shrinking

(B) infection

(C) agreement

(D) production

⑧ It can be inferred that which of the following was shipped from Florida in refrigerated railroad cars?

(A) dairy products

(B) vegetables

(C) only milk

(D) ice

⑨ The author elaborates on all of the following terms EXCEPT

(A) "parity years"

(B) improved farm machinery

(C) dry farming

(D) the contraction of farming in the Northeast

題解

文章翻譯

美國農業在 20 世紀前半經歷一系列的改變，突顯出它的許多問題。從「標準年」與一次大戰前後的年代到令人沮喪的 1920 年代、悲劇的 1930 年代以及隨著二次大戰而來的恢復，農民從高峰跌入深谷，然後謹慎地觀察 1940 年代的恢復，以及 1950 年代的產量增加與價格上漲。在此期間，農業大學裡面教的、實驗站裡面做的那種科學農耕在各地都造成了深遠的影響，不只是在比較大或者比較先進的農場。農耕機器改進，尤其是收割機兼打穀機，以及最重要的引進了橡膠輪胎拖拉機、還有供電的普及，導致了農業革命。

在新開發的西部，20 世紀開墾家園者持續推進，主要是進入西德州以及奧克拉荷馬州狹長地帶的半乾旱地區。小麥是主要的作物。研發出乾旱農耕技術，農民可以節約土壤中貧乏的水分。發展出灰塵護根法，而且讓土地休耕以累積來年種農作所需的水分。

在歷史悠久的東北部，農業持續萎縮，至少在農場數目與總耕地面積方面是這樣。雖然拉警報的人大聲疾呼，但農經學家大都認為萎縮是健康的。產量不高的貧瘠土地回復為森林。產量高的土地上農民欣欣向榮。酪農製品需求量日增、柏油路廣泛鋪設，造成城市的牛奶供應範圍擴大，所以東北部的農民，哪怕地點再偏遠也能感受到城市市場的吸引。

在南部，佛羅里達州的農產品用冷凍車廂向北運到快速擴張的都會市場。發展出一套複雜的運輸網，把南部溫暖地區種出來的季節性農產帶到大城市來。特殊農產包括蔬菜、水果與堅果，成為大生意。

練習題翻譯與詳解

① 關於 1900-1920 年間可以推論出什麼？

   (A) 那是美國農業的好年代   (B) 那是農業循環的底部

   (C) 世界大戰傷害到農產價格   (D) 美國農業與歐洲農業表現相同

【答案】**A**

【解析】這是推論題，要找「根據」。第一段說「從標準年與一次大戰前後的年代到令人沮喪的 1920 年代……農民從高峰跌入深谷」，可以看出 1920 之前是高峰，故選 (A)。

② 第一段中的 cautiously 一字意思最接近

   (A) 焦急地   (B) 小心地

   (C) 很少有   (D) 熱烈地

【答案】**B**

【解析】這是單字題。cautiously 的意思是「謹慎地，小心地」。

③ 第一段中的 not just on the larger or more progressive farms 這句話是什麼意思？

    (A) 產量的增加是由小農場領頭

    (B) 有些農場並沒有像預期那樣進步

    (C) 科學農耕技術廣泛應用

    (D) 連小農場也買得起新機器

【答案】C

【解析】這是問細節的題型，要找同義表達。第一段說「農業大學裡面教的、實驗站裡面做的那種科學農耕在各地都造成了深遠的影響，不只是在比較大或者比較先進的農場」。相對於「不只在大農場」，上文講的是「科學農耕在各地都有深遠影響」，這和 (C) 選項是同義表達。

④ 根據本文，1950 年代農產增加，主要原因是什麼？

    (A) 綜合收割與打穀機　　　　　　(B) 農場機器新近獲得改進

    (C) 某些鄉村地區發生革命　　　　(D) 農業區供電增加

【答案】B

【解析】這是問細節的題型，要找同義表達。第一段說到 1950 年代農產增加，之後說：「農耕機器改進，尤其是收割兼打穀機，以及最重要的引進了橡膠輪胎拖拉機，還有供電的普及，導致了農業革命」，這是原因，其中 Improved farm machines 就是 Newly improved farm machines 的同義表達。

⑤ 作者在第二段為何提到 the process of dust mulching？

    (A) 說明農民為何要放棄自己的土地

    (B) 建議一種新辦法可以解決一項農業問題

    (C) 描述奧克拉荷馬州舊有的農耕作法

    (D) 舉例說明乾旱農耕的方式

【答案】D

【解析】這是修辭目的的題型，要看上下文。直接上文是「研發出乾旱農耕技術，農民可以節約土壤中貧乏的水分」，其中 Dry farming techniques 就是 dry farming practice，所以選 (D)。

⑥ 作者暗示東北部農業有下列哪種情況？

    (A) 有些土地改種果樹

    (B) 農場數目減少，但產量增加

    (C) 比較少有農場賣牛奶給城市居民

    (D) 事實證明農經學家錯了

【答案】**B**

【解析】這是推論的題型，要找「根據」。第三段說到「農經學家大都認為萎縮是健康的。產量不高的貧瘠土地回復為森林。產量高的土地上農民欣欣向榮」，這裡暗示雖然農場少了，但產量增加。

⑦ 第三段中的 contraction 一字意思最接近

    (A) 縮小   (B) 感染

    (C) 同意   (D) 生產

【答案】**A**

【解析】這是單字題，contraction（構造：together/pull/(*n*.)）字面上是「收縮」之意，引申為「縮小」。

⑧ 可以推論，下列何者由佛羅里達裝上冷凍火車廂運出？

    (A) 酪農製品   (B) 蔬菜

    (C) 只有牛奶   (D) 冰

【答案】**B**

【解析】這是推論題，要找「根據」。第三段說佛羅里達州的農產品用冷凍車廂運送，後面舉出農產品的例子「包括蔬菜 (including vegetables)、水果與堅果」，故選 (B)。

⑨ 作者除了哪一個名詞之外都有加上解說？

    (A)「標準年」   (B) 改善的農耕機器

    (C) 乾旱農耕   (D) 東北部農業萎縮

【答案】**A**

【解析】這是問細節的題型。第一段的 parity years 未作任何解說，其餘都有。

Reading 5

What causes ocean tides? The same thing that causes the less well-known, but equally important bodily and atmospheric tides—the gravitational action of the moon and sun. At most seaside locations, though certainly not all, high water marks are twelve hours and twenty-five minutes apart. This, however, can vary **significantly**; certain places in the China sea experience intervals of more than twenty-four hours between high water marks. As might be expected, low water marks occur at similar intervals.

At most places, on the average, the high water mark is about as much above the mean sea level as the **succeeding** low water mark is below it. The difference in level between high and low marks is called the range of the tide. The range of a tide may vary daily, and at most places it reaches a maximum once every two weeks. Tidal ranges vary greatly throughout the world. Many Pacific islands experience a range of less than two feet while the Bay of Fundy has a range exceeding fifty feet.

The **swiftness** of tidal currents also varies greatly from place to place. In British Columbia, Canada, the maximum current often exceeds ten knots per hour, while in most areas of Europe's North Sea it rarely exceeds even a single knot. Sometimes, where a large river meets the tide, a large wave may travel up the river like a wall of water. This is called a **bore**. A race is a fast-moving current usually occurring near a headland separating two bays.

✐ Exercise

① What is the main topic of the passage?
  (A) Tidal ranges
  (B) Worldwide tidal patterns
  (C) The sun's gravitational pull on the moon
  (D) The wide range of ocean currents

② What can be inferred from the passage about atmospheric tides?
  (A) They are similar in origin to ocean tides.
  (B) They are not as common as bodily tides.
  (C) They alter the moon's gravitational pull.
  (D) They are not affected by the sun.

③ The word "significantly" in the first paragraph is closest in meaning to
  (A) randomly
  (B) widely
  (C) distantly
  (D) sequentially

④ According to the passage, what is true about some locations in the China sea?
  (A) High water marks are extremely high.
  (B) Low water marks very rarely occur.
  (C) There is half a day between low water marks.
  (D) There is a full day between high water levels.

⑤ In the second paragraph the word "succeeding" is closest in meaning to which of the following words?
  (A) record
  (B) opposite
  (C) next
  (D) preceding

⑥ In the third paragraph the word "swiftness" is closet in meaning to
(A) strength
(B) speed
(C) frequency
(D) location

⑦ In the third paragraph the term "bore" refers to
(A) an uneventful race
(B) a river meeting the tide
(C) a fast moving current in the sea
(D) a large mass of moving water

⑧ According to the passage, what is true about races?
(A) They run back and forth between two bays.
(B) They flow unusually fast.
(C) They usually come before a bore.
(D) They are not found in the North Sea.

⑨ According to the passage, all of the following is true EXCEPT
(A) Low water marks all along the China sea occur more than twenty-four hours apart.
(B) A bore moves against the direction the river usually flows.
(C) Tidal ranges are not the same throughout the world.
(D) In British Columbia the current can exceed ten knots per hour.

題解

文章翻譯

　　海潮是什麼造成的？就是造成比較少人知道但同樣重要的身體潮與大氣潮的同一個因素——月亮與太陽的重力作用。在海邊大部分地區，雖然絕非全部地區，高潮水位間隔時間是 12 小時 25 分。不過，差別可能很大。中國海有些地方高潮水位的間隔時間超過 24 小時。可以想見，低潮水位的間隔時間也差不多。

　　大部分地區，一般來講，高潮水位超過平均海平面的差距，大約相當於下一個低潮水位低於平均海平面的差距。高低水位之間的落差稱為潮水範圍。潮水範圍可能每天都有變動，在大部分地區都是每兩週達到一次最大值。潮水範圍在世界各地有很大的變化。許多太平洋島嶼的潮水範圍不到兩英尺，而在芬迪灣則是超過 50 英尺。

　　潮水流動的速度也是在各地有很大的差距。在加拿大卑詩省，最高流速往往超過每小時 10 節，但是在歐洲濱北海的大部分地區，流速很少能夠超過 1 節。有時候大河碰上潮水，會有一波大浪逆河而上，像一堵水牆，稱為 bore。至於 race 則是快速的水流，經常發生在分隔兩個海灣的岬角附近。

練習題翻譯與詳解

① 本文的主題是什麼？

(A) 潮水範圍　　　　　　　　　　(B) 世界潮水模式

(C) 太陽對月亮的重力作用　　　　(D) 洋流的廣大範圍

【答案】B

【解析】這是問主題的題型，要看主題句（各段第一句）。第一段說的是海潮的成因、第二段是潮水範圍、第三段是潮水流動速度，共同主題是「潮水」。選項 (A) 雖有講到潮水，但 Tidal ranges 只限於「潮水範圍」，是第二段的段落主題而非全文主題，故選 (B)。

② 關於大氣潮，由文中可以推論出什麼？

(A) 它的起源與海潮類似。　　　　(B) 它不像身體潮那麼常見。

(C) 它會改變月球的引力。　　　　(D) 它不受太陽影響。

【答案】A

【解析】這是推論題，要找「根據」。全文第一句「海潮是什麼造成的？就是造成比較少人知道但同樣重要的身體潮與大氣潮的同一個因素」，可知大氣潮與海潮的成因相同，故選 (A)。

③ 第一段中的 significantly 一字意思最接近

(A) 隨機地

(B) 極大地

(C) 遙遠地

(D) 照順序地

【答案】**B**

【解析】這是字彙題。significantly（構造：mark/make/(*adv.*)）可以解釋為「重要」或者「重大」，同義字是 widely。

④ 根據本文，中國海有些地方如何？

(A) 高潮水位極高。

(B) 低潮水位很少發生。

(C) 低潮水位間隔時間為半天。

(D) 高潮水位間隔時間為一整天。

【答案】**D**

【解析】這是問細節的題型，要找同義表達。第一段說「中國海有些地方高潮水位的間隔時間超過 24 小時」，其中 more than 24 hours 就是 a full day 的同義表達，故選 (D)。

⑤ 第二段中的 succeeding 一字意思最接近

(A) 紀錄的

(B) 相反的

(C) 下一個

(D) 前一個

【答案】**C**

【解析】這是字彙題，succeeding（構造：after/go/(*a.*)）的意思是「接下來的，跟在後面的」，同義字是 next。

⑥ 第三段中的 swiftness 一字意思最接近

(A) 強度

(B) 速度

(C) 頻率

(D) 位置

【答案】**B**

【解析】這是字彙題，swiftness 的意思是「快速」，同義字是 speed。

⑦ 第三段中 bore 指的是

(A) 一場平淡無奇的比賽

(B) 河流碰上潮水

(C) 海中快速移動的水流

(D) 大量的水在移動

【答案】**D**

【解析】這是指射題，要找上下文：「有時候大河碰上潮水，會有一波大浪逆河而上，像一堵水牆，稱為 bore」，所以 bore 是逆河水而上的大浪，也就是 (D)。

⑧ 根據本文，關於 races 哪一句話正確？

　　(A) 它在兩個海灣之間來回移動。

　　(B) 它的流速特別快。

　　(C) 它通常發生在 bore 之前。

　　(D) 它在北海不存在。

【答案】**B**

【解析】這是問細節的題型，要找同義表達：「至於 race 則是快速的水流」，其中 fast-moving 是 flow unusually fast 的同義表達，故選 (B)。

⑨ 根據本文，下列何者錯誤？

　　(A) 中國海沿岸所有地區，低水位間隔都超過 24 小時。

　　(B) bore 行進方向與河水一般流動的方向相反。

　　(C) 潮水範圍並不是全世界都一樣。

　　(D) 卑詩省的潮流速度可以超過每小時 10 節。

【答案】**A**

【解析】這是問細節、採用消去法的題型，要找出三個同義表達刪去。第一段說「中國海有些地方高潮水位的間隔時間超過 24 小時……低潮水位的間隔時間也差不多」，其中 certain places 和選項 (A) 的「所有地區」(all along the China sea) 不是同義表達。

93

The U.S. is a democracy, of course, but it is also a republic; in most cases the will of the electorate is expressed through the votes cast by chosen representatives. In some states and cities, however, voters can make law directly or have a determining influence on whether a proposal should become law. The **devices** for such direct expression of the people's will are initiative and referendum issues on the ballot.

The initiative is a relatively recent development: South Dakota was the first state to authorize it, in 1898. Some legislators and organizations are asking Congress to approve a constitutional amendment that would authorize a national initiative. Political scientist Austin Ranney has explained the difference between referendum and initiative: "The referendum is an arrangement whereby a measure that has been passed by a legislature does not go into force until it has been approved by the voters (in some specified proportion) in an election. The initiative, on the other hand, is an arrangement whereby any person or group of persons may draft a proposed law or constitutional amendment and, after satisfying certain requirements of numbers and form, have it referred directly to the voters for final approval or rejection. Thus the referendum enables voters to accept or reject the legislature's proposals, while the initiative allows the voters both to make their own proposals and to pass upon the proposals of other voters."

Although a constitutional amendment to establish a nationwide initiative procedure is still far from being passed by the Congress, there is congressional support for it. However, as would be expected of any measure introducing drastic change into a system with over two centuries of tradition, the proposal has stirred controversy. Those who favor a national initiative say that it would encourage citizens to exercise more responsibility in governing the nation. They cite statistics that indicate that state initiatives have proved to be an **incentive** toward greater voter participation in elections. For example, in California 700,000 more voters cast their ballots on a proposition to cut property taxes than voted for all candidates for governor. Proponents also believe that results of initiatives—as direct expressions of voters' feelings on various issues—will force legislators to be more responsive to the electorate's needs and will stimulate debate on issues that might otherwise go unaddressed. Even initiatives that fail at the polls, advocates claim, educate the people and their leaders on the issues. **To the charge that initiatives may be manipulated by special interests that pour large amounts of money into campaigns, proponents say that elected officials can also be influenced by contributions and that initiatives are an open process, subject to scrutiny by the public and the media, so that the community will be aware of the forces attempting to pass or block an initiative.**

Critics of the proposal argue that an easily intelligible ballot proposition must by its nature be simplistic, and that **subtleties** of law and enforcement which would be worked out by experienced legislators cannot be included in initiatives. **W** They added that once an issue has been voted on by the public, legislators are unlikely to reintroduce it for refinement for years. **X** Another objection by critics is that frivolous or emotional issues that legislators would be obliged to place into perspective after thorough debate are settled in the heat of a partisan election campaign. Voters may choose to cut taxes, for example, without bearing the responsibility for deciding which government services will be **eliminated**. **Y** Sometimes voters have been persuaded that cutting taxes would result in diminishing government services. One public opinion polling organization reported that voters do not object to paying taxes for needed services but they strenuously resist what they perceive as wasteful expenditures of tax money. **Z**

Initiative and referendum issues have had a decided impact on public policy in the states and cities where they are permitted. John Herbers noted in the *New York Times*: "The rise of the initiative seems to be part of the general search for more responsive government. Whatever the extent of its future use, it is likely to remain at least as a way to '**send them a message**.'"

✎ Exercise

① The word "devices" in paragraph 1 is closest in meaning to
(A) excuses   (B) forms
(C) tools   (D) inclinations

② According to Austin Ranney, initiative differs from referendum in that it
(A) requires votes in some specified proportion
(B) arranges for the drafting of laws
(C) enables voters to decide upon the legislature's proposals
(D) allows the voters to recall elected officials

③ According to paragraph 3, why did the proposal for a constitutional amendment for a national initiative cause dispute?
(A) Because Congress is still a long way from passing the proposal
(B) Because there are some Congressmen who support the proposal
(C) Because the proposal involves momentous changes in the Constitution
(D) Because there is wide support for a referendum instead of an initiative

④ The word "incentive" in paragraph 3 is closest in meaning to
(A) consensus   (B) motive
(C) condition   (D) reward

⑤ The author mentions voting statistics in California in order to
(A) support the claim that state initiatives bring out the vote
(B) prove that property taxes are highly unpopular with voters
(C) illustrate the controversy surrounding a national initiative
(D) contrast the effects of state initiatives and national initiatives

⑥ According to the passage, what do advocates of a national initiative say may happen when an initiative is rejected by the ballot?
(A) The defeat may generate serious controversy.
(B) Voters will henceforth participate more in elections.
(C) There may be serious debate over the efficacy of initiatives.
(D) The people may learn more about the issues.

⑦ Which of the sentences below best expresses the essential information in the boldfaced sentence in paragraph 3?

To the charge that initiatives may be manipulated by special interests that pour large amounts of money into campaigns, proponents say that elected officials can also be influenced by contributions and that initiatives are an open process, subject to scrutiny by the public and the media, so that the community will be aware of the forces attempting to pass or block an initiative.

(A) Proponents say that elected officials are in danger of being influenced by campaign contributions.

(B) Initiatives are under surveillance by the public and the media, and therefore beyond control by elected officials.

(C) Advocates claim that initiatives are not in special danger of being swayed by moneyed interests.

(D) Special interests are accused of trying to manipulate initiatives in an openly scrutinized process.

⑧ The word "subtleties" in paragraph 4 is closest in meaning to

(A) difficulties　　　　　　　　　(B) intricacies

(C) complications　　　　　　　　(D) varieties

⑨ The word "eliminated" in paragraph 4 is closest in meaning to

(A) terminated　　　　　　　　　(B) under-funded

(C) injured　　　　　　　　　　　(D) improved

⑩ In which position would the boldfaced sentence best fit in paragraph 4?

Interestingly, not all tax cutting proposals in states that permit initiatives have succeeded.

(A) Position W　　　　　　　　　(B) Position X

(C) Position Y　　　　　　　　　(D) Position Z

⑪ It can be inferred that when John Herbers says "send them a message" in
paragraph 5, he means
(A) express the will of the people
(B) demand a constitutional amendment
(C) notify critics of national initiatives
(D) present a piece of legislation

⑫ According to the passage, all of the following are true of the initiative EXCEPT
(A) It is a direct expression of the people's will
(B) It does not have a long history in the U.S.
(C) It is a wasteful expenditure of tax money
(D) It has exerted a big influence on public policy

題解

[文章翻譯]

　　美國當然是民主國家，但也是共和國。大部分的情況，選民的意旨是經由民選代表投票的方式來表達的。但是在某些州與城市，投票人可以直接制訂法律、或者決定某項提案是否應該成為法律。如此直接表達民意的方式，就是創制權以及選票上的複決議題。

　　創制權是相對近代的發展：南達科塔州是頭一個授權的州，在 1898 年。有些議員與組織正在要求國會通過一項憲法增訂案，授權全國可以創制法律。政治學者蘭尼解釋過複決與創制的差別：「複決的作法是：議會通過的措施尚不能生效，必須先在選舉中獲得投票人同意（達到特定的支持比例）。至於創制權則是任何人與團體都有權起草提出法律或憲法修訂案。若能達到特定的人數或型式要求，就可以直接提出給選民票決是否通過或拒絕。所以，複決權讓投票人可以接受或拒絕議會的提案，而創制權則容許投票人自訂提案並且表決其他投票人的提案。

　　修憲來建立全國創制程序，這個主張要想在國會過關還很遙遠，但國會中的支持者也不在少數。不過，一套歷史超過兩個世紀的制度若想要大幅修改，這種提案想當然爾會引起爭議。支持全國創制權的人表示它可以鼓勵公民對於治理國家行使更多的責任。他們舉出統計顯示：州級的創制權證明是有效的誘因，讓更多選民參與選舉。例如在加

州一場選舉，所有州長候選人得到的總票數，比起一項財產稅減稅的提案得票還少 70 萬張。支持者同時相信，行使創制權的結果（那是投票人對各種議題直接表達態度）將迫使議員更能回應選民的需求，並且刺激辯論，否則一些議題永遠得不到處理。支持者還說，就算是創制法案沒有能夠通過投票，也是關於該議題對人民與其領袖非常好的教育。有人指控創制權可能遭到特殊利益團體的操控，這些團體會投下鉅資來做宣傳。全國創制權的支持者回應說：民選官員同樣會受到捐獻的影響，而且創制權是公開透明的程序，受到民眾與媒體的監督，所以如果有什麼勢力想要通過或阻撓創制法案，民眾會知道。

批評全國創制權的人則主張：印在選票上的創制提案若要容易看懂，勢必會過於簡單化。而且，法律與執行方面有一些複雜的細節，有經驗的議員可以理出頭緒，但是創制提案就無法納入。W 他們還表示，一旦民眾對某議題投下了票，接下來幾年，議員都不大可能再提出來改進。X 批評者還有一項反對意見：瑣碎的、或者情緒化的議題，議員經過徹底辯論之後必須從大局來考量，但是在黨派色彩濃厚的選舉宣傳中會用一時的激情來解決。例如，投票人可能選擇減稅，卻不必負責決定政府是要裁撤掉哪一些服務。Y 有時候投票人會相信：減稅會造成政府服務縮水。有一項公開民調結果是：投票人並不反對為有需要的服務而納稅，但他們強烈反對他們認為是浪費稅金的行為。Z

在准許的州與城市中，創制與複決議題對於公共政策都造成了決定性的衝擊。約翰‧赫柏斯在《紐約時報》上表示：「民眾在尋找更能夠反應民意的政府，創制權的興起似乎是這個潮流的一部分。不論它將來使用程度是大是小，很可能至少都是一個辦法，可以『給他們一個訊息』」。

[練習題翻譯與詳解]

① 第一段中的 devices 意思最接近

    (A) 藉口   (B) 形式

    (C) 工具   (D) 傾向

〔答案〕**C**

〔解析〕這是單字題。device 的意思是「設備，裝置」，引申為「工具」，同義字是 tool。

② 根據蘭尼的說法，創制與複決的差別在於前者

    (A) 需要特定比例的票數   (B) 要安排起草法律

    (C) 讓投票人能夠決定議會的提案   (D) 容許投票人罷免民選官員

〔答案〕**B**

〔解析〕這是問細節的題型，要找同義表達。第二段引述蘭尼說「至於創制權則是任何人與團體都有權起草提出法律或憲法修訂案」，其中 an arrangement whereby any person or group of persons may draft a proposed law or constitutional amendment 就是 arranges for the drafting of laws 的同義表達，故選 (B)。

③ 根據第三段，提議憲法增訂案以施行全國創制權，為何引起爭執？

(A) 因為國會要通過提議還差很遠

(B) 因為有些國會議員支持

(C) 因為提議牽涉到憲法的重大修改

(D) 因為民眾普遍支持的是複決而不是創制

【答案】**C**

【解析】這是問細節的題型，要找同義表達。第三段說「一套歷史超過兩個世紀的制度若想要大幅修改，這種提案想當然爾會引起爭議」，其中 any measure introducing drastic change into a system with over two centuries of tradition 就是 the proposal involves momentous changes in the Constitution 的同義表達，故選 (C)。

④ 第三段中的 incentive 意思最接近

(A) 共識   (B) 動機

(C) 條件   (D) 獎賞

【答案】**B**

【解析】這是單字題。incentive（構造：in/burn/($n.$)）的意思是「刺激，誘因」，同義字是 motive（構造：move/($n.$)）。

⑤ 作者提到加州的投票統計，目的是

(A) 支持「州創制權可以發動選民出來投票」的說法

(B) 證明財產稅非常不受選民歡迎

(C) 說明一件全國性創制權周圍的爭議

(D) 對比州創制權與全國創制權的效果

【答案】**A**

【解析】這是問修辭目的的題型，要看上下文。第三段直接上文說「州級的創制權證明是有效的誘因，讓更多選民參與選舉」，接下來就是舉出加州的投票統計數字來支持，故選 (A)。

⑥ 根據本文，全國創制權的提倡者說，如果一項創制提案遭到選票拒絕，結果會怎樣？

(A) 這項失敗可能產生嚴重的爭議。

(B) 投票人此後會多多參與選舉。

(C) 關於創制的效力會產生嚴肅的辯論。

(D) 人民可能更了解該議題。

【答案】D

【解析】這是問細節的題型，要找同義表達。第三段說「支持者還說，就算是創制法案沒有能夠通過投票，也是關於該議題對人民與其領袖非常好的教育」，其中 educate the people and their leaders on the issues 就是 The people may learn more about the issues 的同義表達，故選 (D)。

⑦ 下列哪個句子最能夠表達第三段黑體字句子的主要內容？

「有人指控創制權可能遭到特殊利益團體的操控，這些團體會投下鉅資來做宣傳。全國創制權的支持者回應說：民選官員同樣會受到捐獻的影響，而且創制權是公開透明的程序，受到民眾與媒體的監督，所以如果有什麼勢力想要通過或阻撓創制法案，民眾會知道。」

(A) 提倡者說民選官員有受到競選捐獻影響的危險。

(B) 創制權受到民眾與媒體的監視，因此不是民選官員可以控制的。

(C) 提倡者說創制權沒有特別大的危險會被有錢的利益團體左右。

(D) 特殊利益團體被指控想要在受到公開監視的過程中操控創制。

【答案】C

【解析】這是句子改寫的題型，要找句中重點的同義表達。原句重點在說並不是只有創制權會受到金錢影響，而且它還有一些使它不易受影響的有利因素，這個意思最接近 (C)。

⑧ 第四段中的 subtleties 意思最接近

(A) 困難　　　　　　　　　　　(B) 錯綜複雜

(C) 複雜化，併發症　　　　　　(D) 種類

【答案】B

【解析】這是單字題，subtlety（構造：under/(*n.*)）的意思是「微妙，精細」，同義字是 intricacy（構造：in/trick/(*n.*)）。

⑨ 第四段中的 eliminated 一字意思最接近

(A) 被終結　　　　　　　　　　(B) 資金不足

(C) 受傷害　　　　　　　　　　(D) 獲改進

【答案】A

【解析】這是單字題。動詞 eliminate（構造：out/limit/(*v.*)）的意思是「消滅，終止」，同義字是 terminate（構造：end/(*v.*)）。

⑩ 下面這個句子最適合放在第四段的什麼位置？

「很有意思的是，允許創制權的州中，並非所有減稅的提案都獲得成功。」

(A) W 位置　　　　　　　　　　　(B) X 位置

(C) Y 位置　　　　　　　　　　　(D) Z 位置

【答案】**C**

【解析】這是安插句子的題型，要看上下文。插入句中說到減稅提案，選項 Y 的上文是「投票人可能選擇減稅，卻不必負責決定政府是要裁撤掉哪一些服務」，與插入句中的「減稅」直接相關。將句子置入 Y 位置，結果是「投票人可能選擇減稅，卻不必負責決定政府是要裁撤掉哪一些服務。很有意思的是，允許創制權的州中，並非所有減稅的提案都獲得成功。有時候投票人會相信：減稅會造成政府服務縮水。有一項公開民調結果是：投票人並不反對為有需要的服務而納稅」。插入句主要內容說減稅案不一定成功，Y 位置的直接下文說的就是為什麼減稅案不一定成功，可以成功銜接，故選 (C)。

⑪ 可以推論，第五段中約翰·赫柏斯說 send them a message，意思是

(A) 表達民眾意旨

(B) 要求制訂憲法增訂案

(C) 通知批評全國創制權的人

(D) 提出一件立法

【答案】**A**

【解析】這是推論題，要找「根據」。整段引述是「民眾在尋找更能夠反應民意的政府，創制權的興起似乎是這個潮流的一部分。不論它將來使用程度是大是小，很可能至少都是一個辦法，可以『給他們一個訊息』」。文中的 send them a message 字面上是「給他們一個訊息」，雖然沒有明言「他們」是誰，但從上文來看顯然是指「政府」，意思是經由創制讓政府知道人民需要的是什麼，所以選 (A)。

⑫ 根據本文，關於創制權，下面每一項都是對的，除了

(A) 它直接表達民意

(B) 它在美國歷史不很長

(C) 它是浪費的稅金支出

(D) 它對公共政策產生了重大影響

【答案】**C**

【解析】這是採用消去法、問細節的題型，要刪去三個同義表達。其中只有「創制權浪費稅金」找不到同義表達，故選 (C)。

第 3 章

"Philosophy" is a difficult word to define, in part because it can mean various things to various people. To Bertrand Russell, author of *History of Western Philosophy*, it is "something intermediate between theology and science." This is a very concise but quite adequate definition. Hence it is worth going into in some detail.

Philosophy is half theology, half science, but it is neither of these. It is like theology in that it deals with speculations on matters for which definite knowledge cannot be obtained. The question "What is the noblest way of life for humans?" for example, is essentially unanswerable. Theology, building on tradition and authority, points to a way of life and asserts, "This is it!" If one accepts the theological answer, all very well. Most modern minds, however, find it difficult to accept on faith the answers of religion. These people may turn to philosophy.

On the other hand, philosophy more often than not **parts ways with** theology and comes closer to science, for it appeals to human reason rather than to religious authority. Russell maintains that all definite knowledge belongs to science, and that all dogma as to what **surpasses** definite knowledge belongs to theology. Between theology and science, however, there is a No Man's Land, exposed to attack from both sides; this No Man's Land is philosophy.

Philosophy attempts to answer unanswerable questions through a scientific approach. Logical reasoning is used where observation or experimentation is impossible. Philosophy may not provide any answers, but it teaches one to live in uncertainty as to the answers without being paralyzed by hesitation, or without having to rely on religious teachings. This is what philosophy can do for those who study it today.

✏ Exercise

① The author's purpose in writing this passage is to
   (A) define a term
   (B) argue for a theory
   (C) criticize a rival
   (D) solve a problem

② The author describes Russell's definition of philosophy as being
   (A) uncertain and difficult
   (B) short but sufficient
   (C) worthy but redundant
   (D) scientific but superstitious

③ According to the author, philosophy is like theology in that
   (A) both demand faith
   (B) both reject the scientific method
   (C) both deal with uncertainties
   (D) both rely on authority

④ The phrase "parts ways with" in the third paragraph is closest in meaning to
   (A) goes part of the way with
   (B) differs from
   (C) demonstrates particular manners with
   (D) partakes with

⑤ According to the passage, philosophy has scientific characteristics in that
   (A) both involve work in the lab
   (B) both require observations of nature
   (C) both look to reason as the ultimate arbiter
   (D) both are subversive to tradition and authority

⑥ The word "surpasses" in the third paragraph is closest in meaning to
(A) excels over
(B) lies beyond
(C) overtakes
(D) overwhelms

⑦ The author implies that one advantage of studying philosophy is that
(A) it provides all the answers that one might need to know
(B) it helps one live in uncertainty without being overcome by despair
(C) it is a good start for subsequent studies in theology and science
(D) it shows one what is the noblest way of life

⑧ According to the passage, all of the following are correct EXCEPT
(A) theology is based on tradition and authority
(B) science appeals to reason
(C) philosophy may employ logical reasoning
(D) religion lies between dogma and definite knowledge

【文章翻譯】

「哲學」不容易下定義，部分原因在於不同的人對它有不同的解釋。對《西洋哲學史》作者伯特蘭‧羅素而言，哲學是「界於神學與科學之間的東西」。這個定義很精簡但又很充分，所以值得進一步探討。

哲學半是神學、半是科學，但兩者都不全是。它與神學相似之處在於它處理的是一些猜測，而猜測之事是無法獲得明確知識的。例如「人類最高尚的生活方式是什麼？」這個問題基本上沒有答案。神學建立在傳統與權威上，指向一種生活方式並且斷言「就是這個！」。若能接受神學的答案，也沒什麼不好的。然而，現代人大都難以憑信心接受宗教給的答案。這些人可以轉向哲學。

另一方面，哲學往往和神學分道揚鑣、比較接近科學，因為它訴諸人類理性而非宗教權威。羅素主張，一切明確的知識屬於科學、一切超越明確知識之外的教條屬於神學。不過，在神學與科學之間有一個三不管地帶，遭到來自兩邊的攻擊，這個三不管地帶就是哲學。

哲學嘗試解答一些無解的問題，用的是科學方法。無法進行觀察或做實驗，就用邏輯推理。哲學或許提不出任何答案，但可以教人在缺乏確定答案的情況下要如何過生活，而不會因為遲疑猶豫而癱瘓、也不必依賴宗教教條。這就是哲學能夠為今天學它的人所做的貢獻。

【練習題翻譯與詳解】

① 作者寫這篇文章之目的在於

  (A) 界定一個詞彙   (B) 為一項理論辯護

  (C) 批判一名對手   (D) 解決一個問題

【答案】**A**

【解析】這是問主題的題型，要看主題句。各段第一句分別是「哲學不容易下定義」、「哲學半是神學、半是科學」、「哲學往往和神學分道揚鑣、比較接近科學」、以及「哲學嘗試解答一些無解的問題，用的是科學方法」。由此可以看出，作者是採取「比較對比」的方式來界定「哲學」一詞，故選 (A)。

② 羅素對哲學的定義，作者說它是

  (A) 不確定與困難   (B) 簡短但充分

  (C) 有價值但重複   (D) 科學但迷信

【答案】**B**

【解析】這是問細節的題型，要找同義表達。第一段說「這個定義很精簡但又很充分」，其中 concise 是 short 的同義字，adequate 是 sufficient 的同義字，故選 (B)。

③ 根據作者，哲學與神學相似之處在於
   (A) 兩者都要求信心
   (B) 兩者都排斥科學方法
   (C) 兩者都處理不確定的問題
   (D) 兩者都依賴權威

【答案】C
【解析】這是問細節的題型，要找同義表達。第二段說「它與神學相似之處在於它處理的是一些猜測，而猜測之事是無法獲得明確知識的」，其中 matters for which definite knowledge cannot be obtained 是 uncertainties 的同義表達，故選 (C)。

④ 第三段中 parts ways with 這個片語的意思最接近
   (A) 共同走一部分路程
   (B) 有差別
   (C) 表現出特別的態度
   (D) 參與

【答案】B
【解析】這是單字題。片語 parts ways with 字面上是「與……分手，走不同的路」的意思，引申為「有差別」。

⑤ 根據本文，哲學具有科學特色，在於
   (A) 兩者都牽涉到實驗室工作
   (B) 兩者都要求觀察大自然
   (C) 兩者都以理智為最終裁判
   (D) 兩者都會顛覆傳統與權威

【答案】C
【解析】這是問細節的題型，要找同義表達。第三段說「哲學往往和神學分道揚鑣、比較接近科學，因為它訴諸人類理性而非宗教權威」，其中 appeals to human reason 與 look to reason as the ultimate arbiter 是同義表達。

⑥ 第三段中的 surpasses 一字意思最接近
   (A) 勝過
   (B) 在……範圍外，超出
   (C) 追上
   (D) 壓倒

【答案】B
【解析】這是單字題。surpass（構造：over/pass）字面上是「超過」之意，在此上下文指的是「超越某個範圍」，同義表達是 lies beyond。

⑦ 作者暗示，研究哲學有一項好處是
   (A) 它提供人所需要知道的一切答案
   (B) 它幫助人在不確定中生活，不會屈服於絕望
   (C) 它是好的開始，可以接著研究神學與科學
   (D) 它教人什麼是最高尚的生活方式

【答案】B
【解析】這是推論題，要找「根據」。第四段說「教人在缺乏確定答案的情況下要如何過生活，而不會因為遲疑猶豫而癱瘓」，意思最接近的是 (B)。

⑧ 根據本文，下列每項皆正確，除了
　(A) 神學基於傳統與權威
　(B) 科學訴諸理智
　(C) 哲學可能用到邏輯推理
　(D) 宗教位於教條與確切知識之間

【答案】D
【解析】這是採用消去法、問細節的題型，要找出三項同義表達刪除。第一段說的是「哲學界於神學與科學之間」，全文並沒有說「宗教位於教條與確切知識之間」，故選 (D)。

3

Reading 2

Alexander Graham Bell (1847-1922), physicist and inventor of the telephone, was born into a British family long noted as an authority on phonetics and speech therapy. He was the son of Alexander Melville Bell, and the grandson of Alexander Bell, a pioneer in the study of phonetics. Although Bell's enduring **renown** stems from the invention of what is now a commonplace mechanical device, for many years he continued the traditions of his forefathers.

Bell was born in Edinburgh, Scotland in 1847. He was educated at Edinburgh University and the University of London before failing health caused him to move to Canada in 1870. By 1872, Bell had moved to Boston, Massachusetts, where he spent most of the rest of his life, and had opened a school for training teachers of the deaf and providing instruction in speech mechanics. The following year he became a professor of vocal physiology at Boston University. In 1876 Bell exhibited an apparatus embodying the results of his studies in the transmission of sounds by electricity. With subsequent improvements and modifications, this would later become the modern telephone and would literally and figuratively **set the world on its ear**. In his later years, Bell immersed himself in the study of the problems involved with mechanical flight. His accomplishments in a variety of fields made him one of the most important researchers of the nineteenth century.

Like his father, Bell was a **prominent** speaker and involved in numerous scientific and philanthropic associations. He was founder of the American Association to promote the Teaching of Speech to the Deaf, and for a time he served as president of the National Geographic Society. He was appointed a Regent of the Smithsonian Institution in 1898. Bell died suddenly at his summer home in Nova Scotia on August 2, 1922.

✎ Exercise

① What is the main topic of the passage?
(A) The powerful parental influences on Alexander Graham Bell
(B) Researchers and inventors of the nineteenth century
(C) Advances in phonetics and speech therapy
(D) The life and works of Alexander Graham Bell

② Which of the following can be inferred about Alexander Melville Bell?
(A) He continued the work of Alexander Graham Bell.
(B) He worked in the field of phonetics and speech therapy.
(C) He remained in Britain while his family moved to America.
(D) He thoroughly researched the history of the Bell family.

③ According to the passage, Bell did all of the following EXCEPT
(A) establishing a school
(B) teaching speech mechanics
(C) inventing the radio
(D) researching mechanical flight

④ The word "renown" in the first paragraph is closest in meaning to
(A) fame
(B) invention
(C) fortune
(D) approval

⑤ In the second paragraph the expression "set the world on its ear" most nearly
means
(A) excite all the people
(B) convince everyone to speak
(C) improve telephone quality
(D) increase Bell's net worth

⑥ As an adult, Bell spent the greatest amount of time in
(A) Edinburgh, Scotland
(B) Boston, Massachusetts
(C) Nova Scotia, Canada
(D) London, England

⑦ In the third paragraph the word "prominent" most nearly means
(A) well paid
(B) appointed
(C) excellent
(D) noted

⑧ Which of the following can be inferred from the passage?
(A) Bell died from complications arising from deafness.
(B) Bell died in a laboratory accident while in Canada.
(C) Bell did not die from a chronic illness.
(D) Bell died as President of the National Geographic Society.

⑨ The author mentions that Bell was involved with all of the following EXCEPT
(A) a school for teacher training
(B) a university teaching position
(C) the first successful plane flight
(D) a number of scientific organizations

題解

文章翻譯

　　亞歷山大‧葛拉罕‧貝爾 (1847-1922)，物理學家、電話發明人，出生在一個英國家庭，這個家庭一直是語音學和言語障礙治療方面的權威。他的父親是亞歷山大‧梅維爾‧貝爾，祖父亞歷山大‧貝爾是語音學研究的先驅。貝爾持續不墜的名聲來自於他發明了一種如今到處可見的機器，但是有許多年他一直持續他先人的傳統。

　　貝爾於 1847 年出生在蘇格蘭艾丁堡，先在艾丁堡大學與倫敦大學就讀，後來因為健康不佳而在 1870 年移居加拿大。到了 1872 年，貝爾已經搬到麻州波士頓市，此後大部分時間就定居於此，並且開辦學校訓練老師教聽障學生，以及教授言語結構學。次年他成為波士頓大學語音生理學教授。1876 年貝爾展出一套裝置，代表他用電力傳送聲音方面的研究成果。經過後續的改進與修正，這裝置後來就成為今天的電話，並且令世人興奮、傾聽。晚年他潛心研究機械飛行方面的問題。他在好幾門領域都有建樹，成為 19 世紀最重要的研究人員之一。

　　像他父親一樣，貝爾也是知名演說家，並且參加許多科學與慈善組織。他創辦「美國聽障教學促進會」，也曾擔任國家地理學會主席。1898 年他被委任為史密森博物館董事。1922 年 8 月 2 日貝爾在新蘇格蘭自家的避暑別墅突然去世。

練習題翻譯與詳解

① 本文的主題是什麼？
　　(A) 父母對亞歷山大‧葛拉罕‧貝爾強大的影響
　　(B) 19 世紀的研究人員與發明家
　　(C) 語音學與言語治療方面的進展
　　(D) 亞歷山大‧葛拉罕‧貝爾的生平與研究

【答案】**D**
【解析】這是問主題的題型，要找出主題句。全文主題句概括貝爾的生平，段落主題句按照時間順序介紹貝爾的生涯與研究，故選 (D)。

② 關於亞歷山大‧梅維爾‧貝爾可以推論出什麼？
　　(A) 他繼續進行亞歷山大‧葛拉罕‧貝爾的研究。
　　(B) 他的研究領域是語音學和言語治療。
　　(C) 家人移居美國之後他仍留在英國。
　　(D) 他徹底研究過貝爾家族歷史。

【答案】**B**

【解析】這是推論題，要找「根據」。第一段說「這個家庭一直是語音學和言語障礙治療方面的權威。他父親是亞歷山大‧梅維爾‧貝爾」。既然整個家庭是 phonetics and speech therapy 方面的權威，那麼父親當然也是研究這方面的。

③ 根據本文，貝爾做過的不包括

    (A) 創辦學校   (B) 教授言語結構學

    (C) 發明收音機   (D) 研究機械飛行

【答案】**C**

【解析】這是問細節、採用消去法的題型，要找出三個同義表達刪去，剩下的就是答案。除了「發明收音機」是無中生有，其他三個選項都有提到，故選 (C)。

④ 第一段中的 renown 一字意思最接近

    (A) 名聲   (B) 發明

    (C) 財富，命運   (D) 贊同，批准

【答案】**A**

【解析】這是單字題，renown（構造：again/know）的意思是「名聲」，同義字是 fame。

⑤ 第二段中的 set the world on its ear 意思最接近

    (A) 令所有人興奮   (B) 說服大家要說話

    (C) 改進電話品質   (D) 增加貝爾的財產淨值

【答案】**A**

【解析】這是單字題。片語 set someone on his ear 字面上是「令某人倒地」（因而單耳貼地），引申為令人非常興奮、強烈震撼某人。原文在前面還有 literally and figuratively 兩個副詞修飾。前者 literally 是「照字面解釋」，也就是實實在在、不誇張、不打比方。意思是說「發明電話之後，世人真的要貼在耳朵上聽」。後者 figuratively 則是「比喻」，也就是「令人興奮」。

⑥ 成年後，貝爾大部分時間是在

    (A) 蘇格蘭艾丁堡   (B) 麻州波士頓

    (C) 加拿大新蘇格蘭   (D) 英國倫敦

【答案】**B**

【解析】這是問細節的題型，要找同義表達。第二段說「到了 1872 年，貝爾已經搬到麻州波士頓市，此後大部分時間就定居在此」，其中 spent most of the rest of his life 就是本題所問 spent the greatest amount of time 的同義表達，故選 (B)。

⑦ 第三段中的 prominent 一字意思最接近

(A) 待遇優渥　　　　　　　　　(B) 被指定的

(C) 極佳的　　　　　　　　　　(D) 知名的

【答案】**D**

【解析】這是單字題。 prominent（構造：forward/project/(a.)）字面上是「突出的」之意，引申為「著名的」，同義字是 noted。

⑧ 根據本文可以推論出哪一項？

(A) 貝爾死於耳聾產生的併發症。

(B) 貝爾在加拿大死於實驗室意外事件。

(C) 貝爾不是慢性病造成死亡。

(D) 貝爾死時擔任國家地理學會主席。

【答案】**C**

【解析】這是推論題，要找「根據」。第三段說他「突然去世 (died suddenly)」，所以應該不是慢性病造成的。

⑨ 作者提到貝爾涉及的事不包括

(A) 教師訓練學校

(B) 大學教職

(C) 第一次成功的飛機飛行

(D) 若干科學組織

【答案】**C**

【解析】這是問細節、採用消去法的題型，要找出三個同義表達刪去。其中只有選項 (C) 是無中生有。原文只說「晚年他潛心研究機械飛行方面的問題」，其中 immersed himself in the study of the problems involved with mechanical flight 和 the first successful plane flight 不是同義表達。

The whale shark, the world's largest fish, feeds on plankton, as does the blue whale, the largest animal in the world. Whereas the blue whale feeds passively, swimming to and fro on the surface with its jaws hanging, and harvesting the plankton like a lawn mower plowing on, picking up whatever lies in its way, the whale shark actively attacks its food. It seeks out high concentrations of plankton, charges directly to where food is densest, and, with its head swinging sideways, inhales like a vacuum cleaner gobbling up the last bit of dust in a corner. The whale shark feeds efficiently because, unlike most other sharks, which have their mouths underneath and behind the snouts, its mouth opens directly at the front of the head.

Although whale sharks have over 3,000 teeth in each of the jaws, they are too tiny to be of any use in chewing. After sucking plankton-rich sea water into its mouth, the whale shark clamps down its huge jaws and proceeds to separate food from water, which it dispels from the ten gill slits, five on each side of the throat. The gill plates inside are made of cartilage covered with a spongy material. The porous material allows sea water to go through but effectively sifts out all the plankton, which the whale shark swallows into the cardiac stomach, at the rate of one gulp every 15 seconds or so.

If the whale shark **inadvertently** swallowed some indigestible object, it has a way to rid itself of the nuisance. Only digested fluids can pass through the small passage that leads from the cardiac stomach to other stomachs, so a foreign object of any considerable size would be left in the cardiac stomach. In what biologists call "gastric eversion," the whale shark can turn its cardiac stomach inside out and send the whole stomach out from the mouth, emptying its contents to the surrounding water before retrieving the stomach. It is as if a person, **while vomiting violently**, literally spat out his stomach in the process!

✏ Exercise

① Which of the following would be the most appropriate title for the passage?
  (A) Whale Sharks and Blue Whales: Cousins in the Sea
  (B) Gastric Eversion: an Amazing Habit of the Whale Shark
  (C) Feeding Habits of the Whale Shark
  (D) Whales and Sharks: How They Find Food in the Ocean

② According to the passage, all of the following are correct EXCEPT
  (A) the whale shark is larger than the blue whale
  (B) the blue whale is not the largest fish
  (C) the whale shark is the largest fish
  (D) the blue whale is the largest animal

③ According to the author, what feature in a whale shark's anatomy makes for efficiency in feeding?
  (A) a frontal location of the mouth
  (B) a stomach that takes in only fluids
  (C) 6,000 teeth in the mouth
  (D) a hidden "vacuum cleaner" in the body

④ Which of the following does the author compare to a lawn mower working?
  (A) A whale shark feeding on small fish
  (B) A whale shark feeding on plankton
  (C) A blue whale feeding on small fish
  (D) A blue whale feeding on plankton

⑤ The author mentions all of the following as useful to a whale shark while it is feeding EXCEPT
  (A) its teeth
  (B) its jaws
  (C) its gill plates
  (D) some spongy material

⑥ It can be inferred that, when a whale shark feeds on plankton, it swallows food about how many times a minute?
(A) 4
(B) 5
(C) 10
(D) 15

⑦ The word "inadvertently" in the third paragraph is closest in meaning to
(A) inappropriately
(B) accidentally
(C) intentionally
(D) irrevocably

⑧ Which of the following can be inferred bout the whale shark?
(A) The passage from its mouth to the cardiac stomach is relatively wide
(B) It can discard its stomach and regenerate one easily
(C) It eats only fluid food and spits out anything solid
(D) Its cardiac stomach leads directly to the intestines

⑨ In the third paragraph, the author describes what happens to an imaginary person "while vomiting violently" in order to do which of the following?
(A) Caution against vomiting too hard
(B) Explain a biological term
(C) Suggest a similarity between humans and whale sharks
(D) Prove that a whale shark cannot really spit out its stomach

題解

文章翻譯

　　鯨鯊是世界最大的魚類，以吃浮游生物為生，世界最大的動物藍鯨也是。藍鯨覓食是被動的，在水面來回游動、下巴垂下，收獲浮游生物有如剪草機往前推，碰到什麼就是什麼。而鯨鯊則是積極攻擊食物。牠尋找高濃度聚集的浮游生物、直接衝向密度最高處，頭向左右晃動，像吸塵器吞食角落最後一點灰塵那樣把食物吸進來。鯨鯊覓食效率高，因為它和別的鯊不一樣。別的鯊魚，嘴巴長在下方、位於鼻尖後面。鯨鯊的嘴則是在頭的前方直接打開。

　　鯨鯊上下顎雖然各有 3,000 多顆牙齒，但是太小，無助於咀嚼。把富含浮游生物的海水吸入口中之後，鯨鯊緊閉巨大的下顎，開始分離食物與海水。牠有 10 條鰓裂，喉嚨兩邊各有 5 條，海水由此排出。裡面的鰓板由軟骨構成，上覆海綿狀物質。這種多孔物質可以讓海水通過，但能有效篩出所有的浮游生物、吞到胃賁門，速率是每 15 秒左右吞一口。

　　如果鯨鯊不小心吞下無法消化的物體，也有辦法排除掉這種討厭的東西。從胃賁門通往另外幾個胃的狹窄通道只容許消化過的液體通過，所以太大的外來物體就留在胃賁門。有一種動作，生物學家稱為「胃反轉」：鯨鯊可以把胃賁門反過來、整個從口中吐出，裡面的東西全部淨空到周圍海水中，然後再把胃收回。情況彷彿是有人大吐，結果真的把胃都吐出來！

練習題翻譯與詳解

① 下面哪一個是本文最佳標題？

　　(A) 鯨鯊與藍鯨：大海表兄弟

　　(B) 胃反轉：鯨鯊的驚人習慣

　　(C) 鯨鯊的覓食習慣

　　(D) 鯨與鯊：如何在大海覓食

【答案】C
【解析】這是問主題的題型，要找主題句（各段第一句）。第一段「鯨鯊是世界最大的魚類，以吃浮游生物為生，世界最大的動物藍鯨也是」說到兩種動物的覓食。第二段與第三段的主題句分別講到鯨鯊的牙齒與鯨鯊吞下異物時的處理方式，都和鯨鯊的覓食有關。三段共同的主題是鯨鯊的覓食，故選 (C)。

② 根據本文，下列都是正確的，除了

　　(A) 鯨鯊比藍鯨大

　　(B) 藍鯨不是最大的魚類

　　(C) 鯨鯊是最大的魚類

　　(D) 藍鯨是最大的動物

【答案】A

【解析】這是問細節、採用消去法的題型，要找三個同義表達排除。(B) (C) (D) 三個選項都在第一段可以找到同義表達，只有 (A) 說鯨鯊比藍鯨大，這和第一段「世界最大的動物藍鯨」一語有牴觸，故選 (A)。

③ 根據作者，鯨鯊生理構造上有何特徵使牠覓食效率高？

(A) 嘴位於前方　　　　　　　　(B) 胃只能接受流體

(C) 嘴裡有 6,000 顆牙　　　　(D) 體內藏有「吸塵器」

【答案】A

【解析】這是問細節的題型，要找同義表達。第一段說「鯨鯊覓食效率高，因為……鯨鯊的嘴是在頭的前方直接打開」，其中 its mouth opens directly at the front of the head 和 a frontal location of the mouth 是同義表達。

④ 作者把下列哪一項比為剪草機在工作？

(A) 鯨鯊吃小魚　　　　　　　　(B) 鯨鯊吃浮游生物

(C) 藍鯨吃小魚　　　　　　　　(D) 藍鯨吃浮游生物

【答案】D

【解析】這是問細節的題型，要找同義表達。第一段說到「藍鯨覓食……收獲浮游生物有如剪草機往前推」，故選 (D)。

⑤ 作者提到下列各項都對鯨鯊覓食有幫助，除了

(A) 牙齒　　　　　　　　　　　(B) 下巴

(C) 鰓裂　　　　　　　　　　　(D) 某種海綿狀物質

【答案】A

【解析】這是問細節、採用消去法的題型，要找三個同義表達刪去，剩下的就是答案。第二段說「鯨鯊上下顎雖然各有 3,000 多顆牙齒，但是太小，無助於咀嚼」，沒有說牙齒對覓食有幫助，故選 (A)。

⑥ 可以推論，鯨鯊吃浮游生物時每分鐘大約吞嚥幾次食物？

(A) 4　　　　　　　　　　　　　(B) 5

(C) 10　　　　　　　　　　　　(D) 15

【答案】A

【解析】這是推論題，要找「根據」。第二段說「速率是每 15 秒左右吞一口」，換算就是每分鐘 4 次。

⑦ 第三段中的 inadvertently 一字意思最接近
(A) 不恰當
(B) 意外
(C) 故意
(D) 無法挽回

【答案】**B**
【解析】這是單字題。 inadvertently（構造：not/toward/turn/(*adv.*)）的意思是「不注意」，同義字是 accidentally。

⑧ 關於鯨鯊，可以推論出下列哪一項？
(A) 從口到胃賁門的通道相對較寬
(B) 牠可以拋棄胃、很容易再生一個
(C) 牠只吃液態食物、固體一律吐出
(D) 牠的胃賁門直通小腸

【答案】**A**
【解析】這是推論題，要找「根據」。第三段說「從胃賁門通往另外幾個胃的狹窄通道只容許消化過的液體通過，所以太大的外來物體就留在胃賁門」，可知較大的物體仍能從口吞入胃賁門，亦即這一段的通道較寬。

⑨ 第三段作者描述到想像有人「劇烈嘔吐時」發生的事情，目的是要做什麼？
(A) 警告讀者不得嘔吐太用力
(B) 解釋一個生物學詞彙
(C) 提出人類與鯨鯊之間一個共同點
(D) 證明鯨鯊不能真正把胃吐出來

【答案】**B**
【解析】這是修辭目的的題型，要找上下文。直接上文說到「有一種動作，生物學家稱為胃反轉」，下文就是為了說明「胃反轉」這個詞彙，故選 (B)。

William Harnett, the 19th century American artist known for his uncanny realism, was born in 1848, the son of an immigrant Irish shoemaker. Harnett grew up in Philadelphia, and went to New York City as a journeyman artist and engraver. He was in Munich for a while, studying art. There is evidence that he exhibited his paintings at beer halls and art galleries there. He died in 1892, at the age of 44, and did not leave any writings on art, only an abundance of paintings. The sole documented comment of Harnett on his own art is one short sentence: "I endeavor to make the composition tell a story."

Harnett worked in the tradition of the 17th century Flemish masters, who demonstrated the potential for realistic **renditions** of oil colors, their invention. More recent influences on Harnett included his fellow 19th century countrymen Eakins, Audubon and Homer.

Harnett is the American **version** of the ancient-Greek artist Zeuxis, who produced a painting of a bunch of grapes that was so life-like that birds came down to peck at it. The story goes on and relates that Zeuxis, encouraged, did a painting of a man holding a bunch of grapes. When birds again came down to peck at the grapes, Zeuxis conceded failure—he couldn't give life-like qualities to his portraits!

Like the legendary Zeuxis, Harnett disliked painting portraits. Among his paintings today, only one is a portrait—all others are vivid still-life. At an art museum, in 1886, a special guard had to be assigned to watch over his *The Old Harnett's*, for the visitors refused to believe it was a painting and kept trying to pick up the violin and the bow!

Harnett is not considered a great artist today, because today we are not impressed with photographic verisimilitude. Yet, Harnett's paintings never fail to evoke a sense of wonder in the viewer, and a liking for the artist, who evidently took such delight in toying with his viewers' perception of reality.

✏ Exercise

① The primary concern of the author is to
  (A) introduce an artist
  (B) define a school of painting
  (C) compare Greek and American art
  (D) describe a painting

② According to the passage, William Harnett had been to all of the following places EXCEPT
  (A) Munich
  (B) Flanders
  (C) New York City
  (D) Philadelphia

③ The word "renditions" in the second paragraph is closet in meaning to
  (A) repetitions
  (B) depictions
  (C) translations
  (D) renovations

④ Who is NOT mentioned in the passage as having an influence on Harnett's art?
  (A) Eakins
  (B) Audubon
  (C) Homer
  (D) Zeuxis

⑤ The word "version" in the third paragraph can best be replaced by
  (A) reverse
  (B) counterpart
  (C) vision
  (D) conversion

⑥ It can be inferred that Zeuxis would consider which of the following as proof that he had made a life-like portrait of a man holding grapes?

(A) Birds were scared of the portrait

(B) Birds disliked those grapes

(C) Birds pecked at those grapes

(D) Birds perched on the portrait

⑦ According to the passage, which of the following is an accurate comparison of Harnett and Zeuxis?

(A) Both painted violins that looked real

(B) Both fooled birds with paintings

(C) Both disliked doing portrait-painting

(D) Both learned from Flemish masters

⑧ Why is Harnett no longer considered a great artist?

(A) Because we no longer appreciate art that merely reproduces objects

(B) Because Harnett was not a likable man

(C) Because Harnett cheated everyone

(D) Because his art and Zeuxis' art are very similar

⑨ Which of the following questions CANNOT be answered with information in the passage?

(A) How long did Harnett live?

(B) Who invented oil colors?

(C) Did Zeuxis live before Homer?

(D) How many paintings did Harnett leave behind?

↱ 題解

　　威廉‧哈奈特是 19 世紀以驚人的寫實著稱的美國畫家，1848 年出生在愛爾蘭移民鞋匠之家。哈奈特成長於費城，以實習畫家與雕刻家身分來到紐約市。他在慕尼黑停留過一段時間學藝術。有證據顯示他在慕尼黑的啤酒館、畫廊等處展過畫。他在 1892 年去世，享年 44 歲，沒有留下藝術方面的寫作，只有一大堆畫作。哈奈特對本身畫作的評語見於記錄的只有短短一句：「我努力讓構圖說故事」。

　　哈奈特作畫遵循 17 世紀佛萊明區大師的傳統，這些大師發明了油彩，並展現出油彩在寫實描繪方面的潛力。比較近代對哈奈特的影響包括同屬 19 世紀的美國畫家伊金斯、奧杜邦與荷馬。

　　哈奈特是古希臘畫家宙西斯的美國版，宙西斯畫過一串葡萄很像真的，鳥會下來啄食。故事繼續說：宙西斯大獲鼓舞，又畫了個人手持一串葡萄。鳥還是飛下來啄食，宙西斯於是承認失敗──他沒法把人物肖像畫得像活人！

　　跟傳說中的宙西斯一樣，哈奈特也不喜歡畫人像。今日現存的哈奈特作品中只有一張人物肖像──其餘都是栩栩如生的靜物。1886 年有家美術館得派出特別警衛監看他的《老哈奈特》，因為觀眾不肯相信那是幅畫，一直想把畫中的小提琴與琴弓拿起來！

　　哈奈特今天已經不被認為是偉大藝術家，因為今天我們對照相般的寫實已經不再欽佩。不過，哈奈特的畫一定會令觀眾感到不可思議、也一定會喜歡上這位畫家，因為此人顯然非常喜愛玩弄觀眾對真實的認知。

① 作者主要的目的在於

(A) 介紹一名畫家　　　　　　　　(B) 界定一個畫派

(C) 比較希臘與美國藝術　　　　　(D) 描述一幅畫

【答案】**A**

【解析】這是問主題的題型，要看主題句。開頭「哈奈特是 19 世紀以驚人的寫實著稱的美國畫家」是全文主題句，後面各段第一句（段落主題句）也都在介紹哈奈特，所以這是篇人物介紹。

② 根據本文，威廉‧哈奈特去過下列所有地方，除了

(A) 慕尼黑　　　　　　　　　　　(B) 法蘭德斯

(C) 紐約市　　　　　　　　　　　(D) 費城

【答案】B

【解析】這是問細節、採用消去法的題型，要刪去三個同義表達。第二段說哈奈特作畫遵循 17 世紀佛萊明區 (Flemish) 大師的傳統」，其中 Flemish 就是 Flanders 的形容詞，但並沒說哈奈特去過此地，故選 (B)。

③ 第二段中的 renditions 一字意思最接近

    (A) 重複　　　　　　　　　　　(B) 描繪

    (C) 翻譯　　　　　　　　　　　(D) 翻新

【答案】B

【解析】這是單字題。renditions 的意思是「呈現，描繪」，最接近的同義字是 depictions（構造：down/paint/(*n.*)）。

④ 本文說對哈奈特藝術產生影響的人不包括下列何者？

    (A) Eakins　　　　　　　　　　(B) Audubon

    (C) Homer　　　　　　　　　　(D) Zeuxis

【答案】D

【解析】這是問細節、採用消去法的題型，要刪去三個同義表達。第二段結尾提到三人，刪去後剩下的就是 Zeuxis。

⑤ 第三段中的 version 一字可以換成

    (A) 相反　　　　　　　　　　　(B) 相對之另一半

    (C) 視力，願景　　　　　　　　(D) 轉換

【答案】B

【解析】這是單字題。version（構造：change/(*n.*)）的意思是「版本」，最接近的同義字是 counterpart（構造：against/part）。

⑥ 可以推論，宙西斯會認為下列何種情況可以證明他畫「人拿葡萄」畫活了？

    (A) 鳥會怕這幅肖像畫　　　　　(B) 鳥不喜歡這些葡萄

    (C) 鳥來啄這些葡萄　　　　　　(D) 鳥棲息在這幅肖像上

【答案】A

【解析】這是推論題，要找「根據」。第三段說「宙西斯……又畫了個人手持一串葡萄。鳥還是飛下來啄食，宙西斯於是承認失敗─他沒法把人物肖像畫得像活人」。從這段敘述可以看出宙西斯的心理：要是人畫得像真的，鳥會因為怕人而不敢下來。故選 (A)。

⑦ 根據本文，下列何者是哈奈特與宙西斯正確的比較？

    (A) 兩人都畫過可以亂真的小提琴

    (B) 兩人都曾用畫騙過鳥

    (C) 兩人都不喜歡畫肖像

    (D) 兩人都向佛萊明區大師學畫

【答案】**C**

【解析】這是問細節的題型，要找同義表達。第四段說「跟傳說中的宙西斯一樣，哈奈特也不喜歡畫人像」，其中 Like the legendary Zeuxis, Harnett disliked painting portraits. 就是 Both disliked doing portrait-painting 的同義表達，故選 (C)。

⑧ 哈奈特為何不再被視為偉大藝術家？

    (A) 因為我們不再欣賞只是複製物體的藝術

    (B) 因為哈奈特此人不討人喜歡

    (C) 因為哈奈特欺騙所有人

    (D) 因為他的畫和宙西斯的畫太相似

【答案】**A**

【解析】這是問細節的題型，要找同義表達。第五段說「哈奈特今天已經不被認為是偉大藝術家，因為今天我們對照相般的寫實已經不再欽佩」，其中 because today we are not impressed with photographic verisimilitude 是 Because we no longer appreciate art that merely reproduces objects 的同義表達，故選 (A)。

⑨ 用本文提供的資料無法回答下列哪個問題：

    (A) 哈奈特活了幾年？

    (B) 誰發明油畫？

    (C) 宙西斯是否生活在荷馬之前？

    (D) 哈奈特留下幾幅畫作？

【答案】**D**

【解析】這是問細節的題型，要刪去三項有提到的資料。第一段說「1892 年他去世，享年 44 歲，沒有留下藝術方面的寫作，只有一大堆畫作 (an abundance of paintings)」，並沒說是幾幅，故選 (D)。

A police officer on the streets typically feels a high degree of psychological stress and insecurity. A look at statistics will explain why. In 2017, a total of 135 US police officers died on duty. The largest group, 46, were killed by gunfire. The second largest, 32, perished in automobile and motorcycle crashes. Others died by drowning, exposure to toxins, or stabbing. It would hardly be surprising to learn that as many as 15 died of heart attack—this line of work is simply too stressful.

One element that intensifies the sense of insecurity for the police officer is that he or she has no way to tell the likely cop killer from ordinary, law-abiding citizens. FBI experts have come up with detailed depictions of a number of **felons**, including the serial killer and the rapist. Yet, they have failed to provide characteristics of the cop killer. All the experts can say is: he may be **the last person** a police officer perceives to be a threat.

An important source of stress to a police officer is the large number of cases to handle and the lack of manpower or time to handle them. There were 10.3 million crimes of all sorts in the U.S. for 2010, including property crime, murder, rape, robbery, assault, burglary, vehicle theft, and others. That figure fell slightly, to 9.2 million in 2016, but the percentage of violent crimes increased. In the meantime, police forces have not expanded their numbers, with the policeperson-to-citizen ratio staying at roughly two to 1,000. Faced with the high incidence of crime and **escalated** degrees of violence in crime, the police officer simply cannot fulfill the ideal role of active prevention of crime. He or she can only passively respond to it, and barely, at that.

✎ Exercise

① The passage is mainly about
(A) sources of stress and insecurity for U.S. police officers
(B) crime statistics and crime control for 2010
(C) worsening security on the streets of the U.S.
(D) a serious shortage of police officers

② It can be inferred that all of the following are true of police fatality statistics for 2017 EXCEPT
(A) in all, 135 policemen were killed on the streets
(B) nearly 50 policemen were shot to death
(C) more than 10% died of heart attack
(D) most were killed in their cars

③ The word "felons" in the second paragraph probably means
(A) criminals
(B) cop killers
(C) serial killers
(D) rapists

④ The phrase "the last person" in the second paragraph most closely means
(A) the least suspected person
(B) the previous person
(C) the latest person
(D) the nearby person

⑤ It can be inferred that, in the United States, each police officer has to look after how many citizens on average?
(A) 119
(B) 500
(C) 1,000
(D) 9.2 million

⑥ The word "escalated" in the third paragraph most closely means
(A) unrelated
(B) moderated
(C) increased
(D) distinguished

⑦ The author says that the ideal role of the policeman is one of
(A) immediate reaction to crime
(B) protection of political liberty
(C) active prevention of crime
(D) enforcement of punishment

⑧ A paragraph following the passage would probably deal with which of the following subjects?
(A) A psychological profile of the typical rapist
(B) Crime statistics of the early 1980s
(C) The danger of drugs to the juvenile population
(D) Another source of stress for the police officer

⊡ 題解

文章翻譯

　　街頭上的警察通常會感到高度的心理緊張與不安全感，看看統計數字就知道原因了。2017 年總共有 135 名美國警察因公殉職。其中最大宗（46 人）被槍枝射殺。第二是死於汽車與機車事故。還有人死於溺水、接觸毒素、或刀傷。聽到有多達 15 人死於心臟病發就不足為奇了──這行的壓力太大了。

　　會增加警察不安全感的一項因素是：他無法判斷誰是可能殺警的人、誰是奉公守法的普通公民。聯邦調查局的專家為幾種重刑犯提出了詳細的描繪，包括連續殺人犯、強暴犯。但是一直無法提出殺警凶手的特徵。專家只能說：那可能是警察最料想不到會有威脅的人。

　　警察一大壓力來源在於要處理的案件太多、人手和時間不夠。2010 年美國總共發生 1 千零 30 萬起各式犯罪，包括財產犯罪、謀殺、強暴、搶劫、攻擊、竊盜、偷車等等。這個數字到了 2016 年有稍稍下降，來到 9 百 20 萬起，但其中暴力犯罪的比率增加了。同時，警力並沒有擴張，警察對公民之比仍然保持在大約 2 比 1,000。面對高犯罪率以及犯罪暴力程度升高，警察無法達成理想的角色：積極預防犯罪。只能消極回應，而且是勉強才能回應。

練習題翻譯與詳解

① 本文的主題是

　(A) 美國警察壓力與不安全感的來源

　(B) 2010 年犯罪統計與犯罪管制

　(C) 美國街頭的安全性越來越差

　(D) 警察嚴重短缺

【答案】**A**
【解析】這是問主題的題型，要找出主題句。全文主題句（第一段開頭）是「街頭上的警察通常會感到高度的心理緊張與不安全感」，段落主題句（後面各段第一句）則分別發展心理緊張與不安全感的兩個原因，故選 (A)。

② 可以推論，2017 年警察死亡的統計數字有哪一項是錯的？

　(A) 總計有 135 名警察陣亡在街頭

　(B) 將近 50 名警察被槍打死

　(C) 超過 10% 死於心臟病發

　(D) 大多數死在車上

【答案】**D**
【解析】這是推論題，採用消去法，要找「根據」來刪除三項正確的選項。第一段說「第二是死於汽車與機車事故」，所以死在車上的不應該是最多，故選 (D)。

③ 第二段中的 felons 一字可能是指

    (A) 罪犯　　　　　　　　　　　(B) 殺警凶手

    (C) 連續殺人犯　　　　　　　　(D) 強暴犯

【答案】**A**
【解析】這是單字題。felon 是指「重刑犯」，這個意思從下文的例子「包括連續殺人犯、強暴犯」也可以推出。同義字是 criminals。

④ 第二段中的 the last person 意思最接近

    (A) 最不被懷疑的人　　　　　　(B) 前一個人

    (C) 最新的人　　　　　　　　　(D) 附近的人

【答案】**A**
【解析】這是單字題。the last person 字面上是指「最後一人」，也就是別的人選都沒了才會想到的人。

⑤ 可以推論：在美國，每名警察平均得照顧多少名公民？

    (A) 119　　　　　　　　　　　(B) 500

    (C) 1,000　　　　　　　　　　(D) 920 萬

【答案】**B**
【解析】這是推論題，要找「根據」。第三段說「警察對公民之比仍然保持在大約 2 比 1,000」，由此可推算出 1 名警察分配到 500 名公民。

⑥ 第三段中的 escalated 一字意思最接近

    (A) 無關的　　　　　　　　　　(B) 有調節的

    (C) 增加的　　　　　　　　　　(D) 有區別的，傑出的

【答案】**C**
【解析】這是單字題。escalated 字面上是指「升高的」，同義字是 increased。

⑦ 作者說警察的理想角色是

    (A) 立即反應犯罪　　　　　　　(B) 保護政治自由

    (C) 積極預防犯罪　　　　　　　(D) 強制執行懲罰

【答案】C

【解析】這是問細節的題型，要找同義表達。第三段說「警察無法達成理想的角色：積極預防犯罪」，故選 (C)。

⑧ 本文下一段可能會處理下列哪一項主題？

(A) 典型強暴犯的心理素描　　　　(B) 1980 年代初的犯罪統計

(C) 毒品對青少年族群的危害　　　(D) 警察壓力的另一來源

【答案】D

【解析】這是問組織結構的題型。首先要由全文主題句中看出本文的主題：警察壓力，並從段落主題句中看出已經探討了兩個壓力來源，接下來應該繼續探討下一個壓力來源，故選 (D)。

3

Adoption touches almost every conceivable aspect of American society and culture. Adoption commands our attention because of the enormous number of people who have a direct, intimate connection to it—some experts put the number as high as six out of every ten Americans. Others estimate that about one million children in the U.S. live with adoptive parents and that 2% to 4% of American families include an adopted child. According to incomplete 1992 estimates, a total of 126,951 domestic adoptions occurred, 53,525 of them (42%) kinship or stepparent adoptions. Because of the **dearth** of healthy U.S. infants for adoption, 18,477 adoptions in 2000 were intercountry adoptions, with slightly more than half of those children coming from Russia and China. In short, adoption is a ubiquitous social institution in American society, creating invisible relationships with biological and adoptive kin that touch far more people than we imagine.

Any social organization that touches so many lives in such a profound way is bound to be complicated. Modern adoption is no exception. That is why it is so important to have a historical perspective on this significant social and legal institution. Newspapers, television news shows, and magazines frequently carry stories about various **facets** of adoption. Numerous online chat rooms focus on issues related to the subject. There is a reason for this prominence of adoption. While raising any family is inherently stressful, adoption is filled with additional tensions that are unique to the adoptive relationship.

_W_ First comes the problem of state regulation. _X_ A host of state laws govern every aspect of legal adoptions: who may adopt, who may be adopted, the persons who must consent to the adoption, the form the adoption petition must take, the notice of investigation and formal hearing of the adoption petition, the effect of the adoption decree, the procedure for appeal, the confidential nature of the hearings and records in adoption proceedings, the issuance of new birth certificates, and adoption subsidy payments. _Y_ Second, since World War II, the entire edifice of modern adoption has been enveloped in secrecy. Records of adoption proceedings are confidential, closed both to the public and to all the parties involved in the adoption: birth parents, adoptees, and adoptive parents. Third, in a nation that sanctifies blood kinship, adoptive families and adoptees are stigmatized because of their lack of biological relationship. **Z**

With the onset of World War II, a revolution began in the world of adoption that only a historical perspective can explain. A few examples will illustrate this point. In reaction to the stigmatization, rationalization, and secrecy associated with adoption, **the adoptee search movement** emerged and began to demand the opening of adoption records. Opposing these adoptees, some birth mothers argued that they had been promised secrecy when they relinquished their children for adoption and that abrogating that promise constituted an invasion of privacy. Since World War II, intercountry adoptions have increased tremendously, but critics have denounced such adoptions as shameful in admitting a nation's inability to care of its own people, exploitative of its poorest class, destructive of children's cultural and ethnic heritage, and rife with baby-selling scandals.

Since the mid-nineteenth century, formal adoption—the legal termination of the birth parents' (traditionally defined as a heterosexual couple) parental rights and the taking into the home of a child—has been the way Americans have created substitute families. Through most of the twentieth century, the adoptive parents were assumed to be middle-class couples who wanted children in order to fill out a more-or-less traditional family. But nontraditional families are becoming more common now. Fully 30% of adoptive parents are single mothers, and gay and lesbian couples are increasingly winning the legal right to become adoptive parents. And as an outgrowth of in vitro fertilization technology, researchers have developed "embryo adoption" in which an infertile couple can adopt a donated frozen embryo, bringing into question the very meaning of the institution of adoption. The embryo is implanted into the uterus of the adopting mother, who then gestates and gives birth to the baby. Embryo adoption **obviates** the need for legal adoption because many state laws maintain that a woman who gives birth to a child is the biological parent.

The growth of assisted reproductive technologies, along with almost every aspect of modern adoption—whether the state's intervention into the family or removal of children from their country of origin—raises profound emotional and ethical considerations that only the history of adoption can begin to illuminate.

✐ Exercise

① According to paragraph 1, why is adoption too important an issue to be ignored?
- (A) Because so many people are influenced by adoption
- (B) Because many societies are connected through adoption
- (C) Because adoption commands our attention
- (D) Because six out of every 10 Americans were adopted

② The word "dearth" in paragraph 1 is closest in meaning to
- (A) dearness
- (B) depth
- (C) scarcity
- (D) expensiveness

③ Which of the following can be inferred from paragraph 1 about U.S. adoptions in 2000?
- (A) Some 126,951 children were adopted.
- (B) Some 42% were kinship or stepparent adoptions.
- (C) There were 18,447 adoptions in total
- (D) More than 9,000 adoptees came from Russia and China.

④ According to paragraph 2, which of the following is true about adoption?
- (A) Adoption need not be complicated in the modern society as long as one keeps a historical perspective on it.
- (B) The issue of adoption has taken up too much newspaper space, TV news time, and Internet chat room.
- (C) The stress of raising a family finds an outlet in adoption.
- (D) A family with adopted children faces extra stress which is absent from a "normal," biological family.

⑤ The word "facets" in paragraph 2 is closest in meaning to
- (A) faces
- (B) aspects
- (C) facts
- (D) arguments

⑥ The author mentions all of the following in paragraph 3 as being under the control of state legislation EXCEPT
- (A) the kind of person that may adopt a child

(B) the kind of child that may be adopted

(C) the country an adoptee may come from

(D) the need for secrecy in the adoption process

⑦ In which position would the boldfaced sentence best fit in paragraph 3?

From the moment they decide they wish to adopt a child, couples begin to confront a series of challenges.

(A) Position W   (B) Position X

(C) Position Y   (D) Position Z

⑧ The author mentions "the adoptee search movement" in paragraph 4 in order to

(A) illustrate the stigmatization, rationalization, and secrecy surrounding adoption

(B) give an example of a significant change in adoption practices

(C) argue that World War II was a revolution

(D) present a historical perspective on revolutions

⑨ According to the author, what was the goal of the adoptee search movement?

(A) To search foreign countries for possible adoptees

(B) To lift the veil of secrecy from adoption records

(C) To end the stigmatization of adopted children

(D) To satisfy the requirements of the birth mothers

⑩ According to paragraph 5, what kind of couple stood the best chance of adopting a child in the 20th century?

(A) a middle-class couple

(B) a single mother

(C) a gay couple

(D) a nontraditional couple

⑪ The word "obviates" in paragraph 5 is closest in meaning to

(A) makes obvious   (B) precludes

(C) necessitates   (D) establishes

⑫ Which of the sentences below best expresses the essential information in the boldfaced sentence in paragraph 6?

The growth of assisted reproductive technologies, along with almost every aspect of modern adoption—whether the state's intervention into the family or removal of children from their country of origin—raises profound emotional and ethical considerations that only the history of adoption can begin to illuminate.

(A) Technologies and government regulations have facilitated adoption so that historical considerations of emotion and ethics are no longer necessary.

(B) Faced with new technologies and various facets about adoption, one has to ponder moral and emotional issues and look for answers in the history of adoption.

(C) Because the government may intervene and remove children, the history of adoption must be considered profoundly.

(D) Every aspect of modern adoption is emotionally and ethically profound when examined from a historical perspective.

⬛ 題解

[文章翻譯]

　　領養影響到美國社會文化幾乎每一個想像得到的層面。領養要求我們注意，因為與其直接、密切相關的人數眾多——有些專家估計高達 10 分之 6 的美國人都是。也有人估計，美國約有 100 萬兒童和養父母生活，而且美國家庭 2% 到 4% 都有一個養子女。根據不完整的 1992 年估計，國內領養案總數有 126,951 件，其中有 53,525 件 (42%) 是親戚或繼父母領養。因為可供領養的健康美國嬰兒稀少，2000 年有 18,477 件領養案是跨國領養，其中比半數稍多一點都來自俄羅斯與中國。簡單講，領養在美國社會是無所不在的制度，和血親與養親之間都創造出無形的關係，影響到的人數超出我們的想像。

　　一種社會組織如果對這麼多人產生如此深遠的影響，一定是相當複雜的事，現代的領養制度也不例外。所以，對這種重要的社會與法律制度，我們得要有歷史觀才行。報紙、電視新聞節目、以及雜誌，經常報導關於領養的各方面。也有許多線上聊天室專注在與此主題有關的議題上。領養會如此突出是有原因的。生兒育女本身固然是很有壓力的事，可是領養充滿外加的張力，那是領養關係專有的。

W 首先是州政府規定的問題。X 有一堆州政府法律在規範合法領養的每一個層面：誰有資格領養、誰有資格被領養、由誰同意領養、領養申請的形式、領養申請的調查通知與正式聽證會、領養令的效力、上訴的程序、領養程序的聽證與記錄的保密程度、新出生證明的發給、以及領養補助金的支付。Y 其次，自二次世界大戰以來，現代領養的整個架構一直包裹在祕密中。領養程序的記錄屬於機密，民眾無法取得、涉及領養的各方人士也一樣，包括生父母、被領養人、以及養父母。第三，美國這個國家崇尚血親關係，領養家庭與被領養人會因為沒有血緣關係而蒙上污點。Z

　　隨著二次世界大戰來到，領養界也掀起革命，只有從歷史觀點才能夠解釋。舉幾個例子可以說明這點。領養因為被蒙上污名、辯解、以及包裹在祕密中，所以「被領養人搜尋運動」應運而生、開始要求公開領養記錄。有些生母反對這些被領養人的要求，表示當初放棄小孩供人領養時曾經承諾她們會保密，一旦破壞那項承諾就會構成侵犯隱私。二次大戰以來，跨國領養件數大增，但批評者譴責這種領養，說它很不光采地承認一個國家沒有能力照料自己的人民、剝削最貧窮的階級、破壞兒童的種族文化傳承、並且充斥賣小孩的醜聞。

　　自 19 世紀中葉以來，正式領養——依法結束生父母（傳統定義為異性夫婦）的親權、將小孩帶到家中撫養——一直都是美國人創造替代家庭的辦法。大半個 20 世紀，養父母一般認為都是中產階級夫婦、想要有小孩來充實一個多多少少算是傳統的家庭。但是，非傳統家庭如今越來越常見。多達 30% 的養父母如今是單親媽媽，而且有越來越多的男同性戀、女同性戀伴侶贏得合法權力可以當養父母。另外，拜試管嬰兒科技之賜，研究人員已經開發出「胚胎領養」，不孕的夫婦可以領養別人捐贈的冷凍胚胎，所以何謂「領養」都成了問題。胚胎移植到領養母親的子宮中，然後懷胎、產下嬰兒。胚胎領養排除了依法領養的必要，因為許多州的法律認定產下嬰兒的女人就是生母。

　　協助生育科技的發展，加上現代領養的幾乎每一個層面——不論是州政府對家庭的干預還是將小孩帶出原本的國家——都引起深刻的情感與倫理關切，只有通過領養的歷史才能稍加闡明。

　　[練習題翻譯與詳解]

① 根據第一段，領養為何是非常重要不容忽視的議題？
　(A) 因為有許多人受到領養的影響
　(B) 因為許多社會因為領養而連結
　(C) 因為領養令我們不得不注意
　(D) 因為每 10 個美國人有 6 個被領養

【答案】A
【解析】這是問細節的題型，要找同義表達。第一段說「領養影響到美國社會文化幾乎每一個想像得到的層面。領養要求我們注意，因為與其直接、密切相關的人數眾多」，其中 the enormous number of people who have a direct, intimate connection to it 就是 so many people are influenced by adoption 的同義表達，故選 (A)。

② 第一段中的 dearth 意思最接近

    (A) 親密   (B) 深度

    (C) 稀少   (D) 昂貴

【答案】C
【解析】這是單字題。名詞 dearth 的意思是「稀少」，同義字是 scarcity。

③ 由第一段可以推論，美國在 2000 年的領養如何？

    (A) 約 126,951 名兒童被領養。

    (B) 約 42% 是親戚或繼父母的領養。

    (C) 總共有 18,447 件領養。

    (D) 超過 9,000 名被領養人來自俄羅斯與中國。

【答案】D
【解析】這是推論題，要找「根據」。第一段說「2000 年有 18,477 件領養案是跨國領養，其中比半數稍多一點都來自俄羅斯與中國」，而 18,477 的半數已經超過 9,000，所以可以推論出 (D)。

④ 根據第二段，下列關於領養的哪一句話是對的？

    (A) 在現代社會，領養不必很複雜，只要有歷史觀就行。

    (B) 領養議題已經佔據太多的報紙版面、電視新聞時間、以及網路聊天室的空間。

    (C) 養兒育女的壓力在領養中可以找到一個出口。

    (D) 有養子女的家庭面對額外的壓力，那是「正常」血緣家庭沒有的。

【答案】D
【解析】這是問細節的題型，要找同義表達。第二段說「生兒育女本身固然是很有壓力的事，可是領養充滿外加的張力，那是領養關係專有的」，其中 additional tensions that are unique to the adoptive relationship 就是 extra stress which is absent from a "normal," biological family 的同義表達，故選 (D)。

⑤ 第二段中的 facets 一字意思最接近

    (A) 臉   (B) 層面

    (C) 事實   (D) 論證

【答案】B
【解析】這是單字題。名詞 facet（構造：face/small）的意思是「層面，方面」，同義字是 aspect（構造：toward/look）。

⑥ 作者在第三段提到下列每一項都屬於州法管轄，除了

(A) 哪種人可以領養小孩　　　　　　(B) 哪種小孩可以被領養

(C) 被領養人可以來自什麼國家　　　(D) 領養程序中的保密需要

【答案】C

【解析】這是採消去法、問細節的題型，要刪去三項同義表達。第三段只有「被領養人的國家」沒有規範，故選 (C)。

⑦ 下面這個黑體字句子最適合放在第五段什麼位置？

「從他們決定要領養小孩那一刻起，這對夫婦就開始面對一系列的挑戰。」

(A) W 位置　　　　　　　　　　　(B) X 位置

(C) Y 位置　　　　　　　　　　　(D) Z 位置

【答案】A

【解析】這是安插句子的題型，要看上下文。插入句句尾說「開始面對一系列的挑戰」，下文應該要交代是哪些挑戰。W 位置的下文說「首先是州政府規定的問題」，其中 First 一字很明顯表示這是第一項挑戰，應該銜接在後，成為：「從他們決定要領養小孩那一刻起，這對夫婦就開始面對一系列的挑戰。首先是州政府規定的問題」，故選 (A)。

⑧ 作者在第四段提到 the adoptee search movement 的目的是

(A) 說明領養周圍的污名化、辯解、以及祕密

(B) 舉例說明領養的作法有一項重大的改變

(C) 主張二次世界大戰是一場革命

(D) 為革命提出一個歷史觀點

【答案】B

【解析】這是修辭目的的題型，要看上下文。第四段說「隨著二次世界大戰來到，領養界也掀起革命，只有從歷史觀點才能夠解釋。舉幾個例子可以說明這點。領養因為被蒙上污名、辯解、以及包裹在祕密中，所以『被領養人搜尋運動』應運而生、開始要求公開領養記錄」。前面是段落主題句，重點是「領養界掀起革命」，接下來說要「舉例說明」，而舉出來的例子就是下文的「被領養人搜尋運動」，所以作者提到該運動的目的是作為例子，用以說明領養界掀起的革命，最接近的答案是 (B)（革命就是重大改變的同義表達）。

⑨ 根據作者，被領養人搜尋運動的目標何在？

(A) 到外國去找可供領養的對象　　　(B) 揭開領養記錄的神秘面紗

(C) 結束被領養兒童的污名化　　　　(D) 滿足生母的要求

【答案】B

【解析】這是問細節的題型，要找同義表達。第四段說「被領養人搜尋運動應運而生、開始要求公開領養記錄」，其中 demand the opening of adoption records 就是 lift the veil of secrecy from adoption records 的同義表達，故選 (B)。

⑩ 根據第五段，20 世紀哪種夫婦最有機會領養到小孩？

(A) 中產階級夫婦   (B) 單親媽媽

(C) 同性戀伴侶   (D) 非傳統伴侶

【答案】A

【解析】這是問細節的題型，要找同義表達。第五段說「大半個 20 世紀，養父母一般認為都是中產階級夫婦」，故選 (A)。

⑪ 第五段中的 obviates 一字意思最接近

(A) 使……明顯   (B) 排除

(C) 使……有必要   (D) 建立

【答案】B

【解析】這是單字題，動詞 obviate（構造：against/way/($v.$)）的意思是「使……無必要」，同義字是 preclude（構造：before/close）。

⑫ 下列哪個句子最能夠表達第六段黑體字句子的主要內容？

「協助生育科技的發展，加上現代領養的幾乎每一個層面——不論是州政府對家庭的干預還是將小孩帶出原本的國家——都引起深刻的情感與倫理關切，只有通過領養的歷史才能稍加闡明。」

(A) 科技與政府規範造成領養的便利，所以情感與倫理的歷史考量已不再有必要。

(B) 面對新科技以及領養的各個層面，我們必須衡量道德與情感議題、並且在領養史中尋找答案。

(C) 因為政府可能會干預並且帶走小孩，所以領養史要作深刻思考。

(D) 現代領養的每一層面都有情感與倫理深度，如果從歷史角度檢驗。

【答案】B

【解析】這是句子改寫的題型，要找句中重點的同義表達。原句兩個破折號之間是屬於不重要的細節（一對破折號的功能相當於一組括弧），可以捨去，剩餘部分的同義表達就是 (B)。

The increasing world population has been both a blessing and a curse. Between 1930 and 1975, global population increased from two to four billion persons. From 1975 to 2000, it increased to six billion. Now, in 2018, there are a total of 7.6 billion people in the world, and counting. The sharpest increases have generally been in developing nations that are least able to provide food, education, and jobs for all.

Arguably, **averting** world famine depends on the relatively few countries able to export food; literally millions of hungry souls count on them. Many nations, like Indonesia and Thailand, now have effective population control programs, but the control of infectious diseases and an increase in the food supply have combined to encourage continued population growth.

Demographers vary widely in their estimates of the earth's maximum **sustainable** population, but they all agree that population control is a necessity and that there are limits to the planet's capacity. Excessive population density and overcrowding have been implicated in a variety of ills ranging from increased crime and pollution to environmental degradation and political instability. One of mankind's most important **challenges** is to control **the ticking population time bomb**.

✎ Exercise

① What is the main idea of the passage?
   (A) The blessings of the population increase
   (B) The problems of developing nations
   (C) The importance of the population issue
   (D) Mankind's ability to feed itself.

② In the second paragraph the word "averting" is closest in meaning to which of the following?
   (A) controlling
   (B) ending
   (C) avoiding
   (D) replacing

③ Which of the following can be inferred as having the potential to disrupt population growth?
   (A) Jobs for all
   (B) Averting world famine
   (C) Uncontrolled infectious diseases
   (D) Political instability

④ The word "sustainable" in the third paragraph is closest in meaning to
   (A) supportable
   (B) contemporary
   (C) knowledgeable
   (D) developing

⑤ According to the passage, which of the following is NOT a possible consequence of an uncontrollable increase in world population?
   (A) A wide range of new diseases
   (B) Increased level of crime
   (C) Dangerous food shortages
   (D) Disruptions of governments

⑥ It can be inferred from the passage that population growth
    (A) first began increasing in 1930
    (B) has reached the earth's full capacity
    (C) is in line with demographic estimates
    (D) is fastest in developing countries

⑦ In the third paragraph the word "challenges" is closest in meaning to
    (A) adventures
    (B) risks
    (C) difficulties
    (D) tasks

⑧ The phrase "ticking population time bomb" in the third paragraph suggests that
    (A) population increases may lead to war
    (B) time is running out on finding a solution
    (C) terrorists threaten people 24 hours a day
    (D) the author has had extensive military experience

題解

4

文章翻譯

　　世界人口不斷增加，是福也是禍。從 1930 年到 1975 年，全球人口從 20 億增加到 40 億。1975 年到 2000 年增加到 60 億。如今，2018 年，全球人口有 76 億，而且持續增加中。增加幅度最大的大致都是開發中國家，這些國家最沒有能力為全體國民提供食物、教育與工作。

　　可以這樣說：要想避免全球饑荒，得靠相對少數能夠出口糧食的國家，真正有幾百萬饑餓的人在指望這些國家。許多國家如印尼與泰國，如今都已經實施了有效的人口管制計畫，但是因為傳染性疾病控制成功、食物供應量增加，這些因素結合起來造成人口持續成長。

　　人口統計學家對於全球人口能夠維持的上限在哪裡，這項估計有很大的差異，但大家都同意人口管制有其必要、以及地球可以負荷的人口有其限制。人口密度過高、過度擁擠，與各種弊端都有關係，包括犯罪率升高、污染增加、環境破壞、以及政治不安定。人類面臨的一大挑戰就是要控制這顆滴答作響的人口定時炸彈。

練習題翻譯與詳解

① 本文的主題是什麼？

　　(A) 人口增加的好處　　　　　　　　(B) 開發中國家的問題

　　(C) 人口問題的重要　　　　　　　　(D) 人類餵飽自己的能力

【答案】C

【解析】這是問主題的題型，要找主題句。全文主題句（第一段開頭）點出「世界人口不斷增加」這個主題。後面兩個段落主題句（各段第一句）分別發展的是人口增加造成的糧食供應問題與其他問題，所以共同主題是「人口增加造成的問題」，故選 (C)。

② 第二段的 averting 一字意思最接近

　　(A) 控制　　　　　　　　　　　　　(B) 結束

　　(C) 避免　　　　　　　　　　　　　(D) 取代

【答案】C

【解析】這是單字題。avert（構造：away/turn）的意思是「避免，躲開」，同義字是 avoid。

③ 可以推論，下列何者有可能打斷人口增長？

　　(A) 全民就業　　　　　　　　　　　(B) 避免全球饑荒

　　(C) 傳染病無法控制　　　　　　　　(D) 政治不安定

【答案】**C**

【解析】這是推論題，要找「根據」。第二段說「因為傳染性疾病控制成功、食物供應量增加，這些因素結合起來造成人口持續成長」，可知傳染性疾病控制成功是人口持續成長的原因之一。據此可以推論：若傳染性疾病失控，人口成長會受到打擊，故選 (C)。

④ 第三段的 sustainable 一字意思最接近

  (A) 可維持的   (B) 同時代的

  (C) 有知識的   (D) 開發中的

【答案】**A**

【解析】這是單字題。sustainable（構造：under/hold/able）的意思是「永續的，可持續的」，同義字是 supportable。

⑤ 根據本文，下列何者不是世界人口增加失控會造成的後果？

  (A) 許多新疾病出現   (B) 犯罪升高

  (C) 糧食短缺嚴重   (D) 政府遭到破壞

【答案】**A**

【解析】這是問細節、採用消去法的題型，要刪去三個同義表達。第二段說到人口增加帶來饑荒的危險，第三段說到犯罪增加與政治不安定，分別是 (B) (C) (D) 的同義表達，只有選項 (A) 找不到同義表達（第二段說到疾病管制成功，那是人口增加的原因而非結果），故選 (A)。

⑥ 根據本文可以推論，人口成長

  (A) 在 1930 年首度開始增加   (B) 已經達到地球的負荷量

  (C) 符合人口學家的預估   (D) 在開發中國家最快

【答案】**D**

【解析】這是推論題，要找「根據」。第一段說「增加幅度最大的大致都是開發中國家」，可推知開發中國家的人口成長最快，故選 (D)。

⑦ 第三段的 challenges 一字意思最接近

  (A) 冒險   (B) 風險

  (C) 困難   (D) 工作

【答案】**C**

【解析】這是單字題。challenge 的意思是「挑戰」，也就是困難的、不易成功的工作，最接近的同義字是 difficulty。

⑧ 第三段的 ticking population time bomb 暗示

(A) 人口增加可能導致戰爭

(B) 要找出解決方案的時間越來越少了

(C) 一天 24 小時恐怖分子都在威脅世人

(D) 作者有豐富的軍事經驗

【答案】**B**

【解析】這是單字題。a ticking time bomb 是「滴答作響的定時炸彈」，把 population 嵌在裡面，表示人口問題隨時可能引爆，暗示時間緊迫，故選 (B)。

The Navajo were probably the first people to set foot in the Grand Canyon. They left there the oldest artifact found in the Canyon—a small twig figure of an animal, dating back 4,000 years. Their legends also preserve interesting accounts of the creation of the Grand Canyon. They believe it was formed by the gods to drain a devastating flood. The gods also turned the Navajos' ancestors into fish to escape drowning. To this day many Navajo do not eat fish.

Spanish explorers reached the Grand Canyon in 1540, with some Hopi as their guides. The Spaniards came looking for gold, and moved on when they failed to find it in the Canyon. Major John Wesley Powell, a one-armed Civil War veteran, was a man in love with the Canyon who won undying fame in connection with it. He made two boat descents through the Canyon, in 1869 and 1871, and left fascinating notes on both expeditions.

After the explorers came the prospectors, lured by the precious metals exposed on the Canyon's walls. When they failed to strike it rich, some miners started guide services on the side. In 1883, John Hance came to the Canyon near Grandview Point, dug a trail down to his asbestos mine at the Canyon bottom, built a cabin on the Canyon rim, and started his mining-tourism business, the first tourism business in the Grand Canyon.

Other miners came to Grandview Point, digging for copper in the Canyon, of which there was an abundance. The first hotel in the Grand Canyon was built at Grandview Point in 1892. Grandview Point remained a focal point of Grand Canyon tourism until the railroad came, in 1901. The latest and fanciest facilities were established near the railhead, and Grand Canyon Village soon replaced Grandview Point as the **star** resort.

✏ Exercise

① What is the passage mainly about?
  (A) History of human activities in the Grand Canyon
  (B) Spanish explorers in the Grand Canyon
  (C) History of Grandview Point
  (D) Native Americans in the Grand Canyon

② The passage implies that many Navajo do not eat fish because of
  (A) the scarcity of fish in the Grand Canyon
  (B) frequent and devastating floods in the Grand Canyon
  (C) some legendary accounts about their ancestors
  (D) their natural vegetarian inclinations

③ All of the following are true about Native Americans in the Grand Canyon
  EXCEPT
  (A) Hopi led Spaniards to the Canyon
  (B) Navajo were most likely the first to get there
  (C) they left the oldest artifact found in the Grand Canyon
  (D) they first came to the Grand Canyon looking for gold

④ The author suggests that Spanish explorers did not stay on in the Grand
  Canyon because
  (A) they considered the Grand Canyon holy ground
  (B) they did not find gold there
  (C) they failed to find any hotels there
  (D) there were plenty of canyons in Spain

⑤ According to the passage, which of the following is true about Major Powell's
  notes on the Grand Canyon?
  (A) They were permanently lost during the Civil War
  (B) They are too technical for the general reader
  (C) They were written in Spanish and then translated
  (D) They were taken on two separate expeditions

⑥ It is mentioned in the passage that the first man to run a tourist business in the Grand Canyon was
(A) a Spaniard
(B) John Wesley Powell
(C) John Hance
(D) a Navajo

⑦ The author mentions that the Grand Canyon is rich in
(A) fossils
(B) precious stones
(C) gold
(D) copper

⑧ The word "star" in the fourth paragraph is closest in meaning to
(A) most expensive
(B) leading
(C) most distant
(D) show business

⑨ The events mentioned in the passage are organized by
(A) order of importance
(B) order of time
(C) order of space
(D) random order

⤵ 題解

納瓦荷人可能是最早進入大峽谷的人。他們留下了大峽谷找到的最古老文物——一個用樹枝做的動物小像，大約是 4,000 年前的東西。他們的傳說還保留了關於大峽谷創造的有趣的說明。他們相信大峽谷是神明創造的，為了給一次毀滅性的洪水洩洪。神明還把納瓦荷的祖先變成魚以免淹死。直到今天許多納瓦荷人還是不吃魚。

西班牙探險家在 1540 年來到大峽谷，有幾名霍皮族當嚮導。西班牙人是來找黃金的，在大峽谷裡沒找到，所以就離開了。約翰‧威斯利‧鮑威爾少校是位獨臂的南北戰爭老兵，愛上了大峽谷，也因為大峽谷贏得了不朽的名聲。他搭船漂下大峽谷兩次，分別在 1869 與 1871 年，兩次探險都留下了引人入勝的筆記。

探險家之後，來的是淘金客，受到峽谷壁上露出的貴重金屬引誘而來。他們沒能發財，其中有些開礦的就兼職當起導遊。1883 年，約翰‧漢斯來到「大景點」附近的大峽谷、開了條小路下去通到峽谷底部他的石棉礦、在峽谷邊沿蓋了棟小木屋，開始經營起他的採礦兼旅遊生意，那是大峽谷頭一家旅遊公司。

還有別的採礦者來到大景點，為了在峽谷內挖銅礦，這裡的蘊藏豐富。大峽谷第一家旅館於 1892 年在大景點興建。大景點一直是大峽谷觀光業的重鎮，直到 1901 年鐵路開通。火車站附近蓋了最新、最豪華的設施，「大峽谷村」很快取代了大景點成為明星級的勝地。

① 本文的主題是什麼？

   (A) 大峽谷人類活動史   (B) 大峽谷的西班牙探險家

   (C) 大景點歷史   (D) 大峽谷的美洲原住民

【答案】**A**

【解析】這是問主題的題型，要看主題句。第一段開頭是全文主題句：「納瓦荷人可能是最早進入大峽谷的人」。後面各段第一句（段落主題句）按照時間先後順序分別介紹來到大峽谷的探險家、淘金客、旅遊業者，共同主題是人類在大峽谷活動的歷史，故選 (A)。

② 本文暗示許多納瓦荷人不吃魚是因為

   (A) 大峽谷魚很少   (B) 大峽谷洪水多、破壞力強

   (C) 一些關於他們祖先的傳奇故事   (D) 他們天性偏好素食

【答案】**C**

【解析】這是推論題型，要找「根據」。第一段說「他們的傳說還保留了關於大峽谷創造的有趣的說明……神明還把納瓦荷的祖先變成魚以免淹死。直到今天許多納瓦荷人還是不吃魚」，所以他們不吃魚是跟這種傳說有關。

③ 下列關於大峽谷內美洲原住民的敘述，哪一句是錯的？

　　(A) 霍皮人帶領西班牙人進入大峽谷

　　(B) 納瓦荷人可能是最早到此的

　　(C) 他們留下大峽谷內找到的最古老文物

　　(D) 他們最初來大峽谷是為了找黃金

【答案】**D**

【解析】這是問細節、採用消去法的題型，要刪去三個同義表達。第二段說「西班牙人是來找黃金的」，選項 (D) 卻說是納瓦荷人，所以 (D) 不是同義表達。

④ 作者暗示西班牙探險家沒有留在大峽谷是因為

　　(A) 他們認為大峽谷是聖地

　　(B) 他們在那裡沒找到黃金

　　(C) 他們在那裡沒找到旅館

　　(D) 西班牙多得是峽谷

【答案】**B**

【解析】這是推論題，要找「根據」。第二段說「西班牙人是來找黃金的，在大峽谷裡沒找到，所以就離開了」，故選 (B)。

⑤ 根據本文，關於鮑威爾少校留下的大峽谷筆記，哪一項是對的？

　　(A) 筆記在內戰中永遠喪失

　　(B) 筆記太技術性，一般讀者不適合

　　(C) 筆記用西班牙文寫作然後翻譯

　　(D) 筆記分別在兩次探險寫下

【答案】**D**

【解析】這是問細節的題型，要找同義表達。第二段說「他搭船漂下大峽谷兩次，分別在 1869 與 1871 年，兩次探險都留下了引人入勝的筆記」，其中 left fascinating notes on both expeditions 就是 They were taken on two separate expeditions 的同義表達。

⑥ 文中提到，最早在大峽谷經營旅遊業的是

　　(A) 一位西班牙人　　　　　　　　(B) 約翰・威斯利・鮑威爾

　　(C) 約翰・漢斯　　　　　　　　　(D) 一位納瓦荷人

【答案】**C**

【解析】這是問細節的題型。第三段說「漢斯……開始經營起他的採礦兼旅遊生意，那是大峽谷頭一家旅遊公司」，所以是 (C)。

⑦ 作者提到大峽谷有很豐富的

    (A) 化石   (B) 寶石

    (C) 黃金   (D) 銅

【答案】**D**

【解析】這是問細節的題型。第四段說「還有別的採礦者來到大景點，為了在峽谷內挖銅礦，這裡的蘊藏豐富」，所以選 (D)。

⑧ 第四段的 star 一字意思最接近

    (A) 最貴的   (B) 領先的

    (C) 最遙遠的   (D) 演藝事業的

【答案】**B**

【解析】這是單字題。star 字面上是指「星星」，暗示「明星級」，同義字是 leading。

⑨ 文中提到的事件，組織順序是依

    (A) 重要性順序   (B) 時間順序

    (C) 空間順序   (D) 隨機順序

【答案】**B**

【解析】這是組織結構的題型，要看各段主題句。各段主題句由最古老的美洲原住民一直講到現代，所以是時間順序。

Reading 3

Sleep is a recurring state of inactivity, reduced consciousness, and decrease in responsiveness to events in the environment. The ease with which sleep can be terminated differentiates it from coma, general anesthesia, drug induced stupor, and the seasonal hibernation of certain animals. On the other hand, there are conditions of semiwakeness (hypnotic trance, for example) that are intermediate in character, possessing some features of both sleep and wakefulness. Moreover, in the routine of living there are regular diurnal gradations in the depth of **slumber** and the degree of alertness, which alternate with one another like the crest and trough of a 24-hour wave.

A conspicuous characteristic of sleep is the horizontal posture of repose which permits a relaxation of the body musculature. When an individual is awake, muscular contractions not only produce **overt** movement but also maintain a state of partial contraction which produces resistance to passive or externally imposed movement. This is noticeably absent during sleep. However, muscular relaxation and immobility are not absolute. Unless artificially restrained, a sleeper from time to time moves one part of the body or another. As a rule, the longer the duration of sleep, the more it entails at least a semiawakening and a partial awareness of environmental details. Most sleepers do not recall these multiple, moving interruptions of sleep. Hence there is the expression "**sleeping like a rock.**" In any case, the total amount of time taken up by this motility is small, amounting to 30 seconds per hour, or about four minutes in an average night. This periodic change in the position of the body is probably brought on by, and relieves, the pressure on the skin in contact with the sleeping surface.

Exercise

① What is the main idea of the passage?

    (A) Advances in controlling sleep disorders

    (B) The role of observational data in sleep research

    (C) A description of the state of sleep

    (D) The monitoring of periodic movements during sleep

② It can be inferred from the passage that drug induced stupors

    (A) lead to long periods of sleep

    (B) are not unlike routine sleep

    (C) are difficult to awaken from

    (D) include elements of wakefulness

③ In the first paragraph the word "slumber" is closest in meaning to which of the following?

    (A) mental activity

    (B) sleep

    (C) movement

    (D) depression

④ The word "overt" in the second paragraph is closest in meaning to

    (A) willful

    (B) finished

    (C) powerful

    (D) visible

⑤ The author implies that the artificial restraint of sleepers will

    (A) affect their level of movement

    (B) decrease the depth of their sleep

    (C) result in periods of wakefulness

    (D) cause them to move more often

⑥ Which of the following statements would the author be LEAST likely to agree with?
(A) Scientists still do not understand all aspects of sleep
(B) Some conditions border on both sleep and wakefulness
(C) Complete lack of movement is a typical characteristic of sleep
(D) Normal sleep movement is not a serious problem

⑦ It can be inferred that most people use the phrase "sleeping like a rock" (in the second paragraph) to indicate that
(A) they moved less than twenty times that night
(B) they cannot recall any of their dreams
(C) they did not stir at all while sleeping
(D) they remember their trouble falling asleep

⑧ The author uses the phrase "sleeping like a rock" in the second paragraph to explain
(A) Sleeping disorder
(B) People's conception of sleep
(C) Sleepwalking
(D) insomnia

睡眠是重複發生的無活動狀態、知覺降低、並且對環境中發生的事件較無反應。睡覺很容易結束，這是它和下列情況不同的地方：長期昏迷、全身麻醉、藥物引起的昏迷、以及某些動物的季節性休眠。另一方面，也有一些半醒半睡的情況（例如催眠造成的出神）具有中間的特質：睡眠的特徵與清醒的特徵都有一些。而且，在日常生活中也會固定出現每天的程度變化，包括睡眠的深淺與警覺的程度都有高低的不同，彼此輪流交替，像波長 24 小時的波峰與波谷。

睡眠有個明顯的特徵是身體平躺的休息姿態，可以放鬆全身肌肉。人醒的時候，肌肉收縮可以產生明顯的動作，還可以維持部分收縮的狀態，對於被動的、或者外來的動作可以做出抵抗。睡眠中這種情況明顯不存在。不過，睡眠的肌肉放鬆與不活動也並非絕對。除非受到人為約束，睡覺的人偶爾還是會動一動身體的某個部分。一般說來，睡眠時間越久，越容易產生至少半清醒狀態、以及對環境細節的半知覺狀態。睡眠時這些反覆發生的打斷睡眠動作，大部分人都不會記得，所以才會有「睡得像塊石頭」這種說法出來。總之，這種動作全部佔的時間也不多，大約是每小時有 30 秒，或者平均每晚有 4 分鐘。身體這般定期改變姿勢，很可能是因為皮膚與所睡的表面接觸的壓力造成的，變換姿勢就可以減輕壓力。

① 本文的主題是什麼？

　(A) 控制睡眠失調方面的進展

　(B) 睡眠研究中觀察資料扮演的角色

　(C) 描述睡眠的狀態

　(D) 監視睡眠中的週期動作

【答案】**C**

【解析】這是問主題的題型，要看主題句。全文主題句（頭一句）是「睡眠是重複發生的無活動狀態……」，這是睡眠的定義。第二段的段落主題句是「睡眠有個明顯的特徵是身體平躺的休息姿態」，開始描寫睡眠的狀態來發展主題。故選 (C)。

② 可以推論得知，藥物引起的昏迷

　(A) 導致比較長時間的睡眠

　(B) 和一般的睡眠沒什麼不同

　(C) 很難醒過來

　(D) 包括清醒的成分在內

【答案】C

【解析】這是推論題，要找「根據」。第一段說「睡覺很容易結束，這是它和下列情況不同的地方：……藥物引起的昏迷」。所以，藥物引起的昏迷和睡覺不同，也就是不容易結束，故選 (C)。

③ 第一段中的 slumber 一字意思最接近下列何者？

    (A) 心智活動   (B) 睡眠

    (C) 動作   (D) 沮喪

【答案】B

【解析】這是單字題。slumber 字面上是指「沉睡」，同義字是 sleep。

④ 第二段的 overt 一字意思最接近

    (A) 任性的   (B) 已結束的

    (C) 有力的   (D) 可見的

【答案】D

【解析】這是單字題。overt 與 open 的字根相同，意思是「明顯的，公開的」，同義字是 visible。

⑤ 作者暗示，將睡覺的人加以人為約束，將會

    (A) 影響他們活動的水平   (B) 減低他們睡眠的深度

    (C) 造成清醒的時段   (D) 使他們動得更頻繁

【答案】A

【解析】這是推論題，要找「根據」。第二段說「除非受到人為約束，睡覺的人偶爾還是會動一動身體的某個部分」，反過來說，真正加以人為約束，就無法動彈，故選 (A)。

⑥ 作者最不可能同意下列哪句陳述？

    (A) 科學家仍不了解睡眠的所有層面

    (B) 有些情況介乎睡與醒之間

    (C) 完全不動是睡眠的典型特質

    (D) 睡眠中的正常動作不是大問題

【答案】C

【解析】這是推論題、並採用消去法的題型，要刪去三個正確的陳述。第二段說「除非受到人為約束，睡覺的人偶爾還是會動一動身體的某個部分」，這和 (C) 的「完全不動」有衝突，故選 (C)。

⑦ 可以推論，大部分人用 sleeping like a rock 一語（在第二段）來表示

(A) 他們當晚動不到 20 次

(B) 他們想不起做過的夢

(C) 他們睡的時候完全沒動

(D) 他們記得當時很難入睡

【答案】**C**

【解析】這是推論題，要找「根據」。直接上文說「睡眠時這些反覆發生的打斷睡眠動作，大部分人都不會記得，所以才會有 sleeping like a rock 這種說法出來」。首先，石頭是完全不動的。其次，會這樣講的原因是「不記得有動」，所以一般用此語是來表示「睡得很熟、完全不動」。

⑧ 第二段中作者用 sleeping like a rock 一語來解釋

(A) 睡眠障礙

(B) 一般人對睡眠的觀念

(C) 夢遊

(D) 失眠

【答案】**B**

【解析】這是修辭目的的題型，要看上下文：「睡眠時這些反覆發生的打斷睡眠動作，大部分人都不會記得，所以才會有 sleeping like a rock 這種說法出來」。從直接上文來看，這個話是睡覺的人說的，用來表達自己對睡眠的記憶，認為自己睡得很熟。所以作者用此語是來說明睡覺的人的看法，故選 (B)。

4

Henry Louis Mencken, better known as H. L. Mencken, U.S. writer and controversialist, was for two decades the most pungent **critic** of American life.

After attending the Baltimore Polytechnic Institute he became a reporter on the Baltimore *Evening Herald*, and later joined the staff of the Baltimore *Sun*. From 1908, when the *Smart Set* magazine hired him to do its book reviews, until 1929, when the stock market crash and subsequent depression made his caustic wit seem out of place, he jabbed his pen at American icons and weaknesses. He often used literary criticism as a point of departure, though he wrote enough reviews and **miscellaneous** essays to fill six volumes of aptly titled *Prejudices* (1919-1927).

Mencken jeered at organized religion, ridiculed business and the middle class, and mocked the citizens of the southern United States. Mencken's view of life changed surprisingly little during his career. Though few others found the Great Depression a **suitable** subject for satire, Mencken reviled President Roosevelt as much as he did Hoover. Likewise, when the German culture that Mencken so appreciated began to be overwhelmed by Hitler and fascism, Mencken was slower than most of his readers to recognize its decline. Perhaps Mencken's most enduring contribution to American literature was his 1919 publication of *The American Language*, a volume that brought together examples of peculiarly American expressions and idioms. By the time of his death in 1956, Mencken was the leading authority on the language of the United States.

Exercise

① What is the main topic of the passage?
(A) The career of a social commentator
(B) The truth about American literature
(C) Writing in the pre-depression years
(D) An author who fought the Germans

② The word "critic" in the first paragraph is closest in meaning to
(A) member
(B) judge
(C) writer
(D) official

③ According to the author, Mencken worked for all of the following EXCEPT
(A) the Baltimore *Sun*
(B) the Baltimore *Evening Herald*
(C) the Baltimore Polytechnic Institute
(D) the *Smart Set*

④ The word "miscellaneous" in the second paragraph is closest in meaning to
(A) scholarly
(B) published
(C) various
(D) collected

⑤ It can be inferred that the author of the passage believes that Mencken
(A) did not have sufficient material for six volumes
(B) incorrectly judged the day's literary trends
(C) actually belonged to an organized church
(D) held very strong opinions and prejudices

⑥ In the third paragraph the word "suitable" is closest in meaning to which of the following?

(A) humorous

(B) fortunate

(C) reputable

(D) appropriate

⑦ It can be inferred that Mencken was probably a

(A) supporter of Hoover

(B) secret Nazi

(C) believer in free press

(D) mediocre literary talent

⑧ It can be inferred that Mencken differed from most other Americans of his time in which of the following way?

(A) He was among the last to denounce Germany.

(B) He was not interested in material success.

(C) He found humor in subjects that others did not.

(D) He did not believe in a distinctive American tongue.

⑨ According to the passage, Mencken

(A) was an admirer of Hitler

(B) preferred Roosevelt to Hoover

(C) was critical of other writers

(D) was an expert on American speech

【文章翻譯】

　　美國作家、爭議人士亨利・路易斯・孟肯，大家比較熟的名字是 H.L. 孟肯，曾經有 20 年之久是批判美國生活最尖銳的批評家。

　　就讀完巴爾的摩科技高中後，他進入巴爾的摩《前鋒晚報》擔任記者，後來加入巴爾的摩《太陽報》工作。從 1908 年《聰明幫》雜誌聘他擔任書評算起，直到 1929 年股市崩盤以及後續的蕭條使他那種尖酸諷刺的機智令人感覺不合時宜為止，這段期間他用筆鋒戳刺美國人的偶像與弱點。他經常是從文學批評寫起，不過他寫的評論與各式各樣的散文足足有 6 大冊，取了個相當貼切的書名《偏見》(1919-1927)。

　　孟肯訕笑組織宗教、揶揄商業與中產階級、並且嘲諷美國南部居民。孟肯的人生觀在他生涯中改變之少令人意外。雖然沒什麼旁人會覺得經濟大蕭條是恰當的諷刺對象，但孟肯謾罵羅斯福總統一如他謾罵胡佛。同樣的，當孟肯非常賞識的德國文化開始被希特勒與法希斯淹沒，孟肯比大部分的讀者都後知後覺，沒有看出德國文化的衰退。孟肯對美國文學最持久不衰的貢獻或許是 1919 年出版的《美國語言》，書中收集了美國特有的表達方式與成語的例子。到 1956 年他去世時，孟肯已經是美國語言的首席權威。

【練習題翻譯與詳解】

① 本文的主題是什麼？

(A) 一位社會評論家的生涯　　　　　　(B) 美國文學真像

(C) 經濟大蕭條時代之前的寫作　　　　(D) 一名對抗德國人的作家

〔答案〕**A**

〔解析〕這是問主題的題型，要看主題句。第一段整個是一句，也就是全文主題句，提出「批評家孟肯」這個主題。後面兩段的段落主題句分別介紹孟肯的生涯背景與主要成就，所以這是一篇人物介紹。

② 第一段中的 critic 一字意思最接近

(A) 成員　　　　　　　　　　　　　　(B) 裁判

(C) 作家　　　　　　　　　　　　　　(D) 官員

〔答案〕**B**

〔解析〕這是單字題，critic 是指「批評家」，最接近的是 judge「裁判，評判者」。

③ 根據作者，孟肯工作過的單位不包括

(A) 巴爾的摩《太陽報》　　　　　　　(B) 巴爾的摩《前鋒晚報》

(C) 巴爾的摩科技高中　　　　　　　　(D)《聰明幫》

【答案】C
【解析】這是問細節、採用消去法的題型，要刪去三個同義表達。第二段說他「讀完巴爾的摩科技高中」，其中 attending 和他在此工作 (work for) 不是同義表達，故選 (C)。

④ 第二段的 miscellaneous 一字意思最接近
　　(A) 學術的　　　　　　　　　　　(B) 出版的
　　(C) 各種的　　　　　　　　　　　(D) 收集的

【答案】C
【解析】這是單字題。 miscellaneous（字根 misc = mix）的意思是「混雜的」，同義字是 various（字根 vari = change）。

⑤ 可以推論，本文作者認為孟肯
　　(A) 沒有足夠材料可以出 6 冊書
　　(B) 對當時的文學趨勢判斷錯誤
　　(C) 其實有參加一個組織教會
　　(D) 個人意見與偏見相當強

【答案】D
【解析】這是推論題，要找「根據」。第二段說他「取了個相當貼切的書名《偏見》」，表示作者認為此人的文章充滿偏見。

⑥ 第三段中的 suitable 一字意思最接近下列哪一個？
　　(A) 幽默的　　　　　　　　　　　(B) 幸運的
　　(C) 名聲好的　　　　　　　　　　(D) 恰當的

【答案】D
【解析】形容詞 suitable 的意思是「合適的」，同義字是 appropriate（字根 proper = one's own）

⑦ 可以推論，孟肯可能是
　　(A) 胡佛的支持者　　　　　　　　(B) 私底下的納粹
　　(C) 出版自由的信奉者　　　　　　(D) 平庸的文學家

【答案】C
【解析】這是推論題，要找「根據」。第三段說孟肯「訕笑組織宗教、挪揄商業與中產階級、並且嘲諷美國南部居民」，還說他兩位總統一般謾罵，由此可以看出他堅信言論自由與出版自由。

⑧ 可以推論，孟肯和當代大部分美國人有何不同？

　　(A) 他是最晚譴責德國的人之一。

　　(B) 他對物質方面的成功沒興趣。

　　(C) 他在別人不覺得幽默的題材中看出幽默。

　　(D) 他不相信美國有獨特的語言。

【答案】**A**

【解析】這是推論題，要找「根據」。第三段說「孟肯比大部分的讀者都後知後覺，沒有看出德國文化的衰退」，所以他譴責德國也應該比別人來得晚。

⑨ 根據本文，孟肯

　　(A) 是希特勒的崇拜者

　　(B) 喜歡羅斯福超過胡佛

　　(C) 對別的作家持批判態度

　　(D) 是美國語言專家

【答案】**D**

【解析】這是問細節的題目，要找同義表達。第三段說孟肯去世時「已經是美國語言的首席權威」，其中 leading authority on the language of the United States 就是 expert on American speech 的同義表達，故選 (D)。

4

Reading 5

Before the European "discovery" of North America, as many as three hundred **distinct** languages were spoken by Native Americans living north of Mexico. There were many languages that covered large geographical areas and included a score or more of closely related dialects. Among these languages were Algonkian, Athabascan, and Siouan. Many other language groups, however, were smaller and the areas containing them correspondingly were more diverse in language. For example, in California alone more than 20 distinct language groups were represented. According to some experts, the continental United States exhibited greater and more numerous language extremes than were found in all of Europe. One must bear in mind, however, that the **speculations of experts** remain only speculations. There is no precise way to determine the range of Native American languages prior to the thorough cataloguing by Europeans.

Although the Native American population of Mexico and Central America was several times greater than the population north of Mexico, **approximately** the same number of languages were spoken. A limited number of these languages, most notably those of the Aztecs of Central Mexico and the Maya of the Yucatan Peninsula and Guatemala, accounted for the vast majority of the native population. The greatest linguistic diversity in this region was in the area now comprising southern Mexico and the small Central American nations.

South America had more inhabitants, roughly nine million, and more spoken languages, almost fifteen hundred, than the other regions combined. Most of the population spoke the Quechuan language of the powerful Inca empire. The Inca's military conquests spread this language from its birthplace in the southern Peruvian highlands to almost the entire Andean area. These conquests also almost certainly resulted in the extinction or reduction of a large number of other Native American tongues. The low-lying tropical areas near present day Venezuela and Brazil exhibited the greatest linguistic diversity in South America. Three South American languages managed to spread northward; the Chibchan, the Cariban, and the Arawakan.

✎ Exercise

① What does the passage primarily discuss?
  (A) The linguistic diversity of the continental United States
  (B) The language migration from North to South America
  (C) Population estimates of various American Native American tribes
  (D) The distribution of languages in pre-European America

② The word "distinct" in the first paragraph is closet in meaning to
  (A) different
  (B) extinct
  (C) written
  (D) surviving

③ According to the passage, the Algongkian and Siouan languages
  (A) were not spoken in California
  (B) were used in South America
  (C) were structurally similar to one another
  (D) were used in large areas

④ It can be inferred from the passage that the linguistic diversity in Europe was
  (A) magnified by its large population
  (B) not as great as that in California
  (C) the first to be studied by experts
  (D) less than that of South America

⑤ The author uses the words "speculations of experts" in the first paragraph to make the point that
  (A) the statistics are highly unreliable
  (B) the experts disagree among themselves
  (C) the numbers are only estimates
  (D) European researchers may be biased

⑥ The word "approximately" in the second paragraph is closet in meaning to
   (A) roughly
   (B) early
   (C) promptly
   (D) totally

⑦ Which of the following can be inferred about the Quechuan language?
   (A) It was eliminated by invaders
   (B) It spread beyond South America
   (C) It was spoken by nine million people
   (D) It replaced many other tongues

⑧ Which of the following was not mentioned as an area of great language diversity?
   (A) The Yucatan Peninsula
   (B) South Mexico
   (C) Venezuela
   (D) The Brazilian tropical lowlands

⑨ In the passage, linguistic diversity is primarily discussed by
   (A) geographic region
   (B) structural similarities
   (C) population density
   (D) date of discovery

⑩ According to the passage, which of the following were South American languages?
   (A) The tongues of the Aztecs and Maya
   (B) Quechuan and Arawakan
   (C) Athabascan and Algonkian
   (D) Chibchan and Siouan

題解

【文章翻譯】

在歐洲人「發現」北美洲之前，居住在墨西哥以北的美洲原住民使用的有多達 300 種不同的語言。有許多語言涵蓋廣大的地理區、並且包含 20 種以上密切相關的方言在內。這些大型語言包括阿爾岡昆語、阿薩巴斯卡語、以及蘇族語。不過，也有許多語言群規模比較小，使用這些語言群的地區因而語言也比較雜亂。例如，光是在加州就有 20 多種不同的語言群。根據一些專家的說法，美國大陸表現出來的語言極端要比整個歐洲的都更大、更多。不過別忘了：專家的猜測只不過是猜測而已。在歐洲人進行徹底的編錄之前，沒有準確的辦法可以判定美洲原住民語言的分佈範圍。

墨西哥與中美洲的原住民人口雖然比墨西哥以北的人口要好幾倍，但是使用的語言數目大致相等。這些語言當中只有少數幾種（特別是中墨西哥阿茲提克人的語言以及猶加敦半島與瓜地馬拉馬雅人的語言）就是絕大部分原住民人口使用的語言。墨西哥與中美洲地區語言變化最大的區域是在今日的南墨西哥與中美洲各小國。

南美洲居民較多，大約 9 百萬，語言也比較多，將近 1,500 種，這都比上述兩個地區加起來還多。大部分人口使用的是強大印加帝國的克丘亞語。印加帝國的軍事征服造成這種語言從南秘魯高原的誕生地擴散到幾乎涵蓋整個安地斯山區。但是征服也幾乎可以確定造成了許多其他原住民語言的滅絕或萎縮。靠近今日委內瑞拉與巴西的低海拔熱帶地區表現出南美洲最大的語言多樣性。有 3 種南美語言成功向北傳播：奇布恰語、卡利班語、以及阿拉瓦克語。

【練習題翻譯與詳解】

① 本文主要討論的是什麼？

   (A) 美國大陸的語言多樣性   (B) 從北美到南美的語言遷移

   (C) 各種美洲原住民部落的人口估計   (D) 歐洲人進入美洲之前的語言分佈

【答案】D

【解析】這是問主題的題型，要找主題句。第一段的主題句是「在歐洲人發現北美洲之前，居住在墨西哥以北的美洲原住民使用的有多達 300 種不同的語言」，第二段是「墨西哥與中美洲的原住民人口雖然比墨西哥以北的人口要多好幾倍，但是使用的語言數目大致相等」，第三段是「南美洲居民較多，大約 9 百萬，語言也比較多」。這三段的共同主題就是「歐洲人進來以前，美洲的語言分佈情況」。

② 第一段中的 distinct 意思最接近

   (A) 不同   (B) 已滅絕

   (C) 被寫下來   (D) 存活的

【答案】**A**

【解析】形容詞 distinct 來自動詞 distinguish（區分），意思是「不同的」，同義字是 different。

③ 根據本文，阿爾岡昆語和蘇族語

    (A) 在加州沒有人說   (B) 在南美洲使用

    (C) 彼此的結構很像   (D) 在廣大地區使用

【答案】**D**

【解析】這是問細節的題型，要找同義表達。第一段說「有許多語言涵蓋廣大的地理區……包括阿爾岡昆語、阿薩巴斯卡語、以及蘇族語」，其中 covered large geographical areas 是 were used in large areas 的同義表達。

④ 由文中可以推論，歐洲的語言多樣性

    (A) 被它廣大的人口放大了   (B) 沒有加州大

    (C) 是專家首先研究的對象   (D) 不及南美洲

【答案】**D**

【解析】這是推論題，要找「根據」。第一段說「美國大陸表現出來的語言極端要比整個歐洲的都更大、更多」。第三段說「南美洲居民較多，大約 9 百萬，語言也比較多，將近 1,500 種，比上述兩個地區加起來還多」。既然南美洲的語言變化大於美國大陸、美國大陸又大於歐洲，那麼南美洲一定大於歐洲，故選 (D)。

⑤ 作者在第一段說到 speculations of experts 是為了要表示

    (A) 這些統計數字極不可靠   (B) 專家之間並無共識

    (C) 數字只是估計   (D) 歐洲研究員可能有偏見

【答案】**C**

【解析】這是修辭目的的題型，要看上下文：「專家的猜測只不過是猜測而已。在歐洲人進行徹底的編錄之前，沒有準確的辦法可以判定美洲原住民語言的分佈範圍」，所以最接近的答案是 (C)。

⑥ 第二段中的 approximately 一字意思最接近

    (A) 粗略地   (B) 早

    (C) 迅速地   (D) 完全

【答案】**A**

【解析】副詞 approximately（構造：to/near/(adv.)）的意思是「大約」，同義字是 roughly。

⑦ 關於克丘亞語，可以推論出下列哪一項？

    (A) 它被侵略者淘汰了   (B) 它散播到南美洲外

    (C) 有 900 萬人使用它   (D) 它取代了許多別種語言

【答案】D
【解析】這是推論題，要找「根據」。第三段說克丘亞語隨著軍事征服擴散，但是征服也造成許多其他語言滅絕，這兩點加在一起可以推知克丘亞語取代了許多別的語言，故選 (D)。

⑧ 下列何處沒有被提到說它是語言多樣性強的地區？

    (A) 猶加敦半島   (B) 南墨西哥

    (C) 委內瑞拉   (D) 巴西熱帶低海拔地區

【答案】A
【解析】這是採消去法、問細節的題型，要刪掉三個有提到的地區。第二段說「這些語言當中只有少數幾種（特別是……猶加敦半島……馬雅人的語言）就是絕大部分原住民人口說的語言」，表示猶加敦半島的語言是主流語言，種類不多。

4

⑨ 本文討論語言多樣性是按什麼方式來談的？

    (A) 地理分區   (B) 結構相似性

    (C) 人口密度   (D) 發現日期

【答案】A
【解析】這是組織結構的題型，要看主題句。由三段的段落主題句來看，分別談北美、中美、南美，所以用的是地理分區。

⑩ 根據本文，下列何者是南美洲語言？

    (A) 阿茲提克人與馬雅人的語言

    (B) 克丘亞語和阿拉瓦克語

    (C) 阿薩巴斯卡語和阿爾岡昆語

    (D) 奇布恰語和蘇族語

【答案】B
【解析】這是問細節的題型。第三段說南美洲「大部分人口說的是強大印加帝國的克丘亞語」，另外還說「有 3 種南美語言成功向北傳播：……阿拉瓦克語」，所以克丘亞語和阿拉瓦克語都是南美洲語言。

Endocrine disorders (malfunctions of the human hormone-producing mechanisms) can have serious consequences. Hormones like insulin or human growth hormone (hGH) are crucial physical messengers, regulating and coordinating such functions as digestion and the balance of serum minerals. Severe shortages of hormones can mean a virtual shutdown of essential bodily processes. Endocrine disorders are routinely treated by administering hormones obtained from sources outside the body of the person suffering the disorder. The supply of such chemicals in nature, however, is far short of that needed in modern medicine. Since hormones are proteins, they are perfect candidates for production by genetically engineered bacteria. This production represents one of the most useful and widespread applications of rDNA (recombinant DNA) technology.

More than 5 million people worldwide take the hormone insulin each day to control some form of diabetes. Most of the insulin sold comes from cow or pig pancreases collected at **abattoirs** as a byproduct of meat production. While insulin from these sources is generally safe, it has slight structural differences from the human form. **Rather than slipping comfortably past the immune defenses of the recipient, these insulin molecules are easily recognized as outsiders.** Consequently, a few people taking bovine or porcine insulin develop allergic reactions as their immune system reject the foreign intrusion. This problem is avoided by substituting human insulin, which, to be available in significant quantities, must be manufactured by genetically altered bacteria.

Insulin was the first therapeutic rDNA product approved by the FDA for sale in the U.S. It went on the market in 1982 under the brand name Humulin. The development work had been done by the pioneering biotech firm Genentech; Eli Lilly and Company produced and marketed Humulin.

The biotechnology used in making insulin involves a complicated process. The insulin molecule is made up of two polypeptide chains, which join to make the active form of insulin. In the production of genetically engineered insulin, the DNA that codes for the A chain is **introduced into** one batch of *E. coli* bacteria and the DNA for the B chain into a different one. The bacteria cells are induced to make the two chains, which are then collected, mixed, and chemically treated to make them link. The linked elements form a whole, usable molecule. The resulting **insulin molecules** are identical to those secreted by the human pancreas.

Human growth hormone (hGH) was another early target of rDNA approaches to hormone deficiency. HGH controls the growth of bones and regulates weight gain. In some children, the pituitary gland fails to produce enough hGH for normal development, and this is evidenced by markedly short stature (perhaps only 60%-70% of normal height for a given age) and other growth deficiencies. The condition can be ameliorated, but only if hormone supplementation takes place during the growth years of childhood. Beyond this critical period, many bones (such as the femur) lose their ability to elongate.

_W_ Early in the development of hGH therapy, the only sources of the hormone were the pituitary glands of human cadavers. _X_ But a more serious problem was that the source was not **prolific** enough. First of all, the number of cadavers from which the pituitary gland could be harvested was very limited and not easily increased (within the bounds of the law). _Y_ Second, each cadaver yielded a very small amount of the hormone—only about 4 mg, whereas one week's treatment for an individual deficient in hGH requires about 7 mg. No successful animal sources were found. Clearly, new sources were needed. _Z_

The supply of human growth hormone is maintained by applying rDNA techniques and achieving high-volume synthesis. A gene for hGH production is spliced into *E. coli*, which are cultured and exploited in very large amounts. **A 500-liter tank** of bacterial culture can produce as much hGH as could have been derived from 35,000 cadavers. Growth hormone produced by this technique was approved for human use in 1985 and is now commonplace.

Exercise

① According to paragraph 1, what may happen if the body lacks hormones to a serious degree?

(A) Important functions of the body may be almost stopped.

(B) Crucial physical messengers may be shut down.

(C) Insulin and hGH may start coordinating hormone supply.

(D) The body may be invaded by bacteria.

② According to paragraph 1, genetically engineered bacteria are ideal for producing

(A) endocrine disorders

(B) any chemical

(C) proteins

(D) medicines for heart disease

③ The word "abattoirs" in paragraph 2 is closest in meaning to

(A) casinos

(B) hospitals

(C) slaughterhouses

(D) courts

④ Which of the sentences below best expresses the essential information in the boldfaced sentence in paragraph 2?

Rather than slipping comfortably past the immune defenses of the recipient, these insulin molecules are easily recognized as outsiders.

(A) The recipient's immune system spots insulin molecules as alien matter trying to enter.

(B) Instead of feeling comfortable with the immune defense, the recipient recognizes insulin molecules from outside.

(C) The immune system guards the body from outside harm.

(D) Insulin molecules defend the recipient from harm by outsiders.

⑤ Which of the following can be inferred from paragraph 3 about rDNA products?

(A) Humulin was an rDNA product made from bovine or porcine insulin.

(B) No rDNA product was legally available for medical use in the U.S. before 1982.

(C) Genentech was the first biotech firm approved by the FDA to manufacture hGH products.

(D) The FDA encouraged U.S. companies to do rDNA research for therapeutic purposes.

⑥ According to the passage, the biotechnology for making insulin involves all of the following EXCEPT
(A) breaking up a DNA into two chains
(B) using two groups of bacteria
(C) manufacturing two polypeptide chains
(D) linking two chains into a molecule

⑦ The expression "introduced into" in paragraph 4 is closest in meaning to
(A) inserted in
(B) made acquainted with
(C) caused to be available to
(D) presented to

⑧ Which of the following can be inferred about the "insulin molecules" mentioned in paragraph 4?
(A) They are not made up of two chains.
(B) They are not detected by the body's defense system as foreign matter.
(C) They are more expensive than bovine or porcine insulin molecules.
(D) They have nothing to do with rDNA technology.

⑨ According to paragraph 5, why must hGH be administered while the patient is still a child?
(A) Because otherwise there will be rejection by the immune system
(B) Because a child's bones still have the ability to grow
(C) Because an adult's pituitary gland has stopped growing
(D) Because hormone supplementation is a critical period

⑩ The word "prolific" in paragraph 6 is closest in meaning to
(A) pro-life   (B) cheap
(C) productive   (D) proximate

⑪ In which position would the following boldfaced sentence best fit in paragraph 6?
Suppliers and marketers worried that drawing a chemical from the glands of the dead might eventually create a public relations problem.
(A) Position W   (B) Position X
(C) Position Y   (D) Position Z

⑫ The author mentions "A 500-liter tank" in paragraph 7 in order to

(A) support the claim that rDNA techniques can synthesize large quantities of hGH

(B) describe how many cadavers are needed

(C) warn of the dangers of genetic engineering to the environment

(D) argue that the use of cadavers should be banned

▣ 題解

文章翻譯

　　內分泌障礙（人體製造荷爾蒙的機制故障）可能造成嚴重後果。像胰島素或人類生長荷爾蒙 (hGH) 是關鍵的生理訊號，調節與統籌像是消化與血清礦物質平衡等功能。荷爾蒙嚴重不足，可能導致重要身體程序形同關機。內分泌障礙一般的治療方式是從病人體外的來源取得荷爾蒙來使用。但是，大自然中這種化學物質的供應遠遠不足現代醫學所需。因為荷爾蒙是蛋白質，所以用基因工程改造細菌來生產就是最佳選擇。這種生產就是 rDNA（組織 DNA）科技最有用、也最普遍的應用之一。

　　全球超過 5 百萬人每天要用胰島素這種荷爾蒙來控制某種糖尿病。市售胰島素大多來自牛或豬的胰臟，從屠宰場收集而來，是肉類生產的副產品。這種來源的胰島素通常很安全，但它與人類胰島素的結構有小小的差異。這些胰島素分子無法輕易溜過接受者的免疫系統把關，而會被輕鬆認出來是外來物。所以，接受豬或牛胰島素的人有一些會出現過敏反應，因為免疫系統排斥外物入侵。如果改用人類胰島素可以避免這個問題，但是人類胰島素若想要大量供應，必須用基因改造細菌來生產。

　　胰島素是美國食品藥物管理局 (FDA) 批准在美國販售的第一種醫療用 rDNA 產品。1982 年以 Humulin 品牌上市。進行研發工作的是走在尖端的生物科技公司 Genentech。由禮來大藥廠生產與行銷 Humulin。

　　生產胰島素的生物科技牽涉到一套複雜的程序。胰島素分子由兩條多肽鍊構成，兩條合起來成為有作用的胰島素型態。生產基因改造胰島素時，為 A 鍊編碼的 DNA 植入一批大腸桿菌中，B 鍊的 DNA 則植入另一批。細菌細胞被導引去生產兩條鍊，生產出來之後收集、混合、加以化學處理使其連結。連結之後就構成一個完整可用的分子。這樣製造出來的胰島素分子和人類胰臟分泌的完全相同。

人類生長荷爾蒙 (hGH) 是早期用 rDNA 來治療荷爾蒙缺乏症的另一項標的。hGH 控制骨骼生長、調節體重增加。有些小孩的腦下垂體不能生產足夠的 hGH 來刺激正常發育，表現出來的就是身高明顯不足（與同年齡小孩正常身高相比大約只有 60%-70%）以及其他的生長不足症狀。這種情況可以改善，但是必須在兒童時代生長期間進行荷爾蒙補充。過了這個關鍵時期，許多骨骼（例如股骨）已經不能再生長。

W 在開發 hGH 療法的初期，這種荷爾蒙唯一的來源是人類屍體的腦下垂體。X 但是更嚴重的問題在於來源不足。首先，可以採取腦下垂體的屍體相當有限，也很難增加（若不違法）。Y 其次，每一具屍體產生的荷爾蒙相當少——大約只有 4 毫克。一個人治療 hGH 缺乏症一週就要用掉 7 毫克。一直找不到成功的動物來源。很明顯，需要新的來源。Z

人類生長荷爾蒙的供應，因為應用了 rDNA 科技、達到大量合成，才得以維持。生產 hGH 的一種基因被剪接到大腸桿菌中、大量培養來運用。容量 500 公升的細菌培養槽可以生產相當於 3 萬 5 千具屍體採集的 hGH 量。這種技術生產的生長激素在 1985 年批准供人類使用，現在已經相當普遍。

[練習題翻譯與詳解]

① 根據第一段，如果人體嚴重缺乏荷爾蒙，會發生什麼事？

(A) 身體重要功能可能幾乎停止。

(B) 關鍵生理訊號可能關閉。

(C) 胰島素與 hGH 可能開始協調荷爾蒙供應。

(D) 身體可能遭細菌入侵。

〔答案〕**A**

〔解析〕這是問細節的題型，要找同義表達。第一段提到「荷爾蒙嚴重不足，可能導致重要身體程序形同關機」，其中 a virtual shutdown of essential bodily processes 就是 Important functions of the body may be almost stopped 的同義表達，故選 (A)。

② 根據第一段，基因改造細菌用來生產什麼很理想？

(A) 內分泌障礙　　　　　　　　　(B) 任何化學物質

(C) 蛋白質　　　　　　　　　　　(D) 心臟病藥物

〔答案〕**C**

〔解析〕這是問細節的題型，要找同義表達。第一段說「因為荷爾蒙是蛋白質，所以用基因工程改造細菌來生產就是最佳選擇」，可知基因改造細菌適合生產蛋白質。

③ 第二段中的 abattoirs 一字意思最接近

(A) 賭場　　　　　　　　　　　　(B) 醫院

(C) 屠宰場　　　　　　　　　　　(D) 法院

④ 下列哪個句子最能夠表達第二段黑體字句子的主要內容?

「**這些胰島素分子無法輕易溜過接受者的免疫系統把關,而會被輕鬆認出來是外來物。**」

(A) 接受者的免疫系統會發現胰島素分子是想要進入的外來物質。

(B) 接受者對免疫防護不能感覺舒適,而會認出外來的胰島素分子。

(C) 免疫系統守衛身體不受外來侵害。

(D) 胰島素分子防衛接受者不受外人傷害。

⑤ 根據第三段,關於 rDNA 產品可以推論出什麼?

(A) Humulin 是用豬或牛胰島素製造的 rDNA 產品。

(B) 在 1982 年以前美國不能合法取得任何 rDNA 產品供醫療用途。

(C) Genentech 是 FDA 批准可以製造 hGH 產品的頭一家生技公司。

(D) FDA 鼓勵美國公司進行 rDNA 的醫療研究。

⑥ 根據本文,生產胰島素的生物科技牽涉到下列各項,除了

(A) 將 DNA 分裂為兩條鍊　　　　　(B) 使用兩批細菌

(C) 生產兩條多肽鍊　　　　　　　　(D) 連結兩條鍊成為分子

⑦ 第四段中的 introduced into 一語意思最接近

(A) 插入　　　　　　　　　　　　　(B) 使……認識

(C) 使……可以取得　　　　　　　　(D) 提供給

【答案】**A**
【解析】這是單字題。動詞 introduce（構造：inward/lead），在此解釋為「引進、置入、插入」。

⑧ 關於第四段提到的「胰島素分子」，可以推論出什麼？
  (A) 它不是兩條鍊構成的。
  (B) 人體的防衛系統不會偵測出它是外來物質。
  (C) 它比豬牛胰島素貴。
  (D) 它與 rDNA 技術無關。

【答案】**B**
【解析】這是推論題，要找「根據」。第四段說「這樣製造出來的胰島素分子和人類胰臟分泌的完全相同」。另外第二段說豬牛胰島素因為和人類的構造不同，會被免疫系統偵測出來。第四段提到的胰島素既然和人類的完全相同，應該是偵測不出來，故選 (B)。

⑨ 根據第五段，hGH 為何必須在病人仍是小孩時使用？
  (A) 因為不然的話會遭到免疫系統排斥
  (B) 因為小孩的骨骼仍具有生長能力
  (C) 因為成人的腦下垂體已經停止生長
  (D) 因為荷爾蒙補充是個關鍵時期

【答案】**B**
【解析】這是問細節的題型，要找同義表達。第五段說「必須在兒童時代生長期間進行荷爾蒙補充。過了這個關鍵時期，許多骨骼（例如股骨）已經不能再生長」，意思就是兒童骨骼還可以生長，故選 (B)。

⑩ 第六段中的 prolific 一字意思最接近
  (A) 擁護生命，反墮胎   (B) 便宜
  (C) 生產力高的   (D) 接近

【答案】**C**
【解析】這是單字題。prolific（構造：forward/make）的意思是「多產」，同義字是 productive。

⑪ 下面這個黑體字句子最適合放在第六段的什麼位置？
  「供應商與行銷人員擔心，從死人的腺體抽取化學物質，最後可能會造成公關問題。」
  (A) W 位置   (B) X 位置
  (C) Y 位置   (D) Z 位置

【答案】**B**

【解析】這是安插句子的題型，要看上下文。插入句說到「從死人的腺體抽取化學物質」，這和 X 位置上文「唯一的來源是人類屍體的腦下垂體」可以銜接。插入句接下來說到「可能會造成公關問題」，這可以銜接 X 位置下文「但是更嚴重的問題在於來源不足」，所以放在 X 位置最通順，成為：「在開發 hGH 療法的初期，這種荷爾蒙唯一的來源是人類屍體的腦下垂體。<u>供應商與行銷人員擔心，從死人的腺體抽取化學物質，最後可能會造成公關問題</u>。但是更嚴重的問題在於來源不足」。

⑫ 作者在第七段提到「一座 500 公升的大槽」目的是

    (A) 支持「rDNA 技術可以合成大量 hGH」的說法

    (B) 描述需要多少具屍體

    (C) 警告基因工程對環境可能造成危險

    (D) 主張應該禁止使用屍體

【答案】**A**

【解析】這是修辭目的的題型，要看上下文。第七段說「人類生長荷爾蒙的供應，因為應用了 rDNA 科技、達到大量合成，才得以維持。生產 hGH 的一種基因被剪接到大腸桿菌中、大量培養來運用。容量 500 公升的細菌培養槽可以生產相當於 3 萬 5 千具屍體採集的 hGH 量」。其中第一句是段落主題句，重點是 rDNA 科技可以大量生產 hGH，後面提到大型培養槽就是為了說明這種技術可以大量生產，故選 (A)。

Reading 1

Sponges, aquatic animals which constitute the phylum *Porifera*, consist of approximately 5,000 species and inhabit all the oceans of the earth. By virtue of their unique organization, they are able to attach themselves to an array of surfaces from the intertidal zone to depths of over 25,000 feet. Only one sponge family, the Spongillidae, is found in fresh water.

Because of their **apparent** lack of movement, sponges were regarded as plants by most early naturalists. Now however, zoologists regard them as either members of the animal subkingdom Parazoa or as closely related to coelenterates like jellyfish and coral. A sponge is a mass of cells and fibers. Its interior is permeated by an **intricate** system of canals that open out as holes of various sizes, like outsized human pores, through the tough skin. The skin is often, though not always, hairy from the fiber endings that pierce it. Only when the millions of living cells are completely removed does the ocean sponge look anything like the commercial sponges we are accustomed to: the sponge's skeletal framework that has been used by humans since at least the time of ancient Greece. Luckily for sponges however, **synthetic** sponges have largely replaced the more traditional natural ones, except for limited use by surgeons and certain types of artisans.

Exercise

① What does the passage primarily discuss?

    (A) The change from natural to synthetic sponges

    (B) Characteristics of a unique sea animal

    (C) A comparison of ocean and fresh water sponges

    (D) The diverse habitats of sea plants and coral

② In the second paragraph the word "apparent" is closest in meaning to which of the following words?

    (A) total

    (B) transparent

    (C) seeming

    (D) habitual

③ According to the passage, sponges are found

    (A) primarily in intertidal areas

    (B) almost exclusively in fresh water

    (C) in a wide range of ocean depths

    (D) only in areas surrounding Greece

④ Which of the following can be inferred from the passage?

    (A) The subkingdom Parazoa includes coelenterates.

    (B) Most naturalists have become zoologists.

    (C) Some sponges are plants while others are not.

    (D) Early naturalists are no longer considered correct.

⑤ What does the author compare to outsized human pores?

    (A) sponges

    (B) a system of canals

    (C) the openings of a sponge

    (D) the large protruding hairs

5

⑥ In the second paragraph the word "intricate" is closest in meaning to
(A) complex
(B) hidden
(C) living
(D) underground

⑦ According to the passage, what happens when the millions of living cells are removed from a sponge?
(A) The hairs begin to pierce the skin.
(B) The sponge starts to dry and toughen.
(C) The sponge becomes more recognizable.
(D) The remaining skeleton becomes useless.

⑧ At the present time natural sponges
(A) are no longer used by medical professionals
(B) are considered less attractive than synthetic ones
(C) are no longer in wide commercial demand
(D) can no longer be taken from ocean waters

⑨ Based on the information in the passage, all of the following statements about sponges are true EXCEPT
(A) in some ways they are similar to coral
(B) their physical organization is not common
(C) they have been used by humans for centuries
(D) they belong to the animal phylum Parazoa

⑩ The word "synthetic" in the second paragraph is closest in meaning to
(A) long-lasting
(B) plant
(C) artificial
(D) cultivated

⟱ 題解

海綿是水生動物，構成「多孔動物門」，約有 5,000 種，居住在地球各大洋中。因為其特殊的構造，海綿可以附著在各種表面上，從潮間帶到超過 25,000 英尺的深海。只有一科海綿（針海綿）生活在淡水。

因為海綿看來好像不會動，所以早期的博物學家大都認為牠是植物。但是今日的動物學家或者視海綿為側生動物亞界的成員、或者認為牠是水母與珊瑚這些腔腸動物的近親。海綿由一堆細胞與纖維構成，內部遍佈複雜的通道，通到硬皮上成為大小不同的開孔，像是超大的人類毛細孔。皮上經常（雖然不一定有）長毛，來自於穿透到皮外的纖維末稍。要先把數百萬的活細胞完全除去，海中的海綿樣子才會像我們習慣的商業海綿：剩下海綿的骨架，至少從古希臘時代起就被人類使用了。不過，有一點對海綿來說很幸運：合成海綿已經大致取代了傳統的天然海綿，除了還有少量天然海綿被外科醫生和幾種工匠使用。

練習題翻譯與詳解

① 本文的主題是什麼？

    (A) 從天然海綿到合成海綿的改變

    (B) 一種獨特海洋動物的特質

    (C) 比較海水與淡水海綿

    (D) 海洋植物與珊瑚的各種棲息地

【答案】**B**

【解析】這是問主題的題型，要找主題句。第一段的主題句內容是海綿的分類，第二段的主題句也和海綿分類有關，接下來發展的就是海綿的特性，故選 (B)。

② 第二段中的 apparent 一字意思最接近

    (A) 完全的   (B) 透明的

    (C) 看似   (D) 習慣的

【答案】**C**

【解析】這是單字題。apparent 在此解釋為「表面上看起來」，因為下文接著說海綿其實不是植物而是動物，所以同義字是 seeming。

③ 根據本文，海綿生活在

    (A) 主要是潮間帶   (B) 幾乎只在淡水

    (C) 許多不同深度的海洋   (D) 只有希臘周圍

【答案】C

【解析】這是問細節的題型，要找同義表達。第一段說「海綿可以附著在各種表面上，從潮間帶到超過 25,000 英尺的深海」，其中 from the intertidal zone to depths of over 25,000 feet 就是 in a wide range of ocean depths 的同義表達。

④ 根據本文，可以推論得知下列何者？
   (A) 側生動物亞界包括腔腸動物在內。
   (B) 多數博物學家都已經成為動物學家。
   (C) 有些海綿是植物、有些不是。
   (D) 早期博物學家的看法目前已經不再被認為是正確的。

【答案】D

【解析】這是推論題，要找「根據」。第二段說「因為海綿看來好像不會動，所以早期的博物學家大都認為牠是植物。但是今日的動物學家或者視海綿為側生動物亞界的成員、或者認為牠是水母與珊瑚這些腔腸動物的近親」，這表示從前博物學家的看法已經被推翻了。

⑤ 作者將下列哪一項比為超大的人類毛細孔？
   (A) 海綿   (B) 一套通道系統
   (C) 海綿洞孔   (D) 粗大突出的毛髮

【答案】C

【解析】這是修辭目的的題型，要找上下文：「內部遍佈複雜的通道，通到硬皮上成為大小不同的開孔，像是超大的人類毛細孔」，由此可以看出比喻的是海綿硬皮上的開孔。

⑥ 第二段中的 intricate 一字意思最接近
   (A) 複雜的   (B) 隱藏的
   (C) 活著的   (D) 地下的

【答案】A

【解析】形容詞 intricate（構造：in/trick/(a.)）的意思是「複雜」，同義字是 complex。

⑦ 根據本文，從海綿上移除數百萬活細胞之後會如何？
   (A) 毛髮開始穿透海綿皮。   (B) 海綿開始乾燥、變硬。
   (C) 海綿成為比較容易辨認。   (D) 剩餘的骨架就沒有用了。

【答案】C

【解析】這是問細節的題型，要找同義表達。第二段說「要先把數百萬的活細胞完全除去，海中的海綿樣子才會像我們習慣的商業海綿」，其中 look anything like the commercial sponges we are accustomed to 就是 becomes more recognizable 的同義表達。

⑧ 目前，天然海綿
  (A) 醫界專業人士已不再使用
  (B) 被認為不如合成海綿漂亮
  (C) 不再有很廣大的商業需求
  (D) 已經不能再從海水中取出

【答案】C
【解析】這是問細節的題型，要找同義表達。第二段說「合成海綿已經大致取代了傳統的天然海綿，除了還有少量天然海棉被外科醫生和幾種工匠使用」，其中 except for limited use 和 no longer in wide commercial demand 是同義表達。

⑨ 根據本文，關於海綿的陳述哪一項是錯的？
  (A) 某些方面海綿很像珊瑚
  (B) 海綿的物理結構並不常見
  (C) 海綿已經被人類使用了好幾個世紀
  (D) 海綿屬於側生動物門

【答案】D
【解析】這是問細節、採用消去法的題型，要刪去三個同義表達。第二段說海綿是「側生動物亞界的成員 members of the animal subkingdom Parazoa」，並非側生動物門 (the animal phylum Parazoa)，所以 (D) 不是同義表達。

⑩ 第二段中的 synthetic 一字意思最接近
  (A) 長久存在的   (B) 植物的
  (C) 人造的   (D) 栽培的

【答案】C
【解析】形容詞 synthetic（構造：together/put/(a.)）的意思是「合成的」，同義字是 artificial（構造：skill/make/(a.)）。

5

The term "moon" can refer to any number of celestial objects, but it most commonly refers to the earth's largest natural satellite. The moon is so large relative to the earth (with a diameter two thirds that of Mercury) that the earth and the moon are often **regarded** as a double planet. The moon's diameter is 2,160 miles and its mass is approximately 1% of that of the earth. The distance of the moon from the earth varies, with an average of about 240,000 miles.

The moon rotates on its axis every 27.322 days, thus constantly keeping the same face towards the earth. However, to a particular observer on the earth, marginally different parts of the moon's disk are visible at different times; because, in accordance with Kepler's second law, the moon's orbital velocity is not constant and thus liberation is exhibited. The fact that there are slight irregularities in the moon's rotational velocity also contributes to this phenomenon. The moon is covered with craters, ranging to 125 miles in diameter, with crater chains as long as 600 miles. It also features rilles, which are trenches a few miles wide and a few hundred miles long; maria, or great plains; and lunar mountain ranges. There are also lunar hotspots, generally associated with those larger craters showing bright rays; these remain cooler than their surroundings during lunar daytime, warmer during the lunar night.

Samples brought back by the Apollo 11 and **subsequent** expeditions show that the smaller lunar craters are generally of meteoritic origin, while the larger ones are of a volcanic nature. Some scientists believe that the earth and moon formed simultaneously, the greater mass of the earth accounting for its higher proportion of metallic iron; the heat of the young earth's atmosphere, which evaporated silicates, accounting for their higher proportion on the moon. Others propose the theory that the earth formed first and was then hit by a huge foreign object such as an asteroid. The ejected silicate-rich matter gradually condensed into the moon, the much heavier iron having sunk to the core of the earth and failing to be ejected.

✎ Exercise

① What does the passage primarily discuss?
(A) The formation of the Moon
(B) Apollo expeditions
(C) Lunar structure and composition
(D) Lunar eclipses

② In the first paragraph the word "regarded" is closest in meaning to
(A) classified
(B) mistaken
(C) ignored
(D) considered

③ The first paragraph is primarily concerned with
(A) definitions of planetary bodies
(B) characteristics of a natural satellite
(C) the largest moon in the solar system
(D) the growing diameter of the moon

④ All of the following are true about the moon EXCEPT
(A) its diameter is roughly 2,000 miles
(B) its mass is much smaller than the earth's
(C) it is not a man-made satellite
(D) it is slightly larger than Mercury

⑤ It can be inferred from the passage that different parts of the moon's disk are visible at different times due to
(A) Kepler's predictions about the earth
(B) at least two different reasons
(C) reasons that are not yet known
(D) the moon's constant orbital velocity

⑥ According to the passage, which of the following is true about lunar hotspots?
   (A) They are often associated with lunar mountains.
   (B) In the daytime they are warmer than nearby areas.
   (C) At night they are cooler than their surroundings.
   (D) They are often related to large lunar craters.

⑦ The word "subsequent" in the third paragraph is closest in meaning to
   (A) simultaneous
   (B) later
   (C) other
   (D) earlier

⑧ Compared to the earth, the moon
   (A) has more metallic iron
   (B) has fewer numbers of silicates
   (C) has a far smaller mass
   (D) has a more heated atmosphere

⑨ The author defines all of the following terms EXCEPT
   (A) moon
   (B) rilles
   (C) trenches
   (D) maria

⑩ A paragraph following the passage would most likely discuss which of the following topics?
   (A) The discoveries of the first Apollo mission
   (B) Consequences of severe volcanic activity
   (C) The chemical composition of Mercury
   (D) An evaluation of two theories

⊡ 題解

文章翻譯

　　「月球」一詞可以指各種天體，但最常用來指地球最大的天然衛星。月球相對於地球而言非常大（直徑是水星的 3 分之 2），所以地球與月球經常被視為雙子星。月球直徑 2,160 英里，質量大約是地球的 1%。它與地球之間的距離會變化，平均是 240,000 英里左右。

　　月球每 27.322 天在本身軸心上自轉一圈，所以保持以同一面朝向地球。不過，從地球上觀察，不同的時間可以看到月盤邊緣上一些不同的部分，因為根據克卜勒第 2 定律，月球的軌道公轉速度不是恆定的，因而會表現出變化。另外，月球自轉速度有小小的不規律性，也是造成這種現象的原因。月球上面遍佈隕石坑，直徑最大到 125 英里，鍊狀排列的隕石坑可以長達 600 英里。還有月溪（寬數英里、長數百英里的溝渠），月海（大平原），以及月球山脈。另外還有月球熱點，通常和發出明亮光芒的大隕石坑有關，在月球白天時它的溫度比周圍低、晚上溫度則比較高。

　　阿波羅 11 號與後續的任務帶回來一些樣品，顯示月球上的小隕石坑大都是隕石造成的，但大隕石坑則是火山形成的。有些科學家認為地球與月球在同時間生成。地球因為質量大，所以含有鐵金屬的比例較高。而地球年輕時代的大氣層溫度高，將矽化物蒸發掉了，所以矽化物在月球上的比例較高。還有一些科學家提出的理論是：地球先形成，後來受到巨大外來物體撞擊，例如小行星。噴出的物質裡面矽化物含量高，逐漸凝聚成為月球。重得多的鐵質早已沉入地心，因而未被噴出。

練習題翻譯與詳解

① 本文討論的主題是什麼？

(A) 月球的形成　　　　　　　　　(B) 阿波羅任務

(C) 月球結構與成分　　　　　　　(D) 月蝕

【答案】 C

【解析】這是問主題的題型，要看主題句（各段第一句）。第一段：「月球一詞可以指各種天體，但最常用來指地球最大的天然衛星」。第二段：「月球每 27.322 天在本身軸心上自轉一圈」。第三段：「阿波羅 11 號與後續的任務帶回來一些樣品，顯示月球上的小隕石坑大都是隕石造成的，但大隕石坑則是火山形成的」。能夠涵蓋這三個主題句的選項是 (C) 月球結構與成分。

② 第一段中的 regarded 一字意思最接近

(A) 被分類　　　　　　　　　　　(B) 被誤認

(C) 被忽略　　　　　　　　　　　(D) 被認為

【答案】D
【解析】這是單字題。regard 的意思是「看待，認為」，同義字是 consider。

③ 第一段主要涉及
  (A) 行星體的定義　　　　　　　　　(B) 一枚天然衛星的特性
  (C) 太陽系最大的月球　　　　　　　(D) 月球逐漸增加的直徑

【答案】B
【解析】這是問主題的題型，第一段的主題要看它的段落主題句：「月球一詞可以指各種天體，但最常用來指地球最大的天然衛星」，這是在界定「月球」，接下來發展的是月球的幾項特性，故選 (B)。

④ 關於月球，下列哪一項是錯的？
  (A) 它的直徑大約 2,000 英里　　　　(B) 它的質量比地球小得多
  (C) 它不是人造衛星　　　　　　　　(D) 它比水星稍大一點

【答案】D
【解析】這是問細節、採用消去法的題型，要找出三個同義表達來刪去。第一段說月球「直徑是水星的 3 分之 2 (with a diameter two thirds that of Mercury)」，也就是比水星小，因而 (D) 不是同義表達。

⑤ 由文中可以推論，不同時間可以看到月盤的不同部分，是因為
  (A) 克卜勒關於地球的預測　　　　　(B) 至少有兩項原因
  (C) 不明原因　　　　　　　　　　　(D) 月球軌道公轉速度恆定

【答案】B
【解析】這是推論題，要找「根據」。第二段說道「月球的軌道公轉速度不是恆定的，因而會表現出變化。另外，月球自轉速度有小小的不規律性，也是造成這種現象的原因」，這裡就提出了兩個原因，故選 (B)。

⑥ 根據本文，關於月球熱點，下列哪一項是正確的？
  (A) 它經常和月球山脈有關。　　　　(B) 白天它比附近地區溫度高。
  (C) 晚上它比周圍地區溫度低。　　　(D) 它經常和大型月球隕石坑有關。

【答案】D
【解析】這是問細節的題型，要找同義表達。第二段說月球熱點「通常和發出明亮光芒的大隕石坑有關」，其中 associated with 與 related to 是同義表達。

⑦ 第三段中的 subsequent 一字意思最接近

(A) 同時的　　　　　　　　　　(B) 後來的

(C) 別的　　　　　　　　　　　(D) 較早的

【答案】**B**

【解析】這是單字題。 subsequent（構造：after/follow/(*a.*)）是指「後續的」，同義字是
later。

⑧ 與地球相比，月球

(A) 含有比較多的鐵金屬　　　　(B) 含有比較少的矽化物

(C) 質量小得多　　　　　　　　(D) 大氣溫度較高

【答案】**C**

【解析】這是問細節的問題，要找同義表達。第一段說月球「質量大約是地球的 1%」，其
中 its mass is approximately 1% of that of the earth 就是 has a far smaller mass 的同義
表達。

⑨ 下列哪一項，作者沒有下定義？

(A) 月球　　　　　　　　　　　(B) 月溪

(C) 溝渠　　　　　　　　　　　(D) 月海

【答案】**C**

【解析】這是問細節的問題。第二段在界定「月溪」時，作者說那是「寬數英里、長數百
英里的溝渠 (which are trenches a few miles wide and a few hundred miles long)」，但是
接下來並沒有再為 trenches 下定義。

⑩ 本文的下一段可能會討論哪一項主題？

(A) 第 1 次阿波羅任務的發現　　(B) 嚴重火山活動的後果

(C) 水星的化學構造　　　　　　(D) 兩種理論的評估

【答案】**D**

【解析】這是組織結構的題型，要先判斷本文主題是什麼。下段必須討論同一個大主題，
並且要能夠銜接文章的結尾。本文主題從第 1 題的答案來看是介紹月球的結構與成分。最
後一段作者提出兩種有關月球形成的不同理論，下一段若是將這兩種理論評估一下優劣，
可以銜接得上，而且同樣屬於介紹「月球」的這個大主題，故選 (D)。

5

An alphabet indicates by written symbols a set of speech sounds. The alphabet was a Greek invention based upon North Semitic writing which indicated only consonants, a procedure suitable enough for a Semitic language but not for an Indo-European one. The oldest known Greek inscriptions, of the second millennium BCE, are written in a syllabary, which includes vowels. They are several centuries older than Greek inscriptions written in the Greek alphabet. The word "alphabet" itself is derived from the names of the first two letters of the Greek alphabet, alpha and beta. Even when a letter in an alphabet represents a single sound, it does so roughly, taking no account of intonation, stress or pronunciation, which vary not only between speakers but even within the speech of an individual according to the position of the sound in a word or phrase and the nature of the phrase.

An alphabet is a highly developed, abstract form of writing. This is not the case with all forms of writing. Pictographs, ideographs and hieroglyphs bear an **essential** relationship to what they represent. Such methods **constitute** a more ancient form of writing than syllabaries and alphabets.

The story of the alphabet from the time it first appeared in Greek inscriptions is not difficult to trace. It is its pre-history that is **disputed**. Two questions remain unanswered. How did the Greeks obtain it from the Semites? And what was its pre-Semitic history?

✎ Exercise

① What is the passage's primary purpose?
   (A) To compare the Greek alphabet with syllabaries
   (B) To explain the pre-history of early alphabets
   (C) To describe the production of the first speech sounds
   (D) To trace the development of the first alphabet

② According to the author, the letters in an alphabet
   (A) represent consonants only
   (B) are all named after the matching Greek letter
   (C) do not represent any particular stress pattern
   (D) are pronounced identically by all speakers

③ In the second paragraph, the word "essential" is closest in meaning to which of the following?
   (A) particular
   (B) mysterious
   (C) important
   (D) academic

④ In the second paragraph, the word "constitute" most nearly means
   (A) hint at
   (B) announce
   (C) prove
   (D) make up

⑤ The word "disputed" in the third paragraph is closest in meaning to
   (A) contested
   (B) researched
   (C) disrupted
   (D) valued

⑥ According to the passage, all of the following are true about the alphabet EXCEPT
(A) it was used earlier than syllabaries
(B) both alphabets and syllabaries represent sound
(C) it differs significantly from ideographs and hieroglyphs
(D) it builds upon symbols used by the Semitic culture

⑦ The passage lends the most support to which of the following conclusions?
(A) Some questions about the alphabet's origin still can't be answered.
(B) The Greeks and Semites both used the modern alphabet.
(C) Only backward societies now fail to use the alphabet.
(D) Scholars have uncovered the roots of the modern alphabet.

◩ 題解

文章翻譯

　　字母是用書寫的符號來表示一套語音。字母是希臘人的發明，建立在北閃族文字上，只表示出子音，這種做法適用於閃族語言，但不適合印歐語言。已知最古老的希臘文字寫於西元前一千多年，是以音節文字寫成的，包含母音在內。這要比採用希臘字母書寫的文字要早好幾百年。「字母」(alphabet) 一語本身來自頭兩個希臘字母，α 與 β。一套字母當中，即使某個字母只代表一種聲音，也不很精確，因為沒有處理音調、重音或者發音。這些因素會因人而異，就算同一個人講話也會有變化，會隨著聲音在單字或片語中的位置而有不同、也隨著片語的性質而有變化。

　　字母是高度發展的抽象文字，但並非所有文字都是這樣。象形符號、寫意文字與象形文字和它所代表的東西基本上還有關聯。這種書寫方式構成比音節文字與字母更古老的文字。

　　字母的故事不難追溯，可以一路追到在希臘文字中最早出現的時候。有爭議的是進入正史之前的字母歷史。有兩個問題仍無答案。希臘人如何從閃族手中取得字母？在閃族之前的字母歷史又是什麼？

5

練習題翻譯與詳解

① 本文的主要目的是什麼？

　　(A) 比較希臘字母與音節文字

　　(B) 解釋早期字母的史前史

　　(C) 描述最早發出的語音

　　(D) 追溯最早字母的發展

【答案】D

【解析】這是問主題的題型，要找主題句。第一段先界定字母作為開場白，然後進入主題句「字母是希臘人的發明，建立在北閃族文字上」。第二段主題句「字母是高度發展的抽象文字，但並非所有文字都是這樣」與第三段主題句「字母的故事不難追溯，可以一路追到在希臘文字中最早出現的時候」都與字母的早期發展有關，故選 (D)。

② 根據作者，一套字母當中的所有字母

　　(A) 只代表子音

　　(B) 都是以相對的希臘字母命名

　　(C) 並不代表任何一種重音模式

　　(D) 每一個人的發音都相同

【答案】C
【解析】這是問細節的題型，要找同義表達。第一段「一套字母當中，即使某個字母只代表一種聲音，也不很精確，因為沒有處理音調、重音或者發音」，其中 taking no account of intonation , stress or pronunciation 是 do not represent any particular stress pattern 的同義表達，故選 (C)。

③ 第二段中的 essential 一字意思最接近
　　(A) 特殊的　　　　　　　　　　(B) 神祕的
　　(C) 重要的　　　　　　　　　　(D) 學術的

【答案】C
【解析】這是單字題。essential（構造：be/(a.)）的意思是「根本的，基本的，必要的」，同義字是 important。

④ 第二段中的 constitute 一字意思最接近
　　(A) 暗示　　　　　　　　　　　(B) 宣告
　　(C) 證明　　　　　　　　　　　(D) 構成

【答案】D
【解析】這是單字題。constitute（構造：together/stand/(v.)）的意思是「構成」，同義字是 make up。

⑤ 第三段中的 disputed 一字意思最接近
　　(A) 有爭議的　　　　　　　　　(B) 被研究過的
　　(C) 被中斷的　　　　　　　　　(D) 被重視的

【答案】A
【解析】這是單字題。disputed（構造：apart/consider/(a.)）的意思是「有爭議」，同義字是 contested。

⑥ 根據本文，關於字母的哪一項敘述是錯的？
　　(A) 它的使用比音節文字更早
　　(B) 字母和音節文字都代表聲音
　　(C) 它和象形符號與象形文字都有重大不同
　　(D) 它建立在閃族文化使用的象徵上

【解析】這是問細節、採用消去法的題型，要找出三個同義表達刪去。第一段「已知最古老的希臘文字寫於西元前一千多年，是以音節文字寫成的，包含母音在內。這要比採用希臘字母書寫的文字要早好幾百年」，由此可知音節文字的使用比字母更早，這和 (A) 有牴觸，故選 (A)。

⑦ 本文最能夠支持下列哪一項結論？

    (A) 關於字母的起源，有些問題仍無法回答。

    (B) 希臘人與閃族都採用現代字母。

    (C) 如今只有落後的社會才不使用字母。

    (D) 學者已經找到了現代字母的根源。

【解析】這是推論題，要找「根據」。第三段的結論說「有爭議的是進入正史之前的字母歷史。有兩個問題仍無答案」，故選 (A)。

5

Reading 4

The Human Genome Initiative (HGI), started under George H. W. Bush in 1990, carried on under Bill Clinton and eventually declared complete under George W. Bush in 2003, was a large-scale project in genetic engineering that absorbed top U.S. and international talents in the field. The goal of the project was nothing less than mapping out the complete genetic blueprint of the human race.

In the human body, every cell equipped with a nucleus, which **rules out** hemoglobin, has a complete set of genetic programming contained in the 23 pairs of chromosomes in the nucleus. Picture **a large stadium**—the nucleus—packed full with thick cables—the chromosomes. Genes are sections of the cables, or chromosomes, that contain meaningful codes that can be **cracked** by scientists in the lab. A chromosome is composed of a large number of genes separated by areas which may contain meaningful information that we do not yet understand. The genes contain all the information that directs the physical and psychological growth of the individual, from the development of the fetus in the womb to physiological changes leading to senility and death. It was the ambition of the HGI to decode all the genes in a human cell nucleus.

Now that the HGI has been completed, a new-born infant can be checked against the HGI blueprint for heredity-related diseases like mental illness or certain types of cancer. The logical next step, of course, is that genetic defects can be surgically removed or altered through gene splicing. Ultimately, the genes responsible for senility and death can be tampered with—wherein lies the key to human immortality.

Rosy as the picture is, many have expressed concern over the HGI, not without cause. Companies and research labs are already patenting one gene after another, so that many genes in your body now belong to commercial interests. In the future, insurance companies might check one's genes and declare certain latent diseases preexisting conditions. Employers might discriminate against workers with bad genes, considering such workers potential financial burdens to the company. Youths might have to undergo a gene check before they could persuade anyone to enter into wedlock with them.

✒ Exercise

① What does the passage mainly discuss?
   (A) Various aspects of the HGI
   (B) Dangers of gene splicing
   (C) The history of the HGI
   (D) A definition of genes

② All of the following statements about the HGI project are true EXCEPT
   (A) it was begun under George H. W. Bush
   (B) Clinton continued the HGI
   (C) it took more than a dozen years
   (D) it engaged U. S. experts only

③ The phrase "rules out" in the second paragraph most closely means
   (A) outlaws
   (B) excludes
   (C) accommodates
   (D) singles out

④ According to the passage, the existence of genetic information in a cell depends on
   (A) the location of the cell
   (B) the age of the cell
   (C) the existence of a nucleus
   (D) the size of its nucleus

⑤ The author mentions "a large stadium" in the second paragraph in order to
   (A) illustrate the nucleus and chromosomes
   (B) indicate where the HGI was carried on
   (C) suggest the need of exercise to maintain healthy genes
   (D) introduce a possible storage space for cables

⑥ Which of the following statements is a correct description of the relationship between genes and chromosomes?
(A) Genes and chromosomes are unrelated.
(B) Genes and chromosomes are the same.
(C) Chromosomes are sections of a gene.
(D) Genes are sections of a chromosome.

⑦ The word "cracked" in the second paragraph is closest in meaning to
(A) studied
(B) smashed
(C) damaged
(D) decoded

⑧ According to the passage, the ultimate goal of the HGI project is
(A) eternal life for humans
(B) the curing of cancer
(C) the elimination of mental illness
(D) the prediction of disease

⑨ The word "Rosy" in the fourth paragraph most closely means
(A) Red
(B) Fragrant
(C) Romantic
(D) Promising

⑩ The passage mentions all of the following as concerns raised by the HGI EXCEPT
(A) insurance policies might be complicated
(B) new discriminations in employment might occur
(C) biological monsters might be created by gene splicing
(D) the right to marriage might be hampered

【文章翻譯】

　　人類基因組計畫 (HGI) 於 1990 年在老布希任內開始，柯林頓政府繼續進行，終於在 2003 年小布希任內宣告完成。這是基因工程方面的重大計畫，吸收了該領域頂尖的美國與世界人才。計畫的目標宏大，要測繪出人類完整的基因藍圖。

　　人體中，每一枚有核細胞（這就排除了紅血球）都有一套完整的基因程式，藏在細胞核 23 對染色體裡面。想像一座大型體育館（代表細胞核）裡面塞滿了粗纜繩（染色體）。基因是纜繩（就是染色體）上的片段，內含一些有意義的程式碼，科學家可以在實驗室中破解。染色體由大量的基因構成，基因與基因之間隔著一些區塊，裡面或許包含一些有意義的資訊，但我們尚不了解。基因含有一切的資訊可以導引個人的身心成長，從子宮內胚胎的發育直到引發衰老與死亡的生理變化。HGI 的野心是要破解人類細胞核中所有的基因。

　　如今 HGI 已經完成，新生嬰兒可以對照 HGI 藍圖檢查是否有遺傳疾病如精神病或某些癌症。當然，合理的下一步是用手術移除基因缺陷或者用基因剪接來改變。到最後，造成衰老與死亡的基因也可以修改——人類長生不老的關鍵就在於此。

　　這幅畫面固然美麗，但也有很多人對 HGI 表示憂慮，這並不是杞人憂天。各大公司與研究實驗室接連取得基因專利，結果你身體裡面的許多基因現在已經屬於商業組織所有。將來，保險公司可能要檢查基因，並且宣告某些潛伏的疾病為投保前存在的病情。僱主可能給予基因不良的員工差別待遇，認為這種員工對公司是潛在的財務包袱。年輕人可能得先做基因檢查才能說服別人共同締結婚姻。

5

【練習題翻譯與詳解】

① 本文的主題是什麼？

(A) HGI 的各方面　　　　　　　　(B) 基因剪接的危險

(C) HGI 歷史　　　　　　　　　　(D) 基因的定義

【答案】A

【解析】這是問主題的題型，要看主題句。第一段開場白介紹 HGI 歷史之後，主題句說它的目標是「要測繪出人類完整的基因藍圖」。第二段說明 HGI 的科學背景。第三段說 HGI 的功用，第四段說 HGI 引起的顧慮。所以最接近的主題是「HGI 的各方面」。

② 關於 HGI 計畫，下列哪一項是錯的？

(A) 它在老布希任內開始　　　　　(B) 柯林頓繼續進行 HGI

(C) 它花了超過 12 年　　　　　　(D) 它只用到美國專家

【答案】D

【解析】這是問細節、採用消去法的題型，要找出三個同義表達消去。第一段說 HGI「吸收了該領域頂尖的美國與世界人才」，這和選項 (D) 說的「只用到美國專家」牴觸，故選 (D)。

③ 第二段中的片語 rules out 意思最接近
  (A) 禁止   (B) 排除
  (C) 包容   (D) 挑出

【答案】B

【解析】這是單字題。片語 rule out 的意思是「排除」，同義字是 exclude。

④ 根據本文，細胞內是否有基因資訊存在，取決於
  (A) 細胞的位置   (B) 細胞的年紀
  (C) 細胞核的存在   (D) 細胞核的大小

【答案】C

【解析】這是問細節的題型，要找同義表達。第二段說「人體中，每一枚有核細胞（這就排除了紅血球）都有一套完整的基因程式，藏在細胞核 23 對染色體裡面」，其中 equipped with a nucleus 是 the existence of a nucleus 的同義表達。

⑤ 作者在第二段提到 a large stadium 的目的是
  (A) 說明細胞核與染色體
  (B) 表示 HGI 計畫進行的場地
  (C) 暗示需要運動才能維持基因健康
  (D) 提出一個可以用來儲藏纜繩的空間

【答案】A

【解析】這是修辭目的的題型，要看上下文。第二段中的直接上文是「人體中，每一枚有核細胞……都有一套完整的基因程式，藏在細胞核 23 對染色體裡面」。接下來把細胞核比為體育館，染色體比為纜繩，這是在用比喻的手法來說明細胞核與染色體，故選 (A)。

⑥ 基因與染色體的關係，下列哪項描述正確？
  (A) 基因與染色體無關。
  (B) 基因就是染色體。
  (C) 染色體是基因上的片段。
  (D) 基因是染色體上的片段。

【答案】**D**

【解析】這是問細節的題型，要找同義表達。第二段說「基因是纜繩（就是染色體）上的片段」，其中 Genes are sections of the cables, or chromosomes 就是 Genes are sections of a chromosome. 的同義表達。

⑦ 第二段中的 crack 一字意思最接近

(A) 研究 　　　　　　　　　　(B) 粉碎

(C) 損害 　　　　　　　　　　(D) 解碼

【答案】**D**

【解析】這是單字題。crack 的意思是「破裂，破解」，同義字是 decode。

⑧ 根據本文，HGI 計畫的終極目標是

(A) 人類的永生 　　　　　　　(B) 治療癌症

(C) 消除精神病 　　　　　　　(D) 預測疾病

【答案】**A**

【解析】這是問細節的題型，要找同義表達。第三段說「到最後，造成衰老與死亡的基因也可以修改—人類長生不老的關鍵就在於此」，其中 wherein lies the key to human immortality 就是 eternal life for humans 的同義表達，故選 (A)。

⑨ 第四段中的 Rosy 一字意思最接近

(A) 紅色 　　　　　　　　　　(B) 芳香

(C) 浪漫 　　　　　　　　　　(D) 有希望的

【答案】**D**

【解析】這是單字題。Rosy 字面上是指「玫瑰色」，暗示「美好、理想」，同義字是 promising。

⑩ 本文提到，HGI 引起的憂慮不包括

(A) 保單可能變複雜 　　　　　(B) 對員工可能產生新的差別待遇

(C) 基因剪接可能創造出怪物 　(D) 婚姻權可能遭到阻礙

【答案】**C**

【解析】這是問細節、採用消去法的題型，要找出三個同義表達消去。「創造出怪物」屬於無中生有，找不到同義表達，故選 (C)。

Newly paved roads stay fresh for a couple of weeks. Within a month, however, cracks and potholes will begin to appear. Often the damage is not due to faulty design or substandard material. According to Professor Lewis Brown, a microbiologist at Mississippi State University, damage to road surface is primarily caused by bacteria in the soil. Brown **claims** that he has found a solution to the problem.

In paving asphalt—which actually contains 95% sand and rock and only 5% asphalt—there are countless numbers of bacteria, which are paved on to the road with the material. After the road is paved over, the bacteria continue to grow, and produce soap-like substances in **the process**. The substances gradually wash the gravel from the asphalt, **undermining** the road surface so that it crumbles and cracks when vehicles pass over it.

Brown's proposal is to put an additive, silane, in the road-paving mixture and let it do the work. Silane binds with the gravel in a watertight seal, leaving no room for bacterial growth between gravel and asphalt. Brown has conducted lab research on the effects of silane, and has come up with very positive results. Whereas in control groups soil bacteria separated asphalt from gravel in just 10 days, in experimental groups, where the gravel had been treated with silane before mixing, gravel and asphalt remained **bonded** after 137 days. Silane is not a sterilizer and it does not kill bacteria in the soil, but it does prevent bacteria from stripping asphalt from gravel.

Exercise

① What is this passage mainly about?
- (A) Damage to poorly constructed highways
- (B) The chemical properties of silane
- (C) How to maintain safety on the highways
- (D) A proposal to prevent cracks on highways

② According to the author, newly paved roads typically would show cracks within
- (A) two weeks
- (B) one month
- (C) 10 days
- (D) 137 days

③ Professor Brown believes that broken road surfaces are usually a result of
- (A) actions of soil bacteria
- (B) faulty design
- (C) poor construction
- (D) inferior material

④ The word "claims" in the first paragraph is closest in meaning to
- (A) exclaims
- (B) requests
- (C) asserts
- (D) hopes

⑤ "The process" in the second paragraph refers to that of
- (A) paving
- (B) growing
- (C) producing
- (D) washing

⑥ The word "undermining" in the second paragraph is closest in meaning to
    (A) digging mine pits under
    (B) harming
    (C) lifting
    (D) cleaning

⑦ According to the passage, silane does all of the following EXCEPT
    (A) bind with rock
    (B) bind asphalt to rock
    (C) dispel water
    (D) kill soil bacteria

⑧ The word "bonded" in the third paragraph is closest in meaning to
    (A) bent
    (B) combined
    (C) indebted
    (D) sticky

⑨ Brown's experiment implies that adding silane might extend the life of highways by approximately
    (A) 5 times
    (B) 10 times
    (C) 14 times
    (D) 137 times

題解

文章翻譯

　　新鋪設路面可能兩個星期保持光鮮亮麗。但是不出一個月，裂縫與坑洞就開始出現。這種破壞往往不是因為設計不良或材料不符標準。根據密西西比州立大學微生物學家布朗教授的說法，路面損壞主要是土壤細菌造成的。布朗說他已經找到了問題的解決辦法。

　　鋪路用的柏油（裡面其實 95% 是砂石，只有 5% 是柏油），有數不清的細菌在其中，和材料共同鋪到路上。路面鋪設完成後，細菌繼續生長，同時產生出肥皂狀的物質。這些物質逐漸分離碎石與柏油，破壞路面，一旦有車輛壓過就會崩解破裂。

　　布朗提出來的辦法是添加甲矽烷到鋪路材料中、讓它去工作。甲矽烷和碎石結合、密不透水，所以碎石和柏油之間沒有空隙可以讓細菌生長。布朗對甲矽烷的效果做了實驗室研究，獲得相當肯定的結果。對照組中，土壤細菌短短 10 天就造成柏油與碎石分離。實驗組的碎石在攪拌之前有做過甲矽烷處理，137 天之後碎石與柏油仍然緊密結合。甲矽烷不是消毒劑、也不會殺死土壤細菌，但能夠防止細菌剝離柏油與碎石。

練習題翻譯與詳解

① 本文的主題是什麼？

(A) 建造不良的公路受到的損壞　　　　(B) 甲矽烷的化學性

(C) 如何維持公路安全　　　　　　　　(D) 預防公路龜裂的一項提案

【答案】**D**

【解析】這是問主題的題型，要找主題句。第一段開頭是開場白，主題句是「路面損壞主要是土壤細菌造成的。布朗說他已經找到了問題的解決辦法」，後面兩段就是說明這項解決辦法，故選 (D)。

② 根據作者，新鋪設的路面多久會出現裂縫？

(A) 兩週　　　　　　　　　　　　　　(B) 一個月

(C) 10 天　　　　　　　　　　　　　 (D) 137 天

【答案】**B**

【解析】這是問細節的題型，要找同義表達。第一段說「不出一個月 (within a month)，裂縫與坑洞就開始出現」，所以選 (B)。

③ 布朗相信，路面破損通常是什麼造成的？

(A) 土壤細菌的作用　　　　　　　　　(B) 設計錯誤

(C) 施工不良　　　　　　　　　　　　(D) 材料不好

5

【答案】**A**

【解析】這是問細節的題型，要找同義表達。第一段中提到布朗說「路面損壞主要是土壤細菌造成的」，其中 caused by bacteria in the soil 就是 a result of actions of soil bacteria 的同義表達，故選 (A)。

④ 第一段中的 claims 一字意思最接近
(A) 大呼　　　　　　　　　　　(B) 要求
(C) 主張　　　　　　　　　　　(D) 希望

【答案】**C**

【解析】這是單字題。claim（構造：shout）的意思是「聲稱，主張」，同義字是 assert。

⑤ 第二段中 the process 指的是什麼程序？
(A) 鋪設　　　　　　　　　　　(B) 生長
(C) 產生　　　　　　　　　　　(D) 沖洗

【答案】**B**

【解析】這是指射的題型，要看上下文：the bacteria continue to grow, and produce soap-like substances in the process，這個 process 指的就是上文的 to grow，故選 (B)。

⑥ 第二段中的 undermining 一字意思最接近
(A) 在底下挖礦坑　　　　　　　(B) 傷害
(C) 提高　　　　　　　　　　　(D) 清潔

【答案】**B**

【解析】這是單字題。undermine 字面上是指在底下挖礦，但要引申為「破壞、淘空」解釋，同義字是 harm。

⑦ 根據本文，甲矽烷下面每一件事都會做，除了
(A) 與石頭結合　　　　　　　　(B) 結合柏油與石頭
(C) 排水　　　　　　　　　　　(D) 殺死土壤細菌

【答案】**D**

【解析】這是採消去法、問細節的題型，要找出三項同義表達刪去。第三段說「甲矽烷不是消毒劑、也不會殺死土壤細菌 (it does not kill bacteria in the soil)」，故選 (D)。

⑧ 第三段中的 bonded 一字意思最接近？

    (A) 彎曲   (B) 結合

    (C) 欠債   (D) 黏

【答案】B

【解析】這是單字題。bond 的意思是「結合」，同義字是 combine。

⑨ 布朗的實驗暗示，甲矽烷可以延長公路壽命大約幾倍？

    (A) 5 倍   (B) 10 倍

    (C) 14 倍   (D) 137 倍

【答案】C

【解析】這是推論題，要找「根據」。第三段講到布朗的實驗說「對照組中，土壤細菌短短 10 天就造成柏油與碎石分離。實驗組的碎石在攪拌之前有做過甲矽烷處理，137 天之後碎石與柏油仍然緊密結合」，算起來相差 13.7 倍，大約 14 倍。

5

Reading 6

Speciation is the process in which a species **diverges** into two descendant species. **W** Since the pair of species produced by speciation are equally descended from the ancestral form, it is incorrect to view one daughter species as the "original" and the other the "new" species. **X** However, this mistake is a common misconception about evolution, and gives rise to some erroneous ideas. **Y** Actually humans did not evolve from monkeys—they share a common ancestor with monkeys that was neither human nor monkey. **Z**

In sexually reproducing organisms, speciation results from reproductive isolation and then genealogical divergence. There are four mechanisms for speciation. The most common in animals is allopatric speciation, which occurs in populations that initially become isolated geographically—by habitat fragmentation or migration, for example. Simply by virtue of being geographically separated, selection will act independently in the isolated populations. If isolation is maintained, the separate evolutionary process will result in reproductive incompatibility. **In contrast, the second mode, sympatric speciation, is species divergence without geographic isolation, and its identification is typically controversial, since even a small amount of gene flow may be sufficient to homogenize a potentially diverging species.** Generally, models of sympatric speciation in animals require the evolution of stable polymorphisms associated with non-random assortative mating, in order for reproductive isolation to evolve.

The third mechanism of speciation is peripatric speciation, which occurs as a result of small populations of organisms becoming isolated in a new environment. Here, the founder effect causes rapid speciation through both rapid genetic drift and selection on a reduced gene pool. In peripatric speciation there is no specific **extrinsic** barrier to gene flow. The population is continuous, but nonetheless, the population does not mate randomly. Individuals are more likely to mate with their geographic neighbors than with individuals in a different part of the population's range. In this mode, divergence may happen because of reduced gene flow within the population and varying selection pressures across the population's range. Peripatric speciation is commonly cited as contributing to punctuated **equilibrium**, which describes speciation as proceeding in short "bursts" interspersed with long periods of stasis, in which species remain relatively unchanged. Hence, the majority of the fossil record will correspond to the parental population, with the isolated organisms rarely being preserved and consequently few intermediate forms being fossilized.

Finally, the fourth mechanism of speciation is parapatric speciation, which is similar to peripatric speciation in that a small population enters a new habitat. However, in this type of speciation there is no physical separation between these two populations. Instead, speciation results from the evolution of biological mechanisms that reduce gene flow between the two populations. Generally, this occurs when there has been a drastic change in the environment within the original species' habitat. An example of this is the grass genus *Anthoxanthum odoratum*, which can undergo parapatric speciation in response to localized metal pollution from mines. Here, around the mine, there is selection for resistance to high levels of metals in the soil. Selection against interbreeding with the metal-sensitive parental population produces a change in flowering time of the metal-resistant plants, resulting in reproductive isolation.

Extinction, on the other hand, is the disappearance of entire species. Extinction is not an unusual event on a geological time scale, as species regularly appear through speciation and disappear through extinction. Indeed, virtually all animal and plant species that have ever lived on the earth are now extinct. These extinctions have happened continuously throughout the history of life, although the rate of extinction **spikes** in occasional mass extinction events.

The Permian-Triassic extinction event was the Earth's most severe extinction event, rendering extinct 96% of all species. In the later Cretaceous-Tertiary extinction event, 76% of all species perished, the most commonly mentioned among them being the non-avian dinosaurs. The Holocene extinction event is the mass extinction associated with humanity's expansion across the globe over the last few thousand years and involves the rapid extinction of hundreds of thousands of species and the loss of up to 30% of all species by the mid 21st century. Human activities are probably the cause of the ongoing extinction event, and climate change may further accelerate it in the future.

5

✏ Exercise

① The word "diverges" in paragraph 1 is closest in meaning to

(A) merges

(B) disappears

(C) splits

(D) breaks

② In which position would the following boldfaced sentence best fit in paragraph 1?

Here is one: if humans evolved from monkeys, monkeys should no longer exist.

(A) Position W

(B) Position X

(C) Position Y

(D) Position Z

③ Which of the following can be inferred from paragraph 2 as evidence that a new species has appeared?

(A) This group has migrated to inhabit new locations.

(B) Members of this group are highly selective in their choice of mates with whom to breed offspring.

(C) This group is geographically isolated from others for a period of time.

(D) Members of this group can no longer produce offspring with members of another group.

④ Which of the sentences below best expresses the essential information in the boldfaced sentence in paragraph 2?

In contrast, the second mode, sympatric speciation, is species divergence without geographic isolation, and its identification is typically controversial, since even a small amount of gene flow may be sufficient to homogenize a potentially diverging species.

(A) Sympatric speciation occurs without geographic isolation, and is hard to ascertain because it may easily be disrupted by gene flow.

(B) The second mode is controversial in that even a small amount of gene flow may easily overcome geographic isolation.

(C) Sympatric speciation means species divergence without geographic isolation, and it can only be identified through gene flow.

(D) Identification of the second mode is controversial because a small amount of gene flow is characteristic of this mode.

⑤ The word "extrinsic" in paragraph 3 is closest in meaning to
(A) outside (B) intricate
(C) secure (D) extra

⑥ The word "equilibrium" in paragraph 3 is closest in meaning to
(A) equality (B) balance
(C) calmness (D) development

⑦ It can be inferred from paragraph 3 that few fossils of in-between forms have been found in the case of peripatric speciation because
(A) punctuated equilibrium is difficult to maintain
(B) fossils of the parent population have been carefully preserved
(C) such speciation only occurs occasionally
(D) speciation is punctuated with bursts of stasis

⑧ According to paragraph 4, parapatric speciation differs from peripatric speciation in that in parapatric speciation
(A) a small group goes into a new environment
(B) the new group is isolated from the old one
(C) speciation is the result of changes in biological mechanisms
(D) gene flow continues between the new group and the old one

⑨ The author mentions *Anthoxanthum odoratum* in paragraph 4 in order to
(A) describe one similarity between parapatric and peripatric speciation
(B) illustrate the effect of severe environmental change on speciation
(C) demonstrate that physical separation may lead to the forming of a distinct species
(D) give an example of how flowering time may affect interbreeding

⑩ According to the passage, all of the following may lead to speciation EXCEPT
(A) migration into a new location (B) the founder effect
(C) random mating (D) rapid environmental change

5

⑪ The word "spikes" in paragraph 5 is closest in meaning to

(A) nails

(B) peaks

(C) fastens

(D) plummets

⤵ 題解

[文章翻譯]

　　物種形成指的是一個品種分裂為兩個後代品種的過程。W 因為物種形成產生的兩個品種同樣都是從一個祖先出來的，所以不應該把一個後代品種視為「原」品種、另一個視為「新」品種。X 不過，這個錯誤是關於進化經常產生的誤解，也造成了一些不正確的觀念。Y 其實人類不是從猴子演化出來的——而是和猴子有共同祖先，這個祖先非人非猴。Z

　　有性生殖的生物中，物種形成來自於繁殖的隔離以及其後的世系分岔。物種形成有四種機制。動物界最常見的是異域種化，發生的族群起初是產生地理隔離——例如棲息地分裂，或者因為遷移。只因為有地理隔閡，被孤立的族群就會產生獨立的天擇運作。如果隔離持續下去，分離的進化過程就會產生出彼此無法繁殖後代的結果。相反的，第二種模式稱為同域種化，指的是物種分岔但並沒有地理孤立，它的指認往往會有爭議，因為只要有小量的基因流動可能就足以同質化一個可能會分岔的物種。一般而言，動物同域種化的形式需要先演化出穩定的不同形狀、而且和非隨機的選擇性交配有關，才能演化出繁殖上的孤立。

　　第三種物種形成的機制是邊域種化，來自於小族群的生物孤立在新環境中。在這裡，創立者效應會造成物種加快形成，來自於快速的遺傳漂變以及基因群縮小之後的天擇。

邊域種化並沒有明確的外在障礙阻斷基因流。族群還是連續的，但裡面的生物並非隨機交配。個體比較可能和鄰近的個體交配、不會去找另一個地區的對象。在這種模式中，物種分岔可能產生是因為族群中的基因流動減少，而且在族群分佈的不同區域有不同的天擇壓力。邊域種化經常被引為原因，說它會造成間斷平衡，意思是說物種形成會有短時間的「爆發」，中間隔著長期的停頓，在停頓期間物種相對沒有變化。所以，大多數的化石紀錄對應的都是親代族群，孤立的生物很少能夠保存下來，因此中介的形態很少有機會成為化石。

最後，物種形成的第四種機制是臨域種化，它和邊域種化很像，因為同樣都有一個小族群進入新棲息地。不過，在臨域種化中，兩個族群並沒有實質的分隔。物種形成來自於生物機制的演化，降低了兩個族群之間的基因流動。這通常是因為原始物種的棲息地發生激烈的環境變化。有一個例子是黃花茅屬的草。如果因為採礦而造成局部的金屬污染，黃花茅就可能產生臨域種化。在礦區附近，天擇有利於能夠抵抗土壤中含有高量金屬的物種。原族群仍對金屬敏感，天擇會趨向於使得能夠抗金屬的族群避免和原族群繁殖後代，於是造成花期改變，結果繁殖就分開了。

另一方面，物種滅絕指的是整個品種的消失。滅絕以地質學的時間來衡量絕非罕見現象，因為物種不斷形成、也不斷滅絕。其實，在地球上曾經生活過的所有動植物品種，現在幾乎都已經絕種了。整部生命史中，滅絕持續發生，不過偶爾有大規模滅絕事件出現，滅絕率會激增。

二疊紀—三疊紀滅絕事件是地球上最嚴重的滅絕事件，造成所有物種中 96% 絕種。後來的白堊紀—第三紀滅絕事件中，所有物種有 76% 絕種，其中最常被提到的就是非禽鳥類恐龍。全新世滅絕事件是近幾千年來和人類擴散全球有關的大規模滅絕，牽涉到數十萬種品種快速滅絕，到 21 世紀中葉將消滅掉最多 30% 的物種。人類活動很可能就是造成當前這一波滅絕事件的原因，將來氣候變化也許會進一步加快它的腳步。

练習題翻譯與詳解

① 第一段中的 diverges 意思最接近
(A) 合併，融合   (B) 消失
(C) 分裂   (D) 打破

【答案】C
【解析】這是單字題。動詞 diverge（構造：apart/verge）的意思是「分岔」，同義字是 split。

② 下面這個黑體字句子最適合放在第一段的什麼位置？
「這就有一個：如果人類是猴子演化出來的，那麼猴子就不應該還存在。」
(A) W 位置   (B) X 位置
(C) Y 位置   (D) Z 位置

【答案】C

【解析】這是安插句子的題型，要看上下文。插入句句首說到「這就有一個」，可以接到 Y 位置上文的「一些不正確觀念」。插入句內容說到「如果人類從猴子演化出來」，可以接到 Y 位置下文的「其實人類不是從猴子演化出來」，所以應放到 Y 位置，成為「這個錯誤是關於進化經常產生的誤解，也造成了一些不正確的觀念。這就有一個：如果人類是猴子演化出來的，那麼猴子就不應該還存在。其實人類不是從猴子演化出來的——而是和猴子有共同祖先，這個祖先非人非猴」。

③ 根據第二段可以推論，下列哪一項可以作為證據，證明有新物種出現了？

(A) 這個團體遷移到新地點去居住。

(B) 這個團體的成員在挑選配偶來生育後代時相當挑剔。

(C) 這個團體有一段時間與別的團體有地理隔閡。

(D) 這個團體的成員已經不能和另一個團體的成員生出後代。

【答案】D

【解析】這是推論題型，要找「根據」。第二段中間說「如果隔離持續下去，分離的進化過程就會產生出彼此無法繁殖後代的結果」。另外第二段結尾說「動物同域種化的形式需要先演化出穩定的不同形狀、而且和非隨機的選擇性交配有關，才能演化出繁殖上的孤立」。這兩處都用「無法繁殖後代」或「繁殖孤立」來界定新物種的形成，故選 (D)。

④ 下列哪個句子最能夠表達第二段黑體字句子的主要內容？

「相反的，第二種模式稱為同域種化，指的是物種分岔但並沒有地理孤立，它的指認往往會有爭議，因為只要有小量的基因流動可能就足以同質化一個可能會分岔的物種。」

(A) 同域種化發生並不需要地理孤立，而且不易確定，因為很容易被基因流動打斷。

(B) 第二種模式的辨認會有爭議，因為小量的基因流動就可以輕易克服地理孤立。

(C) 同域種化指的是物種分岔而沒有地理孤立，而且只能靠基因流動來辨認。

(D) 第二種模式的辨認會有爭議，因為小量的基因流動是這種模式的特色。

【答案】A

【解析】這是句子改寫的題型，要找句中重點的同義表達。只有選項 (A) 包含原句所有重點，並且沒有節外生枝。

⑤ 第三段中的 extrinsic 一字意思最接近

(A) 外面的   (B) 複雜的

(C) 安全的   (D) 多出來的

【答案】A

【解析】這是單字題，形容詞 extrinsic（構造：outward/(a.)）的意思是「外在的」，同義字是 outside。

⑥ 第三段中的 equilibrium 一字意思最接近

(A) 平等   (B) 平衡

(C) 冷靜   (D) 發展

【答案】**B**

【解析】這是單字題。equilibrium（構造：equal/scales/(*n.*)）的意思是「均衡」，同義字是 balance。

⑦ 根據第三段可以推論，邊域種化的中介形態化石很少找到，因為

(A) 間斷平衡很難維持

(B) 親種族群化石被仔細保存下來

(C) 這種物種形成只會偶爾發生

(D) 物種形成間雜有爆發性的停頓

【答案】**C**

【解析】這是推論題，要找「根據」。第三段說「間斷平衡，意思是說物種形成會有短時間的爆發，中間隔著長期的停頓……因此中介的形態很少有機會成為化石」，而「短時間的爆發」就是「只會偶爾發生」，故選 (C)。

5

⑧ 根據第四段，臨域種化與邊域種化的差別在於，在臨域種化中

(A) 一小群進入新環境

(B) 新族群與老族群有隔離

(C) 物種形成是生物機制改變的結果

(D) 新族群與老族群之間持續有基因流動

【答案】**C**

【解析】這是問細節的題型，要找同義表達。第四段說「在臨域種化中，兩個族群並沒有實質的分隔。物種形成來自於生物機制的演化」，其中 speciation results from the evolution of biological mechanisms 就是 speciation is the result of changes in biological mechanisms 的同義表達，故選 (C)。

⑨ 作者在第四段提到黃花茅，目的是

(A) 描述臨域種化與邊域種化的一個相似處

(B) 說明重大環境變化對物種形成的影響

(C) 證明實質隔閡可能導致不同物種的形成

(D) 舉例說明開花時間如何影響到互相交配繁殖

【答案】 **B**
【解析】這是修辭目的的題型，要看上下文。第四段說「這通常是因為原始物種的棲息地發生激烈的環境變化。有一個例子是黃花茅屬的草」，可以看出黃花茅是例子，用來說明上文「激烈環境變化」的影響，故選 (B)。

⑩ 根據本文，下列都可能導致物種形成，除了
    (A) 遷移到新地點
    (B) 創立者效應
    (C) 隨機交配
    (D) 快速環境變化

【答案】 **C**
【解析】這是採消去法、問細節的題型，要刪去三項同義表達。只有「隨機交配」不是物種形成的原因，故選 (C)。

⑪ 第五段中的 spikes 意思最接近
    (A) 釘住
    (B) 達到高峰
    (C) 綁緊
    (D) 直落

【答案】 **B**
【解析】這是單字題。動詞 spike 的意思是「突出成尖形」，引申為「達到高峰」，同義字是 peak。

Frontiersmen in the eighteenth century lived rigorous lives. These pioneers bought land from the government at the price of one or two shillings an acre, or simply took it from Native Americans by force. They practiced slash-and-burn agriculture. That is, they set fire to the trees and bushes on their land, and then planted corn and wheat among the stumps and roots. For accommodation they built log cabins piled up from felled walnut tree trunks and caulked with mud. The floors were usually plain dirt, or covered with twigs. Paper was soaked in lard and stretched over the windows to replace glass, a scarcely affordable **luxury**.

The men wore home-made hunting outfits; the women wove their own cloth and **tailored** their own dresses. Tables, or chairs, were nailed together with wooden pegs. They ate with wooden or tin spoons out of wooden plates. Typical frontier food was pork-and-corn stew, roast venison, wild turkey, and fish from nearby streams. The frontiersmen were widely scattered, but they built forts around important watering places to fight Native Americans.

During religious festivals or fairs, they celebrated with outdoor feasts, often featuring beef cows roasted whole. Dancing and drinking were indispensable, and so were quarreling and fighting. When frontiersmen fought, **they meant business**. Many of the one-eyed men in Virginia and the Carolinas could have told you how they lost an eye.

Exercise

① According to the passage, eighteenth-century pioneers acquired land by
- (A) buying it from Native Americans
- (B) taking it from the government by force
- (C) renting it at a couple of shillings an acre
- (D) purchasing it cheaply from the government

② What is "slash-and-burn agriculture"?
- (A) Burning the plants before planting crops
- (B) Burning last year's crops for fertilizer
- (C) Cutting down corn stems for fuel
- (D) Planting stumps and roots for food

③ It is implied in the passage that the houses of the frontiersmen were
- (A) crudely built
- (B) built only around watering places
- (C) bought cheaply from the government
- (D) cabins built from stumps and roots

④ The word "luxury" in the first paragraph refers to
- (A) lard
- (B) glass
- (C) paper
- (D) window

⑤ The word "tailored" in the second paragraph most closely means
- (A) ordered
- (B) purchased
- (C) made
- (D) spun

⑥ It can be inferred that which of the following was an important material to the pioneer?
(A) Iron
(B) Plastics
(C) Wood
(D) Cement

⑦ All of the following were mentioned in the passage as a common food in the pioneer household EXCEPT
(A) chicken
(B) venison
(C) turkey
(D) pork

⑧ The expression "they meant business" in the third paragraph most likely means
(A) they intended to do trade
(B) they were serious
(C) they wanted to make a profit
(D) they were bluffing

⑨ It is implied in the passage that many one-eyed men in Virginia had lost an eye
(A) in a confrontation with wild animals during hunting
(B) in a dangerous mission in war
(C) in a conflict with Native Americans
(D) in a drunken quarrel during a celebration

⑩ This passage is most probably an excerpt from a book on
(A) American history
(B) eighteenth-century religion
(C) colonial architecture
(D) North American Natives

文章翻譯

　　18 世紀的拓荒者過著嚴苛的生活。這些開路先鋒以每英畝一、兩先令的低價向政府購地，或者直接用武力從美洲原住民手中搶來。他們做的是砍劈焚燒式的農業。也就是說，他們放火焚燒自己土地上的樹木與灌木叢，然後在殘樁與樹根之間種植玉米與小麥。住的地方他們蓋原木小屋，砍倒核桃樹幹後堆起來、用泥填隙。地板通常就是泥土地，或者鋪上小樹枝。用紙浸上豬油就繃在窗戶上當玻璃，很少人買得起真正玻璃這種奢侈品。

　　男人穿的是自家做的獵裝，女人自己織布、自己剪裁衣服。桌椅是用木釘接合的。他們吃飯用木製或錫製湯匙、木盤子。拓荒者典型吃的是豬肉燉玉米、烤鹿肉、野火雞，以及附近溪裡抓來的魚。拓荒者零星分佈，但會在重要的水源地附近興建城堡和原住民作戰。

　　在宗教節慶或市集期間，他們舉辦戶外宴會來慶祝，經常有整頭的烤牛。跳舞與喝酒是少不了的，爭吵與打架也是一定會發生的。拓荒者打起架來是玩真的。當時維吉尼亞州、南北卡羅萊納州有許多獨眼男子可以告訴你他們是怎麼少了一隻眼的。

練習題翻譯與詳解

① 根據本文，18 世紀之拓荒者取得土地的方法是

　　(A) 向美洲原住民購買

　　(B) 用武力從政府手中搶奪

　　(C) 以每英畝一、兩先令的價格承租

　　(D) 向政府廉價購買

【答案】**D**

【解析】這是問細節的題型，要找同義表達。第一段說「這些開路先鋒以每英畝一、兩先令的低價向政府購地」，其中 These pioneers bought land from the government at the price of one or two shillings an acre 就是 purchasing cheaply from the government 的同義表達，故選 (D)。

② 何謂 slash-and-burn agriculture？

　　(A) 燒掉植物然後栽種作物

　　(B) 燒去年的農作物當肥料

　　(C) 砍下玉米桿當燃料

　　(D) 種植樹樁與樹根當食物

【答案】**A**

【解析】這是問細節的題型，要找同義表達。第一段在 slash-and-burn agriculture 後面說「也就是說，他們放火焚燒自己土地上的樹木與灌木叢，然後在殘樁與樹根之間種植玉米與小麥」，其中 they set fire to the trees and bushes on their land, and then planted corn and wheat among the stumps and roots 就是 Burning the plants before planting crops 的同義表達。

③ 原文暗示拓荒者的房屋

(A) 建造粗陋   (B) 只蓋在水源旁邊

(C) 向政府廉價購買   (D) 是用樹樁與樹根蓋的木屋

【答案】**A**

【解析】這是推論題，要找「根據」。第一段關於住屋是這樣說的「住的地方他們蓋原木小屋，砍倒核桃樹幹後堆起來、用泥填隙。地板通常就是泥土地，或者鋪小樹枝。用紙浸上豬油就繃在窗戶上當玻璃」。基本上就是非常簡陋，故選 (A)。

④ 第一段中的 luxury 這個字指的是

(A) 豬油   (B) 玻璃

(C) 紙   (D) 窗戶

【答案】**B**

【解析】這是指射題，要看上下文。第一段說 Paper was soaked in lard and stretched over the windows to replace glass, a scarcely affordable luxury.，其中 luxury 是 glass 的同位格，故選 (B)。

⑤ 第二段中的 tailored 一字意思最接近

(A) 命令，訂購   (B) 購買

(C) 製造   (D) 紡織

【答案】**C**

【解析】這是單字題。名詞 tailor（構造：cut/(n.)）是指「裁縫」，動詞是「剪裁」，同義字是 make。

⑥ 可以推論，下列哪一項是拓荒者的重要材料？

(A) 鐵   (B) 塑膠

(C) 木頭   (D) 水泥

【答案】**C**

【解析】這是推論題，要找「根據」。第一段說拓荒者住的是原木小屋，第二段說「桌椅是用木釘接合的。他們吃飯用木製或錫製湯匙、木盤子」，主要都是木料，故選 (C)。

⑦ 原文提到拓荒者家庭中常吃的食物不包括

(A) 雞肉   (B) 鹿肉

(C) 火雞肉   (D) 豬肉

【答案】**A**

【解析】這是問細節、採用消去法的題型，要找出三個同義表達刪去。第二段說「拓荒者典型吃的是豬肉燉玉米、烤鹿肉、野火雞，以及附近溪裡抓來的魚」，這裡面不包括雞，故選 (A)。

⑧ 第三段中的 they meant business 一語意思可能是

(A) 他們打算做生意   (B) 他們很認真

(C) 他們想賺錢   (D) 他們在唬人

【答案】**B**

【解析】這是單字題。片語 mean business 的意思是「認真的，玩真的」。

⑨ 原文暗示，維吉尼亞州有許多獨眼男子是怎麼少了隻眼的？

(A) 打獵時面對野獸   (B) 戰爭時出危險任務

(C) 和美洲原住民衝突   (D) 在節慶時醉酒吵架

【答案】**D**

【解析】這是推論題，要找「根據」。第三段說「在宗教節慶或市集期間，他們舉辦戶外宴會來慶祝……爭吵與打架也是一定會發生的」，然後就說到獨眼男子，暗示是因為打架而少了隻眼。

⑩ 本文可能選自一本談論什麼主題的書？

(A) 美國歷史   (B) 18 世紀宗教

(C) 殖民地時代建築   (D) 北美原住民

【答案】**A**

【解析】這是問主題的題型，要看主題句。第一段第一句是全文主題句：「18 世紀的拓荒者過著嚴苛的生活」。後面兩段的主題句分別介紹拓荒者的衣食與活動。三段共同的主題是美洲拓荒者，這應該屬於「美國歷史」這個更大的主題之下，也就是選自談美國歷史的書，故選 (A)。

6

Briefly, the greenhouse **model** of global warming goes as follows. The burning of fossil fuels injects carbon dioxide and other gases into the atmosphere. These gases allow the high-energy solar rays to pass through and heat the earth, but trap the reflected, low-energy infrared radiation in the atmosphere. The result is ever-increasing temperatures, or global warming.

Scientists calculate that there has been a 37% rise in atmospheric contents of carbon dioxide from 1900 to the present day. The average temperature has correspondingly risen about 0.8 degree Celsius. Many scientists agree that the greenhouse effect will raise average temperatures by roughly three degrees Celsius by the year 2050. Such an increase in temperature would melt parts of the polar ice caps, cause sea levels to rise, and inundate such places as the coastal towns in Florida and California. In addition, the corn belt and the cotton belt in middle-latitude United States would turn into vast deserts, whereas high-latitude areas such as Canada and Siberia would have the most pleasant climates.

There are skeptics to the greenhouse model of global warming. President Trump of the U.S., for one, dismisses global warming as a figment. The skeptics point out that, first of all, the evidence for a warming trend is **inconclusive** at best. In fact, the cooling trend between 1940 and 1970 once prompted many scientists to predict that a new ice age was coming. Furthermore, **these critics** point to the amazing heat-absorbing capacities of sea water as insurance against any sudden rise in global temperature. Finally, the clouds may actually work toward lowering temperatures. As temperatures rise, more sea water will be evaporated. Besides absorbing more heat, the increased evaporation would form thicker clouds, thus cutting substantial amounts of sunlight from reaching the earth. This would serve to cool off the earth and thus counteract the warming caused by the greenhouse effect.

✎ Exercise

① The author is primarily concerned with
   (A) describing disasters caused by the greenhouse effect
   (B) explaining the relationship between the greenhouse effect and agriculture
   (C) defending the greenhouse effect model of global warming
   (D) introducing the greenhouse effect model and the controversies surrounding it

② The word "model" in the first paragraph most closely means
   (A) fashion
   (B) theory
   (C) ideal
   (D) statue

③ The passage implies that infrared radiation is trapped in the atmosphere because, compared with sunlight, it has
   (A) less energy
   (B) more carbon dioxide
   (C) more water vapor
   (D) less visibility

④ Scientists believe that a three-degree Celsius rise in average temperature by 2050 would result in all of the following EXCEPT
   (A) flooding of seaside towns
   (B) desertification of certain parts of the U. S.
   (C) melting of parts of polar ice caps
   (D) a 37% rise in atmospheric carbon dioxide

⑤ Some scientists predict that Canada would have a pleasant climate by 2050 probably because they believe that
   (A) global warming would make it warmer in Canada
   (B) the clouds would cut off sunlight and cool off the earth
   (C) sea water could absorb enough excess heat
   (D) global temperature would have risen by 0.8 degree Celsius

⑥ The word "inconclusive" in the third paragraph is closest in meaning to
   (A) not constructive
   (B) fruitless
   (C) infinite
   (D) uncertain

⑦ It is implied that global climates between 1940 and 1970 were relatively
   (A) hot
   (B) cool
   (C) dry
   (D) wet

⑧ The phrase "these critics" in the third paragraph refers to
   (A) scientists who predicted a sudden rise in global temperature
   (B) skeptics to the greenhouse effect model
   (C) environmentalists agitating for control of carbon dioxide emission
   (D) Canadians dissatisfied with the international control of greenhouse gases

⑨ Which of the following is mentioned in the passage as a guarantee against any sudden rise in global temperature?
   (A) Average temperature is rising steadily.
   (B) The greenhouse effect moderates temperature.
   (C) A new ice age is coming.
   (D) The water in the seas can absorb heat very well.

➡ 題解

文章翻譯

　　全球暖化的溫室效應理論簡介如下。燃燒化石燃料注入二氧化碳與其他氣體到大氣層中。這些氣體容許高能量的陽光穿過、加熱地球,但捕捉住反射出來的低能量紅外線輻射在大氣層中。結果就是溫度不斷升高,亦即全球暖化。

　　科學家統計,自 1900 年迄今,大氣層中的二氧化碳含量增加了 37%。平均氣溫相對也增加了大約攝氏 0.8 度。許多科學認為,溫室效應到 2050 年將提高平均溫度約攝氏 3 度。這種幅度的增加將造成南北極冰帽部分溶解、海平面上升,諸如佛羅里達州與加州沿海城市這樣的地方會淹沒。而且,美國中緯度玉米帶與棉花帶會變成大沙漠,而加拿大、西伯利亞這種高緯度地區會變得氣候宜人。

　　全球暖化的溫室效應論有人持懷疑看法。例如美國川普總統就說全球暖化根本是想像出來的。懷疑論者指出,首先,暖化趨勢的證據頂多只能說是尚無定論。事實上,1940 到 1970 年間的冷卻趨勢一度引起許多科學家預言新冰河時期即將來臨。此外,這些批評家指出海水具有驚人的吸熱能力,說這是一項保險,不致於發生全球溫度突然上升的現象。最後,雲層還可能會降低溫度。隨著溫度上升,更多海水會蒸發掉。蒸發就會吸熱,而且會形成厚厚的雲層,因而大幅阻斷陽光不致抵達地球表面。這就會造成冷卻作用,因而抵消溫室效應產生的暖化。

練習題翻譯與詳解

① 作者的主要目的在於

　　(A) 描寫溫室效應造成的災難

　　(B) 解釋溫室效應與農業之間的關係

　　(C) 為全球暖化的溫室效應論辯護

　　(D) 介紹溫室效應論以及它周圍的爭議

【答案】**D**

【解析】這是問主題的題型,要找主題句。第一段全文主題句是「全球暖化的溫室效應理論簡介如下」。第二段的段落主題句「自 1900 年迄今,大氣層中的二氧化碳含量增加了 37%。平均氣溫相對也增加了大約攝氏 0.8 度」,繼續介紹全球暖化的溫室效應理論。第三段的段落主題句「全球暖化的溫室效應論有人持懷疑看法」介紹的是同一理論的反對意見。三段共同主題是全球暖化的溫室效應論,但有正反兩面看法,故選 (D)。

② 第一段中的 model 一字意思最接近

　　(A) 式樣　　　　　　　　　　　(B) 理論

　　(C) 理想　　　　　　　　　　　(D) 雕像

6

【答案】**B**

【解析】這是單字題。model（構造：manner/(n.)）可以解釋為「模型，模式」，在此上下文應解釋為「理論模式」，最接近的是 theory。

③ 本文暗示，紅外線輻射會困在大氣層中是因為，比起陽光來，它
   (A) 能量較少　　　　　　　　　　(B) 二氧化碳較多
   (C) 水蒸氣較多　　　　　　　　　(D) 能見度較小

【答案】**A**

【解析】這是推論題，要找「根據」。第一段說「這些氣體容許高能量的陽光穿過、加熱地球，但捕捉住反射出來的低能量紅外線輻射在大氣層中」，其中 low-energy 就是 less energy，故選 (A)。

④ 科學家相信，到 2050 年平均溫若上升攝氏 3 度，造成的結果不包括
   (A) 沿海市鎮淹沒　　　　　　　　(B) 美國有些地區沙漠化
   (C) 兩極冰帽部分溶解　　　　　　(D) 大氣層二氧化碳增加 37%

【答案】**D**

【解析】這是問細節、採用消去法的題型，要找出三個同義表達刪去。第二段說「自 1900 年迄今，大氣層中的二氧化碳含量增加了 37%」，這和「到 2050 年將增加 37%」不同，所以 (D) 不是同義表達。

⑤ 有些科學家預言加拿大到 2050 年將會氣候宜人，可能是因為他們相信
   (A) 全球暖化將造成加拿大變溫暖
   (B) 雲層將阻絕陽光、造成地球冷卻
   (C) 海水將吸收夠多的過剩熱度
   (D) 全球溫度將已上升攝氏 0.8 度

【答案】**A**

【解析】這是推論題，要找「根據」。第二段說「溫室效應到 2050 年將提高平均溫度約攝氏 3 度……加拿大、西伯利亞這種高緯度地區會變得氣候宜人」，所以加拿大的氣候變化與溫度升高 3 度有關。

⑥ 第三段中的 inconclusive 一字意思最接近
   (A) 沒有建設性　　　　　　　　　(B) 沒有結果
   (C) 無限　　　　　　　　　　　　(D) 不確定

【答案】**D**

【解析】這是單字題。inconclusive（結構：not/together/close/(a.)）的意思是「沒有定論」，同義字是 uncertain。

⑦ 原文暗示，1940 至 1970 年間的全球氣候相對

   (A) 熱   (B) 冷

   (C) 乾   (D) 濕

【答案】**B**

【解析】這是推論題，要找「根據」。第三段說「1940 到 1970 年間的冷卻趨勢一度引起許多科學家預言新冰河時期即將來臨」，所以那段時間是比較冷的。

⑧ 第三段中的 these critics 指的是

   (A) 預言全球溫度將突然上升的科學家

   (B) 懷疑溫室效應論的人

   (C) 鼓吹管制二氧化碳排放的環保人士

   (D) 對國際管制溫室效應氣體心懷不滿的加拿大人

【答案】**B**

【解析】這是指射題，要看上下文。第三段第二句說 There are skeptics to the greenhouse model of global warming.，先提出來說有人懷疑溫室效應論。接下來說 The skeptics point out that, first of all, the evidence for a warming trend is inconclusive at best.。下文的 these critics 指的就是 the skeptics，也就是懷疑溫室效應論的人。

⑨ 本文有提到下列哪一點，說它是保障，可以防止全球溫度突然上升？

   (A) 平均溫度穩定上升中。

   (B) 溫室效應會調節氣溫。

   (C) 新冰河時代快來了。

   (D) 海水能夠吸很多熱。

【答案】**D**

【解析】這是問細節的題型，要找同義表達。第三段說「這些批評家指出海水具有驚人的吸熱能力，說這是一項保險，不致於發生全球溫度突然上升的現象」，其中 the amazing heat-absorbing capacities of sea water 就是 The water in the seas can absorb heat very well. 的同義表達，故選 (D)。

The Civilian Conservation Corps (CCC) was conceived by Franklin D. Roosevelt to serve **a dual purpose**. It had been an important part of Roosevelt's campaign platform to "develop land and water resources." The Great Depression and massive unemployment, however, **diverted** Roosevelt's attention from conservation until he hit upon the idea of employing jobless men to do conservation work. Such an arrangement would at once reduce unemployment and contribute to conservation.

The CCC Bill was passed in May, 1933, not long after Roosevelt's inauguration. Roosevelt immediately issued orders to get the CCC started, and set the goal of sending 250,000 people to the camps before summer was over. He also decided to restrict participation to unmarried men between 18 and 25 who were from families on relief.

By the middle of June, 1,300 camps were established, and before August, over 300,000 young men were working in the woods. Their jobs included planting trees, building dams and reservoirs, digging ditches, fighting plant diseases and pests, restoring historic sites and cleaning beaches. More important than developing natural resources, however, they developed themselves. The CCC boys came from every corner of America. Many of them had never left home before. Now they waded brooks, climbed mountains, and camped in national parks. And they had plenty to eat, which to many people was far from a guaranteed thing at the **peak** of Depression years. Even more important than food, their self-respect was restored through work. They learned trades with which they later earned a living, and they learned about their country and their countrymen. Through all this, they learned about themselves, which was the most valuable knowledge they brought back home.

In all, more than two and a half million young men came to the Corps. The highest number of enrollment was 500,000, in 1935. Participants typically stayed from six months to a year, were proud of the job, and missed the experience when it was over.

Exercise

① The best title for this passage would be
- (A) Franklin D. Roosevelt and the Great Depression
- (B) An Inspired Project during Depression Years
- (C) The Civilian Conservation Corps: How It Failed Expectations
- (D) Energy Conservation and Economic Depression

② The expression "a dual purpose" in the first paragraph refers to the purposes of
- (A) curing the Great Depression and eliminating unemployment
- (B) developing both land and water resources
- (C) helping conservation and combating unemployment
- (D) winning the campaign and founding the CCC

③ The word "diverted" in the first paragraph could best be replaced by
- (A) reverted
- (B) distracted
- (C) rerouted
- (D) focused

④ It can be inferred from the passage that a person who had the best chance of being accepted by the CCC would have been
- (A) A boy of 17, from a double-income family
- (B) A woman of 21, from a rich family
- (C) A man of 23, from a poor family
- (D) A woman of 28, from a single-parent family

⑤ Compared with the goal set by Roosevelt for the summer of 1933, the number actually recruited that summer was
- (A) lower
- (B) the same
- (C) higher
- (D) 1,300

⑥ According to the passage, the CCC boys did all of the following in the camps EXCEPT
(A) look after sick plants
(B) construct reservoirs
(C) clean buildings
(D) renovate places of historic significance

⑦ The word "peak" in the third paragraph most closely means
(A) mountain range
(B) uncontrollable wrath
(C) deep pit
(D) high point

⑧ The author seems to feel that the most important thing the CCC participants earned was
(A) plenty of food to eat
(B) skills to earn a living
(C) an understanding of America
(D) a knowledge of themselves

⑨ According to the passage, all of the following are true EXCEPT
(A) the total number of CCC participants was over 2,500,000
(B) the largest enrollment at the CCC occurred in 1935
(C) the CCC participants usually stayed from half a year to one full year
(D) the CCC participants planted 500,000 trees

▶ 題解

文章翻譯

　　公民保育團 (CCC) 是小羅斯福總統的構想，有雙重目的。羅斯福競選時有一重要政見是「開發水陸資源」。但是經濟大蕭條與大規模失業令羅斯福轉移注意無暇顧及保育，直到他想到可以聘用失業男子來做保育工作。這樣安排可以同時降低失業又能對保育有貢獻。

　　CCC 提案在 1933 年 5 月通過，當時羅斯福剛就任不久。他立即發出命令開辦 CCC，訂下的目標是在夏季結束之前要派 250,000 人進入工作營區。他同時決定只限 18 到 25 歲、領救助金家庭的未婚男性才可參加。

　　到了 6 月中已經成立了 1,300 處營區。還不到 8 月，就已經有 300,000 年輕男子在森林中工作。他們做的事包括種樹、建水壩與水庫、挖溝渠、對抗植物病蟲害、歷史古蹟復舊、以及淨灘。不過，比開發天然資源更重要的是這些人開發了自我。CCC 青年來自全美國每一個角落，其中有許多人從來沒離開過家。如今他們在涉溪、爬山，在國家公園露營。而且他們不缺食物，這在大蕭條時代的高峰對許多人來說絕非易事。還有比食物更重要的：他們的自尊經過工作而恢復。他們學會了謀生本事，後來靠這個本事過活，而且他們了解了國家、了解了國人。經由這一切，他們了解了自己，這才是他們帶回家的最寶貴的知識。

　　總計有 250 多萬人來到 CCC。最高的單年註冊紀錄是 1935 年的 50 萬人。參加者一般停留 6 個月到 1 年，對工作很驕傲，結束後也很懷念這段經驗。

練習題翻譯與詳解

① 本文的最佳標題是
　　(A) 小羅斯福總統與經濟大蕭條　　　　(B) 大蕭條年代一項英明的計畫
　　(C) 公民保育團：它怎樣令人失望　　　(D) 節約能源與經濟蕭條

【答案】**B**
【解析】這是問主題的題型，要找主題句。第一段全文主題句是「公民保育團 (CCC) 是小羅斯福總統的構想，有雙重目的」，提出主題是 CCC。第二段與第三段都是介紹 CCC 的內容與成就。選項 (C) 用 CCC 當標題本來是好的，但後面說它令人失望，與主題有牴觸，故選 (B)。

② 第一段的 a dual purpose 指的是哪兩項目的？
　　(A) 治癒經濟大蕭條以及消除失業　　　(B) 開發水資源以及陸資源
　　(C) 幫助保育以及對抗失業　　　　　　(D) 贏得大選以及創立 CCC

【答案】**C**
【解析】這是指射題，要看上下文。第一段說「這樣安排可以同時降低失業又能對保育有貢獻」，兩項目的就在此，故選 (C)。

6

③ 第一段中的 diverted 可以換成哪個字？

    (A) 回復   (B) 打岔，使分心

    (C) 改道   (D) 聚焦

【答案】**B**

【解析】這是單字題。動詞 divert（構造：apart/turn）的意思是「轉移注意」，同義字是 distract。

④ 由文中可以推論，最有機會被 CCC 接受的人是

    (A) 17 歲男孩，來自雙薪家庭

    (B) 21 歲女人，來自有錢家庭

    (C) 23 歲男人，來自貧窮家庭

    (D) 28 歲女人，來自單親家庭

【答案】**C**

【解析】這是推論題，要找「根據」。第二段列出參加 CCC 的條件是「只限 18 到 25 歲、領救助金家庭的未婚男性才可參加」，選項 (C) 符合條件。

⑤ 比起羅斯福為 1933 年夏季訂定的目標，實際徵召來的人數

    (A) 較低   (B) 一樣

    (C) 較高   (D) 是 1,300

【答案】**C**

【解析】這是推論題，要找「根據」。第二段提到說「訂下的目標是在夏季結束之前要派 250,000 人進入工作營區……還不到 8 月，就已經有 300,000 年輕男子在森林中工作」，所以結果是超出原訂目標。

⑥ 根據本文，CCC 青年在營區做的事不包括

    (A) 照顧有病的植物   (B) 建造水壩

    (C) 打掃建築   (D) 翻新有歷史價值的場所

【答案】**C**

【解析】這是問細節、採用消去法的題型，要找出三個同義表達刪去。第二段說「他們做的事包括種樹、建水壩與水庫、挖溝渠、對抗植物病蟲害、歷史古蹟復舊、以及淨灘」，其中找不到 clean buildings 的同義表達。

⑦ 第三段中的 peak 一字意思最接近

    (A) 山脈   (B) 無法控制的忿怒

    (C) 深坑   (D) 高點

【答案】D

【解析】這是單字題，peak 字面是「山峰」，在此上下文是用來比喻「最高點」，同義字是 high point。

⑧ 作者似乎覺得，CCC 參加者最重要的收獲是

(A) 有許多食物吃　　　　　　　　(B) 謀生技能

(C) 了解美國　　　　　　　　　　(D) 認識自我

【答案】D

【解析】這是推論題，要找「根據」。第二段說「他們了解了自己，這才是他們帶回家的最寶貴的知識」，故選 (D)。

⑨ 根據本文，下列哪一項是錯的？

(A) CCC 參加者總數超過 2,500,000

(B) CCC 最大的註冊人數發生在 1935 年

(C) CCC 參與者通常停留半年到 1 年

(D) CCC 參與者種了 500,000 棵樹。

【答案】D

【解析】這是問細節、採用消去法的題型，要找出三個同義表達刪除。第三段提到 500,000 這個數字是指「最高的單年註冊紀錄是 1935 年的 500,000 人」而非樹木，所以 (D) 不是同義表達。

Reading 4

Human hearing, like other human senses, has evolved over hundreds of thousands of years. With the exception of vision, hearing is the most acutely developed of our senses. Because our ancestors were hunters, as well as prey for **carnivorous** predators, a highly refined sense of hearing was indeed often rewarded.

Hearing takes place in the ear, a special sense organ that is also concerned with balance. It is divided into the outer ear, extending from the tympanic membrane or ear drum to the pinna; the middle ear, embedded in the skull bones, consisting of the cochlea and labyrinth; and the inner ear, containing small bones or ossicles. The ear drum, which is the most important structure in the ear, has a very delicate membrane, and it can be easily **punctured**.

It must be remembered that the human ear is capable of receiving only a certain number of different types of vibrations. Vibrations occurring above or below this range cannot be interpreted by humans as sound because of the limitations of our faculty. Other animals, for example dogs, can interpret a much wider range of vibrations, hence the familiar dog whistle that manufactures a sound that is **painful to dogs** yet inaudible to humans. However, since there are few important sounds in today's world that humans cannot hear, in the long run human hearing is probably more likely to deteriorate than to improve. Interestingly, however, some anatomists believe that the **traces** of muscle attached to the human ear indicate that at one time humans could move their ears to catch sound waves, as do horses.

✎ Exercise

① What is the main topic of the passage?
   (A) The ear drum
   (B) Human hearing
   (C) Eyes and ears
   (D) Hearing of mammals

② Why does the author mention our human ancestors in the first paragraph?
   (A) To illustrate how excellent hearing was beneficial
   (B) To suggest that human hearing has become less efficient
   (C) To compare human hearing with the hearing of animals
   (D) To describe the dwellings of the earliest human society

③ In the first paragraph, the word "carnivorous" most nearly means which of the following?
   (A) dangerous
   (B) now forgotten
   (C) man eating
   (D) meat eating

④ According to the passage, what is true of the ear drum?
   (A) It is another name for the pinna
   (B) It is found inside the skull bones
   (C) It is a relatively unimportant structure
   (D) It is considered part of the outer ear

⑤ In the second paragraph, the word "punctured" is closest in meaning to
   (A) located
   (B) restored
   (C) pierced
   (D) vibrated

⑥ It can be inferred from the passage that human hearing is limited because
  (A) of excessive vibrations occurring in the ear drum
  (B) ancient humans relied on dogs to hear certain sounds
  (C) we have eliminated dangerous high-pitched sounds
  (D) we detect only a portion of all possible vibrations

⑦ In the third paragraph, what does the author mean by stating that a dog whistle produces a sound that is "painful to dogs"?
  (A) Dog whistles are a good form of protection
  (B) Dogs obey commands given in a loud voice
  (C) Dogs make an inaudible howl when they are attacked
  (D) Dogs can hear some noises that humans cannot

⑧ The word "traces" in the third paragraph is closest in meaning to
  (A) outlines
  (B) fibers
  (C) small amounts
  (D) absence

⑨ According to the author, the ability to move the ears to catch sound waves
  (A) is now found only in horses
  (B) is still found in most humans
  (C) is likely to soon be a human trait
  (D) may have once existed in humans

⤵ 題解

文章翻譯

人類聽覺和其他的感官一樣，都歷經數十萬年的發展。僅次於視覺，聽覺是人類發展最敏銳的感官。因為我們的祖先是獵人、同時也是肉食狩獵者的獵物，所以高度發展的聽覺確實經常帶來好處。

聽覺發生在耳中，耳朵這個特殊的感官同時也和平衡感有關。耳朵分為外耳（從鼓膜，或稱耳鼓，延伸到外面的耳殼），中耳（埋在頭骨內，由耳蝸與迷路構成），以及內耳（包含小骨頭，或稱聽小骨）。鼓膜是耳朵裡最重要的構造，有一層很精細的薄膜，很容易被刺穿。

別忘了，人耳只能接收幾種不同的振動。在此範圍之上或之下的振動，人類無法解讀為聲音，因為我們的能力有限。別種動物，例如狗，能夠詮釋的振動範圍要大得多，所以才會有大家知道的狗哨子這種東西，它能夠產生狗聽起來很痛苦的聲音，但是人類聽不到。不過，在今日世界，很少有什麼重要的聲音是人類聽不到的，所以長遠來看，人類聽覺退化的可能性大於進化。有一件事很有意思：有些解剖學家相信，人耳附有的殘留肌肉顯示從前人類可以轉動耳朵捕捉聲音，就像馬一樣。

練習題翻譯與詳解

① 本文的主題是什麼？

    (A) 耳鼓   (B) 人類聽覺

    (C) 眼睛與耳朵   (D) 哺乳類的聽覺

【答案】B
【解析】這是問主題的題型，要找主題句。第一段全文主題句「人類聽覺和其他的感官一樣，都歷經數十萬年的發展」；第二段段落主題句「聽覺發生在耳中」；第三段「人耳只能接收幾種不同的振動」。全篇共同的主題是人類聽覺，故選 (B)。

② 作者在第一段為何提到人類祖先？

    (A) 說明敏銳的聽覺為何有好處

    (B) 暗示人類聽覺已經變成比較差了

    (C) 比較人類聽覺與動物聽覺

    (D) 描述最早人類社會的住所

【答案】A
【解析】這是修辭目的的題型，要看上下文。第一段說「因為我們的祖先是獵人、同時也是肉食狩獵者的獵物，所以高度發展的聽覺確實經常帶來好處」，這裡提到人類祖先，是為了說明下文「聽覺有好處」的原因，故選 (A)。

③ 第一段中的 carnivorous 一字意思最接近
　　(A) 危險的　　　　　　　　　　(B) 現在已經被遺忘的
　　(C) 吃人的　　　　　　　　　　(D) 吃肉的

【答案】D
【解析】這是單字題。carnivorous（構造：flesh/swallow/(a.)）意思是「肉食的」，相當於 meat eating。

④ 根據本文，下列關於耳鼓的哪一句話是對的？
　　(A) 它又稱耳殼　　　　　　　　(B) 它埋在頭骨裡面
　　(C) 它是相對不重要的構造　　　(D) 它被視為外耳的一部分

【答案】D
【解析】這是問細節的題型，要找同義表達。第二段說「耳朵分為外耳（從鼓膜，或稱耳鼓，延伸到外面的耳殼）」，可知耳鼓是外耳的一部分。

⑤ 第二段中的 punctured 一字意思最接近
　　(A) 找到　　　　　　　　　　　(B) 恢復
　　(C) 穿透　　　　　　　　　　　(D) 振動

【答案】C
【解析】這是單字題。動詞 puncture（構造：point/(v.)）的意思是「戳破」，同義字是 pierce。

⑥ 由文中可以推論，人類聽覺有限是因為
　　(A) 耳鼓裡面的振動過多
　　(B) 古人靠狗來聽某些聲音
　　(C) 我們已經消除掉危險的高頻率聲音
　　(D) 在所有可能的振動中我們只能偵測到一部分

【答案】D
【解析】這是推論題，要找「根據」。第三段說「人耳只能接收幾種不同的振動。在此範圍之上或之下的振動，人類無法解讀為聲音，因為我們的能力有限」，故選 (D)。

⑦ 第三段中作者說到狗哨子發出的聲音是 painful to dogs，這是什麼意思？
　　(A) 狗哨子是一種很好的防護
　　(B) 狗會服從大聲下達的指令
　　(C) 狗受到攻擊會發出聽不到的嚎叫
　　(D) 狗可以聽到人類聽不到的一些聲音

【答案】D

【解析】這是修辭目的的題型，要找上下文。第三段說「別種動物，例如狗，能夠詮釋的振動範圍要大得多，所以才會有大家知道的狗哨子這種東西，它能夠產生狗聽起來很痛苦的聲音，但是人類聽不到」，可以看出重點在於「狗聽得到、人聽不到」，故選 (D)。

⑧ 第三段中的 traces 一字意思最接近

    (A) 大綱，輪廓   (B) 纖維

    (C) 小量   (D) 缺席，不存在

【答案】C

【解析】這是單字題。名詞 trace 的意思是「痕跡」，喻「小量」。

⑨ 根據作者，轉動耳朵接收聲波的能力

    (A) 如今只有馬還擁有

    (B) 大部分人仍然具有

    (C) 可能很快會成為人類一種特質

    (D) 從前人類可能擁有過

【答案】D

【解析】這是問細節的題型，要找同義表達。第三段說「人耳還附有一些殘留的肌肉，顯示從前人類可以轉動耳朵捕捉聲音」，其中 at one time humans could move their ears to catch sound waves 和 the ability to move the ears to catch sound waves may have once existed in humans 是同義表達，故選 (D)。

6

Reading 5

Hidden deep inside the jungle of the Amazon basin that covers so much of Brazil, Ecuador, and Peru is the magnificent Manu Wildlife Reserve. Normally accessible only by boat, and then only in the dry season, the Manu Reserve remains an almost pristine portion of rain forest even as more and more wilderness areas feel the **relentless** encroachment of man.

The Peruvian government first attempted to establish a park in the Manu region in 1972, when opposition from business interests and Native American Rights activists forced the government to **postpone** the park's creation. By 1978, however, the Peruvian government had succeeded in creating a national wildlife sanctuary—larger than the combined areas of Rhode Island and Connecticut—unrivaled in the entire world. Construction of any type is completely banned within the park's borders, except for that by the park's sparse indigenous population, which makes its living largely by hunting, fishing, and gathering.

The wildlife reserve is home to an **incredible array** of flora and fauna, some of it found virtually nowhere else in the world. As such, the Manu attracts a large number of scientists and researchers of various sorts, ornithologists being especially common, as well as a very limited number of green, or environmentally friendly tourists. All visitors reside in one of several small compounds scattered throughout the park and obey strict guidelines aimed at minimizing the impact of human habitation.

✏ Exercise

① The passage primarily discusses
  (A) the discovery of new plant species
  (B) the establishment of "green" tourism
  (C) the creation of a wilderness park
  (D) people's encroachment on pristine areas

② According to the passage, the Manu Reserve is
  (A) part of an international nature park
  (B) slowly losing ground to nearby developers
  (C) connected to passable roads in the dry season
  (D) only accessible by boat for part of the year

③ The word "relentless" in the first paragraph is closest in meaning to
  (A) unnatural
  (B) ceaseless
  (C) illegal
  (D) increasing

④ It can be inferred from the passage that the Peruvian government
  (A) eventually gave in to business lobbyists
  (B) spent years trying to establish the Manu Reserve
  (C) moved most of the native inhabitants to nearby lands
  (D) brought in experts from several US states

⑤ The word "postpone" in the second paragraph is closest in meaning to
  (A) abandon
  (B) rethink
  (C) advertise
  (D) put off

⑥ The phrase "incredible array" in the third paragraph is closest in meaning to which of the following?
(A) incredible variety
(B) incredible color
(C) endangered group
(D) increasing number

⑦ According to the passage, most of the native inhabitants of the Manu Reserve
(A) are employed by construction firms
(B) are assistants to field researchers
(C) provide guide services to tourists
(D) collect and hunt their own food

⑧ For which of the following terms does the author give a definition?
(A) "wildlife sanctuary"
(B) "unrivaled"
(C) "ornithologists"
(D) "green"

⑨ It can be inferred that the purpose of restricting the number of visitors to the park is to do which of the following?
(A) Reduce the disruption brought by people
(B) Keep visitors from interfering with scientists' work
(C) Keep peace between visitors and natives
(D) Charge higher entrance fees

〔文章翻譯〕

亞馬遜盆地涵蓋巴西、厄瓜多爾與秘魯的極大部分,壯觀的馬努野生動物保護區就藏在叢林深處。馬努保護區通常只有乘船才可以通,而且還得是乾季。至今仍然是幾乎完好無損的一片雨林,雖然別處有越來越多的荒野地區都遭到人類無情的入侵。

秘魯政府在 1972 年首度嘗試在馬努地區建立園區,但商業利益與美洲原住民權益運動人士群起反對,迫使政府延後計畫。不過到了 1978 年,秘魯政府成功創造出一處國家級的野生生物保護區(面積超過羅德島州加上康乃迪克州),全世界無與倫比。園區內禁止任何形式的建築,除了園區內稀疏的原住民族群例外,原住民的謀生方式是打獵、捕魚與採集。

這處野生生物保護區裡面有多到令人難以置信的動植物,其中有一些可以說全世界就只有這裡找得到。所以,馬努吸引來大批各式各樣的科學家與研究人員,最多的就是鳥類學家,還有人數嚴格管制的綠色(亦即環保)觀光客。所有訪客都住在散落在園區各地的幾處小營區內,他們必須遵守嚴格的指導方針,目的在於盡量降低人類居住帶來的衝擊。

〔練習題翻譯與詳解〕

① 本文討論的主題是

    (A) 新植物品種的發現   (B) 建立「綠色」觀光

    (C) 一座荒野園區的創造   (D) 人類侵入原始地區

【答案】**C**

【解析】這是問主題的題型,要找主題句。第一段全文主題句「亞馬遜盆地涵蓋巴西、厄瓜多爾與秘魯的極大部分,壯觀的馬努野生動物保護區就藏在叢林深處」,點出馬努保護區這個主題。第二段段落主題句介紹園區的創造歷史,第三段介紹園區的管理。涵蓋三段的共同主題是「園區的創造」,故選 (C)。

② 根據本文,馬努保護區

    (A) 屬於國際自然公園的一部分

    (B) 土地逐漸喪失於附近開發商之手

    (C) 乾季有可以通行的道路連接

    (D) 一年中只有部分時段可以乘船抵達

【答案】**D**

【解析】這是問細節的題型,要找同義表達。第一段說「馬努保護區通常只有乘船才可以通,而且還得是乾季」,其中 Normally accessible only by boat, and then only in the dry season 是 only accessible by boat for part of the year 的同義表達,故選 (D)。

③ 第一段中的 relentless 一字意思最接近

    (A) 不自然的   (B) 不停的

    (C) 違法的   (D) 不斷增加的

【答案】**B**

【解析】這是單字題。relentless（構造：back/slow/without）的意思是「不放鬆的，不留情的」，暗示「不停的」，同義字是 ceaseless。

④ 由文中可以推論，秘魯政府

    (A) 終於向商業說客屈服

    (B) 花了好幾年嘗試建立馬努保護區

    (C) 把大部分原住民遷到鄰近地區

    (D) 從美國幾個州請來專家

【答案】**B**

【解析】這是推論題，要找「根據」。第二段說秘魯政府在 1972 年首度嘗試在馬努地區建立園區，直到 1978 年才成功，中間經過了 6 年，故選 (B)。

⑤ 第二段中的 postpone 一字意思最接近

    (A) 放棄   (B) 重新思考

    (C) 廣告   (D) 延後

【答案】**D**

【解析】這是單字題。postpone（構造：after/place）的意思是「延期」，同義字是 put off。

⑥ 第三段的片語 incredible array 意思最接近

    (A) 種類多到令人難以置信

    (B) 令人難以置信的色彩

    (C) 瀕臨危險的團體

    (D) 越來越多的數目

【答案】**A**

【解析】這是單字題。incredible（構造：not/believe/able）的意思是「令人難以置信」。array 的意思是「排列」，整個片語意為「一大排，多到令人難以置信」，亦即「種類繁多」。選項 (A) 中的 variety 意思是「種類，變化」。

⑦ 根據本文，馬努保護區中大部分的原住民
  (A) 受聘於營造公司
  (B) 是田野研究員的助手
  (C) 為觀光客提供導遊服務
  (D) 採集與狩獵自己的食物

【答案】**D**
【解析】這是問細節的題型，要找同義表達。第二段說「原住民的謀生方式是打獵、捕魚與採集」，其中 makes its living largely by hunting, fishing, and gathering 就是 collect and hunt their own food 的同義表達，故選 (D)。

⑧ 作者有為下列哪一個詞彙提供了定義？
  (A) 野生生物保護區
  (B) 無與倫比的
  (C) 鳥類學家
  (D) 綠色

【答案】**D**
【解析】這是問細節的題型。第三段說「人數嚴格管制的綠色（亦即環保）觀光客」，其中作者用 environmentally friendly 來說明 green。

⑨ 可以推論，限制入園人數的目的是什麼？
  (A) 減少人類帶來的干擾
  (B) 防止訪客妨礙科學家的研究
  (C) 維持訪客與原住民之間的和平
  (D) 收取較高的入園費

【答案】**A**
【解析】這是推論題，要找「根據」。第三段說到「人數嚴格管制的綠色（亦即環保）觀光客。所有訪客都住在散落在園區各地的幾處小營區內，他們必須遵守嚴格的指導方針，目的在於盡量降低人類居住帶來的衝擊」，其中 minimizing the impact of human habitation 與 Reduce the disruption brought by people 意思相同，故選 (A)。

6

Reading 6

 W Through various methods of research, anthropologists try to fit together the pieces of the human puzzle—to discover how humanity was first achieved, what made it branch out in different directions, and why separate societies behave similarly in some ways but quite differently in other ways. **X** Anthropology, which **emerged** as an independent science in the late eighteenth century, has two main divisions: physical anthropology and cultural anthropology. **Y** Physical anthropology focuses on human evolution and variation and uses methods of physiology, genetics, and ecology. Cultural anthropology focuses on culture and includes archaeology, social anthropology, and linguistics. **Z**

 Physical anthropologists are most concerned with human biology. Physical anthropologists are detectives whose mission is to solve the mystery of how humans came to be human. **They ask questions about the events that led a tree-dwelling population of animals to evolve into two-legged beings with the power to learn—a power that we call intelligence.** Physical anthropologists study the fossils and organic remains of once-living primates. They also study the connections between humans and other primates that are still living. Monkeys, apes, and humans have more in common with one another physically than they do with other kinds of animals. In the lab, anthropologists use the methods of physiology and genetics to investigate the composition of blood chemistry for clues to the relationship of humans to various primates. Some study the animals in the wild to find out what behaviors they share with humans. Others **speculate** about how the behavior of non-human primates might have shaped human bodily needs and habits.

 A well-known family of physical anthropologists, the Leakeys, conducted research in East Africa indicating that human evolution centered there rather than in Asia. In 1931, Louis Leakey and his wife Mary began excavating at Olduvai Gorge in Tanzania, where over the next 40 years they discovered stone tools and hominid evidence that pushed back the dates for early humans to over 3.75 million years ago. Their son, Richard Leakey, discovered yet other types of hominid skulls in Kenya, which he wrote about in *Origins* (1979) and *Origins Reconsidered* (1992).

Like physical anthropologists, cultural anthropologists study clues about human life in the distant past; however, cultural anthropologists also look at the similarities and differences among human communities today. Some cultural anthropologists work in the field, living and working among people in societies that differ from their own. Anthropologists doing fieldwork often produce an ethnography, a written description of the daily activities of men, women, and children that tells the story of the society's community life as a whole. Some cultural anthropologists work not in the field but rather at research universities and museums doing the comparative and interpretive part of the job. These anthropologists, called ethnologists, **sift through** the ethnographies written by field anthropologists and try to discover cross-cultural patterns in marriage, child rearing, religious beliefs and practices, warfare— any subject that constitutes the human experience. They often use their findings to argue for or against particular hypotheses about people worldwide.

A cultural anthropologist who achieved worldwide fame was Margaret Mead. In 1923, Mead went to Samoa to pursue her first fieldwork assignment—a study that resulted in her widely-read book *Coming of Age in Samoa* (1928). Mead published 10 major works during her long career, moving from studies of child rearing in the Pacific to the cultural and biological bases of gender, the nature of cultural change, the structure and functioning of complex societies, and race relations. Mead was a pioneer in her willingness to tackle subjects of major intellectual consequence, to develop new technologies for research, and to think of new ways that anthropology could serve society.

Today ethnography continues to dominate cultural anthropology. Nevertheless, many **contemporary** cultural anthropologists have rejected earlier models of ethnography which they claim treated local cultures as bounded and isolated. These anthropologists continue to concern themselves with the distinct ways people in different locales experience and understand their lives, but they often argue that one cannot understand these particular ways of life solely in the local context; one must analyze them in the context of regional or even global political and economic relations. Notable proponents of this approach include Arjun Appadurai, James Clifford, George Marcus, Sidney Mintz, Michael Taussig and Eric Wolf.

✎ Exercise

① The word "emerged" in paragraph 1 is closest in meaning to
    (A) appeared   (B) excelled
    (C) disguised   (D) matured

② In which position would the following boldfaced sentence best fit in paragraph 1?
Anthropology is the study of the origin, development, and varieties of human beings and their societies.
    (A) Position W   (B) Position X
    (C) Position Y   (D) Position Z

③ Which of the sentences below best expresses the essential information in the boldfaced sentence in paragraph 2?
They ask questions about the events that led a tree-dwelling population of animals to evolve into two-legged beings with the power to learn—a power that we call intelligence.
    (A) People want to know more about the behavior of animals and how some animals acquire the ability to learn.
    (B) Physical anthropologists investigate how intelligent human beings evolved from creatures that lived in trees.
    (C) There are unanswered questions about why some tree-dwelling animals have evolved only two legs.
    (D) Some animal populations have the power to ask questions and to learn from the events of the past.

④ The word "speculate" in paragraph 2 is closest in meaning to
    (A) worry   (B) forget
    (C) disagree   (D) think

⑤ Why does the author discuss the Leakey family in paragraph 3?
    (A) To argue for an increase in the amount of research in Africa
    (B) To contradict earlier theories of human evolution
    (C) To give examples of fieldwork done by physical anthropologists
    (D) To compare hominid evidence from Tanzania with that from Kenya

⑥ According to the passage, which of the following is of major interest to both physical and cultural anthropologists?
(A) Methods of physiology and genetics
(B) Religious beliefs and practices
(C) Child rearing in societies around the world
(D) Evidence about human beings who lived long ago

⑦ According to paragraph 4, cultural anthropologists who do fieldwork usually
(A) discover hominid evidence indicating when humans evolved
(B) write an account of the daily life of the people they study
(C) work at universities and museums interpreting the work of others
(D) develop new technologies for gathering cultural data

⑧ The phrase "sift through" in paragraph 4 is closest in meaning to
(A) avoid   (B) sort
(C) discuss   (D) contradict

⑨ According to the passage, Margaret Mead wrote about all of the following subjects EXCEPT
(A) the nature of cultural change
(B) relations between people of different races
(C) the biological bases of gender
(D) economic systems of pioneer women

⑩ It can be inferred from paragraph 5 that Margaret Mead's work
(A) made an impact on the field of anthropology
(B) contradicted that of the Leakey family
(C) opened Samoa to outside influences
(D) is not widely read by anthropologists today

⑪ The word "contemporary" in paragraph 6 is closest in meaning to
(A) important   (B) modern
(C) competing   (D) conservative

⊡ 題解

W 利用各種研究方法，人類學家設法拼湊出人類的謎團——要了解人性是如何達成的、為何朝不同方向分岔、以及為何不同的社會在有些方面的行為相似但別的方面卻大不相同。X 人類學在 18 世紀晚期作為一門獨立的科學出現，分為兩大枝：體質人類學與文化人類學。Y 體質人類學的研究重點在於人類演進與變化，採用的方法包括生理學、遺傳學、生態學。文化人類學的重點在於文化，包括考古學、社會人類學、語言學。Z

體質人類學家主要關切的是人類生物學。體質人類學家可以說是偵探，他的任務是要解開人之所以成為人的奧祕。他們研究的問題是：哪些事件導致一個樹居的動物族群演化為兩條腿的生物、擁有學習能力——這種能力我們稱為智能。體質人類學家研究從前存活過的靈長類的化石以及有機殘留。他們也研究人類與其他仍然存活的靈長類之間的關聯性。猴、猿、與人類在體質方面的共同點，超過他們與其他動物的共同點。在實驗室中，人類學家採用生理學與遺傳學的方法來研究血液化學成分，尋找線索，了解人類與各種靈長類之間的關係。有些人研究野生動物以了解牠和人類有何共同行為。還有些人在揣測：人類之外的靈長類的行為當初如何塑造出人類的身體需要與習慣。

體質人類學界有一個著名的家族是李奇家族，他們在東非洲進行研究，結果顯示人類的進化以東非為中心而不是在亞洲。1931 年，路易斯‧李奇與夫人瑪麗開始在坦尚尼亞的奧杜威峽谷進行挖掘，接下來的 40 年間他們發現石製工具與人科動物的證據，將早期人類的時代往回推到 375 多萬年前。他們的兒子理查‧李奇在肯亞又發現別種人科動物的頭骨，寫了兩本書來介紹：《起源》(1979) 與《起源再探》(1992)。

和體質人類學家一樣，文化人類學家也研究遙遠過去的早期人類生活的線索。但是文化人類學家還研究今日各種人類社會之間的異同。有些文化人類學家做田野工作，到與自己的社會不同的地方、和當地人共同生活與工作。做田野工作的人類學家經常產生出人種誌，那是用文字描述男、女、小孩的日常活動，介紹出整個社會集體生活的故事。也有一些文化人類學家不是做田野工作而是在研究大學與博物館，進行比較與詮釋的工作。這些人類學家稱為人種學者，篩檢田野人類學家撰寫的人種誌，尋找一些跨越不同文化的模式，包括婚姻、育兒、宗教信仰與做法、戰爭——任何構成人類經驗的主題。他們經常用他們的發現來辯護或反駁關於世界各地人民的一些假說。

有一位聞名世界的文化人類學家是瑪格麗特‧米德。1923 年，米德到三毛亞群島進行她頭一樁田野任務——這項研究產生了她那本擁有廣大讀者的《三毛亞成年祭》(1928)。米德在漫長的職業生涯中出版了 10 部主要的作品，主題包括太平洋地區育兒研究、性別的文化與生物基礎、文化變化的本質、複雜社會的結構與運作、以及種族關係。米德是個拓荒者，因為她願意處理會造成重大影響的知識議題、開發做研究的新技術、以及思考人類學可以為社會服務的新方式。

今天，人種誌仍然是文化人類學的主流。不過，許多當代文化人類學家排斥早期人種誌的模式，他們認為那種模式把地方文化視為孤立與受到限制。這些人類學家持續關切不同地方的人民經歷與理解生活的不同方式，但他們主張：不能只是從地方的角度來了解這些生活方式，而是要放到更大的區域性、甚至全球性的政治經濟關係網裡面來分析。這種作法的重要提倡者包括阿帕杜萊、克利弗、馬可士、敏茲、陶錫、與沃爾夫。

練習題翻譯與詳解

① 第一段中的 emerged 一字意思最接近
　　(A) 出現　　　　　　　　　　　(B) 勝出
　　(C) 偽裝　　　　　　　　　　　(D) 成熟

【答案】**A**
【解析】這是單字題，動詞 emerge 的意思是「浮現、出現」，同義字是 appear。

② 下面這個黑體字句子最適合放在第一段的什麼位置？
　　「人類學研究的對象是人類與人類社會的起源、發展、與種類。」
　　(A) W 位置　　　　　　　　　　(B) X 位置
　　(C) Y 位置　　　　　　　　　　(D) Z 位置

【答案】**A**
【解析】這是安插句子的題型，要看上下文。插入句內容是人類學的定義。談任何主題，第一步是先下定義，界定清楚之後才能夠接下來發展。W 位置後面已經開始發展「人類學家做什麼事」，在此之前要先定義人類學，所以插入句要放在 W 位置，成為<u>人類學研究的對象是人類與人類社會的起源、發展、與種類。</u>利用各種研究方法，人類學家設法拼湊出人類的謎團……」。

③ 下列哪個句子最能夠表達第二段黑體字句子的主要內容？
　　「他們研究的問題是：哪些事件導致一個樹居的動物族群演化為兩條腿的生物、擁有學習能力──這種能力我們稱為智能。」
　　(A) 人們想要多了解動物行為、以及某些動物如何取得學習能力。
　　(B) 體質人類學家研究有智力的人類如何從樹居生物演化出來。
　　(C) 一些樹居動物為何只演化出兩條腿，這方面仍有問題無法解答。
　　(D) 有些動物族群有能力問問題並且從過去的事件中學習。

【答案】**B**
【解析】這是句子改寫的題型，要找句中重點的同義表達。原句中 they 的先行詞是體質人類學家，內容與 (B) 最接近。

④ 第二段中的 speculate 一字意思最接近

(A) 擔心　　　　　　　　　　　(B) 忘記

(C) 不同意　　　　　　　　　　(D) 思考

⑤ 作者在第三段為何談到李奇家族？

(A) 主張要加強在非洲研究

(B) 反駁關於人類演化的早期理論

(C) 舉出體質人類學家田野工作的例子

(D) 比較坦桑尼亞與肯亞的人科動物的證據

⑥ 根據本文，下列哪一項是體質人類學家與文化人類學家共同關注的？

(A) 生理學與遺傳學方法　　　　(B) 宗教信仰與做法

(C) 世界各地不同社會的育兒　　(D) 古代人類的證據

⑦ 根據第四段，做田野工作的文化人類學家通常

(A) 發現人科動物的證據，顯示人類在何時演化出來

(B) 記錄研究對象的日常生活

(C) 在大學與博物館詮釋別人的研究

(D) 開發新技術來採集文化資料

⑧ 第四段中的片語 sift through 意思最接近

(A) 避免　　　　　　　　　　　　(B) 分類

(C) 討論　　　　　　　　　　　　(D) 牴觸，反駁

【答案】 B

【解析】這是單字題，動詞 sift 的意思是「篩檢」，最接近 sort「分類」。

⑨ 根據本文，瑪格麗特‧米德寫過下列所有的主題，除了

(A) 文化變化的本質　　　　　　　(B) 不同種族人民的關係

(C) 性別的生物基礎　　　　　　　(D) 拓荒時代婦女的經濟制度

【答案】 D

【解析】這是採消去法、問細節的題型，要刪去三項同義表達。第五段提到米德寫過的主題不包括 (D)。

⑩ 根據第五段可推論，瑪格麗特‧米德的工作

(A) 對人類學領域造成衝擊

(B) 牴觸李奇家族的研究

(C) 打開三毛亞受到外界影響

(D) 今日人類學家已很少閱讀

【答案】 A

【解析】這是推論題，要找「根據」。第五段說米德世界聞名、讀者廣大、職業生涯漫長、著作豐富、又是拓荒者，這些都暗示她的影響深遠。

⑪ 第六段中的 contemporary 意思最接近

(A) 重要的　　　　　　　　　　　(B) 現代的

(C) 競爭的　　　　　　　　　　　(D) 保守的

【答案】 B

【解析】這是單字題。contemporary（構造：together/time($a.$)）的意思是「同時代的，現代的」，同義字是 modern。

NOTES

閱讀測驗篇

第 7 章

Henry Wadsworth Longfellow, born in Portland, Maine, was one of the most popular U.S. poets of the nineteenth century. He attended Bowdoin College, where he graduated with Nathaniel Hawthorne in 1825, and later taught at Bowdoin as well as at Harvard. He also traveled extensively in Europe; visiting the continent for three years in the late 1820s and for a single year in 1835. His father wanted Longfellow to enter into his law practice, but the future poet was **decidedly** against it, proclaiming "I most eagerly aspire future eminence in literature."

Longfellow's first book, vignettes of life in France, Spain and Italy, was an abject failure. His travel pieces lacked the humor and liveliness of say, Washington Irving's *Sketch Book*. **Undaunted**, in 1839 he published a volume entitled *Voices of the Night*. This included both "The Psalm of Life" and "The Light of the Stars," poems that became immediately popular. The same year he brought out *Hyperion*, a romantic novel based on his European travels.

In 1855 he published the epic poem *The Song of Hiawatha*, which was based on Henry Schoolcraft's scholarly work on Native North American tribes. The poem was another immediate success. Longfellow's **intended masterpiece**, *Christus, a Mystery*, a trilogy of dramatic poems dealing with the subject of Christianity from its very beginning, was published in 1872 and was disappointing, both to readers and to the poet himself. Longfellow's true genius was simply not in drama, but in lyrical poetry.

Exercise

① What is the main idea of the passage?

    (A) A brief description of Longfellow's best work

    (B) Strong foreign influences on an American poet

    (C) Longfellow's career as a poet

    (D) A comparison of Irving, Schoolcraft and Longfellow

② According to the passage, Longfellow was

    (A) an unhappy law student

    (B) Hawthorne's teacher

    (C) a Harvard professor

    (D) an uninspired poet

③ The passage says Longfellow spent time in all of the following places EXCEPT

    (A) Maine

    (B) France

    (C) Spain

    (D) Germany

④ The word "decidedly" in the first paragraph is closest in meaning to

    (A) firmly

    (B) probably

    (C) silently

    (D) violently

⑤ It can be inferred from the passage that Longfellow's

    (A) father was also a well-respected writer

    (B) *Sketch Book* was a national bestseller

    (C) first book was published before 1839

    (D) *Hyperion* featured fictional material only

⑥ The word "Undaunted" in the second paragraph most nearly means
(A) Not deterred
(B) Uninformed
(C) Not learning
(D) Uninspired

⑦ It can be inferred from the second paragraph that
(A) *Voices of the Night* was more popular than *Hyperion*
(B) Irving's poetry was superior to Longfellow's
(C) *Voices of the Night* contained poetry selections
(D) "The Light of the Stars" outsold "The Psalm of Life"

⑧ What does the author imply when he refers to *Christus, a Mystery* as Longfellow's "intended masterpiece"?
(A) The work was longer than any other of Longfellow's works
(B) Longfellow intended to announce his Christian beliefs
(C) Longfellow believed he excelled in romantic novels
(D) Longfellow's intentions were never realized

⑨ What would the author of the passage be most likely to believe about Longfellow?
(A) His reputation exceeded his true ability
(B) Some of his works were very widely read
(C) Other poets are more worthy of scholarly study
(D) Longfellow had a very unexpressive personality

題解

文章翻譯

　　亨利‧沃茲沃思‧朗費羅出生在緬因州波特蘭市，是 19 世紀美國人氣最旺的詩人之一。他就讀波多恩大學，在 1825 年與納撒尼爾‧霍桑一同畢業，後來在波多恩與哈佛兩處任教。他也曾在歐洲廣泛遊歷，於 1820 年代晚期在歐洲停留 3 年、1835 也去了 1 年。他父親希望他投入自己的律師事務所，但這位未來的詩人堅決反對，宣稱「我急切渴望將來在文壇揚名」。

　　朗費羅的頭一本書是旅居法國、西班牙與義大利的生活速寫，失敗得很慘。他的遊記裡欠缺例如華盛頓‧歐文《素描簿》裡的那種幽默與生動感。但他並不氣餒，1839 年出了一本《暗夜人語》。這本詩集裡面收有「人生禮讚」與「星光」這兩首立即轟傳的詩作。同年他又推出了《海伯利安》，這部浪漫小說以他的歐洲旅遊為根據。

　　1855 年他出版了史詩《海華沙之歌》，以亨利‧史庫克拉特研究北美原住民部落的學術著作為藍本。這首詩也是一炮而紅。朗費羅心目中的大作《基督：神祕故事》是戲劇詩歌串成的三部曲，主題是基督教，由誕生開始。這本書在 1872 年出版，結果令人失望（讀者與詩人同樣失望）。朗費羅的真正天才不在於戲劇，而是抒情詩。

練習題翻譯與詳解

① 本文的主題是什麼？
   (A) 簡介朗費羅的一部最佳作品
   (B) 一位美國詩人受到的強烈外國影響
   (C) 朗費羅的詩人生涯
   (D) 比較歐文、史庫克拉特、朗費羅

【答案】**C**
【解析】這是問主題的題型，要找出主題句。第一段全文主題句說「朗費羅……是 19 世紀美國人氣最旺的詩人之一」。第二段從他寫的頭一本書開始介紹他的詩歌創作，第三段按照時間順序繼續介紹他的詩歌創作，共同的主題就是朗費羅的詩人生涯，故選 (C)。

② 根據本文，朗費羅是
   (A) 不快樂的法律系學生　　　　　(B) 霍桑的老師
   (C) 哈佛教授　　　　　　　　　　(D) 沒有靈感的詩人

【答案】**C**
【解析】這是問細節的題型，要找同義表達。第一段說朗費羅「在 1825 年與霍桑一同畢業，後來在波多恩與哈佛兩處任教」，其中 taught at Bowdoin as well as at Harvard 是 was a Harvard professor 的同義表達，故選 (C)。

③ 本文說到朗費羅停留過的地方不包括

(A) 緬因州　　　　　　　　　(B) 法國

(C) 西班牙　　　　　　　　　(D) 德國

【答案】 **D**

【解析】這是問細節、採用消去法的題型，要找出三個同義表達消去。第一段說他出生在緬因州，第二段說「朗費羅的頭一本書是旅居法國、西班牙與義大利的生活速寫」，四個選項當中唯獨沒有提到德國。

④ 第一段中的 decidedly 一字意思最接近

(A) 堅定地　　　　　　　　　(B) 可能地

(C) 默默地　　　　　　　　　(D) 暴力地

【答案】 **A**

【解析】這是單字題。動詞 decide（構造：away/cut）的意思是「決定」，decidedly 是「很肯定」，同義字是 firmly。

⑤ 由文中可以推論，朗費羅的

(A) 父親也是受人尊敬的作家

(B)《素描簿》是全國暢銷書

(C) 頭一本書出版在 1839 以前

(D)《海伯利安》裡面全都是虛構材料

【答案】 **C**

【解析】這是推論題，要找「根據」。第二段說他的頭一本書失敗得慘，「但他並不怕，1839 年出了一本《暗夜人語》」，所以頭一本書應該在 1839 之前出版。

⑥ 第二段中的 Undaunted 一字意思最接近

(A) 不被嚇阻　　　　　　　　(B) 沒有資訊

(C) 沒有學習　　　　　　　　(D) 沒有靈感

【答案】 **A**

【解析】這是單字題，動詞 daunt 的意思是「嚇怕」，搭配否定字首 un- 成為過去分詞 undaunted，意思是「沒有被嚇怕」，同義字是 undeterred（構造：not/away/terror/(a.)）。

⑦ 從第二段可以推論
 (A)《暗夜人語》的人氣超過《海伯利安》
 (B) 歐文的詩歌勝過朗費羅
 (C)《暗夜人語》裡面有詩選
 (D)「星光」銷售超過「人生禮讚」

【答案】C
【解析】這是推論題，要找「根據」。第二段提到《暗夜人語》，說到「這本詩集裡面收有
『人生禮讚』與『星光』這兩首立即轟傳的詩作」，所以「《暗夜人語》是詩選。

⑧ 作者說《基督：神祕故事》是朗費羅的 intended masterpiece，這是在暗示什麼？
 (A) 這部作品比朗費羅其他的作品都更長
 (B) 朗費羅打算宣告他的基督教信仰
 (C) 朗費羅相信自己擅長浪漫小說
 (D) 朗費羅的用意並未實現

【答案】D
【解析】這是推論題，要找「根據」。第三段說「朗費羅心目中的大作《基督：神祕故事》
……這本書在 1872 年出版，結果令人失望」，從下文的結果可以看出朗費羅心目中的想
法並未實現。

⑨ 作者會相信下列哪種關於朗費羅的說法？
 (A) 他的名聲超過真實的能力
 (B) 他有些作品讀者眾多
 (C) 別的詩人比較值得學者來研究
 (D) 朗費羅的個性相當拙於表達

【答案】B
【解析】這是推論題，要找「根據」。第二段說「詩集裡面收有『人生禮讚』與『星光』這
兩首立即轟傳的詩作。第三段說「史詩《海華沙之歌》……也是一炮而紅」，這幾部作品
都是讀者眾多，故選 (B)。

Weaving is among the oldest of humanity's industrial arts, and, with its sister art of spinning, it launched the Industrial Revolution. There is solid evidence that humans were practicing the art of weaving in the 5th century B.C.E., and that techniques were already fairly **sophisticated** then. It was in the late 18th century that the art of weaving became an industry in the modern sense. The factory system as we now know it was born in the textile industry. With the advent of the factory system, the textiles that could be produced increased vastly, and the increase has continued as the machinery has become more versatile and faster. Meanwhile, hand weaving also continues as a hobby that is currently pursued by thousands of persons for pleasure, as a folk art (as by the Navaho Native Americans), or as a cottage industry (as in Tibet or Turkey).

Weaving is the process of combining horizontal and longitudinal strands to make cloth. The two components—horizontal and longitudinal—need not always cross each other at right angles. Most kinds of cloth, however, do comprise two sets of strands crossing at right angles.

Weaving has a very wide application because it is cheap, **basically** simple, and adaptable. Woven materials are held together not by rigid bonding but by the friction that occurs where the horizontal and longitudinal components **make contact**, a unique feature that makes them softer and more elastic than most other materials, therefore more suitable for clothing, draperies and bedding.

Weaving differs from knitting, braiding, and netmaking in that the latter three make use of only one set of elements. Another difference has to do with geometric structure. Woven cloth is typically smooth and flat, because the strands are bent in a much smaller angle than, say, the yarn is in knitting.

Exercise

① What does the passage primarily discuss?
   (A) Different types of knitting
   (B) The origins of the textile industry
   (C) Various aspects of weaving
   (D) Clothing throughout history

② According to the passage, which of the following is NOT true about the history of weaving?
   (A) Weaving was being done in the 5th century B.C.E.
   (B) Cloth was first woven in the 18th century
   (C) The factory system increased textile production
   (D) Hand weaving is still practiced today

③ In the first paragraph the word "sophisticated" is closest in meaning to
   (A) highly developed
   (B) well known
   (C) mechanized
   (D) ancient

④ Which of the following can be inferred about hand weaving?
   (A) It requires thousands of people working together
   (B) It is only practiced in the U.S.
   (C) It does not use advanced machinery
   (D) It is found primarily in museums

⑤ According to the passage, what is true about most woven structures?
   (A) Their components cross at right angles
   (B) They are inflexible
   (C) They feature only horizontal components
   (D) They are longer than they are wide

⑥ In the third paragraph the word "basically" most nearly means which of the following?

(A) hardly

(B) practically

(C) usually

(D) fundamentally

⑦ It can be inferred from the passage that the components of some kinds of non-woven materials are

(A) always made up of geometrical designs

(B) held in position by rigid bonding

(C) constructed of semi-precious material

(D) too small to be used by industry

⑧ In the third paragraph the phrase "make contact" is closest in meaning to

(A) originate

(B) disappear

(C) touch

(D) contract

⑨ It can be inferred that weaving differs from braiding in which of the following ways?

(A) Braiding is part of knitting

(B) Braiding uses smaller angles

(C) Weaving uses two elements

(D) Weaving components are never bent

⤵ 題解

文章翻譯

　　織布是人類最古老的工業藝術之一，與它的姐妹藝術——紡紗——共同發起了工業革命。有扎實的證據可以證明人類在公元前第 5 世紀就已經在織布了，而且當時採用的技術也相當複雜。不過要到 18 世紀晚期，織布藝術才成為現代人所謂的工業。我們所知道的工廠制就是誕生在紡織工業。隨著工廠制的到來，紡織品的產量大增。機器的功能越來越多、速度也不斷加快，所以產量的增加一直持續不斷。同時，手工織布也持續下來，成為現今數以千計的人追求的嗜好、或者是民俗藝術（例如納瓦荷美洲原住民的作法）、或者是家庭工業（例如在西藏或土耳其）。

　　織布的過程是把水平與垂直兩種線縷結合為布匹。兩項成分——水平與垂直——不一定得垂直相交。不過，大部分的布匹都含有兩套垂直相交的線縷。

　　織布應用廣泛，因為成本低、基本上很容易、而且適應力強。織出來的布料不是用硬邦邦的方式結合固定的，而是靠水平與垂直兩種成分接觸的地方產生的摩擦力接合，這是布匹獨一無二的特色，使它柔軟、有彈性，超過大多數的材料，因而也更適合做衣服、幔帳、床單。

　　織布和編織、編結、製網都不同，因為後三者都只用到一套元素。另一項差別和幾何結構有關。織出來的布匹通常都很光滑平整，因為線縷彎曲的角度遠不及例如編織毛線時的彎曲角度。

練習題翻譯與詳解

① 本文的主題是什麼？
　(A) 不同種類的編織
　(B) 紡織工業的起源
　(C) 織布面面觀
　(D) 歷史上的衣物

【答案】**C**
【解析】這是問主題的題型，要找出主題句。第一段全文主題句說「織布是人類最古老的工業藝術之一」，點出織布為主題。後面的段落分別說到織布的過程、應用、與特色，共同的主題是織布，故選 (C)。

② 根據本文，下面哪一項關於織布歷史的敘述是錯的？
　(A) 織布在公元前第 5 世紀就有人在做了
　(B) 布在 18 世紀最早織出來
　(C) 工廠制增加了紡織品產量
　(D) 手工織布今天還有人在做

【答案】B
【解析】這是問細節、採用消去法的題型，要找出三個同義表達刪去。第一段說「人類在公元前第 5 世紀就已經在織布了」，所以 (B) 是錯誤的。

③ 第一段中的 sophisticated 一字意思最接近
   (A) 高度發展　　　　　　　　(B) 眾所周知
   (C) 機械化　　　　　　　　　(D) 古老

【答案】A
【解析】這是單字題。sophisticated（構造：wise/(a.)）的意思是「複雜的，有智慧的」，最接近 highly developed。

④ 關於手工織布可以推論出什麼？
   (A) 它需要幾千人合作
   (B) 只有在美國有人做
   (C) 它不使用先進的機器
   (D) 它主要存在於博物館中

【答案】C
【解析】這是推論的題型，要找「根據」。第一段說「機器的功能越來越多、速度也不斷加快，所以產量的增加一直持續不斷。同時，手工織布也持續下來」，由此可以看出手工織布不需要機器。

⑤ 根據本文，織出來的構造大部分都是怎樣的？
   (A) 它的成分以直角相交
   (B) 它沒有彈性
   (C) 它只有水平成分
   (D) 它的長大於寬

【答案】A
【解析】這是問細節的題型，要找同義表達。第二段說「大部分的布匹都含有兩套垂直相交的線縷」，其中 comprise two sets of strands crossing at right angles 是 Their components cross at right angles 的同義表達，故選 (A)。

⑥ 第三段中的 basically 一字意思最接近
   (A) 很少　　　　　　　　　　(B) 幾乎
   (C) 通常　　　　　　　　　　(D) 基本上

【答案】**D**
【解析】這是單字題，basically「基本上」的同義字是 fundamentally。

⑦ 可以推論，有一些非織造材料，它的成分是
    (A) 永遠由幾何圖案構成
    (B) 用硬梆梆的結合固定
    (C) 由半珍貴的材料構成
    (D) 太小因而不被工業採用

【答案】**B**
【解析】這是推論題，要找「根據」。第三段說「織出來的布料不是用硬梆梆的方式結合固定的，而是靠水平與垂直兩種成分接觸的地方產生的磨擦力接合，這是布匹獨一無二的特色」，可以推知別的材料並不具有這種特色，故選 (B)。

⑧ 第三段中 make contact 這個片語的意思最接近
    (A) 發源   (B) 消失
    (C) 接觸   (D) 感染，收縮

【答案】**C**
【解析】這是單字題。名詞 contact（構造：together/touch）的意思是「接觸」。

⑨ 可以推論，織布和編結有何不同？
    (A) 編結是編織的一部分
    (B) 編結採用比較小的角度
    (C) 織布用到兩種元素
    (D) 織布的成分永不彎曲

【答案】**C**
【解析】這是推論的題型，要找「根據」。第四段說「織布和編織、編結、製網都不同，因為後三者只用到一套元素」。另外在第二段說到「織布的過程是把水平與垂直兩種線縷結合為布匹」，也就是織布有兩項成分。由這兩句話可以推知織布與編結的差別在於採用的元素數目不同。

Reading 3

The origination of slavery in the New World has been **exhaustively** studied and chronicled and can be outlined quite simply. Columbus did take several European-born black slaves with him to the New World. However, it appears that at first there was no **conscious** design to set up black slavery in the newly discovered territories. On the contrary, the Europeans at first attempted to use the Native American population for labor. Initially, only when the Natives were performing mining work did their condition approach the condition of chattel slavery. At other times, especially when used for agricultural exploitation, the Natives were treated in a manner more reminiscent of European serfdom.

However, difficulties with Native American labor quickly arose. The Natives sometimes rebelled, and frequently just disappeared into the surrounding forests. They also succumbed in large numbers to new diseases brought over from Europe. In addition, the powerful Roman Catholic church was engaged in the evangelization of the Native American population and it wanted the Natives treated gently. Consequently, at the urging of the renowned Bartolome de Las Casas, bishop of Chiapas, the Spanish king Ferdinand issued an edict stating that Native Americans could be forced to work, but only if they received **humane treatment** and fair wages.

A few years later, however, in 1520, the next Spanish king began allowing Spanish nobleman to import a specified number of Africans into the new Spanish colonies each year. These Africans were brought over for the sole purpose of serving as slaves. Soon thousands of African slaves were in the New World, not only in Hispaniola, where slavery was first permitted, but also in the other Caribbean islands and the North American mainland. The number of African slaves increased rapidly, due in part to the almost total extinction of many Native American tribes. This helped create an almost insatiable demand for cheap slave labor.

✎ Exercise

① What does the passage primarily discuss?
   (A) Native American life in the New World
   (B) The Spanish conquest of America
   (C) Slavery in the New World
   (D) The role of African Americans

② The word "exhaustively" in the first paragraph is closest in meaning to which of the following?
   (A) tirelessly
   (B) barely
   (C) exclusively
   (D) thoroughly

③ According to the author, which group was the first to be put to work for the European conquerors?
   (A) Africans
   (B) European serfs
   (C) Native Americans
   (D) Prisoners of war

④ In the first paragraph the word "conscious" most nearly means
   (A) mental
   (B) official
   (C) purposeful
   (D) evil

⑤ It can be inferred from the passage that all of the following about the Native Americans were true EXCEPT that the
   (A) caught dangerous diseases from the Europeans
   (B) disliked working for the Europeans
   (C) built large cities in remote areas
   (D) were sometimes forced to work in the mines

⑥ According to the passage, Bartolome de Las Casas

(A) influenced Spain's Native American policy

(B) eventually ruled all of Spain

(C) refused to pay his slaves any wages

(D) established the first Catholic church in Spain

⑦ In the second paragraph the phrase "humane treatment" is closest in meaning to

(A) medical treatment

(B) family members

(C) decent treatment

(D) educational opportunities

⑧ It can be inferred that black slaves could be found in large numbers in the New World before 1520 in which of the following places?

(A) only in Hispaniola

(B) throughout the Caribbean

(C) in mainland North America

(D) nowhere

⑨ A paragraph following this passage would be most likely to discuss which of the following?

(A) Agriculture in the New World

(B) Slavery in mediaeval Europe

(C) New World slavery in the 17th century

(D) Nineteenth century Native American revolts

「文章翻譯」

　　新世界奴隸制度的起源有人徹底研究與記錄過，可以很簡單列出大要如下。哥倫布是有帶著幾個歐洲出生的黑奴一同到新世界。不過看起來最早並沒有刻意設計要在新發現的地區設立黑奴制度。相反的，歐洲人一開始是嘗試使用美洲原住民人口當勞力。起初，原住民只有在挖礦的時候，工作條件才接近動產奴隸制。別的時間，尤其是用來開發農業時，原住民的待遇比較像是歐洲的農奴制。

　　不過，與美洲原住民勞工之間很快產生了問題。原住民有時會反叛，而且經常消失在周遭的森林中。他們還因為歐洲帶來的新疾病而大量死亡。此外，強大的羅馬天主教會正在向美洲原住民人口宣講福音、希望對原住民的待遇不要太苛。因此，在著名的恰帕斯州巴托洛梅主教的敦促下，西班牙國王斐迪南發佈命令，表示可以逼迫美洲原住民工作，但必須給他們人道待遇以及公平的工資。

　　但是過了幾年來到 1520，下一任西班牙國王開始容許西班牙貴族每年進口指定數目的非洲人到新開發的西班牙殖民地。這些非洲人被帶過來就專為充當奴隸之用。很快就有數以千計的非洲奴隸在新世界，不只在最早准許奴隸制度的伊斯帕尼奧拉島，也在加勒比海的其他島嶼以及北美大陸。非洲奴隸的數目增加得很快，部分原因在於許多北美原住民部落幾乎完全滅絕。這造成對廉價奴隸勞工幾乎無法滿足的需求。

「練習題翻譯與詳解」

① 本文的主題是什麼？

　　(A) 新世界美洲原住民的生活　　　　(B) 西班牙征服美洲

　　(C) 新世界的奴隸制度　　　　　　　(D) 非裔美人的角色

【答案】**C**

【解析】這是問主題的題型，要找主題句。第一段全文主題句「新世界奴隸制度的起源有人徹底研究與記錄過，可以很簡單列出大要如下」明確指出「新世界奴隸制度」這個主題。第二段與第三段按照時間順序說明新世界奴隸制度的發展，共同主題就是新世界奴隸制度，故選 (C)。

② 第一段中的 exhaustively 一字意思最接近

　　(A) 不知疲倦地　　　　　　　　　　(B) 勉強

　　(C) 排他地，獨家地　　　　　　　　(D) 徹底地

【答案】**D**

【解析】這是單字題。動詞 exhaust 是指「耗盡，用光」，exhaustively 的意思是「徹底」，同義字是 thoroughly。

③ 根據作者,哪一群人最早被派去為歐洲征服者工作?

　　(A) 非洲人　　　　　　　　　　(B) 歐洲農奴

　　(C) 美洲原住民　　　　　　　　(D) 戰俘

【答案】 C

【解析】這是問細節的題型,要找同義表達。第一段說「歐洲人一開始是嘗試使用美洲原住民人口當勞力」,故選 (C)。

④ 第一段中的 conscious 一字意思最接近

　　(A) 心理的　　　　　　　　　　(B) 官方的

　　(C) 故意的　　　　　　　　　　(D) 邪惡的

【答案】 C

【解析】這是單字題。conscious(構造:together/know/(a.))的意思是「有意識的」,引申為「有意的」,同義字是 purposeful。

⑤ 從本文可以推論,關於美洲原住民的話哪一句是錯的?

　　(A) 他們從歐洲人身上傳染到危險疾病

　　(B) 他們不喜歡為歐洲人工作

　　(C) 他們在偏遠地區建造大型城市

　　(D) 他們有時被迫到礦區工作

【答案】 C

【解析】這是採用消去法的推論題型,要刪去三個正確的推論。只有選項 (C)「建造大型城市」完全是無中生有,故為正解。

⑥ 根據本文,巴托洛梅

　　(A) 影響到西班牙的美洲原住民政策

　　(B) 最後統治整個西班牙

　　(C) 拒絕付工資給他的奴隸

　　(D) 建立西班牙第一個天主教會

【答案】 A

【解析】這是問細節的題型,要找同義表達。第二段說「在著名的恰帕斯州巴托洛梅主教的教促下,西班牙國王斐迪南發佈命令,表示可以逼迫美洲原住民工作,但必須給他們人道待遇以及公平的工資」,這就是巴托洛梅對西班牙政策的影響。

⑦ 第二段中 humane treatment 這個片語的意思最接近
   (A) 醫療　　　　　　　　　　　　　(B) 家庭成員
   (C) 良好的對待　　　　　　　　　　(D) 教育機會

【答案】**C**
【解析】這是單字題。humane 的意思是「人道的，博愛的」，意思接近 decent「正直的，良好的」。

⑧ 從本文可以推論，1520 年之前新世界什麼地方有大量的黑奴？
   (A) 只有在伊斯帕尼奧拉島
   (B) 整個加勒比海地區
   (C) 在北美大陸
   (D) 都沒有

【答案】**D**
【解析】這是推論的題型，要找「根據」。第三段說「但是過了幾年來到 1520，下一任西班牙國王開始容許西班牙貴族每年進口指定數目的非洲人到新開發的西班牙殖民地。這些非洲人被帶過來就專為充當奴隸之用。很快就有數以千計的非洲奴隸在新世界」，表示新世界 1520 年之後才開始有大量的黑奴，可以推出 1520 之前沒有，故選 (D)。

⑨ 本文的下一段可能談論什麼主題？
   (A) 新世界的農業
   (B) 中古歐洲的奴隸制度
   (C) 17 世紀新世界的奴隸制度
   (D) 19 世紀美洲原住民叛變

【答案】**C**
【解析】這是組織結構的題型，要找出主題，並且要能銜接得上文章結尾。本文主題是新世界的奴隸制度，按照時間順序從源頭起一直介紹到 1520 年之後。接下來繼續照時間順序介紹同一主題，就應該是 16 世紀下旬或 17 世紀的新世界奴隸制度，故選 (C)。

Frederic Edwin Church would be envied by modern painters were he alive today. In 1859, Church exhibited one single painting, *Heart of the Andes*, charging an entry fee of 25 cents per viewer. In three weeks he made three thousand dollars. It was an unusually large painting, five feet by nine, and the showroom was furnished with benches where the viewer could sit down and enjoy the view—the huge painting on the wall was surrounded by woodwork which made it look like a window opening on a magnificent outdoor view. No modern painter can hope to attract such a crowd with a full retrospective, not to mention with one single painting.

Church's subject was nature on a grand scale. He studied art under landscape painter Thomas Cole, the most famous American artist of the 1840s. Other influences on him included Claude Lorraine, John Martin, and the great Turner. Yet he painted in a style distinctly his own. His method was built on scientific fidelity and artistic enhancement. In *Heart of the Andes*, every leaf and tree is botanically accurate, and every feather and beast would qualify as a museum illustration. He made two trips to South America, in 1853 and 1857, and discovered the volcano of Cotopaxi, which became the center piece of *Heart of the Andes*. In one of his letters he wrote thus about Cotopaxi, "The big mountain grimly secludes itself in an immense circle of volcanic and comparatively barren country." To **capture** the huge mountain, however, he needed vegetation in the foreground to add perspective, and so he liberally threw in palm trees that he had observed elsewhere. The result is a magnificent landscape, framed in the foreground with a **profusion** of vegetation, gradually extending through seemingly endless variations to the huge volcano looming behind it all.

✐ Exercise

① What is the topic of this passage?
(A) The life of Frederic Edwin Church
(B) A masterpiece landscape by Frederic Edwin Church
(C) The South American journeys of Frederic Edwin Church
(D) Frederic Edwin Church and American abstract painting

② Which of the following can be inferred about Church's exhibition in 1859?
(A) It showed all Church's paintings up to that time.
(B) It sold many paintings and made a lot of money for Church.
(C) It attracted over 10,000 viewers in all.
(D) It was held in the Andes Mountains in South America.

③ The author implies that modern painters would envy which aspect of Frederic E. Church?
(A) His artistic skills
(B) His travels to South America
(C) His vast wealth
(D) His ability to attract viewers

④ According to the passage, the most famous American painter from 1840 to 1849 was
(A) Frederic E. Church
(B) Thomas Cole
(C) Claude Lorraine
(D) John Martin

⑤ The author says that the basis for Church's method of painting was
(A) botany and zoology
(B) foreign trips and studio work
(C) scientific truthfulness and artistic improvement
(D) perspective and variations

⑥ The word "capture" in the second paragraph most closely means

(A) conquer

(B) arrest

(C) record

(D) memorize

⑦ All of the following can be inferred about *Heart of the Andes* EXCEPT

(A) the birds and animals in it are very life-like

(B) Church faithfully recorded what he saw, without any modifications

(C) the trees in it are painted in scientifically correct detail

(D) there is a large volcano in it

⑧ The word "profusion" in the second paragraph most closely means

(A) production

(B) abundance

(C) mixture

(D) transplant

⑨ A paragraph following this passage would most probably discuss

(A) another painting by Church

(B) Thomas Cole

(C) the Andes

(D) modern art

題解

　　弗雷德里克‧埃德溫‧丘池如果活在今日，現代畫家會很羨慕他。1859 年丘池展出一幅畫《安地斯山脈之心》，每人收取入場費 25 美分。3 週下來他賺了 3 千美元。那是幅超大的畫，5 英尺乘 9 英尺，展覽室安排有長椅讓觀眾坐著欣賞風景──牆上的大畫周圍有木框，看起來像個窗戶，外頭是壯麗的戶外風景。現代畫家就算是一整個回顧展也別想吸引到如此的人潮，更別提只展一幅畫了。

　　丘池的主題是宏偉的大自然。他向風景畫家托馬斯‧柯爾學畫，柯爾是 1840 年代最著名的美國藝術家。另外他還受到克勞德‧洛林、約翰‧馬丁，以及偉大的透納的影響。不過他的畫風獨特，屬於自己。他的技法建立在科學忠實與藝術美化上。在《安地斯山脈之心》中，每片葉子、每棵樹都符合植物學，每支羽毛、每頭野獸也都合格可以當作博物館插畫。他去了南美洲兩趟，分別在 1853 和 1857 年，發現了科托派西火山，拿它當作《安地斯山脈之心》的中央主題。有封信中他如此描寫科托派西火山：「大山冷峻地隔離在中央，四周環繞廣大的一圈火山地，相對缺乏植被」。但是，為了捕捉住大山的形象，他需要有植物在近景來添加透視法的比較，所以他刻意加入在別處觀察到的棕櫚樹。結果是一幅壯麗的風景，近景圈在大量滋生的植物中，逐漸向遠處伸展，看似有無窮的變化，直到隱約呈現在一切後頭的大火山。

練習題翻譯與詳解

① 本文的主題是什麼？

  (A) 丘池的生平　　　　　　　　　　(B) 丘池的一幅風景畫大作

  (C) 丘池的南美洲之旅　　　　　　　(D) 丘池與美國抽象畫

【答案】**B**

【解析】這是問主題的題型，要找主題句。第一段在開場白過後進入全文主題句「1859 年丘池展出一幅畫《安地斯山脈之心》」，第二段段落主題句是「丘池的主題是宏偉的大自然」，兩段共同的主題是介紹這幅畫，故選 (B)。

② 關於 1859 年丘池那場展覽可以推論出什麼？

  (A) 它展出截至當時為止丘池所有的畫作。

  (B) 它賣出許多畫、為丘池賺了不少錢。

  (C) 它總共吸引 1 萬多人參觀。

  (D) 它在南美安地斯山脈舉行。

【答案】**C**

【解析】這是推論的題型，要找「根據」。第一段說「每人收取入場會 25 美分。3 週下來他賺了 3 千美元」，兩個數字除一下就可算出繳費的觀眾超過 1 萬人。

③ 作者暗示，現代畫家會羨慕丘池的哪一方面？

(A) 他的藝術技法 　　　　　　(B) 他的南美洲之旅

(C) 他的龐大財富 　　　　　　(D) 他吸引觀眾的能力

【答案】**D**

【解析】這是推論題，要找「根據」。下文說「現代畫家就算是一整個回顧展也別想吸引到如此的人潮，更別提只展一幅畫了」，所以招人羨慕的應該是他吸引觀眾的能力。

④ 根據本文，1840 到 1849 年間最著名的美國畫家是

(A) 丘池 　　　　　　　　　　(B) 柯爾

(C) 洛林 　　　　　　　　　　(D) 馬丁

【答案】**B**

【解析】這是問細節的題型，要找同義表達。第二段說「柯爾是 1840 年代最著名的美國藝術家」，其中 in the 1840s 就是 from 1840 to 1849 的同義表達，故選 (B)。

⑤ 作者表示，丘池作畫技法的基礎是

(A) 植物學與動物學 　　　　　(B) 外國旅行與畫室工作

(C) 科學真實與藝術改進 　　　(D) 透視法與變化

【答案】**C**

【解析】這是問細節的題型，要找同義表達。第二段說「他的技法建立在科學忠實與藝術美化上」，其中 scientific fidelity and artistic enhancement 就是 scientific truthfulness and artistic improvement 的同義表達，故選 (C)。

⑥ 第二段中的 capture 一字意思最接近

(A) 征服 　　　　　　　　　　(B) 逮捕

(C) 記錄 　　　　　　　　　　(D) 記憶

【答案】**C**

【解析】這是單字題。capture（構造：take/(v.)）字面上意指「捕捉」，但在此上下文指的是用畫筆記錄，同義字是 record。

⑦ 關於《安地斯山脈之心》下列哪一點無法推論得知？

(A) 裡面的鳥獸很逼真

(B) 丘池忠實記錄他看到的東西，沒有任何修改

(C) 裡面的樹木以科學正確的細節繪出

(D) 裡面有座大火山

【答案】**B**

【解析】這是採用消去法的推論題型，要刪除三項正確的推論。第二段說「為了捕捉住大山的形象，他需要有植物在近景來添加透視法的比較，所以他刻意加入在別處觀察到的棕櫚樹」，這裡說明他並非完全忠實記錄所見，故選 (B)。

⑧ 第二段中的 profusion 一字意思最接近

　　(A) 生產　　　　　　　　　　　(B) 豐富
　　(C) 混合　　　　　　　　　　　(D) 移植

【答案】**B**

【解析】這是單字題。profusion（構造：forward/pour/(*n.*)）的意思是「大量、豐富」，同義字是 abundance（構造：away/wave/(*n.*)）。

⑨ 本文的下一段可能談到

　　(A) 丘池的另一幅畫　　　　　　(B) 柯爾
　　(C) 安地斯山脈　　　　　　　　(D) 現代美術

【答案】**A**

【解析】這是組織結構的題型，要找出主題，並且能夠銜接文章結尾。本文主題是介紹丘池的一幅畫，介紹完畢之後繼續介紹他別的畫作，仍舊屬於「丘池的畫」這個大主題之下，故選 (A)。

The term "virtual reality" refers to the kind of interactive computer technology that produces an illusory three-dimensional world for the user. With virtual reality, the user can explore the inside of a volcano, go back in time to the Jurassic age and ride a dinosaur, or pilot a spacecraft to its landing on Venus. With its almost unlimited potential, virtual reality, first developed by VPL Research in Redwood, California, has now become the **hottest** thing in such areas as medicine, teaching, military training and video games. It promises to forever alter entertainment as we have come to know it.

To escape from reality to virtual reality, the user simply puts on a headset, in which a pair of tiny liquid-crystal-display (LCD) TV screens creates stereoscopic images, with earphones producing high-fidelity sound to **add to** the illusion. In some versions, to interact with events in the computer-programmed world she sees, the user puts on a pair of gloves equipped with optic-fiber sensors. With input from the headset and the gloves, the computer records every action and movement of the user, and changes the simulated world according to her perspective.

To make the vision convincing to the user, a special computer conducts computation at incredible speed for every picture frame, each frame consisting of a minimum of 340,000 pixels—the smallest individual picture element. In addition, there must be over 30 picture frames per second to ensure the smooth flow of the images into one another. Ideal effects are not yet attainable. Researchers can produce high quality pictures, but the speed becomes unnaturally slow. The user finds the images halting, as if in slow-motion. On the other hand, if natural speed is achieved, the visual effects are **compromised**, and the image is blurred.

✎ Exercise

① The passage is mainly about
  (A) an interactive computer technology
  (B) imperfections of virtual reality
  (C) how to escape from boring reality
  (D) applied computer science

② The word "hottest" in the first paragraph is closest in meaning to
  (A) of highest temperature
  (B) most fashionable
  (C) most freshly baked
  (D) most controversial

③ The author mentions all of the following as fields in which virtual reality is used
  EXCEPT
  (A) games
  (B) teaching
  (C) medicine
  (D) engineering

④ Which of the following is mentioned by the author as something equipped in the
  headset?
  (A) microphones
  (B) minute television screens
  (C) fiber-optic sensors
  (D) special gloves

⑤ The phrase "add to" in the second paragraph most closely means
  (A) enhance
  (B) combine
  (C) create
  (D) expose

⑥ The author implies that, if there are fewer than 30 picture frames per second, the images
(A) will switch to slow-motion
(B) will fail to be smoothly connected
(C) will be distorted out of shape
(D) will still be sharp and in focus

⑦ The author mentions that, at the present level of technology, maintaining high-quality pictures in virtual reality would mean
(A) lower speed
(B) fewer pixels
(C) more expensive TV's
(D) larger picture frames

⑧ The word "compromised" in the third paragraph most closely means
(A) agreed on
(B) sacrificed
(C) maintained
(D) settled

⑨ A paragraph following the passage would most probably deal with
(A) current research to perfect virtual reality
(B) a definition of virtual reality
(C) personal computers
(D) artificial intelligence

題解

文章翻譯

「虛擬實境」一詞指的是一種互動式電腦科技，可以為使用者產生出虛幻的立體世界。有了虛擬實境，使用者可以探測火山內部、回到過去侏儸紀時代去騎恐龍、或者駕駛太空船登陸金星。虛擬實境可說潛力無窮，最早在加州紅木市 VPL 研究公司研發出來，現在已經是炙手可熱，運用於醫療、教學、軍事訓練與電玩等各領域。它可能會永遠改變我們所知道的娛樂。

要逃脫現實、進入虛擬實境，使用者只需戴上目鏡，裡面有兩具微型液晶電視螢幕可以創造出立體影像、耳機產生出高傳真音響以增強幻象。有些款式為了要和眼見的電腦世界中的事件互動，使用者還要戴上一雙手套、上面配有光纖感應器。目鏡與手套提供輸入，電腦就能記錄使用者的每一個動作、並且隨著使用者的觀點改變模擬世界。

為了使影像逼真，有一台特別的電腦以極快的速度在為每一個畫面進行運算，一個畫面由至少 340,000 個像素構成——像素是最小的個別成像元素。此外，每秒至少要有 30 幅畫面才能確保影像的轉換流暢無礙。理想的效果目前尚無法達到。研究人員可以產生出高品質影像，但速度就會慢得不自然。使用者會感覺動作遲鈍，有如慢動作。另一方面，如果達到自然的速度，視覺效果就要打折扣、影像變得模糊。

練習題翻譯與詳解

① 本文的主題是

(A) 一種互動電腦科技　　　　　　(B) 虛擬實境的缺點

(C) 如何逃脫無聊的現實　　　　　(D) 應用電腦科學

【答案】**A**

【解析】這是問主題的題型，要找主題句。第一段全文主題句「虛擬實境一詞指的是一種互動式電腦科技，可以為使用者產生出虛幻的立體世界」，點出介紹虛擬實境的主題，後面兩段分別介紹它的詳細做法，故選 (A)。

② 第一段中的 hottest 一字意思最接近

(A) 溫度最高的　　　　　　　　　(B) 最時髦的

(C) 最新烤出來的　　　　　　　　(D) 最有爭議的

【答案】**B**

【解析】這是單字題。hot 在此是口語化用法，表示「熱門」，同義字是 fashionable。

③ 作者提到虛擬實境使用的領域，不包括

　　(A) 遊戲　　　　　　　　　　(B) 教學

　　(C) 醫療　　　　　　　　　　(D) 工程

【答案】D

【解析】這是採用消去法、問細節的題型，要刪去三個同義表達。第一段說虛擬實境「運用於醫療、教學、軍事訓練與電玩等各領域」，其中不包括工程。

④ 作者提到下列哪一項說是配備在目鏡中的東西？

　　(A) 麥克風　　　　　　　　　(B) 小電視螢幕

　　(C) 光纖感應器　　　　　　　(D) 特殊手套

【答案】B

【解析】這是問細節的題型，要找同義表達。第二段說「使用者只需戴上目鏡，裡面有兩具微型液晶電視螢幕可以創造出立體影像」，其中 tiny liquid-crystal-display (LCD) TV screens 就是 minute television screens 的同義表達，故選 (B)。

⑤ 第二段中的片語 add to 意思最接近

　　(A) 增進　　　　　　　　　　(B) 結合

　　(C) 創造　　　　　　　　　　(D) 暴露

【答案】A

【解析】這是單字題。add 是「加」，片語 add to 是指「添加、加強」，同義字是 enhance。

⑥ 作者暗示，如果每秒不到 30 幅畫面，那麼影像

　　(A) 會轉為慢動作　　　　　　(B) 不能平滑銜接

　　(C) 會扭曲變形　　　　　　　(D) 仍然清晰聚焦

【答案】B

【解析】這是推論題，要找「根據」。第三段說「每秒至少要有 30 幅畫面才能確保影像的轉換流暢無礙」，由此可以推論，每秒不到 30 幅影像就會不流暢。

⑦ 作者提到，以目前的科技水平而言，在虛擬實境中維持高品質畫面會造成

　　(A) 速度慢　　　　　　　　　(B) 像素少

　　(C) 電視貴　　　　　　　　　(D) 畫面大

【答案】A

【解析】這是問細節的題型，要找同義表達。第三段說「研究人員可以產生出高品質影像，但速度就會慢得不自然」，所以是速度會變慢。

⑧ 第三段中的 compromised 一字意思最接近

    (A) 有共識　　　　　　　　　　　(B) 被犧牲

    (C) 被維持　　　　　　　　　　　(D) 被決定

【答案】**B**

【解析】這是單字題。動詞 compromise（構造：together/promise）的意思是「妥協」，引申為「犧牲、傷害」。

⑨ 本文下一段可能談的主題是

    (A) 當前改善虛擬實境的研究

    (B) 定義虛擬實境

    (C) 個人電腦

    (D) 人工智慧

【答案】**A**

【解析】這是組織結構的題型，要先整理出主題，並且要能銜接結尾。本文主題是介紹虛擬實境，最後說到的是它的一項缺點。下一段的主題若是談目前如何改善虛擬實境的缺點，與本文同屬於「虛擬實境」這個大主題之下，並且最能夠銜接上結尾，故選 (A)。

7

When President Bill Clinton's approval ratings **plummeted** in 1994, **the cartoonist Herblock** drew him staring in shock at his cat, Socks, who was resolutely walking out of the White House with his possessions in a bundle on his shoulder. This image would have been inconceivable a century ago. It is based on the assumption that a cat can be a valued friend, who can be counted on to provide solace during affliction.

Four centuries ago, few people could have conceived of a cat as a friend at all. Common English-language expressions from long ago make clear that our ancestors viewed the cat as a hunter of rodents and did not approve of its methods. Instead of forthrightly chasing down its prey, like a dog, a cat lies in wait, stalks, and pounces on its unsuspecting victim; instead of immediately killing its prey and **wolfing it down**, it may prefer to defer eating and play with its catch. Accordingly, *catty* means slyly spiteful, and *feline* **connotes** stealth. To *play cat and mouse with* is to toy heartlessly with a victim in one's power, and the children's game *puss in the corner* involves surrounding and teasing one of the players by offering and withdrawing opportunities to escape.

Only in recent times, as we have come increasingly to like and value cats, has the English language begun to reflect any appreciation of the animal's beauty, coordination, poise, and style. Although a woman would still object to being called a *cat*, she may like to be praised for feline grace and **seductiveness**. The great baseball player Johnny Mize, a large but well-coordinated man, was called "the big Georgia cat"; and "**Harry the Cat Brecheen**" was a particularly lithe and graceful pitcher.

In the 1930s, African-Americans began to describe a smart man who appreciates swing or jazz music as a *cat* or *hepcat*. This sense has been extended to refer to any streetwise, self-assured, stylishly dressed man-about-town—one who has the cool sophistication suggested by the cat's poise and elegant detachment, along with the defiance of mainstream social conventions suggested by its refusal to conform. Public figures who projected a tough, straightforward image began to enjoy having cat-related nicknames. A cat may also be a member of the *avant-garde* that defies traditional artistic conventions.

Finally, a whole family of expressions reflects a general perception of the cat as fortunate and superior: if something is really special, it is described as *the cat's whiskers*, *the cat's meow*, or *the cat's pajamas*. Fat cats enjoy luxury and special privileges, and *the cat that swallowed the canary* is a proverbial example of triumphant satisfaction. One who sits *in the catbird seat* is in an enviable or controlling position.

In contrast, dog terms are almost invariably used to demean. A *dog* is a despicable man or a crude woman, a worthless thing or an utter failure. *Bitch* has almost lost its primary meaning of female dog as it has become a handy term of abuse. A *bitch* can also be an ill-tempered complaint or an unpleasantly difficult task; *to bitch* is to gripe or grumble. A *puppy* is a pert, conceited, empty-headed young man. A *dog-eat-dog* competition is particularly destructive and ruthlessly self-interested. A *yellow dog* (a mongrel of undistinguishable ancestry) is synonymous with abject cowardice.

Even when the terms are based on actual canine behavior, they are used negatively. To *dog* or *hound* is to pursue remorselessly. A human who behaves in a *hangdog* manner is crestfallen and abject, and usually guilty and ashamed as well. **Even if we admire the fidelity and self-abnegation implied in *doglike devotion*, we find something contemptible in its uncritical, subservient nature and would not like to see our own love characterized in this way.** **W** Another set of expressions—to *lead a dog's life*, *it shouldn't happen to a dog*, *in the doghouse*, and *die like a dog*—suggests that dogs lead a substandard life because they are inferior beings. Why should the animal that is most loved by people be so negatively presented in our language? **X** Why should cats, which despite their popularity are neither so beloved nor so morally esteemed, fare so much better? **Y** Probably it is because dogs are closer to us, both from our warmer attachment to them and from their constant efforts to be part of our world. **Z**

7

✎ Exercise

① The word "plummeted" in paragraph 1 is closest in meaning to
   (A) soared   (B) stabilized
   (C) collapsed   (D) expanded

② Why does the author mention the drawing by "the cartoonist Herblock" in paragraph 1?
   (A) To make fun of President Clinton
   (B) To present an anecdote as an introduction to the passage
   (C) To cite Socks as an example of an ungrateful cat
   (D) To point out a contrast between cats and dogs

③ By saying "wolfing it down" in paragraph 2, the author means
   (A) pinning the prey
   (B) teasing the prey
   (C) swallowing the prey
   (D) throwing away the prey

④ The word "connotes" in paragraph 2 is closest in meaning to
   (A) connects   (B) means
   (C) notices   (D) implies

⑤ According to paragraph 2, which of the following is a game played by children?
   (A) *Catty*   (B) *Feline*
   (C) *Cat and mouse*   (D) *Puss in the corner*

⑥ The word "seductiveness" in paragraph 3 is closest in meaning to
   (A) attractiveness   (B) slyness
   (C) sedateness   (D) coolness

⑦ Why does the author mention "Harry the Cat Brecheen" in paragraph 3?
   (A) To establish a connection between cats and baseball
   (B) To illustrate the way good pitchers pitch
   (C) To give an example of a positive use of the word "cat"
   (D) To show that "Cat" has become a nickname

⑧ It can be inferred that someone called a "cat" in the sense described in paragraph 4 is probably

(A) stylish   (B) African-American
(C) conformist   (D) a public figure

⑨ According to paragraph 5, someone who has just successfully gratified a desire may be called

(A) *the cat's whiskers*
(B) *a fat cat*
(C) *the cat that swallowed the canary*
(D) *one who sits in the catbird seat*

⑩ According to paragraph 6, to say someone is "bitching" would be the same as saying the person is

(A) a female dog   (B) abusive
(C) complaining   (D) empty-headed

⑪ Which of the sentences below best expresses the essential information in the boldfaced sentence in paragraph 7?

Even if we admire the fidelity and self-abnegation implied in *doglike* *devotion*, we find something contemptible in its uncritical, subservient nature and would not like to see our own love characterized in this way.

(A) We may like the phrase *doglike devotion* because it implies faithfulness, but we would not like to use the phrase to describe our loved ones.
(B) Though the phrase *doglike devotion* has a negative connotation, we still love the faithfulness and self-debasement it implies.
(C) Despite the positive connotations in the expression *doglike devotion*, we find the phrase overly abject to our liking.
(D) The expression *doglike devotion* is both admirable and contemptible, so it is useless in any description of love.

⑫ In which position would the following boldfaced sentence best fit in paragraph 7?
We therefore think of them as second-class humans; we judge them by human standards and assume they are entitled to fewer privileges.
(A) Position W　　　　　　　　　(B) Position X
(C) Position Y　　　　　　　　　(D) Position Z

題解

文章翻譯

　　1994 年比爾‧柯林頓總統的民意支持度大跌，漫畫家赫布羅克畫出柯林頓震驚地瞪著他的貓「襪子」，這隻貓義無反顧地走出白宮，東西打成一個包袱扛在肩頭。若是往回推一個世紀，這幅景象絕無可能想出，因為它建立在一項假設上：貓也能是可貴的朋友，可以指望牠在苦難來臨的時刻給人提供安慰。

　　四個世紀以前，很少人會把貓想像成朋友。英語中從很久以前留傳下來的一些常用片語可以看出，我們的祖先把貓當作是捕老鼠的東西而已，並且對牠的手法不予苟同。貓不像狗，不是直截了當地追逐獵物，而是潛藏等待、跟蹤、然後突然撲向不疑有它的受害者。貓不是直接殺死獵物、大口吞下肚，而是寧可晚點吃、先玩弄牠抓來的東西。因此，「像貓」意思是狡滑又惡毒，「貓式」暗示偷偷摸摸。「玩貓捉老鼠」是冷酷地玩弄全受自己掌控的受害者。童玩「角落的貓」玩法是包圍並逗弄其中一人、給他逃跑的機會又收回。

　　一直要到近代，我們開始比較喜歡、重視貓，英語才開始反映出賞識貓的美、協調、平穩、與格調。如果直接稱女人為「貓」她還是會反對，不過如果稱讚她說有貓般的優雅與誘惑，她可能會很高興。棒球好手邁茲是個塊頭雖大但是協調甚佳的人，外號是「喬治亞大貓」。還有「哈利阿貓布利欽」是位特別靈活優雅的投手。

　　1930 年代，非裔美國人開始描述喜愛搖擺樂、爵士樂的精明男子為「貓」或「時髦貓」。後來擴充為泛指任何適應都市生活、有自信、衣著時髦、吃得開的男子──這種人擁有很酷的世故感，像貓同樣的沉穩、同樣優雅地置身事外，而且反抗主流社會風俗，就像貓那樣不合流俗。公共人物如果投射出強悍、直來直往的形象，會開始喜歡與貓有關的綽號。被稱為貓的人也可能指的是前衛藝術家，這種人反抗傳統的藝術習俗。

最後，有一整批片語反映出大家的看法，認為貓是幸運的、高超的。如果有個東西非常特別，會被描述為「貓鬍鬚」、「貓叫」、或者「貓睡衣」。「肥貓」享受奢侈與特權，「吞了金絲雀的貓」是形容得意自滿的俗語。「坐在貓鳥座位」的人就是處境令人羨慕或者掌握局面的人。

相反的，帶有狗的詞彙幾乎永遠是貶抑語。「狗」是卑劣的男子、粗俗的女子、無價值的東西、或者徹底的失敗。「母狗」幾乎已經喪失「雌狗」的本義、成為一句常用的罵人話。「母狗」還可以表示壞脾氣的抱怨、或者艱難麻煩的工作。「當母狗」就是發牢騷、抱怨。「小狗」是莽撞、自以為是、腦袋空空的年輕人。「狗咬狗」的競爭特別有破壞性、無情而又自私自利。「黃狗」（原指血統不明的雜種狗）等同於卑下的懦怯。

即使有真正的犬科動物行為當作基礎，含有狗的詞語都還是負面的。「當狗」意思是一心一意地追逐。若說某人的行為如同「吊死狗」，就是說他像鬥敗的公雞、低聲下氣，而且往往還有罪又丟臉。「像狗一樣的效忠」一語暗示忠實與抹殺自我，這種暗示我們或許會賞識，但此語的本質是毫不質疑、完全順從，會令我們感覺不屑。要是我們自己對人的感情被這樣形容，也會不高興的。W 另外有一批片語──「活得像狗一樣」、「狗都不該碰到的事」、「在狗屋裡」、「死得像條狗」──暗示狗過的是次等的生活，因為牠是次等生物。狗是人類最喜愛的動物，為什麼在我們的語言中呈現得如此負面？X 貓雖然很多人喜歡，但絕不及狗那樣受人寵愛、德行令人尊重，為什麼貓的處境就好得多？Y 或許原因是狗跟人比較親近，因為我們跟狗比較有感情、也因為狗不斷努力想成為我們世界中的一分子。Z

練習題翻譯與詳解

① 第一段中的 plummeted 一字意思最接近
   (A) 高飛
   (B) 穩定
   (C) 倒塌
   (D) 擴大

【答案】C
【解析】這是單字題。動詞 plummet（構造：lead/(v.)）的意思是「直線下墜」，同義字是 collapse（構造：together/fall）。

② 作者在第一段為何提到「漫畫家赫布羅克」？
   (A) 為了挖苦柯林頓總統
   (B) 為了提供一個小故事作為文章的開場白
   (C) 為了舉出「襪子」為忘恩負義的貓的例子
   (D) 為了指出貓和狗的一項對比

【答案】B
【解析】這是修辭目的的題型，要看上下文。這則故事是在全文開頭，由此導入「人對貓的態度」，再進入「英語中的貓狗詞語」的主題，所以是作為開場白之用。

③ 作者在第二段說到 wolfing it down，意思是

(A) 按住獵物 　　　　　　　　(B) 逗弄獵物

(C) 吞下獵物 　　　　　　　　(D) 丟棄獵物

【答案】C

【解析】這是單字題。名詞 wolf 是「狼」。動詞片語 wolf down 是指「狼吞虎嚥」，同義字是 swallow。

④ 第二段中的 connotes 意思最接近

(A) 連結 　　　　　　　　　　(B) 表示……意思

(C) 注意到 　　　　　　　　　(D) 暗示

【答案】D

【解析】這是單字題。connote（構造：together/note）的意思是「暗示，有……弦外之音」，同義字是 imply（構造：in/fold/(v.)）。

⑤ 根據第二段，下面哪一項是童玩？

(A) *Catty* 　　　　　　　　　(B) *Feline*

(C) *Cat and mouse* 　　　　　(D) *Puss in the corner*

【答案】D

【解析】這是問細節的題型，要找同義表達。第二段結尾說到「童玩『角落的貓』玩法」，故選 (D)。

⑥ 第三段中的 seductiveness 意思最接近

(A) 吸引力 　　　　　　　　　(B) 狡猾

(C) 鎮定 　　　　　　　　　　(D) 冷酷

【答案】A

【解析】這是單字題。seductiveness（構造：apart/lead/(n.)）的意思是「誘惑力」，同義字是 attractiveness（構造：to/draw/(n.)）。

⑦ 作者在第三段提到 Harry the Cat Brecheen 的目的是

(A) 建立貓與棒球的關係

(B) 說明好投手的投球方式

(C) 舉例說明 cat 字的正面用法

(D) 顯示 Cat 已成為綽號

【答案】C

【解析】這是修辭目的的題型，要看上下文。第三段的段落主題句說「一直要到近代，我們開始比較喜歡、重視貓，英語才開始反映出賞識貓的美、協調、平穩、與格調」，然後舉出幾個英語中 cat 這個字正面用法的例子，Harry the Cat Brecheen 也是一例，故選 (C)。

⑧ 可以推論，以第四段中的解釋，叫作 cat 的人很可能是

    (A) 很時髦   (B) 非裔美國人

    (C) 認同傳統者   (D) 公共人物

【答案】A

【解析】這是推論題，必須找出根據。第四段講到以 cat 字描述人，都有「時髦」的共同點，故選 (A)。

⑨ 根據第五段，剛剛成功滿足一項欲望的人可以稱為

    (A) *the cat's whiskers*

    (B) *a fat cat*

    (C) *the cat that swallowed the canary*

    (D) *one who sits in the catbird seat*

【答案】C

【解析】這是問細節的題型，要找同義表達。第五段說「『吞了金絲雀的貓』是形容得意自滿的俗語」，其中 triumphant satisfaction 就是題目中 has just successfully gratified a desire 的同義表達，故選 (C)。

⑩ 根據第六段，若說某人在 bitching，相當於說此人

    (A) 是母狗   (B) 虐待人

    (C) 在抱怨   (D) 腦袋空空

【答案】C

【解析】這是問細節的題型，要找同義表達。第六段說「to bitch 就是發牢騷、抱怨」，其中 gripe or grumble 就是 complaining 的同義表達，故選 (C)。

⑪ 下列哪個句子最能夠表達第七段黑體字句子的主要內容？

「像狗一樣的效忠」一語暗示忠實與抹殺自我，這種暗示我們或許會賞識，但此語的本質是毫不質疑、完全順從，會令我們感覺不屑。要是我們自己對人的感情被這樣形容，也會不高興的。

(A) 我們會喜歡「像狗一樣效忠」一語，因為暗示忠實，但我們不會想用此語來描述我們喜愛的人。

(B) 雖然「像狗一樣效忠」一語有否定暗示，我們仍然喜愛隱含的忠誠與抹殺自我。

(C) 雖然「像狗一樣效忠」一語有正面暗示，但我們會覺得此語太過卑劣而不喜歡。

(D)「像狗一樣效忠」一語既令人欽佩又讓人輕蔑，所以用來描述感情毫無用處。

【答案】 C

【解析】這是句子改寫的題型，要找句中重點的同義表達。原句對「像狗一樣效忠」一語基本上是持否定態度，故選 (C)。

⑫ 下面這個黑體字句子最適合放在第七段什麼位置？

「**所以我們會把牠當作次等人類看待。我們用人的標準衡量牠、假定牠能夠享有的特權比較少。**」

(A) W 位置

(B) X 位置

(C) Y 位置

(D) Z 位置

【答案】 D

【解析】這是安插句子的題型，要看上下文。插入句開頭「所以……」表達因果關係，符合因果關係的是 Z 位置，填入成為：「或許原因是狗跟人比較親近，因為我們跟狗比較有感情、也因為狗不斷努力想成為我們世界中的一分子。所以我們會把牠當作次等人類看待。我們用人的標準衡量牠、假定牠能夠享有的特權比較少。」

In addition to the exaggerated acclaim given Columbus' achievements by scholars, there are a number of stories surrounding Columbus that are simply untrue. He did not attempt to prove the earth was round by sailing westward. Any 15th-century intellectual knew for a fact that the earth was round. Nor did Queen Isabella of Spain sell her jewelry to sponsor Columbus' adventures. Likewise, the *Santa Maria*, Columbus' flagship on his first voyage west, was not manned by convicts and murderers released from jails in Spain.

Strictly speaking, Columbus did not discover America, even from a European viewpoint. The earliest Europeans to reach North America were **Scandinavian pirates**, who had a colony in Newfoundland at the **dawn** of the eleventh century. Columbus came 500 years later, to the West Indies and Central America only. He never landed on the North American continent.

This is not to say that Columbus had no impact on history. It was through him that the various peoples of Europe became aware of the New World, and started emigrating to it. He opened up a route to the New World, thereby permanently altering the history of both worlds, old and new.

✎ Exercise

① What is the main topic of this passage?
  (A) Inexplicable mysteries surrounding Christopher Columbus
  (B) The discovery of America by Scandinavians
  (C) The truth about Christopher Columbus
  (D) The unwarranted fame of Christopher Columbus

② What would a paragraph preceding this passage most probably deal with?
  (A) Researchers' exaggerated praise of Columbus
  (B) Columbus' landing on the American continent
  (C) Native American culture prior to Columbus
  (D) Other stories about Columbus which are false

③ According to the passage, which of the following is a true statement about Christopher Columbus?
  (A) He sailed westward to prove that the earth was round.
  (B) Queen Isabella sold her jewelry to buy ships for him.
  (C) The crew on his ship was composed of criminals and murderers.
  (D) One ship he used in his first voyage west was the *Santa Maria*.

④ The author mentions Scandinavian pirates in the second paragraph probably in order to
  (A) hint that Columbus was once a pirate
  (B) prove that Columbus did not discover the New World
  (C) illustrate that Columbus' crew was mostly convicts and murderers
  (D) explain why Newfoundland has always had a lot of Scandinavians

⑤ The word "dawn" in the second paragraph most closely means
  (A) daybreak
  (B) soft feather
  (C) underside
  (D) beginning

⑥ According to the passage, Columbus had been to
(A) North America
(B) Central America
(C) South America
(D) India

⑦ Which of the following is implied by the author as Columbus' impact on history?
(A) He changed the history of the world forever.
(B) He helped Spain become a major sea power in the 16th century.
(C) He opened up a route of trade with India.
(D) He proved to the European peoples that the earth was round.

題解

文章翻譯

　　除了學者對哥倫布的成就給予過高的好評之外，還有幾則關於哥倫布的故事根本是假的。他向西航行並不是要證明地球是圓的。15 世紀隨便哪個知識分子都知道地球是圓的。西班牙伊莎貝拉女王也沒有變賣首飾來資助哥倫布的探險。同樣的，哥倫布第一次西行的旗艦「聖塔瑪麗亞號」也不是從西班牙監獄中放出囚犯與殺人凶手來當水手。

　　嚴格講起來，哥倫布也沒有發現美洲，即使是從歐洲觀點來看。最早來到北美洲的歐洲人是北歐海盜，他們 11 世紀初在紐芬蘭有個殖民地。哥倫布晚到了 500 年，而且只來到西印度群島和中美洲。他從未在北美大陸上岸。

　　這樣說並不表示哥倫布對歷史沒有造成衝擊。是經過他，歐洲各民族才知道有新世界、而且開始移民過去。他打開了一條通新世界的路線，因而永遠改變了兩個世界的歷史，一舊一新。

練習題翻譯與詳解

① 本文的主題是什麼？

(A) 包圍哥倫布的一些不可解的神祕

(B) 北歐人發現美洲

(C) 哥倫布的真相

(D) 哥倫布浪得虛名

【答案】C

【解析】這是問主題的題型，要找主題句。第一段的主題句「有幾則關於哥倫布的故事根本是假的」指出要揭發哥倫布的真相。第二段的段落主題句「嚴格講起來，哥倫布也沒有發現美洲」繼續做揭發的工作。第三段「這樣說並不表示哥倫布對歷史沒有造成衝擊」則是說到哥倫布的真實影響，所以三段的共同主題是「哥倫布的真相」。

② 在本文的前一段可能是什麼主題？

(A) 研究人員對哥倫布的溢美之詞

(B) 哥倫布在美洲大陸登陸

(C) 哥倫布之前的美洲原住民文化

(D) 關於哥倫布的另一些不真實的故事

【答案】A

【解析】這是組織結構的題型，要整理出主題，並且要能銜接文章開頭。從上一題得知，本文主題是「哥倫布的真相」，前一段也應該和同一主題有關。第一段開頭「除了學者對哥倫布的成就給予過高的好評之外，還有幾則關於哥倫布的故事根本是假的」，其中「學者的過高好評」是銜接上文的轉折語 (Transition)，最能銜接得上的就是「研究人員對哥倫布的溢美之詞」。

8

③ 根據本文，下列哪項關於哥倫布的陳述是真的？

(A) 他向西航行為了證明地球是圓的。

(B) 伊莎貝拉女王賣掉首飾為了給他買船。

(C) 他的船員都是罪犯與殺人凶手。

(D) 他首次西行用的船有一艘名叫「聖塔瑪麗亞號」。

【答案】D

【解析】這是問細節的題型，要找同義表達。第一段說到「哥倫布第一次西行的旗艦聖塔瑪麗亞號」，故選 (D)。

④ 作者在第二段提到北歐海盜可能是為了

(A) 暗示哥倫布曾當過海盜

(B) 證明哥倫布沒有發現新世界

(C) 說明哥倫布的船員大多是囚犯與凶手

(D) 解釋紐芬蘭為何一向有許多北歐人

【答案】B

【解析】這是修辭目的的題型，要看上下文。第二段「嚴格講起來，哥倫布也沒有發現美洲，即使是從歐洲觀點來看。最早來到北美洲的歐洲人是北歐海盜」，其中北歐海盜的直接上文是「哥倫布沒有發現美洲」，也就是沒有發現新世界，故選 (B)。

⑤ 第二段中的 dawn 一字意思最接近

(A) 天亮

(B) 軟羽毛

(C) 下方

(D) 開始

【答案】D

【解析】這是單字題。dawn 字面上指的是「破曉，黎明」，在此引申為「開始」，同義字是 beginning。

⑥ 根據本文，哥倫布到過

(A) 北美洲

(B) 中美洲

(C) 南美洲

(D) 印度

【答案】B

【解析】這是問細節的題型，要找同義表達。第二段說「哥倫布晚到了 500 年，而且只來到西印度群島和中美洲。他從未在北美大陸上岸」，所以答案是中美洲。

⑦ 作者暗示下列哪一項是哥倫布對歷史造成的衝擊？

(A) 他永久改變了世界歷史。

(B) 他幫助西班牙成為 16 世紀的海上強權。

(C) 他打開了與印度的貿易路線。

(D) 他向歐洲各民族證明地球是圓的。

【答案】A

【解析】這是推論題，要找「根據」。第三段說「他打開了一條通新世界的路線，因而永遠改變了兩個世界的歷史」，故選 (A)。

Evolution has produced giants among all varieties of animals. The most evident instances, however, are found among vertebrates, whose internal bone structure and circulatory systems can support great weight and supply large amounts of oxygen. Each major division of vertebrates has produced its giants.

The most famous huge vertebrates are of course the reptiles. In the Upper Jurassic Age, roughly 150 million years ago, there was the 80-ton, 90-foot-long vegetarian Brachiosaurus. In the late Cretaceous Age, about 70 million years ago, Tyrannosaurus rex was the mightiest predator ever developed on earth—40 feet long, standing 19 feet tall, with teeth reaching six inches. Flying reptiles included giants such as the Pteranodon, with a wingspan of 25 feet. The dinosaurs, of course, **became extinct** at the end of the Cretaceous period.

The largest birds were those too large to fly. Some examples that had survived until recently included the plant-eating moas of New Zealand, which stood at an amazing 13 feet, and the 10-foot-tall elephant birds of Madagascar. The latter laid enormous, two-gallon eggs.

Among mammals, the largest land-dwelling member was Baluchitherium, which lived about 50 million years ago in Asia. It was a rhino-like animal standing 18 feet tall to the shoulder. The blue whale, a mammal, is the champion of them all—a 100-foot-long water monster that weighs three times as much as the largest dinosaur. Unfortunately, this creature is on the verge of extinction, primarily due to whale-hunting. Among fish, there are twenty-foot mantas and some equally large sharks still swimming in the oceans today.

Giant animals evolved for several reasons. Some plant-eating animals found safety in size. That is, they tried to grow large enough to deter predators. On the other hand, predators such as Tyrannosaurus rex also evolved toward greater size, so that they could hunt larger prey. This competition propelled predator and prey on a race toward supremacy in bulk. Other reasons for large size may have been competitions for territory, food or mates.

Exercise

① With what is the passage mainly concerned?
   (A) A comparison of various kinds of dinosaurs
   (B) The way very large animals became endangered species
   (C) Competition for resources among various species of animals
   (D) Varieties of huge animals among vertebrates

② According to the passage, very large members have evolved among vertebrates because, more than other kinds of animals, vertebrates
   (A) need to compete fiercely for territory, food and mate
   (B) have strong bones and efficient circulatory systems
   (C) have many divisions among themselves
   (D) eat a lot of food

③ According to the passage, all of the following are correct statements about Brachiosaurus EXCEPT
   (A) it was a predator
   (B) it lived 150 million years ago
   (C) it was a member of the reptile family
   (D) it sometimes grew to 90 feet long

④ The passage says that the most powerful hunter on earth was
   (A) Brachiosaurus
   (B) Tyrannosaurus rex
   (C) Pteranodon
   (D) Baluchitherium

⑤ Which of the following was an animal that could fly?
   (A) Pteranodon
   (B) The moa
   (C) The elephant bird
   (D) The manta

8

⑥ The expression "became extinct" in the second paragraph is closest in meaning
to
(A) went into hiding
(B) died out
(C) were extant
(D) experienced genetic mutation

⑦ According to the passage, elephant birds
(A) laid huge eggs
(B) were 13 feet tall
(C) had a wingspan of 25 feet
(D) can still be found flying today

⑧ Which of the following does the author mention as the largest mammal?
(A) Baluchitherium
(B) The elephant
(C) Tyrannosaurus rex
(D) The blue whale

⑨ According to the passage, if a grass-eating animal grew to be significantly
larger than a predator,
(A) it could rob the predator of a mate
(B) it would soon be extinct
(C) it might scare off the predator
(D) it could feed on the predator

⑩ According to the passage, all of the following are reasons why animals evolved
to be extremely large EXCEPT
(A) competition between predator and prey
(B) competition for habitat
(C) competition for mates
(D) competition for better race

題解

文章翻譯

　　進化在每一種動物都有造成巨人出現，不過最明顯的例子要屬脊椎動物，牠的內骨骼構造與循環系統可以支撐龐大的體重、供應大量的氧氣。脊椎動物中每一種重要分類都有產生出巨人。

　　最著名的巨大脊椎動物當然是爬蟲類。在上侏儸紀，大約 1 億 5 千萬年前，有 80 噸重、90 英尺長，素食的腕龍。在白堊紀晚期，大約 7 千萬年前，暴龍是地球上出現過最有力的掠食者──40 英尺長、站起來有 19 英尺高，牙齒長達 6 英吋。飛行爬蟲類的巨人有無齒翼龍，展翼 25 英尺。當然，恐龍在白堊紀末期絕種了。

　　最大型的鳥類是大到不能飛的。存活到不久以前的例子包括紐西蘭吃植物的恐鳥，站立高達 13 英尺，以及馬達加斯加 10 英尺高的象鳥。後者產的蛋大到有兩加侖。

　　哺乳類中最大的陸地成員是巨犀，大約 5 千萬年前存活於亞洲。牠是長得像犀牛的動物，站立起來肩部高 18 英尺。藍鯨也是哺乳類，是總冠軍──身長 100 英尺的水中怪獸，重量有最大恐龍的 3 倍。很不幸，這種動物已經瀕臨絕種，主要因為捕鯨。魚類中有長達 20 英尺的鬼蝠魟以及同樣大的鯊魚，今天仍在海中游動。

　　巨大動物演化出來有幾個原因。有些吃植物的動物要大才安全。也就是說，牠努力長大到能夠嚇阻掠食者的地步。另一方面，掠食者如暴龍也朝向大體型演化，目的是可以獵捕大型獵物。這種競爭推動掠食者與獵物進行體型的競賽。別的原因可能是為了競爭地盤、食物、或配偶。

練習題翻譯與詳解

① 本文的主題是什麼？

　(A) 比較各種恐龍

　(B) 巨大動物如何成為瀕臨絕種的品種

　(C) 各種動物之間的資源競爭

　(D) 脊椎動物中的各種巨大動物

【答案】**D**

【解析】這是問主題的題型，要找主題句。第一段在開場白過後，全文主題句是「脊椎動物中每一種重要分類都有產生出巨人」，後面各段的段落主題句分別介紹爬蟲類、鳥類、哺乳類等各種脊椎動物裡面的巨人，最後一段則是分析巨大動物出現的原因。共同的主題是「脊椎動物中的巨人」，故選 (D)。

② 根據本文，脊椎動物中演化出巨大成員是因為脊椎動物比起別種動物

　(A) 更有需要激烈競爭地盤、食物與配偶

　(B) 有更強壯的骨骼與更有效率的循環系統

(C) 有更多的內部分類

(D) 吃更多食物

【答案】**B**

【解析】這是問細節的題型，要找同義表達。第一段說「進化在每一種動物都有造成巨人出現，不過最明顯的例子要屬脊椎動物，牠的內骨骼構造與循環系統可以支撐龐大的體重、供應大量的氧氣」，其中 internal bone structure and circulatory systems can support great weight and supply large amounts of oxygen 這個部分就是 have strong bones and efficient circulatory systems 的同義表達，故選 (B)。

③ 根據本文，下列哪一項關於腕龍的陳述是錯的？

   (A) 牠是狩獵者   (B) 牠生活在 1 億 5 千萬年前

   (C) 牠屬於爬蟲科   (D) 牠可以長到 90 英尺長

【答案】**A**

【解析】這是採用消去法、問細節的題型，要刪去 3 個同義表達。第二段說「在上侏儸紀，大約 1 億 5 千萬年前，有 80 噸重、90 英尺長，素食的腕龍」，其中 vegetarian「素食」和 (A) 的 predator「狩獵者」抵觸，故選 (A)。

④ 本文說地球上最有力的狩獵者是

   (A) 腕龍   (B) 暴龍

   (C) 無齒翼龍   (D) 巨犀

【答案】**B**

【解析】這是問細節的題型，要找同義表達。第二段說「暴龍是地球上出現過最有力的掠食者」，其中 the mightiest predator 就是 the most powerful hunter 的同義表達，故選 (B)。

⑤ 下列何者是會飛的動物？

   (A) 無齒翼龍   (B) 恐鳥

   (C) 象鳥   (D) 鬼蝠魟

【答案】**A**

【解析】這是問細節的題型，要找同義表達。第二段說「飛行爬蟲類的巨人有無齒翼龍」，故選 (A)。

⑥ 第二段中的 became extinct 這個片語的意思最接近

   (A) 躲藏起來   (B) 死絕

   (C) 現存   (D) 經歷基因突變

【答案】B
【解析】這是單字題。形容詞 extinct（構造：out/prick）的意思是「滅絕」。

⑦ 根據本文，象鳥

  (A) 產的蛋很大   (B) 有 13 英尺高

  (C) 展翼 25 英尺   (D) 今天還看得到牠在飛

【答案】A
【解析】這是問細節的題型，要找同義表達。第三段說象鳥「產的蛋大到有兩加侖」，其中 laid enormous, two-gallon eggs 是 laid huge eggs 的同義表達，故選 (A)。

⑧ 作者提到下列哪一個是最大的哺乳類？

  (A) 巨犀   (B) 大象

  (C) 暴龍   (D) 藍鯨

【答案】D
【解析】這是問細節的題型，要找同義表達。第四段雖然說巨犀是最大的陸地哺乳類，但接著說「藍鯨也是哺乳類，是總冠軍——身長 100 英尺的水中怪獸，重量有最大恐龍的 3 倍」，所以是藍鯨。

⑨ 根據本文，草食動物若長到比掠食動物大得多，

  (A) 牠可以搶奪掠食動物的配偶   (B) 牠就快要絕種了

  (C) 牠可以嚇走掠食動物   (D) 牠可以捕食掠食動物

【答案】C
【解析】這是問細節的題型，要找同義表達。第五段說「有些吃植物的動物要大才安全。也就是說，牠努力長大到能夠嚇阻掠食者的地步」，其中 plant-eating animals 是 grass-eating animals 的同義表達，deter predators 是 scare off the predator 的同義表達，故選 (C)。

⑩ 根據本文，下列都是動物演化成巨大的原因，除了

  (A) 掠食者與獵物之間的競爭   (B) 爭奪棲息地

  (C) 爭奪配偶   (D) 爭奪較佳的品種

【答案】D
【解析】這是採消去法、問細節的題型，要刪去三個同義表達。第五段可以找到 (A) (B) (C) 的同義表達，但 competition for better race 為無中生有，不是同義表達。

The colonial experience left the young United States with an invaluable cultural heritage. To begin with, the earliest setters in New England brought the English language, which became the common language for the **various** peoples that came to America. A common language, even more than a common culture, is a prerequisite to the building of any nation. Another precious legacy from colonial times was the shaping of a representative form of government. The British government had allowed the colonists to elect their legislators and to establish sufficiently autonomous local governments. The colonists could therefore participate in the management of public affairs by electing legislators and officials. This prepared them for the establishment of a representative form of government after the Revolution.

A third inheritance from colonial America was a respect for basic human rights. Rights to free speech, publication and association were as entrenched in America as they had been in Britain. It is to be **lamented**, however, that human rights did not extend to slaves, partly because no precedents of slavery existed in Britain. In ancient Egypt and Rome, on the other hand, slaves' rights were adequately protected by law and by convention. A fourth legacy was a healthy tolerance for different religious beliefs. As the pilgrims had fled England to seek liberty in practicing their own religion, they could readily sympathize with people following different religions from their own.

An aggressive individualism was yet another gift from colonial days. As colonists carved homes for themselves out of the wilderness, they learned the meaning of independence. That was how individualism was built into the American character.

Exercise

① What is the main topic of the passage?
   (A) Government and politics in colonial America
   (B) British heritage in colonial America
   (C) Colonial traditions in early United States
   (D) Life in the colonial period of North America

② The word "various" in the first paragraph is closest in meaning to
   (A) homogeneous
   (B) changeable
   (C) different
   (D) immigrant

③ The author specifically mentions which of the following as a necessary condition to the founding of a country?
   (A) A common language
   (B) The same race
   (C) A constitution
   (D) A representative government

④ The author implies that the colonists could run public affairs because
   (A) they spoke the English language, wherever they came from
   (B) the British government had given them some degree of autonomy
   (C) the earliest settlers had a common cultural background
   (D) public affairs in colonial America were relatively simple

⑤ The word "lamented" in the second paragraph is closest in meaning to
   (A) regretted
   (B) corrected
   (C) commented on
   (D) noted

⑥ The passage implies that part of the reason slaves had no rights in colonial America was that

(A) the slaves had no representation in the British Parliament

(B) there was no right to free speech for the slaves

(C) there had never been any slaves in England

(D) The slaves came to America too late

⑦ The passage implies that the colonists tolerated different religions because

(A) they did not find religion all that important

(B) they knew what it was like to be deprived the freedom of belief

(C) they were interested to learn from other religions

(D) they were independents and individualists

⑧ In the third paragraph, the author mentions how colonists set up their homes in order to

(A) express sympathy with colonists over their difficulties

(B) explain the origins of individualism in the United States

(C) persuade the reader to be more independent

(D) show his admiration for the intrepid colonists

文章翻譯

　　殖民地經驗留給年輕美國一筆無價的文化遺產。首先，最早來到新英格蘭的移民帶來英語，成為此後來到美洲各種民族的共同語言。共同語言的重要性超過共同文化，是打造國家的先決條件。殖民地時代的另一項寶貴遺產是塑造出代議式的政府。英國政府容許殖民地人民選舉自己的議員、建立有足夠自治權的地方政府。殖民地人民因而可以通過選舉議員與官吏，參與公共事務的管理。這讓他們有充分的準備，可以在革命之後建立代議式的政府。

　　美洲殖民時代的第三項遺產是對基本人權的尊重。言論自由、出版自由與集會結社自由，這三項權利在美洲就像在英國同樣的根深蒂固。但是很令人遺憾，人權並沒有及於奴隸，部分原因在於英國沒有奴隸制度的先例可循。相反的，在古埃及與羅馬，奴隸權都受到法律與傳統的充分保障。第四宗遺產是容忍不同宗教信仰的健康態度。清教徒當年逃出英國是為了追求信奉自己宗教的自由，所以很能夠同情別人追求不同的宗教信仰。

　　強烈的個人主義又是一項殖民時代的禮物。殖民地人民為自己在荒野中努力打造出家園，同時也了解到獨立的重要。個人主義就是這樣建立在美國人性格中的。

練習題翻譯與詳解

① 本文的主題是什麼？
　(A) 殖民地美洲的政府與政治
　(B) 殖民地美洲的英國遺產
　(C) 美國早期的殖民地傳統
　(D) 北美洲殖民地時代的生活

【答案】**C**
【解析】這是問主題的問題，要找主題句。第一段全文主題句是「殖民地經驗留給年輕美國一筆無價的文化遺產」，後面各段的段落主題句分別介紹這筆文化遺產有哪幾項，共同主題是殖民地經驗留給美國的文化遺產，最接近的答案是 (C)。

② 第一段中的 various 一字意思最接近
　(A) 同質性高的　　　　　　　(B) 可變的
　(C) 不同的　　　　　　　　　(D) 移民的

【答案】**C**
【解析】這是單字題，various（構造：change/(a.)）的意思是「各式各樣的」，同義字是 **different**。

③ 作者明確提到下列哪一項，說是創建國家的必要條件？

    (A) 共同語言   (B) 共同血統

    (C) 憲法   (D) 代議式政府

【答案】**A**

【解析】這是問細節的題型，要找同義表達。第一段說「共同語言的重要性超過共同文化，是打造國家的先決條件」，其中 a prerequisite 是 a necessary condition 的同義表達，the building of any nation 是 the founding of a country 的同義表達，故選 (A)。

④ 作者暗示，殖民地人民可以管理公共事務是因為

    (A) 他們不論來自何方都說英語

    (B) 英國政府給了他們一些自治權

    (C) 最早的移民有共同的文化背景

    (D) 美洲殖民地的公共事務相對簡單

【答案】**B**

【解析】這是推論題，要找同義表達。第一段說「英國政府容許殖民地人民選舉自己的議員、建立有足夠自治權的地方政府。殖民地人民因而可以通過選舉議員與官吏，參與公共事務的管理」，可以看出殖民地人民可以管理公共事務的原因和英國政府給予的地方自治權有關，故選 (B)。

⑤ 第二段中的 lamented 一字意思最接近

    (A) 遺憾   (B) 矯正

    (C) 評論   (D) 注意

【答案】**A**

【解析】這是單字題。動詞 lament 的意思是「哀嘆」，同義字是 regret。

⑥ 本文暗示，奴隸在美洲殖民地沒有權利，部分原因在於

    (A) 奴隸在英國國會沒有代表

    (B) 奴隸沒有言論自由

    (C) 英國沒有過奴隸

    (D) 奴隸太晚來到美洲

【答案】**C**

【解析】這是推論題，要找「根據」。第二段說「人權並沒有及於奴隸，部分原因在於英國沒有奴隸制度的先例可循」，可以推出英國沒有過奴隸是其原因。

⑦ 本文暗示，殖民地人民可以容忍不同的宗教是因為
  (A) 他們不覺得宗教很重要
  (B) 他們知道被剝奪信仰自由是什麼感覺
  (C) 他們有意向別的宗教學習
  (D) 他們是獨立主義者、自由主義者

【答案】**B**
【解析】這是推論題，要找「根據」。第二段說「清教徒當年逃出英國是為了追求信奉自己宗教的自由，所以很能夠同情別人追求不同的宗教信仰」，故選 (B)。

⑧ 第三段中作者提到移民如何建立家園，目的是
  (A) 對移民的困難表示同情
  (B) 說明美國個人主義的起源
  (C) 說服讀者要更加獨立
  (D) 表示對無畏的移民很欽佩

【答案】**B**
【解析】這是修辭目的的題型，要看上下文。第三段說「強烈的個人主義又是一項殖民時代的禮物。殖民地人民為自己在荒野中努力打造出家園，同時也了解到獨立的重要。個人主義就是這樣建立在美國人性格中的」。說到打造家園，上下文同樣都是說到個人主義，可以看出是用來解釋個人主義的，故選 (B)。

The solar system, including the earth, is believed to have been formed from the accretion of dust particles some 4.5 billion years ago. When the earth was about 500 million years old, oceans started appearing on its surface, with chemical properties quite different from those of today's oceans. Scientists divide the chemical history of the oceans into three stages. The first stage spans the period when the oceans first appeared as the earth's crust cooled and ocean basins were formed. The crust reacted with volatile gases to produce highly acidic seawater. This stage ended about 3.5 billion years ago. Exactly what happened, in what order, that led to the formation of the oceans is as yet uncertain, though several theories have been advanced.

The second stage, called the transition stage, lasted approximately 2 billion years. The oceans during this stage can be thought of as a **solution** that resulted from water leaching the acid from basaltic rocks. The seawater was more acidic than modern seawater, with a higher concentration of calcium in it, and more silica.

The third stage started about 1.5 billion years ago, when the oceans acquired their contemporary characteristics. Scientists used to think that the salt in seawater simply came from the erosion of rocks by the elements and other natural processes that carried salt to the sea. More recently, as scientists came to better understand the true geological age of the earth, they realized that, at the speed salt is being delivered to the oceans, the world's oceans would have been saturated with salt millions of years ago. The logical conclusion is that there must be a mechanism that removes salt from seawater, probably in the form of minerals. Therefore, the oceans are no longer regarded as a simple storage space but as a steady-state system capable of maintaining chemical balance. This capability is restricted to open oceans, however. For inland seas of restricted areas, such as Utah's Great Salt Lake, the salinity can fluctuate widely.

✎ Exercise

① The passage primarily discusses
   (A) the chemical composition of water
   (B) the formation of the earth's crust
   (C) the different types of seawater
   (D) the chemical evolution of oceans

② According to the passage, it can be inferred that the initial stage of oceanic development lasted about how many years?
   (A) 500 million
   (B) 1 billion
   (C) 1.5 billion
   (D) 3.5 billion

③ According to the passage, oceans during the transition stage had
   (A) lower calcium concentrations than today's oceans
   (B) little silica
   (C) higher acidity than today's seawater
   (D) high concentrations of salt

④ The word "solution" in the second paragraph could best be replaced by
   (A) consequence
   (B) method
   (C) mixture
   (D) theory

⑤ Which of the following statements about the saltiness of modern oceans can best be inferred from the passage?
   (A) It results strictly from the accumulation of deposited salt
   (B) It is gradually decreasing over time
   (C) It is now known not to result from a natural process
   (D) It probably hasn't changed much in a million years

⑥ What can be inferred from the author's discussion of the saltiness of the oceans in the third paragraph?
(A) Salt delivery stopped about 1.5 billion years ago
(B) Today's rate of salt delivery is not known
(C) Scientists have changed their estimates of the earth's age
(D) The oceans are actually much younger than was believed

⑦ Which of the following do scientists NOT currently believe about the earth's oceans?
(A) They are merely accumulators of salt
(B) Some sea salt is regularly removed from the ocean
(C) They may be chemically different from inland seas
(D) They receive salt from natural processes

⑧ Why does the author mention Utah's Great Salt Lake?
(A) To provide an example of a steady-state system
(B) To introduce the world's largest inland sea
(C) As an example of a sea with variations in salinity
(D) As a comparison to the world's salt-free seas

【文章翻譯】

　　太陽系，包括地球在內，一般認為是在大約 45 億年前由灰塵凝聚而生成的。地球大約 5 億歲時，海洋開始在地表出現，化學性和今日海洋大不相同。科學家把海洋的化學史畫分為三個階段。第一階段涵蓋海洋最早出現的時代，當時地殼冷卻、海洋盆地形成。地殼與不穩定氣體產生反應，製造出高度酸性的海水。這個階段大約在 35 億年前結束。究竟發生了些什麼事、以及先後順序如何，導致海洋形成，這些問題尚無定論，雖然有好幾種理論被提出來。

　　第二個階段稱為過渡期，持續約 20 億年。這個階段的海洋可以視為水在玄武岩中溶出酸性而造成的溶液。海水比今日海水的酸性高，含有的鈣濃度比較高、矽也比較多。

　　第三個階段約在 15 億年前開始，當時海洋取得了現代的特色。科學家從前以為海水中的鹽分只是來自於風雨對岩石的侵蝕，以及其他天然程序，把鹽帶到海中。後來，科學家開始比較了解地球真正的地質年齡，於是才發現：以目前鹽進入海水的速度計算，世界的海洋在幾百萬年前早就應該達到鹽分飽和才對。合理的結論是：一定有一套機制可以從海水中移除鹽分，可能是以礦物質的形式。所以，海洋不再被視為單純的儲存空間，而是一個恆定狀態系統，有能力維持本身的化學平衡。不過這種能力局限於開放的海洋。如果是面積有限的內陸海，像猶他州的大鹽湖，鹽分可以有相當大的起伏。

【練習題翻譯與詳解】

① 本文主要討論的是

　(A) 水的化學成分　　　　　　　　(B) 地殼的形成

　(C) 不同種類的海水　　　　　　　(D) 海洋的化學演進

【答案】**D**

【解析】這是問主題的題型，要找主題句。第一段在開場白過後進入全文主題句「科學家把海洋的化學史畫分為三個階段」，接下來的段落主題句依時間先後順序分別介紹這三個階段，共同的主題是 the chemical history of oceans，意思最接近的就是 the chemical evolution of oceans，故選 (D)。

② 根據本文，可以推論海洋發展的最初階段持續了大約多少年？

　(A) 5 億　　　　　　　　　　　　(B) 10 億

　(C) 15 億　　　　　　　　　　　(D) 35 億

【答案】**A**

【解析】這是推論題，要找「根據」。第一段說地球生成於 45 億年前。5 億歲時海洋形成，所以海洋的第一階段開始於 40 億年前。後面說這個階段在 35 億年前結束，所以這個階段歷時應該是 5 億年。

③ 根據本文，過渡時期的海洋裡面有

    (A) 比今日海洋較低的鈣濃度

    (B) 很少的矽

    (C) 比今日海水更高的酸性

    (D) 高濃度的鹽

【答案】**C**

【解析】這是問細節的題型，要找同義表達。第二段說過渡期的海洋「海水比今日海水的酸性高」，故選 (C)。

④ 第二段中的 solution 一字可以替換成

    (A) 後果   (B) 方法

    (C) 混合   (D) 理論

【答案】**C**

【解析】這是單字題。solution（構造：loosen/(*n.*)）在此解釋為「溶液」（動詞 dissolve 是指「溶解」），同義字是 mixture。

⑤ 關於現代海洋的鹹度，下面哪一項陳述可以推論出來？

    (A) 它完全來自於儲存鹽分的累積

    (B) 它隨時間逐漸降低

    (C) 現在了解它不是天然程序造成的

    (D) 它可能有 1 百萬年都沒出現大變化了

【答案】**D**

【解析】這是推論題，要找「根據」。第三段說，如果海洋只是單純儲存鹽分，幾百萬年前就該達到飽和。所以「海洋不再被視為單純的儲存空間，而是一個恆定狀態系統，有能力維持本身的化學平衡」。其中 a steady-state system 表示它可以維持狀態的穩定，主要是維持鹽分固定，故選 (D)。

⑥ 作者在第三段討論到海洋的鹹度，可以推論出什麼？

    (A) 鹽的運送在 15 億年前停止

    (B) 今日鹽分運送的狀態未知

    (C) 科學家改變過對地球年齡的估計

    (D) 海洋其實比從前認為的要年輕許多

【答案】**C**

【解析】這是推論題，要找「根據」。第三段說「後來，科學家開始比較了解地球真正的地質年齡」，這表示從前的了解是錯的，因而要修正，故選 (C)。

⑦ 關於地球的海洋，科學家目前不相信下列哪一項？

    (A) 它只是儲存鹽的地方

    (B) 有些海鹽會固定從海洋中移除

    (C) 它的化學成分可能和內陸海不同

    (D) 它從天然程序中得到鹽分

【答案】**A**

【解析】這是採用消去法、問細節的題型，要刪除三項同義表達。第三段說「海洋不再被視為單純的儲存空間，而是一個恆定狀態系統」，這和 They are merely accumulators of salt 有牴觸，故選 (A)。

⑧ 作者為何提到猶他州大鹽湖？

    (A) 提供例子說明恆定狀態系統

    (B) 介紹世界最大內陸海

    (C) 當作海水鹽分變化的例子

    (D) 和世界上的無鹽海洋做比較

【答案】**C**

【解析】這是修辭目的的題型，要看上下文。第三段說「這種能力局限於開放的海洋。如果是面積有限的內陸海，像猶他州的大鹽湖，鹽分可以有相當大的起伏」，下文說它的海洋鹽分有變化，故選 (C)。

8

Reading 5

Adirondack State Park, a mountainous region in northeastern New York state, is bounded on the east by Lake Champlain, on the north by the St. Lawrence river and on the south by the Mohawk river. The park covers about 5,000 square miles, about the size of Vermont, and although much of the land is designated as "forever wild," some of it is zoned for **restricted** residential, commercial, or industrial use. How to balance the sometimes competing concerns of residents, businesses, and tourists has long been a critical issue in the park.

Since the park's inception in 1892, a Park Commission, controlled by the provisions of the New York state constitution, has been responsible for overseeing the park's development. The decisions of the Park Commission have historically been highly unpopular with park residents, among the poorest citizens in all of New York. They frequently view the commissioners as ivory tower outsiders, overly influenced by environmental groups, who do not understand the deteriorating economic conditions within the park.

Recently, residents have demanded more input on all matters concerning administration of the park. They have been at least partially successful; local boards have been initiated in many communities to consult with park commissioners on matters of community importance. However, these boards merely posses the power of persuasion, not statutory authority. Moreover, many residents are unhappy with the members of these local boards, claiming that they simply constitute a wealthy business elite with no more **regard** for the average citizen than that shown by the park commissioners. Luckily, however, although the political fighting shows no signs of **abating**, the park remains a region of beauty and tranquility for all who visit it.

✎ Exercise

① What does the passage primarily discuss?
   (A) The bodies of water surrounding Adirondack State Park
   (B) The battle over the management of Adirondack State Park
   (C) Creation of New York State's Park Commission
   (D) Zoning laws abolishing wilderness areas inside New York's parks

② Which of the following does the author imply about the demands of residents, tourists, and business?
   (A) The demands are all basically selfish
   (B) The demands are equally bad for the park
   (C) Only the demands of residents really matter
   (D) It is difficult to balance the demands

③ The word "restricted" in the first paragraph can best be replaced by which of the following?
   (A) limited
   (B) eventual
   (C) aggressive
   (D) possible

④ Historically, the attitude of park residents towards Park Commissioners can best be described as
   (A) cooperative
   (B) distrustful
   (C) informative
   (D) short sighted

⑤ It can be inferred from the passage that, at least in the minds of park residents, economic conditions inside the park
   (A) have improved somewhat in recent years
   (B) are heavily influenced by the mining industry
   (C) result from a lack of consistent tourism
   (D) are not helped by the Park Commission

8

⑥ What evidence does the author supply for the claim that residents have been successful in demanding participation in park management?

(A) They have formed local boards to consult with park commissioners.

(B) They have been invited to join the Park Commission.

(C) Business in the park has prospered.

(D) More residents have become business elites.

⑦ The author claims that park residents have only been partially successful in achieving more management responsibility because

(A) most residents are not interested in political office

(B) local boards do not have any legal authority

(C) some communities have not yet established local boards

(D) businesses are still allowed in many areas of the park

⑧ In the third paragraph the word "regard" is closest in meaning to

(A) concern

(B) hostility

(C) program

(D) protection

⑨ In the third paragraph the word "abating" is closest in meaning to

(A) lessening

(B) concluding

(C) continuing

(D) escalating

題解

阿第倫達克州立公園是紐約州東北部一處山區，東臨尚普蘭湖、北界聖勞倫斯河、南濱莫霍克河。公園佔地約 5,000 平方英里，大小和佛蒙特州相仿。雖然裡面大部分土地標示為「永保荒野」，但是也有一部分規畫作有限的住宅區、商業區、或者工業區之用。居民、商業、與觀光客不同的需求時有衝突，要如何拿捏平衡點，這個問題長久以來一直是園區的重要議題。

自從 1892 年開辦園區以來，園區委員會（要受紐約州憲法條款的約束）一直負責監督公園的發展。園區委員會所做的決定歷來一直很不受園區居民支持，這些人屬於全紐約州最貧窮的公民。他們經常視委員為象牙塔裡頭的外人，過度受到環保團體的影響，不了解園區內每況愈下的經濟處境。

最近，居民要求對於園區管理的各方面能夠加強參與。他們至少成功了一部分。許多社區都開辦了地方理事會，就社區重要事務向園區委員提供意見。不過，這些理事會只有建議權，沒有法定的權威。而且，許多居民對這些地方理事會的成員也不滿意，表示這些理事只是富有的商業菁英階級，和園區委員同樣不關心小老百姓。幸好，雖然政治鬥爭毫無平息的跡象，但是公園仍然是美麗安詳的地方，開放給所有訪客享用。

練習題翻譯與詳解

① 本文的主題是什麼？

(A) 阿第倫達克州立公園四周的水域

(B) 阿第倫達克州立公園管理權的鬥爭

(C) 紐約州公園委員會的成立

(D) 在紐約州公園內廢除荒野地區的區域規畫法

【答案】B

【解析】這是問主題的題型，要找主題句。第一段開場白過後進入全文主題句：「居民、商業、與觀光客不同的需求時有衝突，要如何拿捏平衡點，這個問題長久以來一直是園區的重要議題」，點出園區管理的主題。第二段與第三段分別介紹園區委員會與園區居民，重點在這兩方面對園區管理的爭執。涵蓋全文的主題就是園區管理方面的衝突，故選 (B)。

② 關於居民、觀光客、商業這三方面的要求，作者暗示了什麼？

(A) 這些要求基本上都是自私的

(B) 這些要求對園區同樣有害

(C) 只有居民的要求才重要

(D) 很難平衡這些要求

【答案】D

【解析】這是推論的題型，要找「根據」。第一段說「居民、商業、與觀光客不同的需求時有衝突，要如何拿捏平衡點，這個問題長久以來一直是園區的重要議題」。既然長久以來無法拿捏一個恰當的平衡點，可以推論很難平衡這些要求，故選 (D)。

③ 第一段中的 restricted 一字可以替換成哪個字？

    (A) 有限的   (B) 最後的

    (C) 侵略性的，積極的   (D) 可能的

【答案】A

【解析】這是單字題。動詞 restrict（構造：back/tighten）的意思是「限制」，同義字是 limit。

④ 從歷史看，園區居民對園區委員的態度可以說是

    (A) 合作的   (B) 不信任的

    (C) 有啟發性的   (D) 短視的

【答案】B

【解析】這是問態度的題型，要看用字。「園區委員會所做的決定歷來一直很不受園區居民支持，這些人屬於全紐約州最貧窮的公民。他們經常視委員為象牙塔裡頭的外人，過度受到環保團體的影響，不了解園區內每況愈下的經濟處境」，這裡透露出來的是對委員的否定態度，故選 (B)。

⑤ 從文中可以推論，至少在園區居民的眼中，園區內的經濟情況

    (A) 近年來略有改善

    (B) 嚴重受到採礦業的影響

    (C) 是觀光業方針不一致的產物

    (D) 園區委員會沒有幫到忙

【答案】D

【解析】這是推論題，要找「根據」。第二段說園區居民「經常視委員為象牙塔裡頭的外人，過度受到環保團體的影響，不了解園區內每況愈下的經濟處境」，可知居民認為委員對經濟沒有幫助。

⑥ 作者說居民要求參與園區管理，這種要求獲得成功，作者為這種說法提供了什麼證據？

    (A) 他們組成了地方理事會為園區委員提供意見。

    (B) 他們受邀參加園區委員會。

    (C) 園區內的商業蓬勃發展。

    (D) 更多居民成為商業菁英。

【答案】**A**

【解析】這是修辭目的的題型，要找上下文。第三段說「最近，居民要求對於園區管理的各方面能夠加強參與。他們至少成功了一部分。許多社區都開辦了地方理事會，就社區重要事務向園區委員提供意見」。作者在「成功」的直接下文提供的證據就是地方理事會的成立。

⑦ 作者說園區居民要求多承擔管理責任，這方面只獲得部分的成功，原因在於

    (A) 大部分居民對政治職位興趣缺缺

    (B) 地方理事會沒有法律實權

    (C) 有些社區尚未成立地方理事會

    (D) 園區許多地方仍然允許商業

【答案】**B**

【解析】這是問細節的題型，要找同義表達。第三段說到園區居民爭取參與管理「至少成功了一部分……不過，這些理事會只有建議權，沒有法定的權威」。在「不過」後面說明的就是沒有完全成功的原因，故選 (B)。

⑧ 第三段中的 regard 一字意思最接近

    (A) 關切   (B) 敵意

    (C) 計畫   (D) 保護

【答案】**A**

【解析】這是單字題。regard 的意思是「看待，關切」，在此的同義字是 concern。

⑨ 第三段中的 abating 一字意思最接近

    (A) 減輕   (B) 結束

    (C) 繼續   (D) 升高

【答案】**A**

【解析】這是單字題。動詞 abate（構造：to/beat）的意思是「降低，緩和，減低」，同義字是 lessen。

8

Developing societies contain within them 85% of the world's population. Between the poorest and relatively most prosperous, there are more differences in average living conditions than among developed societies. The ratio between average incomes in the relatively poorest developed country and the richest is about one to three. In contrast, the ratio between average incomes in the poorest developing countries and the relatively most prosperous is about one to twelve. This difference results, to some degree, from the size of the category (there are more developing countries than developed ones), but some commentators attribute it to a sort of "**critical income level**," below which a country is forced to live poor even if it seems wealthy in comparison to its neighbors.

It is also worth remembering that people in any given developing country are likely to have a sense of pride in their own system and may not focus on those systemic problems that would cause an economic theorist to classify it as "developing." The people of a given developing country may also **take great offense at** being grouped with another country whose circumstances they consider vastly inferior to their own. Even an attempt to address these issues from a value-neutral, science-based perspective can cause considerable offense. Caution must therefore be exercised in drawing generalizations about developing countries. Nevertheless, it can be concluded that certain characteristics are common to most of them.

One defining characteristic is an economic profile that includes low GNP per capita, a low average income, and very limited accumulations of capital. **W** A history of having been a colony is also typical, although the same could also be said for several of the world's developed countries (e.g., the U.S., Singapore, and Australia). **X** Nevertheless, the proportion of former colonies among the developing societies is great (and the proportion of them among developed countries small). Some economists, as we shall see below, see causality in this pattern. **Y** Finally, the typical developing country imports not only **significant** amounts of finished goods but also significant amounts of capital in the form of loans and foreign investments, while it exports a limited number of raw materials and goods that have been assembled in foreign-owned factories. **Z**

The typical developing country has a foreign-dominated economy, with its economic functioning being dependent on continual infusions of foreign investments, loans, and aid from developed countries, for which it pays a high price in profit repatriations, interest payment, and economic sovereignty. Its economy thus functions at, and is integrated into, a lower level of the world economy and division of labor.

There is considerable debate among social scientists regarding the historical origins of Third World inequality. Dependency theorists such as Baran (1957), Frank (1969), Wallerstein (1974), and Amin (1980) hold that as the capitalist world economy developed, European countries seized control through conquest, colonialism, and other forms of domination of large parts of the economies of Asia, Africa, and Latin America. They forced Third World economies into molds which served their own development interests. **The agriculture of Caribbean island countries**, for example, was oriented toward production of sugar for export rather than all-around production for domestic needs. Modernization theorists such as Rostow (1960), Hagan (1962), and Eisenstadt (1966) hold that the causes of Third World poverty and misery are primarily domestic, lying in pre-capitalist and pre-industrial institutional structures which are **antithetical to** development needs. Still other social scientists blame rising population growth rates for continuing poverty in the developing countries.

Virtually all these development theorists agree that agricultural efficiency is the primordial first step toward development. The more technologically efficient the agriculture of a country, the more the agricultural workers can be shifted to industrial and service occupations. The more developed a country, the proportionally fewer agricultural workers in its labor force and the smaller the contribution of agricultural production toward its economic production. Hence, the World Bank has reported that agricultural production accounts for only 3% of the total GDP of developed countries (in aggregate), compared to 29% for all low-income countries combined—nearly 10 times as high.

Exercise

① The word "critical" in paragraph 1 is closest in meaning to

(A) condemnatory   (B) appraising

(C) crucial   (D) unacceptable

② The author mentions all of the following as reasons one must be careful while making generalizations about developing countries EXCEPT

(A) people's sense of pride in their own system

(B) people's neglect of their nation's problems

(C) people's reluctance to be classified with people worse off than they are

(D) people's attempt to be neutral and scientific

③ In stating "take great offense at" in paragraph 2, the author means

(A) feel very angry about

(B) be on the offensive at

(C) very carefully guard against

(D) launch a massive attack on

④ Which of the following can be inferred from paragraph 3 about the U.S., Singapore, and Australia?

(A) They used to have low GDP per capita.

(B) They have all been colonies before.

(C) They all have typical histories.

(D) They are among the richest of the world's developed countries.

⑤ The word "significant" in paragraph 3 is closest in meaning to

(A) important   (B) meaningful

(C) substantial   (D) ominous

⑥ In which position would the following boldfaced sentence best fit in paragraph 3?

A third characteristic of most developing societies is that a relatively high proportion of the labor force is still in agriculture.

(A) Position W   (B) Position X

(C) Position Y   (D) Position Z

⑦ Which of the sentences below best expresses the essential information in the boldfaced sentence in paragraph 4?

The typical developing country has a foreign-dominated economy, with its economic functioning being dependent on continual infusions of foreign investments, loans, and aid from developed countries, for which it pays a high price in profit repatriations, interest payment, and economic sovereignty.

(A) The typical developing country is controlled by foreign powers and needs constant foreign aid.

(B) A foreign-dominated economy typically relies on continual imports of capital and pays high interests.

(C) A developing country usually has a foreign-controlled economy and pays a high price for foreign capital and aid.

(D) The economy of a developing country is typically controlled by foreign powers that give aid to it.

⑧ According to paragraph 5, what is one reason given by experts why Third World countries have been economically inferior to developed countries?

(A) They have been forced by European countries to modernize.

(B) They have had trouble fitting into the molds set by the capitalist world.

(C) They have institutional structures that are oriented to sugar production.

(D) They have populations that have been growing too fast.

⑨ Why does the author mention "The agriculture of Caribbean island countries" in paragraph 5?

(A) to support one belief held by dependency theorists

(B) to support one belief held by modernization theorists

(C) to name one belief that all development theorists hold

(D) to name one belief that is based on inaccurate information

⑩ By saying "antithetical to" in paragraph 5, the author means

(A) theoretical to   (B) similar to

(C) contrary to   (D) conducive to

⑪ According to paragraph 6, what do experts believe to be the first thing an underdeveloped nation must do for economic development?

(A) It must achieve industrial efficiency.

(B) It must have a primarily industrial or service population.

(C) It must report to the World Bank.

(D) It must become efficient in agriculture.

⑦ 題解

[文章翻譯]

　　開發中社會包括全球 85% 人口。在最窮與相對最富之間，平均生活水平的差異要大過已開發社會的情況。已開發國家中，相對最貧窮的國家與相對最富裕的國家，平均所得比例大約是 1 比 3。相反的，在開發中國家，相對最貧窮國家的平均所得比起相對最富裕國家，比例大約是 1 比 12。這樣的差異，某種程度可以說是因為兩個種類有大有小（開發中國家的數目大於已開發國家）。但也有一些評論家歸因於一種「關鍵收入水平」，國家在此水平之下就不得不過貧窮生活，儘管比起鄰國好像自己很富裕。

　　另外也別忘了：任何一個開發中國家的人民很可能對自己的體制感到驕傲，也可能不會特別注意一些體制性的問題，這些問題會令經濟理論家把該國歸類為「開發中」。某個開發中國家的人民，如果聽到自己國家被人歸為和一個自己認為差得多的國家同類，也可能會很生氣。就算是從價值中立、以科學為基礎的角度來嘗試解決這些問題，都會嚴重得罪到人。所以，如果要為開發中國家歸納出什麼通則，一定要很小心。不過，還是可以下結論說大部分開發中國家有某些共同的特點。

　　一項獨特的特色就是這樣的經濟結構：人平均 GDP（國內生產毛額）低、平均所得低、財富累積相當有限。W 還有一項特色是曾經當過殖民地，不過世界上有幾個已開發國家也是（例如美國、新加坡、澳洲）。X 但是，在開發中社會裡面，前殖民地的比例極

高（而在已開發國家中這個比例極低）。有些經濟學家（下面將會看到），認為其中有因果關係。Y 最後，典型的開發中國家不只進口大量的成品、還進口大量的資本，以貸款與外資的形式，同時出口有限的原料與產品，這些產品都是在外資擁有的工廠裡組裝起來的。Z

典型的開發中國家，經濟由外國主導，經濟運作要仰賴已開發國家持續注入外資、貸款、與援助，而且要付出高昂的代價，包括利潤還給外國、支付利息、以及犧牲經濟自主權。因此，它的經濟運作屬於世界經濟與分工的較低層次、也被整合在這個層次。

關於第三世界不平等的歷史源由，社會學家之間有相當大的辯論。依賴理論家如巴蘭 (1957)、法蘭克 (1969)、瓦勒斯坦 (1974) 與阿敏 (1980) 主張，隨著資本主義世界的經濟發展，歐洲國家經由征服、殖民、以及其他方式的主宰，掌握住亞洲、非洲、拉丁美洲大部分的經濟體。他們迫使第三世界經濟體進入某些模子，以利他們自己的發展需要。例如加勒比海島國的農業，導向於生產糖以供外銷，而不是為了內需的各種生產。現代化理論家諸如羅斯托 (1960)、哈根 (1962) 與艾森斯達 (1966) 主張，第三世界貧窮苦難的原因主要在於國內：制度結構屬於前資本主義、前工業革命時代，與發展的需要相反。還有一些社會科學家則認為人口成長率越來越高才是開發中國家持續貧窮的原因。

幾乎所有的開發理論家都同意：農業效率是走上發展最為根本的第一步。一國的農業技術效率越高、農民就越能夠轉移到工業與服務業的職業。國家開發越高、勞動力中農民佔的比例相對就越低、農業生產對經濟產量的貢獻也就越小。所以，世界銀行提出報告說：已開發國家（總計）的 GDP，只有 3% 是農業生產，但是所有低所得國家總合起來的農業生產佔比則是 29% ——將近高出 10 倍。

┌─────────────────────┐
│ 練習題翻譯與詳解 │
└─────────────────────┘

① 第一段中的 critical 意思最接近

   (A) 譴責的   (B) 評估的

   (C) 關鍵的   (D) 不可接受的

【答案】**C**
【解析】這是單字題。critical 在此指的是「關鍵的，臨界點的」，同義字是 crucial。

8

② 在為開發中國家歸納通則時，作者提出下列作為必須要小心的原因，除了

   (A) 人民對自己的體制有驕傲感

   (B) 人民對自己國家的問題會忽略

   (C) 人民不願被分為和比他們差的人同一類

   (D) 人民嘗試中立、科學的態度

【答案】**D**
【解析】這是採消去法、問細節的題型，要找出三個同義表達刪去。第二段提出各種原因，不包括 (D)。

③ 作者在第二段說到 take great offense at，意思是
　　(A) 對……感覺很生氣　　　　　　(B) 對……採取攻勢
　　(C) 對……小心防範　　　　　　　(D) 對……發起大規模攻擊

【答案】A
【解析】這是單字題。片語 take offense 是「受到冒犯，生氣」。

④ 根據第三段可以推論出美國、新加坡、澳洲如何？
　　(A) 從前的人平均 GDP 很低。　　　(B) 從前都是殖民地。
　　(C) 都具有典型的歷史。　　　　　(D) 都是世界最富有的已開發國家。

【答案】B
【解析】這是推論題，要找「根據」。第三段說「還有一項特色是曾經當過殖民地，不過世界上有幾個已開發國家也是（例如美國、新加坡、澳洲）」，可知這三國曾經當過殖民地，故選 (B)。

⑤ 第三段中的 significant 一字意思最接近
　　(A) 重要　　　　　　　　　　　　(B) 有意義
　　(C) 重大　　　　　　　　　　　　(D) 不祥

【答案】C
【解析】這是單字題。significant（構造：mark/make/(a.)）在此解釋為「重大的」，同義字是 substantial（構造：under/be/(a.)）。

⑥ 下面這個黑體字句子最適合放在第三段的什麼位置？
　「大部分開發中國家的第三項特質是相當高比例的勞動力仍然務農。」
　　(A) W 位置　　　　　　　　　　　(B) X 位置
　　(C) Y 位置　　　　　　　　　　　(D) Z 位置

【答案】C
【解析】這是安插句子的題型，要看上下文。插入句開頭說到「第三項特質」，表示前面說過兩項特質。在 X 位置前面說到兩項特色，但是 X 位置後面繼續在說第二項特色（前殖民地），所以第三項特色應該放在後面的 Y 位置，成為：「一項獨特的特色就是這樣的經濟結構：人平均 GDP（國內生產毛額）低、平均所得低、財富累積相當有限。還有一項特色是曾經當過殖民地，不過世界上有幾個已開發國家也是（例如美國、新加坡、澳洲）。但是，在開發中社會裡面，前殖民地的比例極高（而在已開發國家中這個比例極低）。有些經濟學家（下面將會看到），認為其中有因果關係。大部分開發中國家的第三項特質是相當高比例的勞動力仍然務農。最後，典型的開發中國家不只進口大量的成品、還進口大量的資本……」。

340

⑦ 下列哪個句子最能夠表達第四段黑體字句子的主要內容？

「典型的開發中國家，經濟由外國主導，經濟運作要仰賴已開發國家持續注入外資、貸款、與援助，而且要付出高昂的代價，包括利潤還給外國、支付利息、以及犧牲經濟自主權。」

(A) 典型的開發中國家被外國勢力控制、需要持續外援。

(B) 外國主宰的經濟典型要倚賴持續進口資本，並且要支付高利息。

(C) 開發中國家的經濟通常由外國把持、並且要為外資與外援付出高昂代價。

(D) 開發中國家的經濟通常由給它援助的外國勢力把持。

【答案】C
【解析】這是句子改寫的題型，要找句中重點的同義表達。刪除不重要的細節後，最接近的同義表達是 (C)。

⑧ 根據第五段，第三世界國家經濟方面不及已開發國家，專家提出的一個原因是什麼？

(A) 他們被歐洲國家強迫現代化。

(B) 他們要適應資本主義世界設定的模子有困難。

(C) 他們有一些產糖導向的制度結構。

(D) 他們的人口成長太快。

【答案】 D
【解析】這是問細節的問題，要找同義表達。第五段說「還有一些社會科學家則認為人口成長率越來越高才是開發中國家持續貧窮的原因」，其中 rising population growth rates 就是 populations that have been growing too fast 的同義表達，故選 (D)。

⑨ 在第五段，作者為何提到「加勒比海島國農業」？

(A) 為了支持依賴論者的一項理念

(B) 為了支持現代化論者的一項理念

(C) 為了說出所有開發論者共有的一項理念

(D) 為了說出一項建立在錯誤資訊上的理念

【答案】A
【解析】這是修辭目的的題型，要看上下文。第五段說「依賴理論家……主張，隨著資本主義世界的經濟發展，歐洲國家經由征服、殖民、以及其他方式的主宰，掌握住亞洲、非洲、拉丁美洲大部分的經濟體。他們迫使第三世界經濟體進入某些模子，以利他們自己的發展需要。例如加勒比海島國的農業」，可知加勒比海島國的農業是作為例子，說明「依賴理論家」的主張，故選 (A)。

8

⑩ 第五段中作者說 antithetical 的意思是

    (A) 對……是理論性的

    (B) 與……相似

    (C) 和……相反

    (D) 對……有引導作用

【答案】**C**

【解析】這是單字題。形容詞 antithetical（構造：against/put/(*a.*)）的意思是「對立的，相反的」。

⑪ 根據第六段，專家認為低度開發國家要想發展經濟，必須做的頭一件事是什麼？

    (A) 必須達成工業效率。

    (B) 必須要以工業或服務業人口為主。

    (C) 必須向世界銀行報告。

    (D) 必須加強農業效率。

【答案】**D**

【解析】這是問細節的題型，要找同義表達。第六段說「農業效率是走上發展最為根本的第一步」，其中 agricultural efficiency 就是 efficient in agriculture 的同義表達，故選 (D)。

The Industrial Revolution, a term used in the United States to refer to the industrial development from roughly 1760 to 1840, actually consisted of new developments in both the industrial sphere and the socio-economic-cultural sphere. Technological developments like **improved** spinning and weaving machines, the steam engine, and the railway locomotive generally receive the most attention, but these are merely the best known of a long series of industrial advances. The non-industrial developments, however, were equally as important. Additionally, **it is not at all clear** whether the industrial developments spurred changes in the other sphere or vice versa.

Advancements outside the industrial sphere included agricultural improvements that made possible the provision of food for a larger non-agrarian population and economic changes that resulted in a wider distribution of wealth. Furthermore, land began to decline as a source of wealth in face of rising industrial production and increased international trade. By removing large numbers of men and women from the agricultural pursuits that had formed humankind's main occupation since the beginnings of civilization, and by introducing them to novel ways of living and working, the Industrial Revolution transformed Western societies. It thus became one of the chief determinants of the modern way of life.

✏ Exercise

① The passage primarily discusses
    (A) the vast influences of the Industrial Revolution in the U.S.
    (B) the results of increased numbers of agricultural laborers
    (C) the numerous developments that brought about the Industrial Revolution
    (D) how wealthy Americans lived in the 18th and 19th centuries

② In the first paragraph the word "improved" is closest in meaning to which of the following?
    (A) enhanced
    (B) less expensive
    (C) produced
    (D) automated

③ It can be inferred from the passage that, with regards to the industrial sphere of the Industrial Revolution,
    (A) agricultural developments were major causes
    (B) many advances were made over a period of time
    (C) only the railroad locomotive and steam engine remain important
    (D) changes in the transportation industry were the first to occur

④ In the first paragraph the phrase "it is not at all clear" is closest in meaning to which of the following?
    (A) most people agree
    (B) it is obvious
    (C) it is uncertain
    (D) it is not worth discussing

⑤ According to the author, one of the non-industrial advancements made during the Industrial Revolution was that
    (A) urban dwellers consumed less farm produce
    (B) more families were forced to work on farms
    (C) farmers became the wealthiest class of citizens
    (D) some agricultural techniques were improved

⑥ According to the passage, which of the following happened during the Industrial Revolution?

(A) Farm land became less productive

(B) International trade grew

(C) Many citizens were forced to move

(D) Foreign investors purchased much land

⑦ The author mentions all of the following as related to the Industrial Revolution EXCEPT

(A) industrial development

(B) agricultural improvement

(C) economic changes

(D) computer technology

⑧ It can be inferred from the passage that for many years most people

(A) did not benefit from civilization

(B) earned their living from the land

(C) reaped fortunes from international trade

(D) fought against rapid industrial growth

【文章翻譯】

　　工業革命一詞在美國指的是大約 1760 至 1840 年間的工業發展，其實涵蓋的不只工業領域，還有社會經濟文化領域的新發展。科技進步諸如改良的紡織機、蒸汽引擎、以及火車頭，一般受到最大的注意，但這些只是一長串工業進步當中最知名的幾件。然而，非工業方面的發展也同樣重要。此外，到底是工業發展刺激到另一領域的改變、還是反過來，這個問題完全沒有定論。

　　工業領域之外的進步包括農業改良（可以為更大的非農業人口提供糧食）以及經濟變化（帶來了財富普及）。此外，土地不再是那麼重要的財富來源，因為工業生產增加、國際貿易繁榮。自有文明伊始，人類主要的工作就是務農。工業革命解放了大量男男女女不必從事農耕、讓他們認識到新的生活與工作方式，所以工業革命改造了西方社會，也因而成為現代生活方式的主要決定因素之一。

【練習題翻譯與詳解】

① 本文的主題是

　　(A) 工業革命在美國的廣大影響

　　(B) 農業勞工人數增加的結果

　　(C) 造成工業革命的眾多發展

　　(D) 富裕美國人在 18 與 19 世紀的生活方式

【答案】**A**

【解析】這是問主題的題型，要看主題句。第一段全文主題句是「工業革命……涵蓋的不止工業領域，還有社會經濟文化領域的新發展」，指出工業革命在兩個領域造成的影響。接下來兩段分別討論在這兩方面的影響，故選 (A)。

② 第一段中的 improved 一字意思最接近

　　(A) 促進的　　　　　　　　　　(B) 較不貴的

　　(C) 被生產出來的　　　　　　　(D) 自動化的

【答案】**A**

【解析】這是單字題。動詞 improve 的意思是「改善」，同義字是 enhance。

③ 從文中可以推論，關於工業革命的工業領域

　　(A) 農業發展是主要的原因

　　(B) 經過一段時間達成了許多進展

　　(C) 只有火車頭與蒸汽引擎至今仍然重要

　　(D) 運輸產業的改變是頭一個發生的

【答案】**B**

【解析】這是推論題，要找「根據」。第一段說「科技進步諸如改良的紡織機、蒸汽引擎、以及火車頭，一般受到最大的注意，但這些只是一長串工業進步當中最知名的幾件」，其中 a long series of industrial advances 與 many advances were made over a period of time 是同義表達，故選 (B)。

④ 第一段中的 it is not at all clear 一語意思最接近

    (A) 大部分人同意　　　　　　　　(B) 很明顯

    (C) 不確定　　　　　　　　　　　(D) 不值得討論

【答案】**C**

【解析】這是單字題。not clear 就是 uncertain。

⑤ 根據作者，工業革命期間有一項非工業進展是

    (A) 都市居民消耗的農產品減少

    (B) 更多家庭被迫到農場工作

    (C) 農民成為最富有的公民階級

    (D) 有些農耕技術改進了

【答案】**D**

【解析】這是問細節的題型，要找同義表達。第二段說「工業領域之外的進步包括農業改良」，其中 agricultural improvements 就是 some agricultural techniques were improved 的同義表達，故選 (D)。

⑥ 根據本文，工業革命期間發生了什麼事？

    (A) 農地產量降低

    (B) 國際貿易成長

    (C) 許多公民被迫搬家

    (D) 外國投資人購買大量土地

【答案】**B**

【解析】這是問細節的題型，要找同義表達。第三段說到「工業生產增加、國際貿易繁榮」，其中 increased international trade 就是 International trade grew 的同義表達，故選 (B)。

⑦ 作者提到以下各項都與工業革命相關，除了

    (A) 工業發展   (B) 農業進步

    (C) 經濟改變   (D) 電腦科技

【答案】**D**

【解析】這是採用消去法、問細節的題型，要刪去三個同義表達。全文沒有提到電腦科技，故選 (D)。

⑧ 從文中可以推論，有許多年的時間，大部分人

    (A) 沒有獲得文明的好處

    (B) 靠土地謀生

    (C) 從國際貿易取得財富

    (D) 對抗快速的工業成長

【答案】**B**

【解析】這是推論題，要找「根據」。第三段說「自有文明伊始，人類主要的工作就是務農」，可以推論出很長時間大部分人都靠土地謀生，故選 (B)。

9

Many mammals and some birds spend at least part of the winter in hiding, but remain no more drowsy than in normal sleep. On the other hand, some mammals undergo a **drastic** decrease in metabolic rate and physiological function during the winter, with a body temperature approaching the freezing point. This condition, sometimes known as deep hibernation, is the only state in which the warm-blooded vertebrate, with its complex mechanisms for temperature control, **abandons** its warm-blooded state and chills to the temperature of the environment. Between the drowsy condition and deep hibernation are gradations about which little is known.

The deep hibernators are confined to five orders of mammals; marsupials, Chiroptera or bats, insectivores, rodents, and, most likely, primates. With all deep hibernators, except **bats**, hibernation is seasonal, usually occurring in the cold winter months. In all cases, it occurs in animals which would face extremely difficult conditions if they had to remain active and search for food. A few desert species disappear during the hottest, driest months, and they probably enter into a stage of hibernation inside their cool burrows, although no studies have been done on this, or on the hibernation of primates during the tropical rainy season. Hibernators are typically restricted to more temperate zones, but the Alaskan ground squirrel lives near the Arctic Circle.

Exercise

① What is the main topic of the passage?
   (A) Unusual features of land mammals
   (B) Hibernation in mammals
   (C) Animals that do not hibernate
   (D) The need for studies on hibernation

② The word "drastic" in the first paragraph is closest in meaning to which of the following?
   (A) permanent
   (B) rare
   (C) extreme
   (D) mysterious

③ In the first paragraph the word "abandons" is closest in meaning to
   (A) lowers
   (B) gives up
   (C) revises
   (D) checks on

④ According to the passage, what is true about the state of deep hibernation?
   (A) It occurs only in insectivores
   (B) It is triggered by air temperatures below 0 degree C
   (C) It also occurs commonly in many bird species
   (D) It results in a significantly reduced body temperature

⑤ In the second paragraph the author mentions "bats" as an example of a species that
   (A) is not one of the five orders of mammals
   (B) engages in seasonal hibernation
   (C) lives only in cold climates
   (D) is different from other deep hibernators

⑥ According to the passage, all of the following are true about bats EXCEPT
  (A) they belong to the order Chiroptera
  (B) they hibernate to avoid difficult conditions
  (C) they are not seasonal hibernators
  (D) they need cool desert burrows to hibernate in

⑦ Which of the following can best be inferred from the passage?
  (A) No research has been done on hibernation
  (B) Most desert animals migrate in the dry season
  (C) The Arctic Circle's climate is not temperate
  (D) Tropical primates do not hibernate

⤷ 題解

文章翻譯

　　許多哺乳類和一些鳥類冬天至少有一段時間會躲起來，但並沒有比正常睡眠時更昏睡。相反的，也有一些哺乳類到了冬天會經歷新陳代謝率與生理功能大幅降低，體溫接近冰點。這種狀況有時稱為深度冬眠。溫血脊椎動物具有複雜的溫度調節機制，只有在深度冬眠時才會放棄溫血狀態、溫度降到與環境溫度相同。一個極端是昏昏欲睡、另一個極端是深度冬眠。這兩端之間有各種各樣的程度變化，但我們所知無幾。

　　深度冬眠在哺乳類中限於五目：有袋類、翼手目（就是蝙蝠）、食蟲目、齧齒類，很可能還包括靈長類。所有的深度冬眠者（除了蝙蝠）都是季節性冬眠，通常發生在寒冬。而且所有的冬眠動物都一樣，若仍然必須清醒覓食，都會面對極端艱困的環境。有少數幾種沙漠品種是在最熱最乾的幾個月躲起來，可能是在陰涼的洞穴中冬眠，不過沒有人研究過這個主題，也沒有研究過靈長類在熱帶雨季的冬眠。冬眠動物通常局限於氣候比較溫和的地區，不過阿拉斯加的地松鼠生活在接近北極圈的地區。

練習題翻譯與詳解

① 本文的主題是什麼？
   (A) 陸地哺乳類的罕見特徵
   (B) 哺乳類的冬眠
   (C) 不冬眠的動物
   (D) 冬眠需要進一步研究

【答案】B
【解析】這是問主題的題型，要找主題句。第一段在開場白之後進入全文主題句「有一些哺乳類到了冬天會經歷新陳代謝率與生理功能大幅降低，體溫接近冰點。這種狀況有時稱為深度冬眠」。第二段的主題句把哺乳類動物的冬眠做了分類。兩段共同的主題是哺乳類動物的冬眠，故選 (B)。

② 第一段中的 drastic 一字意思最接近何者？
   (A) 永久的
   (B) 罕見的
   (C) 極端的
   (D) 神祕的

【答案】C
【解析】這是單字題。drastic 的意思是「劇烈的」，同義字是 extreme。

9

③ 第一段中的 abandons 一字意思最接近

    (A) 降低

    (B) 放棄

    (C) 修改

    (D) 檢查

【答案】**B**

【解析】這是單字題。abandon 的意思是「拋棄」，同義字是 give up。

④ 根據本文，關於深度冬眠哪一句是對的？

    (A) 它只發生在食蟲目

    (B) 溫度低於攝氏零度就會引起它發生

    (C) 它也經常發生在許多鳥類品種

    (D) 它的結果是體溫大幅降低

【答案】**D**

【解析】這是問細節的題型，要找同義表達。第一段說「也有一些哺乳類到了冬天會經歷新陳代謝率與生理功能大幅降低，體溫接近冰點。這種狀況有時稱為深度冬眠」，其中 with a body temperature approaching the freezing point 就是 a significantly reduced body temperature 的同義表達，故選 (D)。

⑤ 作者在第二段提到蝙蝠作為哪種品種的例子？

    (A) 不屬於提到的五目哺乳類

    (B) 從事季節性冬眠

    (C) 只生活在寒冷氣候

    (D) 和別的深度冬眠動物不同

【答案】**D**

【解析】這是修辭目的的題型，要看上下文。第二段說「所有的深度冬眠者（除了蝙蝠）都是季節性冬眠」，這表示蝙蝠和所有的深度冬眠者不同，故選 (D)。

⑥ 根據本文，下列有關蝙蝠的話都是對的，除了

    (A) 牠屬於翼手目

    (B) 牠冬眠是為了躲避艱困的環境

    (C) 牠不是季節性冬眠動物

    (D) 牠需要陰涼的沙漠地穴好冬眠

【答案】D

【解析】這是採用消去法、問細節的題型，要找出三個同義表達刪除。第二段說「有少數幾種沙漠品種是在最熱最乾的幾個月躲起來，可能是在陰涼的洞穴中冬眠」，但不是蝙蝠，故選 (D)。

⑦ 根據本文可以推論出什麼？

  (A) 冬眠無人做過研究

  (B) 大部分沙漠動物都在乾季遷移

  (C) 北極圈的氣候不是溫和的

  (D) 熱帶靈長類不會冬眠

【答案】C

【解析】這是推論題，要找「根據」。第二段說「冬眠動物通常局限於氣候比較溫和的地區，不過阿拉斯加的地松鼠生活在接近北極圈的地區」，可以看出地松鼠是例外，生活地區不在氣候溫和處，故選 (C)。

9

Between 1450 and 1550 the foundations for the Renaissance and modern science were laid in Europe. Two partially conflicting discoveries were of **paramount** importance in this process: first, the practical rediscovery of the works of the ancient authors like Plato and Aristotle, and second, the realization that these revered sources required both partial correction and sometimes wholesale revision. From this simultaneous acceptance and rejection came the modern scientific method so well exemplified by Galileo.

Medieval thought on the material world was **solidly** based on that of the Greeks, especially Aristotle, and other notable historic authors. By 1450 the complete works of Plato and Aristotle were available in Latin translations direct from Greek. Copernicus, despite the vastness of the change involved in his theory of the earth's revolution around the sun, retained the belief of many Greek astronomers of the spherical nature of the universe and its limitation by the sphere of the fixed stars. He also retained the ancient idea of the uniform circular motion of all heavenly bodies. The same applies to the field of medicine. Even such a towering Renaissance figure as the father of modern anatomy, Andreas Vesalius, consciously based his research on the then 1,300-year-old findings of the dusty Galen.

But for all the respect paid to the luminaries of the past, scientific thought was in motion. Traditional notions were subjected to freshly designed experiments and rigorous debates before they were accepted. Although in the opening years of the Renaissance Platonic thought was revived and Aristotle was **confirmed** as the unrivaled master in biology, cracks began to appear in his systems of cosmology and mechanics. By the middle of the seventeenth century, Aristotle's physics and cosmology had both completely collapsed, while his biology was being laboriously rebuilt. The Greek science of alchemy had effectively been replaced by chemistry built mainly on the technological traditions of artisans and craftsmen, and the exploration of the structure and function of the human body had become a new profession based on observation and experimentation rather than scholarly memorization. Science itself had emerged as a vocation supported by its specialized philosophers, its specialized advocates in the art of discovery, and its highly skilled instrument makers. **Science had evolved from its more primitive stages and was ready for the glittering gains of the following period.**

✏ Exercise

① What is the main idea of the passage?
(A) The problems with a dual conception of ancient authors
(B) A scientific rejection of Greek and Roman thought
(C) The use of the ancients by early Renaissance scientists
(D) Why the works of Aristotle replaced first-hand observation

② In the first paragraph the word "paramount" is closest in meaning to which of the following?
(A) primary
(B) debated
(C) historical
(D) academic

③ According to the first paragraph, Galileo
(A) ignored the findings of the Greeks
(B) deferred to the works of ancient scholars
(C) was never satisfied with his research
(D) is representative of the scientific method

④ The word "solidly" in the second paragraph is closest in meaning to
(A) squarely
(B) mathematically
(C) probably
(D) linearly

⑤ In the second paragraph, the author mentions Copernicus in order to demonstrate that
(A) the Greek science of cosmology was incredibly accurate
(B) Copernicus was the most influential of the ancient Greeks
(C) at one time cosmology and anatomy were closely allied
(D) Greek ideas influenced even original scientific thinkers

9

⑥ According to the passage, which of the following is true of Galen?

　(A) Some of his work deals with cosmology

　(B) He was the father of Andreas Vesalius

　(C) His work came before that of Vesalius

　(D) He studied the subconscious and human psychology

⑦ The word "confirmed" in the third paragraph is closest in meaning to

　(A) condemned

　(B) replaced

　(C) affirmed

　(D) tested

⑧ According to the passage, which of the following is true about the state of scientific thought by the middle of the seventeenth century?

　(A) Aristotle's work in cosmology had been verified

　(B) The science of alchemy was no longer widely practiced

　(C) Science had returned to the level of the ancient Greeks

　(D) Craftsmen had largely replaced professional scientists

⑨ What does the author imply by saying in the third paragraph "Science had evolved from its more primitive stages and was ready for the glittering gains of the following period"?

　(A) Galileo is the most brilliant scientist ever produced

　(B) Evolution was an important topic during the Renaissance

　(C) The author is disappointed in the work of specialized philosophers

　(D) Science was ready for an era of great progress

文章翻譯

　　在 1450 到 1550 年間，歐洲為文藝復興與現代科學奠定了基礎。在這個過程中，有兩項互相有點衝突的發現特別重要：第一，古代作家如柏拉圖、亞理斯多德等人的作品等於是重新發現；第二，大家明白這些受人崇敬的資料來源有些部分需要訂正、有時候還得全盤修改。在這同時又接受、又排斥的過程中，產生了現代的科學方法，最佳典範就是伽利略。

　　中古時代關於物質世界的思想穩固地奠基在希臘人上面，特別是亞理斯多德，另外還有一些知名的古代作家。到了 1450 年，柏拉圖與亞理斯多德的完整作品已經直接從希臘文翻譯為拉丁文、可以使用。哥白尼的地球繞太陽理論造成了廣大的改變，但是他仍然保留許多希臘天文學家的觀念，相信宇宙本質是球形、恆星固定在大球體上構成宇宙的邊界。他也保留古老的想法，認為所有的天體都是作規律的圓形運動。同樣的情況也發生在醫學界。維薩里是現代解剖學之父，就連像他這麼崇高的文藝復興人物也還刻意把他的研究奠定在 1,300 年前老骨董蓋倫的發現之上。

　　不過，雖然尊重過去的名人，但是科學思想已經起動。傳統觀念要受到新設計的實驗檢驗、經過嚴格的辯論，然後才能接受。雖然在文藝復興初年，柏拉圖思想復興、亞理斯多德被肯定為生物學無與倫比的大師，但是他的宇宙論與力學系統裡面都開始出現裂痕。到了 17 世紀中葉，亞理斯多德的物理學和宇宙論都已經完全垮台，他的生物學則被仔細地重新打造。希臘的煉金術基本上已經被化學取代，主要建立在工匠與技師的技術傳統上。對於人體結構與功能的探索也成為一門新專業，建立在觀察與實驗上、不再靠學者的背誦。科學本身也成為一門行業，後援是它的專業哲學家、鼓吹發現藝術的專業提倡者、以及技巧高超的工具製造者。科學從比較原始的階段演化出來，準備好要迎接下一階段閃亮的收穫。

練習題翻譯與詳解

① 本文的主題是什麼？
　(A) 對古代作家持雙重看法的問題所在
　(B) 以科學排斥希臘羅馬思想
　(C) 文藝復興初期的科學家如何運用古人
　(D) 為何亞理斯多德的作品取代了第一手觀察

【答案】**C**
【解析】這是問主題的題型，要找主題句。第一段說到歐洲文藝復興時代對古代作家「同時又接受、又排斥的過程中，產生了現代的科學方法」。第二段描述「接受」的情況，第三段描述「排斥」的情況。所以全文主題是「文藝復興科學家如何運用古人」。

② 第一段中的 paramount 一字意思最接近何者？

    (A) 主要的　　　　　　　　　　(B) 有爭議的

    (C) 歷史的　　　　　　　　　　(D) 學術的

【答案】A

【解析】這是單字題。paramount（構造：beside/mountain）的意思是「最高的」，引申為「最主要的」，同義字是 primary。

③ 根據第一段，伽利略

    (A) 忽略希臘人的發現

    (B) 順從古代學者的作品

    (C) 對自己的研究一直不滿意

    (D) 代表科學方法

【答案】D

【解析】這是問細節的題型，要找同義表達。第一段說「在這同時又接受、又排斥的過程中，產生了現代的科學方法，最佳典範就是伽利略」，其中 the modern scientific method so well exemplified by Galileo 就是 Galileo is representative of the scientific method 的同義表達，故選 (D)。

④ 第二段中的 solidly 一字意思最接近

    (A) 直接地，堅定地　　　　　　(B) 數學地

    (C) 可能地　　　　　　　　　　(D) 線形地

【答案】A

【解析】形容詞 solid 是「穩固」的意思，solidly 是指「穩固地」，同義字是 squarely。

⑤ 第二段中作者提到哥白尼的目的是要說明

    (A) 希臘的宇宙論極為精確

    (B) 哥白尼是古希臘人中影響力最大的一位

    (C) 宇宙論與解剖學一度緊密相連

    (D) 希臘觀念影響到甚至很有原創性的科學思想家

【答案】D

【解析】這是修辭目的的題型，要看上下文。上文說「中古時代關於物質世界的思想穩固地奠基在希臘人上面」，接下來舉哥白尼為例：這個提出地球繞太陽這種原創想法的人卻仍然相信古希臘人的許多觀念，故選 (D)。

⑥ 根據本文，下面哪一句關於蓋倫的話是對的？

　　(A) 他有一些研究處理的是宇宙論

　　(B) 他是維薩里之父

　　(C) 他的研究工作是在維薩里之前

　　(D) 他研究潛意識與人類心理學

【答案】**C**

【解析】這是問細節的題型，要找同義表達。第二段說「維薩里……還刻意把他的研究奠定在 1,300 年前老骨董蓋倫的發現之上」，可看出蓋倫比維薩里早得多。

⑦ 第三段中的 confirmed 一字意思最接近

　　(A) 譴責　　　　　　　　　　　　(B) 取代

　　(C) 肯定　　　　　　　　　　　　(D) 測驗

【答案】**C**

【解析】這是單字題。動詞 confirm 的意思是「確認」，同義字是 affirm。

⑧ 根據本文，關於 17 世紀中葉科學思想的狀況，下列哪一句是對的？

　　(A) 亞理斯多德的宇宙論作品已獲得證實

　　(B) 煉金術不再被人廣泛採用

　　(C) 科學回復到了古希臘的水平

　　(D) 工匠大致取代了專業科學

【答案】**B**

【解析】這是問細節的題型，要找同義表達。第三段說「到了 17 世紀中葉……煉金術基本上已經被化學取代」，其中 had effectively been replaced by chemistry 與 was no longer widely practiced 是同義表達，故選 (B)。

⑨ 作者在第三段說「科學從比較原始的階段演化出來，準備好要迎接下一階段閃亮的收穫」，這話是在暗示什麼？

　　(A) 伽利略是史上最卓越的科學家

　　(B) 進化論是文藝復興時代的重要主題

　　(C) 作者對專業哲學家的研究工作很失望

　　(D) 科學準備進入偉大進步的時代

【答案】**D**

【解析】這是推論題。原句中的 glittering gains of the following period 就是 an era of great progress 的同義表達。

Liquid Crystal Displays (LCDs) is the way of the future. They have the advantage of being lightweight, thin, flat, energy-efficient, and versatile in application. Computers, cellphones and high-definition TV sets have largely switched over to using LCD screens.

Liquid crystals are half solid, half liquid. They flow as liquids do, but their molecules have a regular formation, as do those in solid crystals. They are **sensitive** to light, heat, electric currents or magnetic fields. LCDs are made primarily of nematic crystals—crystals made up of long, rod-like molecules that are arranged parallel to each other. Nematic crystals easily stick to glass. When stimulated with electric currents, they can be made to block light or to allow light to pass through. It is this characteristic that makes liquid crystals ideal for display screens.

Nematic crystals themselves do not provide crisp and sharp displays. To increase contrast and enhance sharpness, a sheet of glass is placed above nematic crystal-coated glass. When the overlying glass is twisted, the optical properties of the liquid crystal are **exalted**, and clarity is improved. To get the screen to display desired numbers or graphics, designers of LCD screens placed a **fine** mesh of wire under the glass. The wire is used to convey electric currents to each pixel, or light-producing unit, while an integrated circuit (IC) board controls the flow of currents to produce the desired images. To give color displays, a color filter has to be added on top of each pixel. The colors as they are, however, are seldom of satisfactory quality. They are either blurred or mixed up along borderlines. The solution is to power each pixel with a transistor. The addition of transistors makes the picture vivid and sharp, but the control of the transistors is technically complicated and requires huge computing powers to achieve. Large color LCD screens are therefore still rather expensive.

✎ Exercise

① Which of the following would be the best title for the passage?
(A) LCD Screens and Conventional Screens
(B) Liquid Crystals: a Contradiction in Terms
(C) Liquid Crystal Displays: the Way of the Future
(D) Problems with Liquid Crystal Displays

② The author mentions all of the following as merits of LCD screens EXCEPT their
(A) minimal weight
(B) low energy consumption
(C) numerous uses
(D) reasonable price

③ Which of the following is mentioned in the passage as a characteristic of liquid crystals that they have in common with solid objects?
(A) The ability to flow around
(B) A regular molecular formation
(C) A rod-like shape
(D) Conductivity to electricity

④ The word "sensitive" in the second paragraph most closely means
(A) delicate
(B) insightful
(C) fragile
(D) responsive

⑤ According to the passage, why are liquid crystals excellent materials for display screens?
(A) They easily stick to glass.
(B) They come with a variety of colors.
(C) They can be twisted into any shape.
(D) They can vary in transparency.

⑥ The word "exalted" in the third paragraph most closely means
(A) increased
(B) resulted
(C) minimized
(D) elongated

⑦ The word "fine" in the third paragraph most closely means
(A) punitive
(B) graceful
(C) thin
(D) healthy

⑧ In order to get LCDs to display numbers on the screen, all of the following are needed EXCEPT
(A) a mesh of wire
(B) a number of pixels
(C) an integrated circuit board
(D) a lot of filters

⑨ It can be inferred from the passage that a number of transistors are added to LCD screens in order to
(A) raise the quality of color pictures
(B) expand computing power
(C) cut down production cost
(D) create stereo sound

⑩ All of the following questions about LCDs can be answered according to information in the passage EXCEPT
(A) Are LCDs solid or liquid?
(B) How can nematic crystal displays be made sharper and crisper?
(C) How do LCD screens compare with traditional TV screens in terms of color?
(D) Why are large color LCD screens expensive?

題解

【文章翻譯】

液晶顯示 (LCD) 是未來之道。它的好處是輕、薄、扁、省電、以及應用多端。電腦、手機與高解析電視機大致都已經轉換為液晶顯示螢幕。

液晶半是固體、半是液體。它會像液體那樣流動，但它的分子結構規律，和固態晶體一樣。它對光、熱、電流或磁場都有敏感度。液晶顯示主要採用向列型晶體——這種晶體由長棒狀分子作平行排列構成。向列型晶體很容易黏附到玻璃上。受到電流刺激，可以有阻光或透光的變化。就是因為這個特質，液晶才是展示幕的理想原料。

向列型晶體本身不能提供清晰的展示。為了增加對比、增強清晰度，在塗有向列型晶體的玻璃上還要加一層玻璃。如果扭轉上層玻璃，液晶的光學性質會提升，清晰度就增加。為了讓螢幕展示想要的數字或圖形，液晶螢幕設計師在玻璃下面放了一面細電網。電網用來傳導電流到每個像素（發光單位）上，另有一塊積體電路 (IC) 板控制電流以產生想要的影像。為了做彩色展示，得在每個像素上加一個濾色器。不過，這樣產生的色彩品質很難令人滿意：或者模糊不清、或者會在邊緣混淆。解決方案是每個像素用一枚電晶體發動。加了電晶體，畫面鮮明清晰，但控制電晶體的技術很複雜，要巨大的電腦運算能力來達成。所以大型彩色液晶螢幕仍不便宜。

【練習題翻譯與詳解】

① 下列哪一個是本文最佳標題？

(A) 液晶螢幕與傳統螢幕　　　　　(B) 液晶：矛盾的名稱

(C) 液晶顯示：未來之道　　　　　(D) 液晶顯示的問題

【答案】**C**

【解析】這是問主題的題型，要找主題句。第一段「液晶顯示是未來之道」是全文主題句。後面兩段進一步說明液晶顯示的原理，共同的主題是液晶顯示，而且語氣是肯定的，故選 (C)。

② 作者說到下列各項都是液晶螢幕的好處，除了它的

(A) 重量輕　　　　　　　　　　　(B) 耗電少

(C) 用途多　　　　　　　　　　　(D) 價格合理

【答案】**D**

【解析】這是採用消去法、問細節的題型，要刪去三個同義表達。(A) (B) (C) 三項在第一段都能找到同義表達，但最後一段說到大型液晶螢幕仍不便宜，與 (D) 有抵觸，故選 (D)。

③ 文中提到下列哪一項說是液晶和固體的共同特性？

(A) 能夠流動　　　　　　　　(B) 有規律的分子構成

(C) 棒形　　　　　　　　　　(D) 導電性

【答案】**B**

【解析】這是問細節的題型，要找同義表達。第二段說液晶「分子結構規律，和固態晶體一樣」其中 their molecules have a regular formation 與 a regular molecular formation 是同義表達，故選 (B)。

④ 第二段中的 sensitive 一字意思最接近

(A) 精細　　　　　　　　　　(B) 有觀察力

(C) 脆弱　　　　　　　　　　(D) 有反應

【答案】**D**

【解析】這是單字題。sensitive 字面意思是「敏感」，在此上下文是說能夠感光、感電，這和「有反應」相同，故選 responsive。

⑤ 根據本文，液晶為何是展示幕的理想材料？

(A) 它很容易黏上玻璃。　　　(B) 它有許多色彩。

(C) 它可以扭成任何形狀。　　(D) 它的透明度可以變化。

【答案】**D**

【解析】這是問細節的題型，要找同義表達。第二段說液晶「受到電流刺激，可以有阻光或透光的變化。就是因為這個特質，液晶才是展示幕的理想原料」，其中 they can be made to block light or to allow light to pass through 就是 They can vary in transparency. 的同義表達，故選 (D)。

⑥ 第三段中的 exalted 一字意思最接近

(A) 增加　　　　　　　　　　(B) 產生結果

(C) 最小化　　　　　　　　　(D) 拉長

【答案】**A**

【解析】動詞 exalt（構造：intensifier/high）的意思是「升高，提升」，引申為「增加」，同義字是 increase。

⑦ 第三段中的 fine 一字意思最接近

(A) 懲罰性的　　　　　　　　(B) 優雅的

(C) 細的　　　　　　　　　　(D) 健康的

【答案】C
【解析】形容詞 fine 的意思很多，在此上下文只能解釋為「細」，同義字是 thin。

⑧ 為了要讓液晶螢幕顯示數字，下列都有需要，除了
   (A) 一張電網
   (B) 若干像素
   (C) 一塊積體電路板
   (D) 大量過濾器

【答案】D
【解析】這是採用消去法、問細節的題型，要刪去三項同義表達。第三段說「為了做彩色展示，得在每個像素上加一個濾色器」，但是顯示數目並不需要過濾器，故選 (D)。

⑨ 從文中可以推論，加了若干電晶體到液晶螢幕上是為了
   (A) 提升彩色影像品質
   (B) 擴大運算能力
   (C) 降低生產成本
   (D) 創造立體音響

【答案】A
【解析】這是推論題，要找「根據」。第三段說到，液晶螢幕的色彩效果不佳。「解決方案是每個像素用一枚電晶體發動」，所以電晶體是為了解決色彩問題，故選 (A)。

⑩ 本文的資訊可以回答下列所有問題，除了
   (A) 液晶是液體還是固體？
   (B) 向列型液晶顯示要如何增加清晰度？
   (C) 在色彩方面，液晶顯示和傳統電視相比如何？
   (D) 為什麼大型液晶顯示仍然很貴？

【答案】C
【解析】這是採消去法、問細節的題型，要刪去三個同義表達。只有選項 (C) 的問題原文找不到答案，故選 (C)。

Reading 5

Ernest Hemingway was born in the last year of the nineteenth century. In high school he was a good student and an all-around athlete. He played the cello in the school orchestra and contributed short stories and poems to magazines. Despite a busy and enviable student life, Hemingway was remembered by his classmates as **versatile** but "lonely."

Grace Hall Hemingway, his mother, was a very religious woman who nevertheless had strong passions for art, music and literature. Artists often gathered at Oak Park, the Hemingway residence, with Grace playing hostess of a cultural saloon. It was she who insisted on Ernest's taking cello lessons. As a result, Ernest **cultivated** a love for music, especially that of Bach and Mozart. He also maintained a life-long fondness for art. As he **confessed** later on, "**I learn as much from painters how to write as from writers.**"

Dr. Clarence Edmonds Hemingway, Ernest's father, was a famous physician, an accomplished sportsman, and an outstanding naturalist. The doctor initiated his son into the joys of the outdoors. In fact, the doctor seems to have been an ideal father. In summer he often took his son fishing and hunting from their lakeside house in northern Michigan. Sometimes he even took Ernest along on his visits to Ojibway Native American patients across Walloon Lake. Thanks to his father, Ernest grew up to be a hunter, swimmer, football player and boxer, with an undying love for nature.

✏ Exercise

① The best title for the passage would be
   (A) Hemingway's Early Years
   (B) Hemingway's Literary Career
   (C) Hemingway the Artist
   (D) Hemingway the Sportsman

② It is implied that Hemingway was born in
   (A) the early 1890s
   (B) the late 1890s
   (C) the early 1900s
   (D) the late 1900s

③ According to the author, Hemingway was all of the following in high school EXCEPT
   (A) a musician in the orchestra
   (B) a skillful athlete
   (C) a short-story writer
   (D) a fairly good boxer

④ The word "versatile" in the first paragraph is closest in meaning to
   (A) solitary
   (B) popular
   (C) many-talented
   (D) fickle

⑤ According to the passage, Oak Park was
   (A) where the Hemingways lived
   (B) where the Hemingways often went
   (C) where Dr. Hemingway had his clinic
   (D) where Hemingway took cello lessons

9

⑥ The word "cultivated" in the second paragraph is closest in meaning to
(A) planted
(B) inherited
(C) developed
(D) civilized

⑦ The word "confessed" in the second paragraph most closely means
(A) acknowledged his sins
(B) told everything to a priest
(C) concealed a secret
(D) admitted candidly

⑧ In the second paragraph the author quotes Hemingway's saying about painters in order to
(A) prove that Hemingway learned writing from a painter
(B) suggest that Hemingway could have become a painter
(C) demonstrate Hemingway's long-lasting passion for art
(D) prepare the reader for the discussion about Hemingway's father

⑨ According to the passage, all of the following are correct statements about Hemingway's father EXCEPT
(A) he was a man of various interests
(B) he was a loving father to Hemingway
(C) his patients included Ojibway Native Americans
(D) he initiated Hemingway into music

⊡ 題解

文章翻譯

　　厄尼斯特 · 海明威出生在 19 世紀最後一年。高中時他是個好學生、全能運動員。在學校樂團拉大提琴、並且向雜誌投稿短篇小說與詩。雖然學生生活過得忙碌又令人羨慕，海明威在同學的回憶中卻是多才多藝但「很寂寞」。

　　他母親葛瑞絲·霍爾·海明威是虔誠的教徒，但是對藝術、音樂、文學都有狂熱。藝術家經常聚集在橡樹園，就是海明威宅，由葛莉絲主持文藝沙龍。就是她堅持要海明威去上大提琴課。結果，海明威培養出對音樂的愛好，尤其是巴哈與莫札特。同時他終生喜愛藝術。後來他坦白：「我學寫作，畫家教給我的不比作家少」。

　　海明威之父，克萊倫斯·愛德蒙茲·海明威是位名醫、有成就的運動員、也是傑出的博物學家。是海明威醫生為兒子啟蒙，喜歡上戶外。事實上，海明威醫生好像是個理想父親。夏天他常常帶兒子到密西根州北部他們的湖畔別墅去釣魚、打獵。有時還帶兒子到瓦隆湖對岸去給歐吉布威原住民的病人看診。因為父親的關係，海明威長大後喜歡打獵、游泳、打美式足球、拳擊，對大自然的喜愛終身不變。

練習題翻譯與詳解

① 本文的最佳標題是
　　(A) 海明威早年　　　　　　　　　(B) 海明威的文學生涯
　　(C) 藝術家海明威　　　　　　　　(D) 運動員海明威

【答案】A
【解析】這是問主題的題型，要找出主題句。第一段「海明威出生在 19 世紀最後一年」從出生說起，後面談到海明威的學生生活。第二段與第三段分別說到母親與父親對他的影響，所以最佳標題應該是「海明威早年」。

② 本文暗示海明威出生在
　　(A) 1890 年代初期　　　　　　　　(B) 1890 年代晚期
　　(C) 1900 年代初期　　　　　　　　(D) 1900 年代晚期

【答案】B
【解析】這是推論題，要找「根據」。第一段說「海明威出生在 19 世紀最後一年」，那就是 1899，也是 1890 年代最後一年，故選 (B)。

③ 根據作者，海明威在高中時不是下面哪一項？
　　(A) 樂團的樂手　　　　　　　　　(B) 高超的運動員
　　(C) 短篇小說作家　　　　　　　　(D) 相當好的拳擊手

【答案】**D**

【解析】這是採用消去法、問細節的題型，要刪去三項同義表達。第一段可以找到 (A) (B) (C) 的同義表達，只有拳擊手這項是第三段說他長大後的事，並不是在高中，故選 (D)。

④ 第一段中的 versatile 一字意思最接近

(A) 單獨的   (B) 熱門的

(C) 多才多藝的   (D) 善變的

【答案】**C**

【解析】這是單字題。versatile（構造：change/(*a.*)）的意思是「多才多藝，多功能，多用途」，同義字是 many-talented。

⑤ 根據本文，橡樹園是

(A) 海明威一家居住的地方

(B) 海明威一家常去的地方

(C) 海明威大夫開診所的地方

(D) 海明威上大提琴課的地方

【答案】**A**

【解析】這是問細節的題型，要找同義表達。第二段說「藝術家經常聚集在橡樹園，就是海明威宅」，其中 the Hemingway residence 就是 where the Hemingways lived 的同義表達，故選 (A)。

⑥ 第二段中的 cultivated 一字意思最接近

(A) 種植   (B) 繼承

(C) 培養   (D) 文明化

【答案】**C**

【解析】這是單字題，動詞 cultivate（構造：cover/(*v.*)）的意思是「開發，栽培」，同義字是 develop。

⑦ 第二段中的 confessed 一字意思最接近

(A) 承認他的罪   (B) 把一切告訴神父

(C) 隱藏一個祕密   (D) 坦白承認

【答案】**D**

【解析】這是單字題。confess（構造：together/speak）的意思是「坦白，承認」。在此上下文就是指「坦白說出」。

⑧ 第二段中，作者引述海明威關於畫家那段話，目的是

　　(A) 證明海明威是向畫家學寫作的

　　(B) 暗示海明威本來可以當畫家的

　　(C) 證明海明威長久愛好藝術

　　(D) 準備讓讀者接受要談海明威之父了

【答案】**C**

【解析】這是修辭目的的題型，要看上下文。第二段說「他終生喜好藝術。後來他坦白：『我學寫作，畫家教給我的不比作家少』」。引述那句話的直接上文說到海明威對藝術的喜愛，所以這句引言應該是為上文提供佐證，故選 (C)。

⑨ 根據本文，關於海明威之父，下面每一句是對的，除了

　　(A) 他是興趣廣泛的人

　　(B) 他是疼愛海明威的父親

　　(C) 他的病人包括歐吉布威原住民

　　(D) 他給海明威啟蒙、讓他愛好音樂

【答案】**D**

【解析】這是採消去法、問細節的題型，要刪去三項同義表達。在第二段說到海明威對音樂的興趣是因為母親的關係，這和 (D) 有牴觸，故答案選 (D)。

Off the northeastern shore of North America, from the island of Newfoundland in Canada south to New England in the U.S., there is a series of shallow areas called banks. Several large banks off Newfoundland are together called the Grand Banks, huge shoals on the edge of the North American continental shelf, where the warm waters of the Gulf Stream meet the cold waters of the Labrador Current. As the currents brush each other, they stir up minerals from the ocean floor, providing nutrients for plankton and tiny shrimp-like creatures called krill, which feed on the plankton. Herring and other small fish rise to the surface to eat the krill. Groundfish, such as the Atlantic cod, live in the ocean's bottom layer, **congregating** in the shallow waters where they prey on krill and small fish. **This rich environment has produced cod by the millions and once had a greater density of cod than anywhere else on Earth.**

Beginning in the eleventh century, boats from the ports of northwestern Europe arrived to fish the Grand Banks. For the next eight centuries, the entire Newfoundland economy was based on Europeans arriving, catching fish for a few months in the summer, and then taking fish back to European markets. Cod laid out to dry on wooden "flakes" were a common sight in the fishing villages dotting the coast. Settlers in the region used to think the only sea creature worth talking about was cod, and in the local speech the word "fish" became synonymous with cod. **Newfoundland's national dish** was a putting whose main ingredient was cod.

By the nineteenth century, the Newfoundland fishery was largely controlled by merchants based in the capital at St. John's. They marketed the catch supplied by the fishers working out of more than 600 villages around the long coastline. In return, the merchants provided fishing equipment, clothing, and all the food that could not be grown in the island's thin, rocky soil. This system kept the fishers in a continuous state of debt and dependence on the merchants.

Until the twentieth century, fishers believed in the cod's ability to **replenish** itself and thought that overfishing was impossible. However, Newfoundland's cod fishery began to show signs of trouble during the 1930s, when cod failed to support the fishers and thousands were unemployed. The slump lasted for the next few decades. Then, when an international agreement in 1977 established the 200-mile offshore fishing limit, the Canadian government decided to build up the modern Grand Banks fleet and make fishing a viable economic base for Newfoundland again. All of Newfoundland's seafood companies were merged into one conglomerate. By the 1980s, the conglomerate was prospering, and cod were **commanding** excellent prices in the market. Consequently, there was a significant increase in the number of fishers and fish-processing plant workers.

However, while the offshore fishery was prospering, the inshore fishermen found their catches dropping off. _W_ In 1992 the Canadian government responded by closing the Grand Banks to groundfishing. _X_ Newfoundland's cod fishing and processing industries were shut down in a bid to let the vanishing stocks recover. _Y_ The moratorium was extended in 1994, when all of the Atlantic cod fisheries in Canada were closed, except for one in Nova Scotia, and strict quotas were placed on other species of groundfish. _Z_ Canada's cod fishing industry collapsed, and around 40,000 fishers and other industry workers were put out of work.

Atlantic cod stocks had once been so plentiful that early explorers joked about walking on the backs of the teeming fish. Today, cod stocks are at historically low levels and show no signs of imminent recovery, even after drastic conservation measures and severely limited fishing. Fishermen often blame the diminishing stocks on seals, which prey on cod and other species, but scientists believe that decades of overfishing are to blame. Studies of fish populations have shown that cod disappeared from Newfoundland at the same time that stocks started rebuilding in Norway, raising the possibility that the cod had migrated. Still, no one can predict whether the cod will return to the Grand Banks.

9

✏ Exercise

① According to paragraph 1, what physical process occurs in the region of the Grand Banks?
(A) Underwater hot springs heat the water
(B) Waters of widely different temperatures come together
(C) Nutrient-rich water flows in from rivers
(D) Currents wash up plankton and krill

② The word "congregating" in paragraph 1 is closest in meaning to
(A) mating   (B) hunting
(C) gathering   (D) growing

③ Which of the sentences below best expresses the essential information in the boldfaced sentence in paragraph 1?
This rich environment has produced cod by the millions and once had a greater density of cod than anywhere else on Earth.
(A) Millions of cod come to the Grand Banks every year to feed on the abundant supplies of herring and other small fish.
(B) The Grand Banks used to have the world's largest concentration of cod because of favorable natural conditions.
(C) The Grand Banks is the only place on Earth where cod are known to come together in extremely large groups.
(D) The environmental resources of the Grand Banks have made many people wealthy from cod fishing.

④ Which of the following can be inferred from paragraph 2 as the economic mainstay of Newfoundland in the 17th century?
(A) Foreign trade   (B) Immigration
(C) European fishermen   (D) Cod-processing factories

⑤ Why does the author mention "Newfoundland's national dish" in paragraph 2?
(A) To encourage the development of tourism in Newfoundland
(B) To describe the daily life of people in Newfoundland
(C) To stress the economic and cultural significance of cod to Newfoundland
(D) To show that Newfoundland used to be a separate country

⑥ According to the passage, all of the following statements characterized Newfoundland's cod fishery in the past EXCEPT

(A) Fishers were dependent on merchants in the capital.

(B) Cod were the foundation of the island's economy.

(C) Fishers competed with farmers for natural resources.

(D) Cod were placed on wooden "flakes" for drying.

⑦ The word "replenish" in paragraph 4 is closest in meaning to

(A) defend   (B) repair

(C) restock   (D) improve

⑧ According to paragraph 4, what event first signaled the overfishing of the Atlantic cod?

(A) The failure of cod to support thousands of fishers in the 1930s

(B) The establishment of the 200-mile offshore fishing limit

(C) The merging of seafood companies into one huge conglomerate

(D) An increase in the number of fishers and fish-processing plants

⑨ Which of the following can be inferred from paragraph 4 as the reason the Canadian government decided to build up the Grand Banks fishing fleet?

(A) The 200-mile limit was seen as an economic opportunity.

(B) There had not been enough boats to handle all the fish.

(C) The shipbuilding sector of the economy was in a slump.

(D) Canada faced stiff competition from other fishing nations.

⑩ The word "commanding" in paragraph 4 is closest in meaning to

(A) suggesting   (B) ordering

(C) defying   (D) fetching

⑪ In which position would the following boldfaced sentence best fit in paragraph 5?

They suspected this was because the offshore draggers were taking so many cod that the fish did not have a chance to migrate inshore to reproduce.

(A) Position W   (B) Position X

(C) Position Y   (D) Position Z

⑫ It can be inferred from paragraph 6 that the author probably believes which of the following about the future of the Atlantic fishery?

(A) The fishery will improve if the government lifts the fishing ban.

(B) It may be a long time before cod stocks recover from overfishing.

(C) The center of the Atlantic cod fishery will shift to Norway.

(D) The cod will return to the Grand Banks if seal hunting is allowed.

題解

文章翻譯

　　在北美洲東北沿海，從加拿大紐芬蘭島往南到美國新英格蘭，有一連串的淺水區稱為淺灘。紐芬蘭附近有幾座大型淺灘總稱為「大淺灘」，那是巨大的沙洲在北美洲大陸棚邊緣，墨西哥灣流的溫暖海水在此碰上拉布拉多洋流的冷水。洋流擦肩而過，攪起海底的礦物質，為浮游生物與小小的蝦狀生物稱為磷蝦的提供了營養素，磷蝦吃浮游生物。鯡魚和其他小魚浮到水面來吃磷蝦。底棲魚類像大西洋鱈魚生活在海洋最底層，聚集到淺水區來吃磷蝦和小魚。這個豐饒的環境提供了數以百萬計的鱈魚，曾經有一度鱈魚的密度高居全球之冠。

　　從 11 世紀開始，就有船從歐洲西北港口來到大淺灘捕鱈魚。接下來 8 個世紀，整個紐芬蘭的經濟基礎就是靠歐洲人抵達、夏天捕幾個月的魚、然後把魚帶到歐洲市場。鱈魚擺在木製「魚架」上曬乾，在沿海分佈的漁村是常見的景像。來此定居的人一度認為唯一值得談的海洋生物就是鱈魚，在當地用語中「魚」與「鱈魚」成為同義字。紐芬蘭的國菜是一道布丁，主要成分是鱈魚。

　　到了 19 世紀，紐芬蘭漁業大致由首府聖約翰市的商人把持。他們行銷漁民捉來的鱈魚，長長的海岸線上有 600 多個漁村是漁民的據點。商人相對要提供漁具、衣物，以及島上多岩石、薄薄的土壤種不出來的食物。這套制度造成漁民持續負債、依賴商人。

一直到 20 世紀，漁民都相信鱈魚有能力自我補充，認為不可能過度捕撈。但是，1930 年代紐芬蘭的鱈魚業開始出現問題，鱈魚不再能夠維持漁民的生活，有數以千計的漁民失業。接下來幾十年頹勢都持續。然後，1977 年一項國際協定設立了 200 英里的沿海漁業限制，加拿大政府於是決定打造現代化的大淺灘船隊、讓漁業再度成為紐芬蘭可行的經濟基礎。紐芬蘭所有的海產公司合併為一家大集團。到了 1980 年代，這家集團生意鼎盛，鱈魚在市場賣到很好的價錢。所以，漁民和漁產加工廠工人的人數大增。

不過，沿海漁業雖然興盛，近海漁民卻發現漁獲量下跌。W 1992 年加拿大政府採取對策，封閉大淺灘、禁止捕撈底棲魚類。X 紐芬蘭的鱈魚捕撈與加工產業也都關閉，希望消失中的漁源能夠復元。Y 1994 年，禁漁令延長，加拿大所有的大西洋鱈魚場全部封閉，只有在新蘇格蘭留下一處，並且對別種的底棲魚類也實行嚴格的配額管制。Z 加拿大的鱈魚產業崩潰，大約 4 萬名漁民與漁產業人員失業。

大西洋鱈魚量從前極多，早期探險家開玩笑說踩在擁擠的魚背上可以走路。今天，鱈魚量在歷史低點，也看不出即將復元的跡象，雖然採取了嚴苛的保育措施與嚴格限制捕魚。漁民經常把漁量減少怪在海豹的頭上，海豹會吃鱈魚與其他品種，但科學家相信應該怪的是幾十年的過度捕撈。對魚類族群的研究顯示，鱈魚從紐芬蘭消失的時間正好就是挪威漁量開始恢復的時間，因而有一種可能性：鱈魚遷走了。不過，沒有人能夠預測鱈魚會不會重回大淺灘。

練習題翻譯與詳解

① 根據第一段，在大淺灘地區有何物理程序發生？
   (A) 水底熱泉加熱海水
   (B) 溫差極大的海水交會
   (C) 營養豐富的水從河中流入
   (D) 洋流沖起浮游生物與磷蝦

【答案】**B**
【解析】這是問細節的題型，要找同義表達。第一段說「墨西哥灣流的溫暖海水在此碰上拉布拉多洋流的冷水」，其中 the warm waters of the Gulf Stream meet the cold waters of the Labrador Current 就是 Waters of widely different temperatures come together. 的同義表達，故選 (B)。

② 第一段中的 congregating 一字意思最接近
   (A) 交配   (B) 獵捕
   (C) 聚集   (D) 生長

【答案】**C**
【解析】這是單字題。動詞 congregate（構造：together/grow/(v.)）的意思是「聚集」，同義字是 gather。

③ 下列哪個句子最能夠表達第一段黑體字句子的主要內容？

「這個豐饒的環境提供了數以百萬計的鱈魚，曾經有一度鱈魚的密度高居全球之冠。」

(A) 每年有數百萬的鱈魚來大淺灘吃大量的鯡魚與其他小魚。

(B) 大淺灘曾擁有全球密度最高的鱈魚，因為天然環境有利。

(C) 大淺灘是地球上唯一有極大群鱈魚聚集的地方。

(D) 大淺灘的環境資源讓許多人因為捕鱈魚而致富。

【答案】B

【解析】這是句子改寫的題型，要找句中重點的同義表達。最接近的同義表達是 (B)。

④ 從第二段可以推論，17 世紀紐芬蘭的經濟支柱是什麼？

(A) 外貿　　　　　　　　　　(B) 移民

(C) 歐洲漁民　　　　　　　　(D) 鱈魚加工廠

【答案】C

【解析】這是推論題，要找「根據」。第二段說「從 11 世紀開始，就有船從歐洲西北港口來到大淺灘捕鱈魚。接下來 8 個世紀，整個紐芬蘭的經濟基礎就是靠歐洲人抵達、夏天捕幾個月的魚、然後把魚帶到歐洲市場」，所以 17 世紀也是同樣的情況，靠的是歐洲漁民。

⑤ 作者在第二段為何提到「紐芬蘭的國菜」？

(A) 為了鼓勵紐芬蘭發展觀光

(B) 為了描述紐芬蘭人民的日常生活

(C) 為了強調鱈魚對紐芬蘭經濟與文化的重要性

(D) 為了表示紐芬蘭從前是獨立國家

【答案】C

【解析】這是修辭目的的題型，要看上下文。第二段的段落主題句是「從 11 世紀開始，就有船從歐洲西北港口來到大淺灘捕鱈魚」，下文開始發展鱈魚對紐西蘭的重要性，「國菜」之語也是在發展這個主題，故選 (C)。

⑥ 根據本文，下面每項都是從前紐芬蘭鱈魚業的特色，除了

(A) 漁民依賴首都的商人

(B) 鱈魚是島上經濟的基礎

(C) 漁民和農民競爭天然資源

(D) 鱈魚放在木製「魚架」上曬乾

【答案】C

【解析】這是採消去法、問細節的題型，要刪去三項同義表達。選項中只有「漁民和農民競爭」是無中生有，故選 (C)。

⑦ 第四段中的 replenish 意思最接近

(A) 防衛   (B) 修理

(C) 補充   (D) 改善

【答案】**C**

【解析】這是單字題，replenish（構造：again/fill/(v.)）的意思是「補充、添加」，同義字是
restock。

⑧ 根據第四段，是什麼事件最早顯示出大西洋鱈魚捕撈過度？

(A) 1930 年代鱈魚不再能夠維持數千漁民的生活

(B) 建立了沿海 200 英里的漁業限制

(C) 海產公司合併為一家大集團

(D) 漁民與漁產加工廠工人數目增加

【答案】**A**

【解析】這是問細節的題型，要找同義表達。第四段說「1930 年代紐芬蘭的鱈魚業開始出
現問題，鱈魚不再能夠維持漁民的生活，有數以千計的漁民失業」，其中 cod failed to
support the fishers and thousands were unemployed 就是 The failure of cod to support
thousands of fishers in the 1930s 的同義表達，故選 (A)。

⑨ 根據第四段可以推論下列哪一項是加拿大政府決定打造大淺灘船隊的原因？

(A) 200 英里限制被視為經濟機會。

(B) 船隻太少，不足以處理那麼多魚。

(C) 造船業經濟不景氣。

(D) 加拿大面對其他漁業國的強烈競爭。

【答案】**A**

【解析】這是推論題，要找「根據」。第四段說「1977 年一項國際協定設立了 200 英里的
沿海漁業限制，加拿大政府於是決定打造現代化的大淺灘船隊、讓漁業再度成為紐芬蘭可
行的經濟基礎」，可知加拿大政府視限制為經濟機會，故選 (A)。

⑩ 第四段中的 commanding 一字意思最接近

(A) 建議   (B) 命令

(C) 反抗   (D) 取得

【答案】**D**

【解析】這是單字題。動詞 command（構造：intensifier/order）字面上是「命令」之意，
但是在此上下文應解釋為「取得，得到」，同義字是 fetch。

⑪ 下面這個黑體字句子最適合放在第五段的什麼位置？

「他們猜測這是因為沿海拖網漁船抓了太多鱈魚以致於魚群沒有機會到近海來繁殖。」

(A) W 位置　　　　　　　　　　　　(B) X 位置

(C) Y 位置　　　　　　　　　　　　(D) Z 位置

【答案】**A**

【解析】這是安插句子的題型，要看上下文。插入句內容說到沿海與近海漁業的衝突，W位置前面有說到這個衝突，可以銜接，成為：「沿海漁業雖然興盛，近海漁民卻發現漁獲量下跌。他們猜測這是因為沿海拖網漁船抓了太多鱈魚以致於魚群沒有機會到近海來繁殖。1992 年加拿大政府採取對策，封閉大淺灘、禁止捕撈底棲魚類」。

⑫ 從第六段可以推論，作者對於大西洋漁業的前途可能認為如何？

(A) 漁業會改善，只要政府取消捕魚禁令。

(B) 可能要過很久，鱈魚才能從過度捕撈中復元。

(C) 大西洋鱈魚業的中心將轉移到挪威。

(D) 鱈魚將回到大淺灘，如果准許獵捕海豹。

【答案】**B**

【解析】這是問態度的題型，要看用字，以及判斷肯定、中立、否定。第六段說「今天，鱈魚量在歷史低點，也看不出即將復元的跡象，雖然採取了嚴苛的保育措施與嚴格限制捕魚」，由此判斷作者對漁業的復元持否定態度（不樂觀），故選 (B)。

閱讀測驗篇

第 10 章

Reading 1

The writers of the Constitution created an extremely complicated form of government. **The three divisions of government**—administrative, legislative and judicial—were independent of each other but subject to an intricate web of checks and balances. Bills passed by Congress could not become laws without the President's signature. The President's appointment of important personnel and the treaties he made with foreign governments were not valid without the consent of the Senate. In addition, Congress had the power to impeach the President. The Supreme Court had jurisdiction over all legal disputes arising out of conflicts between state laws and the Constitution. Therefore it **had a say over** both statutes and the Constitution. This seems to have given the Supreme Court overwhelming power; and yet, the Supreme Court Justices were nominated by the President subject to Senate approval, and were impeachable by Congress, despite the fact that Justices enjoyed life tenure. Therefore, no single division of government could have had unrestrained power. Elected government officials had terms of office from two years to life. Therefore, **short of** a revolution, there was no way to change government personnel completely.

Exercise

① What is the main topic of this passage?
- (A) The checks and balances built into the Constitution
- (B) The difficulty of completely changing government personnel
- (C) Unnecessary complications caused by the writers of the Constitution
- (D) Congress and the Supreme Court as defined by the Constitution

② In can be inferred that "The three divisions of government" were represented by
- (A) the Constitution, statutes, and precedents
- (B) Federal, state, and local governments
- (C) bills, acts ,and laws
- (D) the President, Congress, and the Supreme Court

③ According to the passage, the power of Congress over the President did NOT include which of the following?
- (A) The power of approving or disapproving important officials nominated by the President
- (B) The power of accepting or rejecting treaties made by the President while in office
- (C) The power to impeach the President
- (D) The power to enact laws without the President's signature

④ The phrase "had a say over" most closely means
- (A) had to say again
- (B) was very correct about
- (C) had jurisdiction over
- (D) might hold conversations with

⑤ According to the passage, all of the following were checks on the power of Supreme Court Justices EXCEPT
- (A) they must be nominated by the President
- (B) they must have Senate approval
- (C) they could be impeached by Congress
- (D) they had life tenure

10

⑥ The expression "short of" can best be replaced by
    (A) worse than
    (B) in excess of
    (C) except for
    (D) within less distance than

⑦ According to the passage, why was it impossible to change government personnel completely?
    (A) Some government officials held office for two years only
    (B) Government officials held office for various lengths of duration
    (C) Most elected government officials had life tenure
    (D) Revolutions did not occur very often

题解

　　美國憲法撰寫人創造了一種極其複雜的政府。政府的三權——行政、立法、司法——彼此獨立，但受到複雜的制衡網絡的牽制。國會通過的提案沒有總統簽署不能成為法律。總統重要的人事任命以及和外國政府訂定的條約沒有參議院同意就無效。此外，國會還有權彈劾總統。最高法院對於一切因為州法與憲法衝突而產生的法律紛爭都具有司法管轄權，所以最高法院不論是一般法律還是憲法都有權過問。這似乎授予最高法院至高無上的權力，但是最高法院的大法官要由總統提名、經過參議院同意，國會還有權彈劾，儘管大法官享有終身任期的保障。所以，政府三權沒有任何一支可以掌握無限的權力。民選官員有任期限制，兩年到終身。因此，除了搞革命，根本沒有辦法完全更換政府人事。

練習題翻譯與詳解

① 本文的主題是什麼？
   (A) 憲法中內建的制衡
   (B) 完全改變政府人事的困難
   (C) 撰寫憲法者造成的無必要的複雜化
   (D) 憲法界定下的國會與最高法院

【答案】**A**
【解析】這是問主題的題型，要找出主題句。本文只有一段，頭一句開場白過後進入主題句「政府的三權——行政、立法、司法——彼此獨立，但受到複雜的制衡網絡的牽制」，接下來發展的就是這三權如何互相牽制，故選 (A)。

② 可以推論，「政府的三權」是由誰代表？
   (A) 憲法、成文法、先例
   (B) 聯邦政府、州政府、地方政府
   (C) 提案、法案、法律
   (D) 總統、國會、最高法院

【答案】**D**
【解析】這是推論題，要找「根據」。主題句說三權分立、互相制衡。後面的發展說的是總統、國會、最高法院之間的制衡，所以三權就是這三者代表。

10

③ 根據本文，國會對總統的權力不包括哪一項？

　(A) 同意或不同意總統提名的重要官員

　(B) 接受或拒絕總統任內訂定的條約

　(C) 彈劾總統

　(D) 製訂法律不需總統簽署

【答案】**D**

【解析】這是採用消去法、問細節的題型，要刪去三項同義表達。原文說「國會通過的提案沒有總統簽署不能成為法律」，這和選項 (D) 有牴觸，故為本題答案。

④ 片語 had a say over 意思最接近

　(A) 必須再說一次

　(B) 對於……非常正確

　(C) 對……有司法管轄權

　(D) 可以和……對話

【答案】**C**

【解析】這是單字題。have a say over 字面上是指「對……有發言權、可以過問」，也就是「有權管理」。

⑤ 根據本文，下列都對最高法院大法官構成牽制，除了

　(A) 他們必須由總統提名

　(B) 他們必須經過參議院同意

　(C) 他們可能遭國會彈劾

　(D) 他們有終身任期

【答案】**D**

【解析】這是問細節的題型，要找同義表達。原文說「國會還有權彈劾，儘管大法官享有終身任期的保障」，所以國會彈劾對大法官造成牽制，終身任期卻是大法官的保障、不是牽制。

⑥ 片語 short of 可以替換為

　(A) 比……差

　(B) 超過

　(C) 除了……以外

　(D) 比……距離短

【答案】C

【解析】這是單字題。short of 字面上是「比⋯⋯更短」的意思，比喻為「不到⋯⋯地步」或者「除非⋯⋯」。

⑦ 根據本文，為什麼不可能完全改變政府人事？

   (A) 有些政府官員任期只有兩年

   (B) 政府官員任期長短不一

   (C) 大部分民選官員都有終身任期

   (D) 革命不常發生

【答案】B

【解析】這是問細節的題型，要找同義表達。原文說「民選官員有任期限制，兩年到終身。因此，除了搞革命，根本沒有辦法完全更換政府人事」，其中 Elected government officials had terms of office from two years to life. 就是 Government officials held office for various lengths of duration 的同義表達，故選 (B)。

The Lewis and Clark expedition is probably the most celebrated tale of adventure in U. S. history. The expedition set out from St. Louis in May 1804, sailed up the Missouri into no man's land, conquered the Rocky Mountains, crossed over land to the Columbia River, and successfully reached the Pacific coast. After some rest and recuperation, the men headed back for St. Louis by the same route they had come. They turned up in St. Louis in September 1806, **to everyone's great surprise**. President Jefferson and the people had long given up hope of ever seeing them again!

Why did Jefferson order such a dangerous expedition? In 1804, when Jefferson was newly elected President, the United States had 17 states east of the Mississippi. West of the river there was the mysterious Louisiana Purchase, acquired from Napoleonic France only the year before. No one knew how large it was, **let alone** what it contained. Jefferson needed an expedition to **survey** what he had bought for the country, so that the Louisiana Purchase could one day be governed, as one or several states, by the federal government.

Another motive for the expedition had to do with an old dream — Columbus' dream. A westward route of commerce from Eastern America to India could bring vast wealth to the young United States, or so Jefferson believed. He knew that there was a big tributary of the Mississippi, called the Missouri, that extended westward from St. Louis. He was also aware that a certain captain Gray had discovered a large river, the Columbia, that poured into the Pacific from the north-western bank of North America. Rumor had it that a boat could go upstream along the Missouri, reach its headwaters, be carried over land for a day, and then be lowered into the Columbia, which would take it all the way down to the Pacific shore. This would connect Eastern America to the West Coast. Jefferson wanted to test this theory.

Finally, Jefferson wanted this expedition because of his natural curiosity. He was a statesman, an architect, a lawyer, an astronomer, an archeologist, an inventor, and a naturalist. With a stronger curiosity than most, he simply had to know what was out there.

✎ Exercise

① With what is the passage mainly concerned?
   (A) Amazing discoveries of the Lewis and Clark expedition
   (B) Jefferson's goals in sending out the Lewis and Clark expedition
   (C) The Louisiana Purchase and the Lewis and Clark expedition
   (D) The route taken by the Lewis and Clark expedition

② It can be inferred that the Lewis and Clark expedition took
   (A) exactly one year
   (B) just over one year
   (C) exactly two years
   (D) over two years

③ The men on the expedition turned up in St. Louis "to everyone's great surprise" (in the first paragraph) probably because
   (A) the people did not expect them to be back so soon
   (B) the people did not know they would take the same route back
   (C) everyone thought they were dead
   (D) Jefferson had ordered them to go directly to India

④ It can be inferred that Jefferson obtained the Louisiana Purchase from France in
   (A) 1803
   (B) 1804
   (C) 1805
   (D) 1806

⑤ The expression "let alone" in the second paragraph is closest in meaning to
   (A) not to mention
   (B) not even
   (C) not to disturb
   (D) setting aside

10

⑥ The word "survey" in the second paragraph is closest in meaning to
(A) poll
(B) question
(C) experiment on
(D) check out

⑦ Which of the following is true about Jefferson's plan for the Louisiana Purchase?
(A) He planned to trade it for parts of India
(B) He planned to build it into a wildlife reservation
(C) He planned to govern it like other states
(D) He planned to plant cotton in it

⑧ It is implied in the passage that both Jefferson and Columbus
(A) wanted to open up a route to western North America
(B) wanted to find a westward route to commerce with India
(C) wanted to discover new lands on a westward expedition
(D) were impractical dreamers

⑨ According to the passage, Jefferson knew which of the following to be a fact about the Columbia?
(A) It was discovered by Captain Gray
(B) It flowed into the Mississippi at St. Louis
(C) It was connected to the Missouri at its source
(D) It flowed through the southwestern parts of North America

⑩ It is implied in the last paragraph that Jefferson was
(A) a versatile man
(B) a kind president
(C) a famous explorer
(D) not really good at anything

🖃 題解

　　路易斯與克拉克探險可能是美國歷史上最膾炙人口的冒險故事。探險隊在 1804 年 5 月由聖路易市出發、溯密西西比河而上來到三不管地帶、征服洛磯山、走陸路到哥倫比亞河、成功抵達太平洋岸。休養一段時間恢復元氣之後，他們走原路回聖路易市。1806 年 9 月他們在聖路易市出現，大家都很驚訝。傑弗遜總統與人民早已放棄希望，認為再也看不到他們了！

　　傑弗遜為何要下令進行如此危險的探險？1804 年傑弗遜剛當選總統沒多久，美國在密西西比河以東有 17 州。河西邊神祕的路易斯安納購買地，前一年才從拿破崙手中買來。沒有人知道這塊地有多大，更別提裡面有些什麼。傑弗遜需要探險隊去調查他為國家買的這塊地，將來路易斯安納購買地才好成立為一州或數州、由聯邦政府管理。

　　探險隊的另一項動機牽涉到一個古老的夢想──哥倫布的夢想。從美國東岸向西行、打開一條通往印度的商業通道，可以為年輕的美國帶來龐大的財富，這是傑弗遜的想法。他知道密西西比河有一條大支流叫作密蘇里，從聖路易向西延伸。他也知道有位格雷船長發現一條大河叫作哥倫比亞河，從北美洲西北海岸流入太平洋。謠傳可以駕船沿密蘇里河而上、來到源頭、花一天的時間抬船、放進哥倫比亞河，就可以順流而下一直到太平洋岸。這就可以連接美國東部與西海岸。傑弗遜想要檢驗這個理論。

　　最後還有一個原因：傑弗遜想要這趟探險，因為他天性好奇。他是政治家、建築家、律師、天文學家、考古學家、發明家、也是博物學家。他的好奇心超過一般人，只想知道外頭有什麼。

① 本文的主題是什麼？

　　(A) 路易斯與克拉克探險的驚人發現

　　(B) 傑弗遜派出路易斯與克拉克探險的目的

　　(C) 路易斯安納購買地和路易斯與克拉克探險

　　(D) 路易斯與克拉克探險所走的路線

【答案】**B**

【解析】這是問主題的題型，要找出主題句。第一段全文主題句「路易斯與克拉克探險可能是美國歷史上最膾炙人口的冒險故事」，點出「路易斯克拉克探險」的主題。後面三段的段落主題句說的是傑弗遜派出探險隊的三個動機，故選 (B)。

② 可以推論，路易斯與克拉克探險花了

　　(A) 一年整　　　　　　　　　　　(B) 一年多一點

　　(C) 兩年整　　　　　　　　　　　(D) 兩年多

【答案】D

【解析】這是推論題，要找「根據」。第一段說「探險隊在 1804 年 5 月由聖路易市出發……1806 年 9 月他們在聖路易出現」，所以總共是兩年 4 個月。

③ 第一段說探險隊員在聖路易市出現「大家都很驚訝」，可能是因為

    (A) 大家沒想到那麼快就能回來

    (B) 大家不知道他們會走原路回來

    (C) 大家都以為他們早就死了

    (D) 傑弗遜當初是命令他們直接到印度去的

【答案】C

【解析】這是推論題，要找「根據」。第一段直接下文說「傑弗遜總統與人民早已放棄希望，認為再也看不到他們了」，暗示是以為他們早就死了，故選 (C)。

④ 可以推論，傑弗遜向法國取得路易斯安納購買地是在

    (A) 1803   (B) 1804

    (C) 1805   (D) 1806

【答案】A

【解析】這是推論題，要找「根據」。第二段說「1804 年傑弗遜剛當選總統沒多久……路易斯安納購買地，前一年才從拿破崙手中買來」，可以看出購買時間是 1804 的前一年，就是 1803 年。

⑤ 第二段中的片語 let alone 意思最接近

    (A) 更別提   (B) 甚至不是

    (C) 不要打擾   (D) 放在一旁

【答案】A

【解析】這是單字題。片語 let alone 的意思是「更別提、遑論」，同義字是 not to mention。

⑥ 第二段中的 survey 一字意思最接近

    (A) 意見調查   (B) 詢問

    (C) 做實驗   (D) 了解

【答案】D

【解析】這是單字題。動詞 survey（構造：over/see）的意思是「測量，調查」，也就是「大致了解一下」，同義字是 check out。

⑦ 關於傑弗遜對路易斯安納購買地的計畫，下列何者正確？

(A) 他計畫拿它來交換印度的一部分

(B) 他計畫成立一處野生動物保護區

(C) 他計畫像別的州一樣治理它

(D) 他計畫拿來種棉花

【答案】 **C**

【解析】這是問細節的題型，要找同義表達。第二段說「傑弗遜需要探險隊去調查他為國家買的這塊地，將來路易斯安納購買地才好成立為一州或數州、由聯邦政府管理」，也就是傑弗遜的計畫是要成立為州，故選 (C)。

⑧ 本文暗示，傑弗遜與哥倫布一樣

(A) 想要打開通往北美洲西部的通道

(B) 想要找到向西行可以和印度通商的路線

(C) 想要向西探險以發現新土地

(D) 都是不實際的夢想家

【答案】 **B**

【解析】這是推論題，要找「根據」。第三段說「探險隊的另一項動機牽涉到一個古老的夢想——哥倫布的夢想。從美國東岸向西行、打開一條通往印度的商業通道，可以為年輕的美國帶來龐大的財富，這是傑弗遜的想法」，可以看出傑弗遜與哥倫布同樣的想法是向西行、找出通商印度的通道。

⑨ 根據本文，傑弗遜知道下列哪一點是關於哥倫比亞河的事實？

(A) 它是格雷船長發現的　　　　　　(B) 它在聖路易市匯流到密西西比河

(C) 它在源頭和密蘇里河相連　　　　(D) 它流經北美洲西南

【答案】 **A**

【解析】這是問細節的題型，要找同義表達。第三段說傑弗遜「也知道有位格雷船長發現一條大河叫作哥倫比亞河」，故選 (A)。

⑩ 最後一段暗示傑弗遜是

(A) 多才多藝的人　　　　　　　　　(B) 仁慈的總統

(C) 著名的探險家　　　　　　　　　(D) 任何事情都非真正擅長

【答案】 **A**

【解析】這是推論題，要找「根據」。第四段說傑弗遜「是政治家、建築家、律師、天文學家、考古學家、發明家、也是博物學家」，可謂多才多藝。

10

The Big Bang theory holds that the universe began with a big explosion some 13.7 billion years ago. Radiation and cosmic materials have been flying outward ever since. These materials first condensed into gas; next, huge clouds of gas gathered around cores where the cosmic materials were denser than average. These cores, or gravitational centers, started pulling at the surrounding materials in a process called gravitational condensation. This process resulted eventually in the birth of galaxies, stars and planets.

The first evidence supporting the Big Bang came in 1964, when scientists detected the gamma ray background radiation, thought to be a **remnant** from the original explosion. A second piece of evidence was **located** by the Cosmic Background Explorer (COBE) satellite. In order for cosmic materials to condense into galaxies, there must first be cores of higher-density materials to function as centers of gravitational condensation. Did these cores really exist? COBE sent back pictures of huge cosmic clouds nearly 13.7 billion light years away, or 13.7 billion years ago. That was just a little while—about 300,000 years—after the birth of the universe. The largest cloud observed by COBE was already 10 billion light years **across**! After computer analysis, a cosmic map was charted which showed spots of higher temperature—and thus of greater density. These were the cores that Big Bang scientists had been looking for.

COBE provided evidence for another celestial controversy. Will the universe go on expanding forever, gradually cease to expand, or fall back on itself? The answer depends on the density of matter in the universe. If the density is low, the gravitational pull will be too slight to **check** the expansion, and the universe will go on flying apart till the end of time. If the density is high enough, gravity will eventually pull cosmic matter—galaxies, stars and planets—back toward a grand collision and another Big Bang. If it is exactly at critical density, the universe will slowly cease to expand and eventually reach a static state. The information sent back by COBE seems to support the last alternative.

Exercise

① What is the author's purpose in writing this passage?
  (A) To introduce various theories of the origin of the universe
  (B) To report on a satellite's findings that support the Big Bang theory
  (C) To question the validity of the Big Bang theory
  (D) To speculate on the ultimate end of our universe

② According to the Big Bang theory, the age of the universe is
  (A) under 13 billion years
  (B) under 14 billion years
  (C) 16 to 19 billion years
  (D) about 20 billion years

③ The word "remnant" in the second paragraph is closest in meaning to
  (A) accumulation
  (B) acceleration
  (C) residue
  (D) debt

④ Scientists believed that the gamma ray radiation discovered in 1964 was
  (A) proof that the Big Bang never happened
  (B) what was left from the birth of the universe
  (C) the material at the cores of gravitational condensation
  (D) evidence for critical density of our universe

⑤ The word "located" in the second paragraph is closest in meaning to
  (A) found
  (B) situated
  (C) placed
  (D) contacted

10

⑥ The COBE pictures are pictures of the universe just after its birth because
  (A) the clouds photographed are almost 13.7 billion light years away
  (B) the clouds photographed are 10 billion light years across
  (C) the COBE satellite photographed the Big Bang itself
  (D) the universe is still very young today

⑦ The word "across" in the second paragraph is closest in meaning to
  (A) opposite
  (B) beyond
  (C) away
  (D) wide

⑧ According to the passage, which of the following statement is true?
  (A) The universe has ceased expansion.
  (B) The universe will definitely fall back on itself.
  (C) COBE provides some evidence about the future of the universe.
  (D) The Big Bang theory is disproved by COBE's discoveries.

⑨ The word "check" in the third paragraph is closest in meaning to
  (A) examine
  (B) cash
  (C) restrain
  (D) ensure

⑩ According to the author, a density of cosmic materials higher than critical density would mean that
  (A) our universe will continue to expand forever
  (B) our universe is heading for another great explosion
  (C) our universe is developing into a static universe
  (D) our universe is younger than scientists now think

題解

文章翻譯

　　大霹靂理論主張：宇宙是在大約 137 億年前由一場大爆炸中開始。然後輻射與宇宙物質就一直往外飛。這些物質先是濃縮成氣體；然後，巨大的氣體雲圍繞著宇宙物質密度較高的核心聚集。這些核心（就是重力中心）開始吸引周遭的物質，產生所謂的重力壓縮。這個過程最終的結果就是誕生了星系、恆星與行星。

　　支持大霹靂說的證據最早在 1964 年出現，當時科學家偵測到伽瑪射線背景輻射，這被認為是最初大爆炸殘留的痕跡。第 2 項證據是宇宙背景探測衛星 (COBE) 找到的。宇宙物質要能夠濃縮成為星系，首先得要有高密度的物質核心當作重力壓縮的中心才行。真的有這種核心嗎？COBE 傳回照片：距離將近 137 億光年之遙（或者距今 137 億年以前）的巨大宇宙雲。那是宇宙剛誕生不久（大約 30 萬年）的時候。COBE 觀察到最大的雲，寬度已經有 100 億光年！電腦分析之後繪出一張宇宙地圖，上面有高溫點——也就是密度高的點。這就是大霹靂論者在尋找的核心。

　　COBE 也為另一樁天體爭議提供了證據。宇宙會永遠擴張下去、或者逐漸停止擴張、還是墜落回來？答案取決於宇宙中物質的密度。如果密度低，重力牽引作用太小，不足以遏止擴張，宇宙就會持續飛散、直到時間盡頭。如果密度夠高，重力到最後會拉扯宇宙物質（星系、恆星、行星）回到一場大衝撞以及另一次大霹靂。如果密度剛好在臨界點，宇宙會逐漸停止擴張、最後達到靜止狀態。COBE 傳回來的資訊似乎支持最後一個選項。

練習題翻譯與詳解

① 作者寫這篇文章的目的是
　(A) 介紹關於宇宙起源的各種理論
　(B) 報導一枚衛星的發現，可以支持大霹靂理論
　(C) 質疑大霹靂理論的有效性
　(D) 猜測宇宙最終的結局

【答案】**B**
【解析】這是問主題的題型，要找主題句。第一段全文主題句「大霹靂理論主張：宇宙是在大約 137 億年前由一場大爆炸中開始」，點出大霹靂理論為主題。第二、三兩段則是提出 COBE 衛星的發現可以支持大霹靂理論，故選 (B)。

② 根據大霹靂理論，宇宙的年齡是
　(A) 不到 130 億年　　　　　　　　(B) 不到 140 億年
　(C) 160 到 190 億年　　　　　　　(D) 大約 200 億年

【答案】**B**

【解析】這是問細節的題型，要找同義表達。第一段說「大霹靂理論主張：宇宙是在大約 137 億年前由一場大爆炸中開始」，其中 some 13.7 billion years 就是 under 14 billion years 的同義表達，故選 (B)。

③ 第二段中的 remnant 一字意思最接近

    (A) 累積   (B) 加速

    (C) 殘留物   (D) 債務

【答案】**C**

【解析】這是單字題。動詞 remain（構造：back/stay）的意思是指「停留，留下」，名詞 remnant 是指「殘留物」，同義字是 residue（構造：back/sit/(n.)）。

④ 科學家相信，1964 年發現的伽瑪射線

    (A) 可以證明大霹靂從未發生過

    (B) 是宇宙誕生時留下來的

    (C) 是重力壓縮核心中的物質

    (D) 可以證明宇宙的臨界密度

【答案】**B**

【解析】這是問細節的題型，要找同義表達。第二段說「支持大霹靂說的證據最早在 1964 年出現，當時科學家偵測到伽瑪射線背景輻射，這被認為是最初大爆炸殘留的痕跡」，其中 a remnant from the original explosion 就是 what was left from the birth of the universe 的同義表達，故選 (B)。

⑤ 第二段中的 located 意思最接近

    (A) 被找到   (B) 位於

    (C) 被放置   (D) 被接觸到

【答案】**A**

【解析】這是單字題。動詞 locate（構造：place/(v.)）可以解釋為「位於，找到」，located 在此上下文應作「被找到」解釋，同義字是 found。

⑥ COBE 傳回的照片是宇宙剛誕生不久的時間，因為

    (A) 照片中的宇宙雲距離將近 137 億光年之遙

    (B) 照片中的宇宙雲寬達 100 億光年

    (C) COBE 衛星拍到大霹靂本身

    (D) 今日宇宙仍很年輕

【答案】**A**

【解析】這是問細節的題型，要找同義表達。第二段說「COBE 傳回照片：距離將近 137 億光年之遙（或者距今 137 億年以前）的巨大宇宙雲。那是宇宙剛誕生不久（大約 30 萬年）的時候」，其中 nearly 13.7 billion light years away 就是 almost 13.7 billion light years away 的同義表達，故選 (A)。

⑦ 第二段中的 across 一字意思最接近

(A) 相反　　　　　　　　　　　　　(B) 超出

(C) 離開　　　　　　　　　　　　　(D) 寬

【答案】**D**

【解析】這是單字題。across 指「橫寬」，同義字是 wide。

⑧ 根據本文，下列哪一項陳述是對的？

(A) 宇宙已經停止擴張　　　　　　　(B) 宇宙確定會掉回去

(C) COBE 為宇宙的未來提供了一些證據　(D) 大霹靂理論被 COBE 的發現推翻

【答案】**C**

【解析】這是問細節的題型，要找同義表達。第三段說「COBE 也為另一樁天體爭議提供了證據。宇宙會永遠擴張下去、還是逐漸停止擴張、還是墜落回來？」其中 another celestial controversy 就是關於 the future of the universe 的爭議，故選 (C)。

⑨ 第三段中的 check 意思最接近

(A) 檢查　　　　　　　　　　　　　(B) 兌現

(C) 節制　　　　　　　　　　　　　(D) 確保

【答案】**C**

【解析】這是單字題。在此上下文中，check 應作「控制、節制」解釋，同義字是 restrain。

⑩ 根據作者，宇宙物質密度若高於臨界密度，結果會是

(A) 宇宙將永遠擴張下去　　　　　　(B) 宇宙將再來一次大爆炸

(C) 宇宙正朝向靜態發展　　　　　　(D) 宇宙比科學家目前所想的更年輕

【答案】**B**

【解析】這是問細節的題型，要找同義表達。第三段說「如果密度夠高，重力到最後會拉扯宇宙物質（星系、恆星、行星）回到一場大衝撞以及另一次大霹靂」，其中 another Big Bang 就是 another great explosion 的同義表達，故選 (B)。

10

Legalized gambling—usually meaning state sponsored lotteries, horse racing, or sports betting—is frequently **hailed** as the answer to state money problems.

For states it does offer increased revenues, easy administration, and a more or less politically painless way to balance tricky budgets. And to citizens, legalized gambling offers an enjoyable and legal substitute for illegal sports betting and the chance to contribute to the running of the state rather than criminal enterprises. In some states, such as Connecticut, Nevada, Mississippi, legalized casino gambling attracts thousands of residents and non-residents every day.

But these supposed benefits to citizens and states do not come without an accompanying list of drawbacks. Here, however, it is often difficult to separate real concerns from fictitious ones.

Many government officials, looking for easy solutions to pressing problems, are seduced by the glitter and glamour of boardwalks, Las Vegas style entertainment, and the rivers of cash that seem to **go hand in hand with** legalized gambling. But the legalization of gambling does more than merely create attractive venues for big-name concerts and sporting events.

A look behind the bright lights shows a much more unsettling face of reality. The casinos in **Atlantic City**, for example, have never improved the local employment situation as much as promised. Indeed, many casino workers are brought in from the outside, even while local unemployment remains high. Also, the growth of a gambling industry is possibly connected with the growth of crime, as the historical connections between **Las Vegas** and organized crime will attest. Some critics of state-sponsored gambling claim that it will spawn a host of new evils, from prostitution to loan sharking and street crime. And all of this leaves aside the strong moral considerations that many people have about gambling. Should the state be involved with, and profit from, a business that conflicts with the moral beliefs of so many of its citizens?

The difficulty of resolving these complex issues probably accounts for the fact that only a few states allow either casinos or sports betting. However, many more offer horse racing, probably for historic reasons, or its more modern cousin of dog racing. But the most popular and profitable games are state run lotteries. A majority of states either run their own lotteries or work in cooperation with neighboring states.

✏ Exercise

① What is the main subject of the passage?
   (A) Money problems in American states
   (B) Casino gambling
   (C) Pros and cons of legalized gambling
   (D) Horse racing

② In the first paragraph the word "hailed" is closest in meaning to
   (A) debated
   (B) proclaimed
   (C) renounced
   (D) allowed

③ Which of the following is NOT mentioned in the passage as a benefit of legalized gambling?
   (A) enhanced revenues
   (B) decreased crime
   (C) administrative ease
   (D) citizen enjoyment

④ Which of the following is NOT specifically mentioned in the passage as a form of legalized gambling?
   (A) betting on sporting events
   (B) betting on lotteries
   (C) betting on cards
   (D) betting on horse races

⑤ In the third paragraph the author implies that it is not easy to
   (A) come up with gambling's drawbacks
   (B) influence state officials
   (C) separate truth from myth
   (D) have revenues exceed expenses

10

⑥ In the fourth paragraph the phrase "go hand in hand with" is closest in meaning to which of the following?

(A) precede

(B) follow on the heels of

(C) hold sway over

(D) accelerate

⑦ In the fifth paragraph, why does the author mention Atlantic City?

(A) To describe America's largest casinos

(B) In order to highlight gambling's benefits

(C) To illustrate the creation of new jobs

(D) To discuss gambling's negative side

⑧ The author mentions Las Vegas in the fifth paragraph in order to

(A) contrast its problems with the success of Atlantic City

(B) list another area with high unemployment

(C) illustrate the consequences of legal prostitution

(D) comment on the relationship between crime and gambling

⑨ The author of the passage could best be described as

(A) a fairly objective observer

(B) an advocate of casino gambling

(C) having moral objections to gambling

(D) writing against legalized gambling

賭博合法化——通常是指由國家主辦樂透、賽馬、或運動簽賭——常常被稱為解決國家財務困難的好辦法。

對州政府而言，賭博合法化確實可以增加稅收，又容易管理，而且是相對比較政治無痛的方式可以平衡麻煩的預算。對人民而言，賭博合法化可以提供好玩的、合法的方式取代非法運動簽賭，也有機會對國家的營運做出貢獻，而不是助長犯罪企業。有些州例如康乃迪克、內華達、以及密西西比，合法賭場的賭博每天吸引數以千計的本州居民與外來客。

但是，上述對人民、對州政府的一些據稱的好處，並不是沒有一長串的缺點伴隨。然而就此問題而言，往往很難區分什麼是真正應該擔心的、什麼是虛構的。

許多政府官員因為要找簡單的辦法來解決迫切的問題，會受到下列因素的吸引：木板步道的光彩與奢華、拉斯維加斯式的娛樂表演、以及好像和合法賭博形影不離的現金洪流。但是，賭博合法化的結果不只是會創造出吸引人的場地來舉辦巨星演唱會與體育盛事而已。

在燦爛的光芒後面看一眼，就會發現令人不安的真實面目。例如大西洋城的賭場，一直沒有能夠改善當地的就業情況，不及當初的承諾。事實上，許多賭場工作人員都是從外面請來的，雖然本地失業率居高不下。而且，賭博業的成長可能和犯罪成長有關聯，歷史上拉斯維加斯和組織犯罪之間的關聯就可以證明。有一些批評國營賭博的人說它會製造一批新問題，包括賣淫、高利貸、街頭犯罪。這都還沒提到很強烈的道德考量，那是很多人談到賭博最關心的。這門行業和眾多人民的道德信念有衝突，那麼國家應該涉入、並且從中謀利嗎？

要解決這些複雜的問題並不容易，或許就是這個原因造成目前只有少數幾個州容許賭場賭博或者運動簽賭。但是有很多州都提供賽馬，可能是有歷史因素，還有就是比較現代化的賽狗。不過最熱門、獲利最豐的還是州營的樂透。大多數的州或者自營樂透、或者和隔壁州合作。

① 本文的主題是什麼？
  (A) 美國州政府的金錢問題
  (B) 賭場賭博
  (C) 賭博合法化的好壞處
  (D) 賽馬

【答案】**C**

【解析】這是問主題的題型，要找主題句。第一段全文主題句「賭博合法化……常常被稱為解決國家財務困難的好辦法」，點出賭博合法化為主題。後面各段分別談的是賭博合法化的好壞處，故選 (C)。

② 第一段中的 hailed 意思最接近

(A) 被辯論   (B) 被宣稱

(C) 被拒絕   (D) 被允許

【答案】**B**

【解析】這是單字題，hail 的意思是「歡呼，大叫」，片語 hail as 的意思是「稱為」。

③ 本文沒有提到下列哪一項說是賭博合法化的好處？

(A) 收入增加   (B) 犯罪減少

(C) 管理容易   (D) 人民享受

【答案】**B**

【解析】這是採消去法、問細節的題型，要刪去三個同義表達。第二段中 (A) (C) (D) 三個選項都找得到同義表達，只有 decreased crime 沒有，故選 (B)。

④ 本文沒有明確提到下列哪一項說是一種合法賭博？

(A) 賭體育活動   (B) 賭樂透

(C) 賭牌   (D) 賭賽馬

【答案】**C**

【解析】這是採消去法、問細節的題型，要刪去三個同義表達。文中只有 betting on cards 完全沒有提到，故選 (C)。

⑤ 在第三段中作者暗示下列哪件事並不容易？

(A) 提出賭博有何缺點   (B) 影響州政府官員

(C) 區分事實與神話   (D) 使收入超過開銷

【答案】**C**

【解析】這是推論題，要找「根據」。第三段說「就此問題而言，往往很難區分什麼是真正應該擔心的、什麼是虛構的」，故選 (C)。

⑥ 第四段中的 go hand in hand with 這個片語意思最接近

(A) 領先，在……之前   (B) 緊跟

(C) 控制   (D) 加速

【答案】**B**

【解析】這是單字題，片語 go hand in hand with 字面上是指「攜手同行」，引申為「伴隨」。follow on the heels of 字面上是指「緊跟在後」，但兩個片語暗示相同。

⑦ 第五段中作者為何提到大西洋城？
  (A) 為了描述美國最大的幾家賭場
  (B) 為了突顯賭博的好處
  (C) 為了說明新工作的創造
  (D) 為了討論賭博的負面

【答案】**D**
【解析】這是修辭目的的題型，要看上下文。第五段說「在燦爛的光芒後面看一眼，就會發現令人不安的真實面目。例如大西洋城的賭場，一直沒有能夠改善當地的就業情況，不及當初的承諾」，可以看出作者是舉大西洋城賭場為例，說明上文「賭場不良的真相」，故選 (D)。

⑧ 作者在第五段提到拉斯維加斯是為了
  (A) 將它的問題與大西洋城的成功對比
  (B) 列出另一個高失業率的地區
  (C) 舉例說明合法賣淫的後果
  (D) 評論犯罪與賭博之間的關聯

【答案】**D**
【解析】這是修辭目的的題型，要看上下文。第五段說「賭博業的成長可能和犯罪成長有關聯，歷史上拉斯維加斯和組織犯罪之間的關聯就可以證明」，可以看出作者是舉拉斯維加斯為例，說明上文「賭博與犯罪」的關聯，故選 (D)。

⑨ 本文作者可以被描述為
  (A) 相當客觀的觀察者
  (B) 賭場賭博的提倡者
  (C) 對賭博基於道德立場反對
  (D) 撰文反對合法賭博

【答案】**A**
【解析】這是語氣與態度的題型，要看用字以及判斷肯定、中立、否定。因為作者對合法賭博這個主題做了正面與負面兩方面的探討，不是全力支持、也不是完全反對，所以是站在中立客觀的立場，應選 (A)。

10

Reading 5

Henry Miller's prose, frequently autobiographical, ranges from the **earthy** and colloquial to the lyric and surrealistic in language. It is notable for its candor, vitality and commitment to the "natural man." Miller, born in the United States in 1891, is best known as the author of *Tropic of Cancer* and *Tropic of Capricorn*, narratives published in Paris in the 1930s, and because of their uninhibited relation of Miller's personal experiences, banned in Britain and the United States until the 1960s.

Miller was born in New York City and raised in its borough of Brooklyn. In 1924 he left his job with Western Union to devote himself exclusively to writing. Six years later he went to France, launching a decisive decade in his career.

Tropic of Cancer was based on these years, while *Tropic of Capricorn*, although it was published later, draws on his earlier experiences in New York. The eventual publication of these works in the United States provoked a series of obscenity trials that ended with a 1964 Supreme Court decision in favor of the author. However, most current readers would be puzzled by the furor over these, at least by modern standards, relatively **tame** novels.

Miller's visit to Greece in 1939 inspired his travel book *The Colossus of Maroussi*. In 1940 and 1941 he toured the United States and wrote a sharply critical account of it, *The Air-conditioned Nightmare*. Literary critics were shocked by Miller's condemnation of American ideals. Miller later settled in California where he penned an autobiographical trilogy and wrote **prolifically**, combining homey insights with metaphysical proclamations. In the 1950s Miller became a major inspiration to the writers of the Beat Generation, a short-lived movement that protested against complacent middle-class values. Miller died in Los Angeles in 1980, after earning a reputation as one of the most outspoken and creative American writers of the twentieth century.

✎ Exercise

① What is the main topic of the passage?
   (A) Obscenity in the work of Henry Miller
   (B) The literary contributions of Henry Miller
   (C) Henry Miller's lasting artistic influence
   (D) Henry Miller's travel commentaries

② The word "earthy" in the first paragraph is closest in meaning to
   (A) solid
   (B) traditional
   (C) coarse
   (D) spoken

③ It can be inferred from the passage that which of the following characterizes the work of Henry Miller?
   (A) a diversity of language
   (C) a focus on nature
   (C) a reliance on notes
   (D) an emphasis on tropical areas

④ According to the passage, *Tropic of Cancer* was banned in the United States because
   (A) it was originally published in Europe
   (B) of a 1964 Supreme Court ruling
   (C) of legal troubles with Western Union
   (D) of its controversial content

⑤ Which of the following is true about *Tropic of Capricorn*?
   (A) It was published prior to *Tropic of Cancer*
   (B) It was based on Miller's life in New York
   (C) It was Miller's only illustrated novel
   (D) It was never published until 1964

10

⑥ In the third paragraph the word "tame" could best be replaced by which of the following?
(A) mediocre
(B) mild
(C) similar
(D) refreshing

⑦ According to the passage, Miller visited all of the following places EXCEPT
(A) Paris
(B) Greece
(C) Missouri
(D) California

⑧ The word "prolifically" in the fourth paragraph is closest in meaning to which of the following words?
(A) extensively
(B) personally
(C) unevenly
(D) occasionally

⑨ It can be inferred from the passage that writers of the Beat Generation probably admired Miller because of his
(A) trips abroad
(B) commercial success
(C) unconventional writing
(D) commonplace values

文章翻譯

　　亨利‧米勒的文章經常有自傳式的描述，範圍從俚俗與口語乃至於抒情與超現實的文字都有。值得注意的是它的坦白、活力，以及對「自然人」的認同。米勒於 1891 年出生在美國，代表作是《北回歸線》與《南回歸線》，兩個故事都是 1930 年代在巴黎出版的。因為兩本書口無遮攔地敘述米勒的個人關係，所以在英美兩國一直是禁書，直到 1960 年代才解禁。

　　米勒出生在紐約市、成長在布魯克林區。1924 年他辭去西聯匯款公司的工作、全心投入寫作。6 年後他來到法國，展開他生涯中關鍵性的 10 年。

　　《北回歸線》就是根據這些年的經驗寫成的。《南回歸線》雖然出版較晚，寫的卻是早年在紐約時的經驗。這兩本書後來在美國出版，引起一系列的妨礙風化官司，最後是 1964 年最高法院裁定作者勝訴。不過，今天的讀者會很困惑。這兩本小說至少以現代標準來看是頗溫和的，當年怎麼會引起這麼大的爭議。

　　1939 年米勒出訪希臘給了他靈感，寫出一本遊記《瑪洛西的大石像》。1940 與 1941 年他在美國旅遊，寫了一篇對美國尖銳批判的敘述《空調噩夢》。文學批評家看到米勒對美國理想的譴責感到震驚。米勒後來在加州定居，在那裡寫了一套自傳三部曲，並且創作甚豐，結合了家常的見識與形上學的宣言。1950 年代米勒成為「垮掉的一代」作家的重要啟發，那是曇花一現的運動，主要在抗議中產階級自以為是的價值觀。1980 年米勒在洛杉磯去世，已經被譽為 20 世紀最敢言、最有創意的美國作家之一。

練習題翻譯與詳解

① 本文的主題是什麼？
　　(A) 亨利‧米勒作品中的傷風敗俗
　　(B) 亨利‧米勒的文學貢獻
　　(C) 亨利‧米勒持久的藝術影響
　　(D) 亨利‧米勒的旅遊評論

【答案】B
【解析】這是問主題的題型，要找主題句。第一段全文主題句「亨利‧米勒的文章經常有自傳式的描述，範圍從俚俗與口語乃至於抒情與超現實的文字都有」，點出主題是介紹文學家米勒。後面各段的段落主題句分別發展米勒的生平與重要作品，所以主題是米勒的文學貢獻。

② 第一段中的 earthy 一字意思最接近
　　(A) 堅固的　　　　　　　　　(B) 傳統的
　　(C) 粗糙的　　　　　　　　　(D) 口語的

10

【答案】C

【解析】這是單字題。earthy 字面上是指「帶泥土的」，引申為「粗俗的」，同義字是 coarse。

③ 可以推論亨利‧米勒的作品有何特色？

(A) 語言多樣化　　　　　　　　(B) 聚焦在大自然

(C) 依賴筆記　　　　　　　　　(D) 強調熱帶地區

【答案】A

【解析】這是推論的題型，要找「根據」。第一段說米勒的文章「範圍從俚俗與口語乃至於抒情與超現實的文字都有」，可以推知他的文字多變化，故選 (A)。

④ 根據本文，《北回歸線》在美國被禁是因為

(A) 它原本在歐洲出版

(B) 1964 年最高法院的裁定

(C) 與西聯匯款公司的法律糾紛

(D) 它引起爭議的內容

【答案】D

【解析】這是問細節的題型，要找同義表達。第一段說「因為兩本書口無遮攔地敘述米勒的個人關係，所以在英美兩國一直是禁書」。其中 their uninhibited relation of Miller's personal experiences 屬於書中的內容，故選 (D)。

⑤ 關於《南回歸線》下列哪一項是對的？

(A) 它出版在《北回歸線》之前

(B) 它以米勒的紐約生活為根據

(C) 它是米勒唯一有插圖的小說

(D) 它到 1964 年才首度出版

【答案】B

【解析】這是問細節的題型，要找同義表達。第三段說「《南回歸線》雖然出版較晚，寫的卻是早年在紐約時的經驗」，其中 draws on his earlier experiences in New York 就是 based on Miller's life in New York 的同義表達，故選 (B)。

⑥ 第三段中的 tame 一字可以替換成

(A) 平庸　　　　　　　　　　　(B) 溫和

(C) 類似　　　　　　　　　　　(D) 清新

【答案】**B**
【解析】這是單字題。Tame 字面上是「溫馴，馴服」的意思，引申為「溫和」，同義字是 mild。

⑦ 根據本文，米勒去過下列所有地方，除了
    (A) 巴黎   (B) 希臘
    (C) 密蘇里州   (D) 加州

【答案】**C**
【解析】這是採用消去法、問細節的題型，要刪三個同義表達。全文完全沒提到 Missouri，故選 (C)。

⑧ 第四段中的 prolifically 一字意思最接近
    (A) 廣泛地   (B) 親自
    (C) 不平均地   (D) 偶爾

【答案】**A**
【解析】這是單字題。prolifically（構造：forward/do/(*adv.*)）的意思是「大量地、多產地」，最接近 extensively（構造：out/stretch/(*adv.*)）。

⑨ 可以推論，「垮掉的一代」作家仰慕米勒可能是因為他
    (A) 出國旅遊   (B) 商業成功
    (C) 打破傳統的寫作   (D) 平凡的價值觀

【答案】**C**
【解析】這是推論題，要找「根據」。從本文的敘述可以看出米勒是個反傳統的作家。第四段說垮掉的一代作家「主要在抗議中產階級自以為是的價值觀」，這和米勒的立場相近，故選 (C)。

10

__W__ John Muir's exuberant descriptions of the "fresh, unblighted, unredeemed wilderness" that he found in his explorations of the Sierra Nevada mountains of California popularized an ideal that has shaped American thinking about the value of wilderness and the importance of **preserving** it. __X__ They reflect a revolution in sensibility influenced by English romantic writers and American transcendentalists, most notably Henry David Thoreau. __Y__ Wilderness came to be seen by these writers as desirable, even as a manifestation of the sublime. __Z__

William Bradford's famous characterization of the Cape Cod found by the settlers who arrived on the Mayflower as "a hideous and desolate wilderness, full of wild beasts and wild men," reflects a much older sense of wilderness, going back to the desert wilderness of the Old Testament, as an **inhospitable** and dangerous place. In his story **"Young Goodman Brown"** Nathaniel Hawthorne captured the Puritan sensibility in which the dark forest, the wilderness of the early settlers, became a frightening and disorienting place of evil, haunted by demonic Indians and the devil himself.

By the time Muir wrote, in the later nineteenth century, the appeal of wilderness as a distinctive feature of the American landscape was firmly established. Muir could see the Sierra as a "range of light" and a vibrant, pure, "divine wilderness" ordered and given life by a **benevolent** God. If Muir's particular religion of nature is no longer so likely to be shared, he nonetheless remains a cultural icon, widely quoted and celebrated as the prophet of wilderness preservation and the first president of the Sierra Club. His writing, along with that of such other famous defenders of wilderness as Thoreau and Aldo Leopold and Edward Abbey, can be found in the *Trailside Reader* of the Sierra Club, a pocket-sized book of inspirational reading for backpackers. Reading Muir and others who have meditated on the meaning of wild places has become a part of the American experience of wilderness.

For all the popular fascination with wilderness, which increased dramatically in the later twentieth century, "wilderness" has in recent years become a **contested** and hence problematic term. **Wilderness has long**

seemed an alien concept to Native Americans, a European import that served white culture as a way of signaling the strangeness of a natural world that indigenous peoples found familiar and sustaining, in fact regarded as home.

More recently, Third World critics have attacked the notion of wilderness as an embodiment of a peculiarly American set of attitudes symbolized by a national park ideal that they see as inappropriate for countries in which intense human pressures on available land make preservation seem a luxury. In India and Brazil, for example, critics have advocated "social ecology," a theory of conservation based upon preserving the living patterns of indigenous peoples, in opposition to the emphasis of conservation biologists put upon preserving biological diversity.

Another important critique of the idea of wilderness has come from environmental historians and others who profess support for preserving wild areas but object to what they see as a pervasive habit of pitting nature against culture and consequently neglecting the role of humans in shaping and continuing to live with the natural world. I am thinking particularly of William Cronon's influential "The Trouble with Wilderness; or, Getting Back to the Wrong Nature" and other essays in the collection he edited, *Uncommon Ground: Toward Reinventing Nature* (1990).

Michael Pollan's *Second Nature* (1991) contributed to the reconsideration of the contemporary American attraction to wilderness, which he sees as supported by a "wilderness ethic" deriving ultimately from Thoreau and Muir and "a romantic, pantheistic idea of nature that we invented in the first place." Recent books by Susan G. Davis on the version of "nature" presented by theme parks such as Sea World and by Jennifer Price on such phenomena as the vogue of the plastic pink flamingo and the greening of television offer revealing commentaries on the ways in which we invent versions of nature that serve our various purposes. Americans' relationship with the wilderness, it seems, is still evolving in new directions.

10

✏ Exercise

① The word "preserving" in paragraph 1 is closest in meaning to
- (A) cultivating
- (B) reserving
- (C) protecting
- (D) isolating

② In which position would the following boldfaced sentence best fit in paragraph 1?
Prior to this change, the American wilderness was generally seen as more a threat than a blessing.
- (A) Position W
- (B) Position X
- (C) Position Y
- (D) Position Z

③ The word "inhospitable" in paragraph 2 is closest in meaning to
- (A) unfriendly
- (B) deserted
- (C) wild
- (D) natural

④ In paragraph 2, the author mentions Hawthorne's "Young Goodman Brown" in order to
- (A) prove that the wilderness of Puritan times was more dangerous than today's wilderness
- (B) illustrate how the early settlers of the U.S. regarded the wilderness
- (C) give an example of how literature influenced Puritan attitudes toward the wilderness
- (D) explain that, by Hawthorne's time, attitudes toward the American wilderness had changed

⑤ The word "benevolent" in paragraph 3 is closest in meaning to
- (A) almighty
- (B) omniscient
- (C) kind
- (D) terrible

⑥ It can be inferred from paragraph 3 that modern-day Americans might find Muir's worship of nature
- (A) vibrant and divine
- (B) worthy of celebration
- (C) indicative of their own feelings
- (D) rather old-fashioned

⑦ The word "contested" in paragraph 4 is closest in meaning to

    (A) examined   (B) controversial

    (C) competitive   (D) political

⑧ Which of the sentences below best expresses the essential information in the boldfaced sentence in paragraph 4?

Wilderness has long seemed an alien concept to Native Americans, a European import that served white culture as a way of signaling the strangeness of a natural world that indigenous peoples found familiar and sustaining, in fact regarded as home.

    (A) Native Americans found white culture strange, a threat to their home in the natural world.

    (B) Wilderness was a concept that white Americans brought from Europe and that marked nature as alien.

    (C) Indigenous peoples looked upon wilderness as their home.

    (D) Native Americans considered the natural world friendly, whereas white Americans regarded it as wilderness.

⑨ According to paragraph 5, why do Third World critics oppose the American way of regarding wilderness?

    (A) They think Americans are imperialists bent on exploiting developing countries.

    (B) They don't consider the American view suitable to the needs of poor, populous countries.

    (C) They dislike the theory of social ecology.

    (D) They believe developing countries should consider national parks a priority over luxury items.

⑩ According to paragraph 6, what objections do environmental historians have against the concept of wilderness?

    (A) They claim that they are in favor of preserving natural areas.

    (B) They believe people should be able to change the world of nature.

    (C) They argue that nature and culture cannot coexist.

    (D) They disagree with William Cronon's position.

10

⑪ According to paragraph 7, what did Jennifer Price comment on in her book?
(A) A wilderness ethic deriving from Thoreau and Muir
(B) The version of nature found in Sea World
(C) The popularity of plastic birds
(D) A romantic, pantheistic idea of nature

題解

文章翻譯

　　W 約翰‧穆爾熱情洋溢地描述他在探索加州內華達山脈時發現的「清新、未受破壞、原始的荒野」，造成一種理想普遍流傳，塑造出美國人的思維：荒野是寶貴的、需要保護。X 穆爾的描述反映出一種意識革命，受到英國浪漫作家與美國超越主義哲學家的影響，主要是亨利‧大衛‧梭羅。Y 荒野在這些作家眼中變成是值得追求的，甚至是偉大的表現。Z

　　搭乘五月花號來的移民看到的鱈角，威廉‧布拉德福留下一句著名的描述，說它是「醜陋荒涼的荒野，充滿野獸與野人」，這反映出古老得多的荒野意識，可以追溯到舊約聖經裡面的沙漠荒野，認為那是無法居住的危險處所。納撒尼爾‧霍桑在小說《年輕的布朗大爺》中捕捉住清教徒的意識：黑暗森林（早期移民的荒野）成為邪惡所在，恐怖、令人迷失方向，有惡魔般的印地安人出沒、甚至是魔鬼本身。

　　到 19 世紀晚期穆爾寫作的時代，荒野作為美國地形的特徵，它的吸引力已經建立穩固。穆爾眼中的內華達山脈是「光明山脈」，是活躍、純淨、「神聖的荒野」，由慈善的神下令創造並賦予生命。穆爾特殊的自然信仰或許今天的人不那麼可能共享，但他仍然是個文化偶像，廣泛受到引述，被譽為荒野保護的先知，也是塞拉俱樂部的第一屆會長。他的寫作，還有另外幾位荒野保護名人如梭羅、奧爾多‧利奧波德、艾華‧艾比的作品，

可以在塞拉俱樂部出版的《路邊讀本》裡看到，那是本口袋書，為背包客提供有啟發性的讀物。閱讀穆爾以及另外一些曾經冥想荒野意義的作者，這已經成為美國人荒野體驗的一部分。

民眾對荒野相當迷戀，在 20 世紀晚期還有大幅度的增長，但是「荒野」一詞近年來成為一個因具爭議而有問題的詞語。對美洲原住民而言，荒野一直感覺像是外來的觀念，是歐洲進口貨，為白人文化服務，用來表示自然界的奇怪陌生，但是原住民覺得自然界是熟悉的、維持生命的，事實上就是他們的家。

近年來，第三世界批評者攻擊荒野觀念，說它代表的是一種特屬於美國的態度，以國家公園的理想為象徵。這些批評家認為這種態度並不適合這樣的國家：可用的土地上有強烈的人口壓力，所以保育似乎是一種奢侈。例如在印度與巴西，批評者提倡的是「社會生態學」，這種保護論建立在維護原住民的生活方式上，而不是保育生物學家強調的保護生物多樣性。

關於荒野觀念，還有一項重要的批判來自環境史學家以及另一批人，他們宣稱支持保護荒野地區，但是反對他們眼中那種無所不在的習慣：將自然與文化對立，因而忽略了人類扮演的角色；人類也可以塑造自然界、持續和自然界共存。我想到的主要是威廉・克洛南影響深遠的「荒野的問題，或：回歸錯了自然」，以及其他文章，收在他編輯的文選《非共同立足點：朝向再造自然》(1990)。

麥可・波倫的《第二自然》(1991) 影響到我們重新思考當代美國人對自然的迷戀，他認為那背後有一項支柱，就是「荒野倫理」，歸根究柢來自於梭羅與穆爾，以及「一種浪漫的、泛神論的自然理想，那原本還是人類發明的」。最近有一些書，例如蘇珊・G・戴維斯評論像海洋世界那種主題樂園裡面呈現的「自然」版本，以及珍妮佛・普萊絲評論一些現象諸如塑膠製粉紅火鶴的流行、電視的綠化，也都提供了很有啟發性的評論，關於我們如何發明新版本的自然以配合我們的各種目的。看來美國人與荒野的關係仍然在朝新方向演化中。

練習題翻譯與詳解

① 第一段中的 preserving 一字意思最接近
(A) 開發   (B) 預留
(C) 保護   (D) 孤立

【答案】C
【解析】這是單字題。動詞 preserve（構造：before/keep）的意思是「保存，保護」。

② 下面這個黑體字句子最適合放在第一段的什麼位置？
「在此改變之前，美國荒野通常被視為威脅而非恩賜。」
(A) W 位置   (B) X 位置
(C) Y 位置   (D) Z 位置

10

【答案】**D**

【解析】這是安插句子的題型，要看上下文。插入句句首說到一種「改變」，Z 位置前面說到「荒野在這些作家眼中變成是值得追求的」，可以銜接。插入句句尾說到從前「美國荒野通常被視為威脅」，下文（下一段）說的就是這種威脅，可以銜接，所以插入句要放在 Z 位置，成為：「荒野在這些作家眼中變成是值得追求的，甚至是偉大的表現。<u>在此改變之前，美國荒野通常被視為威脅而非恩賜</u>」。

③ 第二段中的 inhospitable 一字意思最接近

    (A) 不友善   (B) 被遺棄

    (C) 野的   (D) 自然

【答案】**A**

【解析】這是單字題。inhospitable（構造：not/host/able）的意思是「不適居住」，同義字是 unfriendly。

④ 在第二段，作者提到霍桑《年輕的布朗大爺》，目的是

    (A) 證明清教徒時代的荒野比今日的荒野更危險

    (B) 說明美國早期移民如何看待荒野

    (C) 舉例說明文學如何影響到清教徒對荒野的態度

    (D) 解釋說：到了霍桑的時代，對美國荒野的態度已經改變了

【答案】**B**

【解析】這是修辭目的的題型，要看上下文。第二段說「這反映出古老得多的荒野意識，可以追溯到舊約聖經裡面的沙漠荒野，認為那是無法居住的危險處所。納撒尼爾・霍桑在小說《年輕的布朗大爺》中捕捉住清教徒的意識」，直接上下文都說到古老的、清教徒時代的荒野意識，故選 (B)。

⑤ 第三段中的 benevolent 一字意思最接近

    (A) 全能的   (B) 全知的

    (C) 仁慈的   (D) 可怕的

【答案】**C**

【解析】這是單字題。benevolent（構造：good/wish/(*a.*)）的意思是「善意的，慈善的」，同義字是 kind。

⑥ 根據第三段可以推論，今日美國人對於穆爾崇拜自然，會覺得

    (A) 活躍而神聖   (B) 值得歌頌

    (C) 顯示自己的感覺   (D) 有點老式

【答案】**D**

【解析】這是推論題，要找「根據」。第三段說「穆爾特殊的自然信仰或許今天的人不那麼可能共享」，表示穆爾的態度已經過時，故選 (D)。

⑦ 第四段中的 contested 一字意思最接近
    (A) 被檢查   (B) 有爭議
    (C) 有競爭力   (D) 政治性

【答案】**B**

【解析】這是單字題。動詞 contest（構造：together/prove）的意思是「爭辯」，contested 的同義字是 controversial（構造：against/turn/(a.)）。

⑧ 下列哪個句子最能夠表達第四段黑體字句子的主要內容？
    「對美洲原住民而言，荒野一直感覺像是外來的觀念，是歐洲進口貨，為白人文化服務，用來表示自然界的奇怪陌生，但是原住民覺得自然界是熟悉的、維持生命的，事實上就是他們的家。」
    (A) 美洲原住民覺得白人文化奇怪陌生，對他們大自然界的家園構成威脅。
    (B) 荒野是美國白人從歐洲帶來的觀念，把自然視為異類。
    (C) 原住民視荒野為自己的家。
    (D) 美洲原住民認為自然界是友善的，美國白人則視之為荒野。

【答案】**D**

【解析】這是句子改寫的題型，要找句中重點的同義表達。原句對比兩種態度，最接近的同義表達是 (D)。

⑨ 根據第五段，第三世界批評者為何反對美國式的荒野觀？
    (A) 他們認為美國人是帝國主義者，一心要剝削開發中國家。
    (B) 他們不認為美國觀念適合貧窮、人口眾多國家的需要。
    (C) 他們不喜歡社會生態學的理論。
    (D) 他們相信開發中國家應該視國家公園為超過奢侈品的優先議題。

【答案】**B**

【解析】這是問細節的題型，要找同義表達。第五段說「第三世界批評者攻擊荒野觀念，說它代表的是一種特屬於美國的態度，以國家公園的理想為象徵。這些批評家認為這種態度並不適合這樣的國家：可用的土地上有強烈的人口壓力，所以保育似乎是一種奢侈」，其 中 they see as inappropriate for countries in which intense human pressures on available land make preservation seem a luxury 就是 They don't consider the American view suitable to the needs of poor, populous countries. 的同義表達，故選 (B)。

⑩ 根據第六段，環境史學家對荒野觀念有何反對意見？

(A) 他們說自己支持保護自然地區。

(B) 他們相信人應該可以改變自然界。

(C) 他們主張自然與文化不能並存。

(D) 他們不同意克洛南的立場。

【答案】**B**

【解析】這是問細節的題型，要找同義表達。第六段說：「他們宣稱支持保護荒野地區，但是反對他們眼中那種無所不在的習慣：將自然與文化對立，因而忽略了人類扮演的角色；人類也可以塑造自然界、持續和自然界共存」。其中雖然有「他們宣稱支持保護荒野地區」之語，但這不算是反對荒野觀念，所以不能選 (A)。而其中 the role of humans in shaping and continuing to live with the natural world 就是 people should be able to change the world of nature 的同義表達，故選 (B)。

⑪ 根據第七段，普萊絲在書中評論了什麼？

(A) 從梭羅與穆爾傳承下來的荒野倫理

(B) 海洋世界裡面的自然版本

(C) 塑膠鳥的流行

(D) 浪漫、泛神論的自然觀

【答案】**C**

【解析】這是問細節的題型，要找同義表達。第七段說「普萊絲評論一些現象諸如塑膠製粉紅火鶴的流行」，其中 the vogue of the plastic pink flamingo 就是 The popularity of plastic birds 的同義表達，故選 (C)。

NOTES

國家圖書館出版品預行編目資料

閱讀高點：旋元佑英文閱讀通／旋元佑作.
—— 初版. —— 臺北市：波斯納，2019. 03
　面：　公分

　ISBN: 978-986-96852-5-2（平裝）

　1. 英語　　2. 讀本

805.18　　　　　　　　　　　　107019437

閱讀高點：旋元佑英文閱讀通

作　　者／旋元佑
執行編輯／朱曉瑩

出　　版／波斯納出版有限公司
地　　址／台北市 100 館前路 26 號 6 樓
電　　話／(02) 2314-2525
傳　　真／(02) 2312-3535
客服專線／(02) 2314-3535
客服信箱／btservice@betamedia.com.tw
郵撥帳號／19493777
帳戶名稱／波斯納出版有限公司

總 經 銷／時報文化出版企業股份有限公司
地　　址／桃園市龜山區萬壽路二段 351 號
電　　話／(02) 2306-6842

出版日期／2022 年 8 月初版五刷
定　　價／600 元
I S B N／978-986-96852-5-2

貝塔網址：www.betamedia.com.tw

喚醒你的英文語感！

Get a Feel for English !

喚醒你的英文語感！

Get a Feel for English !